The Rogue Tangerine Tablet

BLEUE ROSE

Book cover illustrations and interior image by Bleue Rose
All images digitally enhanced and formatted by Lacegarden
ISBN 978-1-7338194-1-1
ISBN(e) 978-1-7338194-0-4
Edition Copyright 2019
Published by Bleue Rose
Formatting by Istvan Szabo
Printed by Ingram Spark
BleueRose.com
BleueRoseNovels IG

Dedication

This book is dedicated to Ruth, who lovingly supported me in all my crazy endeavors, to Joseph, a master storyteller, who injected humor in the most unexpected situations, to Julia, who sparks my creativity daily by consistently thinking out of the box, and to Joshua, who generates joy with all his heartfelt, smart advice and insights.

Table of Contents

Prologue: Qui n'avance pas, recule. 1

Chapter I: Don't Mute the Messenger.................................2

Chapter II: Pink Slip...7

Chapter III: Portrait of the Artist in New York 12

Chapter IV: The Artist's World 17

Chapter V: Every Thelma needs a Louise.............................21

Chapter VI: The Heat is On 29

Chapter VII: Double Trouble 33

Chapter VIII: Lights! Camera! Action! 38

Chapter IX: Christmas Where?.....................................42

Chapter X: A Sense of the Familiar 46

Chapter XI: Up, Up, and Away 49

Chapter XII: The Fedora Takes Manhattan 52

Chapter XIII: Auction Fiasco.....................................55

Chapter XIV: La Vie Parisienne...................................63

Chapter XV: Joy and Life Along the Costa Brava...................71

Chapter XVI: The Secret to Life? Butter! 74

Chapter XVII: Cause You Gotta Have Friends.......................78

Chapter XVIII: Travel Jitters 88

Chapter XIX: Strange Bedfellows..................................91

Chapter XX: Search for the Perfect Frenchman 95

Chapter XXI: It Takes a Thief... 101

Chapter XXII: Into the Lion's Den 103

Chapter XXIII: The Chance of a Lifetime......................... 107

Chapter XXIV: The Best Laid Plans 111

Chapter XXV: Paths Crossing and Converging...................... 114

Chapter XXVI: Away from the Evil Eye, Life in Paris

Improves 120

Chapter XXVII: Paris is Always a Good Idea.......................... 122

Chapter XXVIII: The Values of Good Help and a Small

World... 126

Chapter XXIX: Paying the Price 135

Chapter XXX: Another Pink Slip 141

Chapter XXXI: Only the Art Dealers Die Young (The

Meringues, Not So Much) 144

Chapter XXXII: The Meaning of Fete in Paris 151

Chapter XXXIII: A Chance Encounter.............................. 154

Chapter XXXIV: Shop till You Drop, Parisian Style.............. 158

Chapter XXXV: Guys Just Want to Have Fun 165

Chapter XXXVI: The Calm Before the Storm 169

Chapter XXXVII: Bad Moon Rising................................. 172

Chapter XXXVIII: Dancing the Night Away 174

Chapter XXXIX: The Morning After and A New Beginning

for All 185

Chapter XL: Art Appreciation or Lust? 190

Chapter XLI: Blue Hair, Strawberry Prosecco and Art

Sparks 193

Chapter XLII: Tying Up Loose Ends 197

Chapter XLIII: Curious and 'Curiouser'............................200

Chapter XLIV: Chance Encounter, Not Entirely by Chance 202

Chapter XLV: Getting Her New York Groove Back 207

Chapter XLVI: Meant to Be? 209

Chapter XLVII: Day of Reflection 217

Chapter XLVIII: Inspiration Can Come from Anywhere..... 218

Chapter XLIX: Suspicions Kill................................ 220

Chapter L: Vive l'Amour and Filmmaking in Paris 223

Chapter LI: Art is in the Eye of the Beholder 226

Chapter LII: Second Date and Whirlwind Romance 229

Chapter LIII: Fantastic Film World in Berlin 236

Chapter LIV: Hooray for Hollywood...Briefly...................... 238

Chapter LV: Dead Starlet and Live Thugs.......................... 240

Chapter LVI: Let it Snow, Let it Snow 245

Chapter LVII: The Dark Side of Berlin............................ 254

Chapter LVIII: The French Connection............................ 258

Chapter LIX: The Plot Thickens 260

Chapter LX: Beat the Press 265

Chapter LXI: The Boys are Back in Town (Soon) 267

Chapter LXII: Free Speech and Wicked Men 270

Chapter LXIII: Trouble in Paradise 272

Chapter LXIV: Turning up like a bad Penny 274

Chapter LXV: Three Heads Are Better Than Two 275

Chapter LXVI: Reality Check, Please! 278

Chapter LXVII: Risky Business 282

Chapter LXVIII: Curse of Clemente— Minding Everyone's
Business 286

Chapter LXIX: Birthdays, Gypsies and Sex Lives, Oh My!... 292

Chapter LXX: No News is Good News................................ 296

Chapter LXXI: Red Herring and Sangria do not Mix Well ... 299

Chapter LXXII: The Sounds of Silence and the Perils of Spanish Coffee ... 303

Chapter LXXIII: Family Secrets and Beyond ... 308

Chapter LXXIV: Paris Sleuthing Times Two ... 310

Chapter LXXV: Never Get Between a Mother Hen and Her Chicks ... 313

Chapter LXXVI: Mother Knows Best or So She Thinks ... 316

Chapter LXXVII: Paris Jitters ... 320

Chapter LXXVIII: Brotherly Love ... 323

Chapter LXXIX: All Rats on Deck ... 325

Chapter LXXX: Burglars, Chatty Supers and Bosses Flying . 328

Chapter LXXXI: Paranoia is Legit If They Really Are Out to Get You ... 336

Chapter LXXXII: Family Meddling Welcome ... 340

Chapter LXXXIII: Dirty Laundry ... 342

Chapter LXXXIV: Paris Idyll Interrupted ... 344

Chapter LXXXV: A Sigh of Relief ... 346

Chapter LXXXVI: On the Crest of the Wave ... 348

Chapter LXXXVII: The Great Escape ... 350

Chapter LXXXVIII: Chasing his Tail ... 352

Chapter LXXXIX: Final Farewell ... 354

Chapter XC: The Usual and Unusual Suspects ... 356

Chapter XCI: Happy Arrivals … Sort of ... 358

Chapter XCII: Paris, Everyone's Home Away from Home .. 364

Chapter XCIII: Negotiating the Maze, Pardon my French … ... 369

Chapter XCIV: Film Basics 101 ... 371

Chapter XCV: Trust No One, Least of all Those Close to

You 375

Chapter XCVI: The Artist's Heart 378

Chapter XCVII: Nightmare in Paris 381

Chapter XCVIII: It Takes a Thief 384

Chapter XCIX: Follow the Money .... Or the Pottery ...
... Or the Drugs? 389

Chapter C: Art Confusion and Book Magic 394

Chapter CI: Love in the Afternoon 400

Chapter CII: The (Nearly) Invisible Man 404

Chapter CIII: Surprising Innermost Thoughts of a Felon 406

Chapter CIV: Standing by her Man 410

Chapter CV: Fernando's Sour Surprise 413

Chapter CVI: Mom Knows Best.. 415

Chapter CVII: Back in the Saddle 417

Chapter CVIII: The Silica Hits the Fan 419

Chapter CIX: I Left My Heart… 422

Chapter CX: Slip, Sliding Away 427

Chapter CXI: Good News Travels Fast 428

Chapter CXII: News Junkies Unite 430

Chapter CXIII: Jasper's Choice 432

Chapter CXIV: Three little words… 434

Chapter CXV: Heaven and Hell… … With No Goodbyes... 437

Chapter CXVI: Jasper's Life Changing Decision, and Cara's
Surprise of a Lifetime 440

Acknowledgement 449

About the Author.. 450

Prologue

Qui n'avance pas, recule.

-Wise French Proverb

Those who do not move forward, recede.

Life is constant movement.
Adaptation. Blossoming. Evolving.
Making strides into new directions.
Courage, flexibility and keeping an open mind
are key to personal growth and good karma.
The end goal is to enjoy the journey and
to look back on a life well-lived.

Carlos Ortiz   Fernando Flores   Jose Flores

Chapter I

Don't Mute the Messenger

Carlos Ortiz sat in his boss's office perusing the company's monthly balance sheet when he discovered a serious discrepancy. He gulped. Finding inadequacies prior to a management meeting was pure pressure. Every few seconds, he looked up through the open office door, from behind a massive mahogany desk, to check on Fernando's whereabouts. Perspiration obliterated the pungent cologne in his open, wilting, crisp white shirt. He felt his throat constrict and a golf-ball-sized lump lodge in his trachea. Knowing where the problem lay and having to disclose it, made him tense. There were many aspects of his job that made his heart hiccup, but finding money missing was the worst scenario.

"We're short a large chunk of cash. I traced it to one of the new distributors. Who wants to tell Fernando?" He looked around at the four male employees sprawled on the leather couch and fiesta-tile, fabric armchairs. Multiple rows of vibrant Mexican pottery lined the office walls displaying the company's exceptional product. Carlos studied the patterns, breathing in deeply, as he waited patiently for a reply. Dirty boots, up on the weathered mahogany coffee table, swung to life and hit the colorful *Talavera* tile floor. The boss's brother, cousin and two nephews meandered their way around the desk to where Carlos was seated beneath a mammoth, bronze ceiling fan. It was hot and the men moved listlessly. He pointed to the missing amount on his spreadsheet and looked up at the surrounding faces. Soft whistles filled the silence. Waiting for a response, Carlos exhaled making a nervous, raspy sound through his teeth. This wouldn't be good.

"I'll tell him, Carlos," Jose volunteered staring at the numbers.

Carlos inhaled a quick shallow breath and let it go with congealed resignation.

The ceramics studio and adjoining warehouse in Tampico, bustled with activity. Their prime location, next to Tampico's active harbor, facilitated the company's business and expansion goals. Fernando Flores, in his trademark black fedora, was surveying rows of his company's prized pottery. The expertly glazed products echoed the rich hues of Mexico's sunbathed landscape. Carlos watched Fernando through the half open office door, as he methodically scanned the stacks of hand-painted pieces, meticulously being wrapped, and carefully wedged, into softly lined crates in anticipation of shipment overseas. Proper packing was key, so the goods would arrive at their final destination intact. Company pride dictated that, and Fernando was all about pride and precision.

Carlos monitored his boss's approach through barely moving eye slits. He watched Fernando finger the finished crates as he counted and computed his profits. Fernando was good that way. The man's brain was a calculator. Unknowingly prolonging Carlos's discomfort, he inched his way toward the back office at a funeral's pace, stopping only long enough to wink at a few select female employees. Carlos nervously tapped his fingers on the desk.

Even on a good day, the atmosphere in the office was tense. Problem solving sessions made Carlos antsy. He despised being holed up in management meetings; they suffocated him. Fernando's management team consisted solely of family members, which put Carlos at an undesirable disadvantage. As the sole company accountant, Carlos worked alone, but every other week his boss randomly called a meeting to "triple check" his profits. Most of the time, Fernando's calculations were remarkably accurate. The man had an uncanny grip on his business finances. Carlos, who preferred working in solitude, ground his teeth through these obligatory disclosure meetings. In his mind, he was in a no-win situation. Basic survival was all he could hope for. Quitting was not an option.

Carlos visualized Fernando's blood percolating, like bubbling lava, when the inaccuracy was revealed. He would be livid, and Carlos would once again want to melt into the rough terrain of the wall plaster. His boss's volatile nature was legendary, and Carlos knew all too well how disagreeable things could get. The last time someone "borrowed" money without permission, Fernando had the thief's facial features rearranged and stuck his hand in a hot kiln. The culprit's fingers fused permanently. Carlos could only imagine how Fernando would handle this digression. He anticipated the pay back with great trepidation. Unless a mistake was an honest, documentable oversight, Fernando Flores did not give second chances. Ever.

Fernando finally entered the office with purposeful strides. He nodded at his 41year old twin brother, his 37 year-old trusted cousin, Jose, his two younger nephews and lastly his eyes met Carlos's. This progression was his annoying way of stating rank.

Carlos ignored it. Business and family honor were closely intertwined at F&S Enterprises and Carlos was constantly reminded of that. He returned Fernando's nod and looked down at his hands, dreading to hear how the score would be settled.

"So? Did everything check out this month?" Fernando directed his question at Carlos.

"No, there's money missing. Five figures." Jose volunteered brusquely. "Check this out, Boss." Jose pointed to the name and balance on the spreadsheet.

Carlos happily let Fernando's cousin take over.

"I take this as a personal affront. This business is my pride and joy, handed down through four generations. Rarely have we encountered theft." Fernando's voice was soft and steely as he dramatically pounded his heart with a closed fist. He circled the room moving only his intense emerald eyes under the shady brim of his fedora. Carlos knew he was scanning his audience for added impact and instinctively, he averted his gaze. He hooked his thumbs into the front pockets of his snug jeans and studied the coffee stains on his white t-shirt, slowly moving to the scratches on his worn tan, cowhide boots. Without looking up, he buttoned his open shirt over the stain.

Head down, eyes alert under long dark lashes, Carlos trailed Fernando as he moved around the desk to view the spreadsheet. A second or two of consideration and Fernando's face clouded as he registered the findings. Carlos could see Fernando's expression change from careful scrutiny to barely controlled anger from one moment to the next. He took a step backward, clearing a path for Fernando to pass to where Jose was standing. As expected, and without hesitation, Fernando dispatched Jose, his number one enforcer, to solve the problem. He tapped his manicured forefinger on the prominent turquoise and silver cross around Jose's neck, the only parting gift from an absent father.

"Handle this and make sure you secure our goods," he growled. "Take Julio and Luis with you. Go. Now."

"Yes, Boss."

The answer came in unison as the three family enforcers filed out of the office. Carlos sighed with relief. He knew Jose thrived on the attention and power bestowed on him. His back up against the wall, Carlos scrutinized Fernando. When the three men exited the room, Carlos followed, turning only once at the door to observe Fernando's hulking frame hover by the window, to ensure his men left without delay. Carlos quietly closed the office door behind Fernando's silent brother, Felipe, and himself.

"Carlos." Fernando barked through the door. "Follow them."

"Damn," he muttered under his breath. He had hoped to forego this drama. Felipe nodded sympathetically and gestured, moving his forefinger across his throat.

Chapter II

Pink Slip

Carlos pulled up behind Jose's pick-up truck and turned off the ignition. How long would they have to wait for the distributor to return to his office? He expelled a ragged breath and turned on music. Turning to his console for his earbuds, he observed Fernando's two nephews chatting away while Jose cleaned his dirty fingernails with the tip of his knife. Sexy *Niia* was singing something jazzy, slowing his pulse to a normal beat. Music was his salvation at times like this.

It was dusk and the narrow cobblestone street had cleared for dinner. The temperature was dropping to a cool 62 degrees. Jose had one evil eye peeled toward the heavy oak door, chilling Carlos to the bone. When Diego finally appeared, the truck door swung open, and Carlos watched Jose and his posse pour out.

"Diego." Jose's voice echoed in the empty street. "We need to talk. Let's go inside."

"*Hola,* Jose. Of course."

Jose and his men escorted Diego into the dilapidated ranch building. The office was dark and empty, but no one turned on the lights. Carlos watched the logs in the fireplace being lit and coaxed into action. He moved his jeep closer to Diego's open office windows, so he could hear and see what transpired, but he elected to stay in the safety of his vehicle. Carlos took an earbud out of one ear.

"What can I do for you, *Amigos*?"

"Sit, Diego."

Diego, not able to control his trembling hands and fearing reprisal, sat on the edge of the cool, cracked leather couch. The rising flames behind him illuminated his profile. His head leaned forward, eyes fluorescing in anticipation, as he glanced back and forth between the men.

"Is there a problem, Jose?" His head shifted back to realign with his spine as he waited for a reply.

"Yes, there is. Let's have a shot of tequila before we discuss business." Jose walked to Diego's bar and poured four shot glasses of premium tequila. He moved in time-loop speed. Carlos could see Diego's nervous twitch accelerate as he waited for Jose to pass him the shot glass. He gulped it down in one swift motion and slammed his glass on the table.

A wave of warm nausea gripped Carlos's soft insides as he listened through the open windows. He would have much preferred to tune everyone out with music, but he felt compelled to listen. He had observed more of these payback schemes than he cared to remember. They always made him feel queasy, which is why Fernando forced him to go. His boss wanted to toughen him up, but Carlos knew he would never adjust to this type of retribution. He was built differently. It was no accident that he was an accountant.

"Is everything ok, Jose?" Diego stammered. His eyebrows rose involuntarily, and he shrugged holding his palms upward in question format. He looked terrified.

"The boss noticed a few accounting mistakes. You only paid us a pittance of what you owed last month. What happened?"

At that moment Diego's terror was justified; the extra money was never worth the flogging that ensued. Carlos witnessed the same scenario over and over, the fear, the regret and the inevitable tumble. He knew the drill and it always ended ugly.

"I needed a little more money for my sick mother. I was planning to pay it back. You know that, right? We're all friends here, are we not?" Diego stuttered, flattening the folds in his shirt. Carlos broke into a cold sweat as he saw the beads of perspiration dripping down Diego's blanched face. The man's troubled bird-like features spelled absolute terror as Jose picked up a hammer, turning it to the sharp edge.

"The boss hates cheaters. Do you know what he does with cheaters?"

"Please. I'm not cheating. I just borrowed some money. I'll repay it as soon as I can."

Diego's eyes were fixated on Jose. His eyes and mouth twitched, and his ears turned the color of an aged burgundy wine. Carlos held his breath.

Jose paused for emphasis. "Let me remind you what happens to cheaters," he snarled. At that moment the family resemblance with Fernando was unmistakable, Carlos thought as he exhaled in measured spurts, his pulse quickening again.

"No, please. I swear I'll repay you. It was a mistake. I'm sorry. So, so sorry."

Diego's pleads echoed inside Carlos's head, making it spin. His captors reached for Diego's trembling hands, and held them palms down, fingers spread on the coffee table. He tried to wriggle free from their iron grips.

"*Amigos*, please. I have a big family to consider. They all depend on me. I had one bad month, but I'll make it up to you," he begged.

Carlos looked away, then reluctantly, riveted back to the window. His hand was massaging his upset stomach.

Diego continued to grovel for mercy. "We can work out a payment plan, can't we? I'll work hard and pay back every penny."

Jose menacingly tapped the hammer into the palm of his free hand as he listened unsympathetically. In a split second the hammer came down. Diego instinctively recoiled, but his hands could not leave the table. They were held firmly in place by Jose's henchmen. The first two fingers on Diego's dominant right hand were fractured with one swift blow. He screamed in agony and begged for forgiveness. Carlos gagged and rubbed his hands together over his mouth.

"Too late. This is for stealing from us. Where is the money?"

"I don't have it," Diego gasped. "I told you; I had family expenses." His breath came in short, labored spurts. "A small amount…bottom desk drawer. Key… in my pants pocket."

"Undress him." Jose ordered with a menacing smirk.

"No," Diego yelled frantically.

Diego's clothes were ripped off, buttons popping everywhere, as he cried for his limbs and life. Hunched over in agony; completely nude, bleeding, and cradling his broken fingers, Diego howled. His stare fixated on Jose, who had discarded the hammer and was approaching him with a hot iron poker. Again, Diego begged for leniency.

"Please, have a heart. My family needs me. I promise to repay you."

"You should have asked Fernando for the money, instead of stealing it."

"I know. I will next time."

"There is no next time."

Carlos opened the jeep door and vomited into the dirt. No matter how often he was forced to witness Fernando and Jose's wrath, he had trouble stomaching it. He said a quick prayer and crossed himself. Seconds later the hot iron poker branded over the skull tattoo on Diego's back. The unfathomable pain searing through Diego's body had him doubled over. His blood curdling screams pierced the balmy night. Again, Carlos swore to himself that one of these days, he would have enough money saved, to leave this misery behind.

Carlos knew that no one would come to Diego's aid. No one dared. Seconds later, the room around Diego went dark and quiet. The fire no longer offered a view, but Carlos knew the poker had pierced Diego's body. If any of the neighbors heard Diego's heart wrenching screams through their open windows, they chose not to look or venture out. The Flores family were an entity not to be messed with in Tampico. When the three men exited Diego's office, Carlos's jeep was gone.

Chapter III

Portrait of the Artist in New York

Early Sunday in New York, Cara Crenston sat in her home office. Her inner clock had woken her around 7am. Moments later, in a pastel fog, she floated to the bathroom for a quick morning regimen. Emerging somewhat refreshed, enveloped in a plush lilac robe and powder puff slippers warming her toes, she shuffled to the cozy office niche in her French country kitchen. Putting the kettle on, she waited.

Cara had traded her morning caffeine jolt for a meditative red bush tea, when her last child left for college. Now that she lived alone and worked in a home studio, she no longer felt the need to kick start her day in a mad rush. Never known for seeing sunrise, she greatly appreciated this small morning luxury. In time, she would go to work in her home studio, but first she needed to get her daily fix of world news and see what her three adult children were up to. She turned on her laptop.

World developments and satisfying, scented tea always eased Cara's transition from dreams to reality. She settled into her comfortable violet, velvet armchair for a comprehensive sweep of world news; it always amazed her what happened in just a few hours while she slept. Today's horrors included a group of college students mysteriously disappearing while on a trip to South America. She also noticed another disheartening cartel killing in Mexico. A man was found skewered. People were mysteriously disappearing or brutally murdered south of the border and drug cartels were nearly always to blame. Something about this fact fascinated and repelled her. Although the news promised to be notoriously grim, she looked forward to her connection with the outside world.

Moving on, she perused her favorite art sites to see what was trending. A gallery in Paris was currently on her radar with an exhibit of ceramic wall constructions. She studied the pieces with great interest and scrolled down for more information. A handsome portrait picture of a man smiled back at her. She studied the peaks and valleys of his face and grinned.

"Now this is a man I would love to discuss art with over a glass of Bordeaux," she muttered out loud. Her life in a New York City bedroom community was simple these days, perhaps too simple she thought as she sipped her tea. When her phone rang, she jumped.

"Hi, Summer. You're up early."

"Hi, Mom. Couldn't sleep. What are you up to?"

"The usual morning fare. Having tea. Planning my day. Reading world news. People in Mexico are disappearing like free cupcakes at a gourmet bake sale."

"Guess we won't be spending our family vacation there. Actually, I was wondering if you have given our holiday plans any thought? It would be nice to spend it with the boys this year. I miss them."

"Yeah. Me too. I don't know. I was hoping they would fly home and we could spend Christmas here."

"That's boring."

"Well, Summer, if I win the lottery, I promise we'll take a fabulous trip to Bora Bora."

"Right. Home it is."

"Sorry, Summer. Business is a bit slow. Speaking of business, let me start my day. I need to get some emails and bills out. Talk to you later? Or did you have something earthshaking to share?"

"No. Talk later."

Cara fingered her generously sized, peony teacup and thought about her ceramics business. She eyed her work wall calendar, the office merely spanning the small alcove at the entrance of her kitchen. She already knew there was nothing major pending. She glanced back at her cluttered desk, nestled in the expansive bay window, and decided to ignore the paperwork. She would not let a few mounting bills deter her from starting her day off right. She took one last look at the face smiling back at her and saved the website, Fereaux Galleries, to her "special artist" file.

After checking her emails for orders and deleting annoying solicitations, Cara focused on her personal mail. Each morning she searched for messages from her family overseas, the fuel that kept the home fire going. Scanning the page, she spotted an email from Jasper, her oldest child. Today's update included a photo with friends in Park Guell. For the past ten months, Jasper worked for a financial firm in Barcelona. As usual, the email was brief, but somewhat informative.

"What are our holiday plans this year?" he inquired before signing off.

Judging from Jasper's photo, enlarged and enhanced, he looked content. Cara was thrilled he had the opportunity to work abroad. Barcelona was a wonderful life experience for him and the city's pace was so much more civilized than New York. Jasper was not the greatest communicator, keeping his life very private, but Cara felt appeased with the brief note and picture.

There was no news from her younger son, Samson, currently residing in Paris. Cara broke into a smile as she looked up and spotted a woodchuck sunning himself outside her bay window. "Morning Harry," she muttered. *Having my lawn for breakfast, are you?*

Lost in thought, Cara allowed the morning sunlight to caress her face. She observed a deer family enjoying her hosta plants along the deck. "Damn these critters," she muttered. *What do they not eat?* Her well-planned garden was being reduced to chewed up stubble. Given the time of year, birds would soon migrate south, however she still saw chipmunks, squirrels and rabbits daily, along with the neighbor's cat. Cara sighed. Was she becoming too complacent? Too dull? Too predictable? Too lonely? She needed some excitement in her life.

Observing nature, reading the day's news and relishing the warm sun on her skin, was a motivating start to her morning. In her cozy, violet cocoon, she assessed the fall temperature. Though the sun felt warm through the windows, ice box weather was around the corner. Morning frost and the leaves' rapid color change encouraged Cara to savor every sunny second.

Soon the dark days of winter would approach, turning the soothing skies into a never-ending hematite sea. Cara dreaded winter gloom. *I must plan our Christmas holiday reunion soon.* She needed something to look forward to. If only sales would pick up. Disdainfully, she regarded the pile of bills on her desk. They unsettled her and were clearly not compatible with a much-desired family vacation. Hopefully, her children would come home this Christmas. A traveling reunion was out of the question.

Chapter IV

The Artist's World

Singing loudly to the radio while lingering beneath the massaging hot stream of water, Cara thought about her weekly schedule, mentally arranging her days around her morning work outs, errands and a few appointments. Her afternoons were generally spent in the studio. She rationalized her leisure mornings out as time well spent on mental health and general maintenance. She could compensate time lost at night. As an artist, late nights were often the times she sketched her best ideas. She dried off her long limbs with a plush white Egyptian spa towel and studied her wardrobe. Cara liked her regimented, self-imposed agenda precisely because she could stray from it whenever she pleased.

As she rummaged for her yoga mat in the foyer closet, her phone rang. She eyed the caller ID and debated. She decided to pick up the call.

"Hi, Mom, I just woke up. I decided to make a few changes to my script. I was listening to TED talks last night and I got a blast of good ideas. Do you have a minute?" Summer's eagerness to chat radiated through the smartphone. Summer, who never seemed to remember Cara's schedule, started chatting with abandon, not waiting for a reply.

"Listen, Summer, I'll have to call you back. I'm rushing off to yoga. And…didn't you already submit that script?" Cara squinted in anticipation.

"Yoga? Again? Yes, I did, but you can always tweak things before and during filming." Summer explained. Cara could hear the stubborn conviction in her daughter's voice.

"Yes, Summer! Again. Like every Monday. And yes, I do know things can be tweaked, but should they be? Doesn't that cost time and money on set? Not that we need to worry about that right now. There is no set. Anyway, talk later? Gotta run."

"Sure, Mom." Cara caught the deflated hum of her daughter's disappointment. "By the way, have you thought about holiday plans yet?"

"Not yet. I'm waiting for a financial windfall."

"Funny, Mom."

"Or for the boys' reply, whichever comes first."

No matter how often Summer called, she always seemed to have something new and pressing to discuss. An unusual idea, a budding story line and today, a revamping of her final script for a movie proposal already submitted.

Cara shook her head. *Why do I bother arguing a point I know she'll ignore anyway?* She reflected on how her daughter, regardless of the subject, always injected humor into her work. It was part of Summer's DNA. Cara found this refreshing and she looked forward to reading Summer's script changes, regardless.

Summer was the ultimate comedian and creator. On the flip side though, Summer stressed obsessively over details, which made Cara her favorite sounding board. Creativity crossed artistic borders, Cara thought. Artists today were versatile and by no means locked into one medium. On the contrary, they easily transitioned from one creative process to another, which morphed them into more interesting human beings. Summer was clearly one example of that.

On her way out, Cara reminded herself, with a post-it-note on her laptop, to group email her children regarding the winter holidays. This year she was determined they spend it together. If they couldn't afford to take a trip, they would gather at home. She was hell-bent on a family reunion everyone would benefit from.

Yoga heightened Cara's senses and soothed her soul. It also got her blood flowing, making her feel alive and energetic. She looked forward to class. All the aches and pains, from being hunched over the potter's wheel for long periods, seemed to melt away. Yoga was a liberating way to start the work week and she never regretted the time spent, no matter how busy she was. As she lay flat on her back, in *shavasana* corpse pose, she tried not to think about the upcoming week.

Back at the studio, Cara started to glaze the soap dishes promised for Bethany's Bath Store. She slid them into the kiln and cleaned off the mammoth, rectangular, reclaimed oak table, in the center of her studio. Her phone sang her favorite tune.

"Hi, honey. I was wondering if I could stop by this morning."

"Hi, Sam. Sure, I'm here, working."

"Good. I'll be there shortly. Actually, I'm around the corner. Put some coffee on."

"Sure. Notice is way over-rated anyway." Cara chuckled. "See you in a few."

Washing her hands in the industrial-sized sink, Cara glanced out of her wall of windows. Her well-planned studio space with its northern exposure, ensured equitable, natural light distribution, an artist's dream. Seconds later, she spotted Sam's red SUV pull into her driveway. Cara sprung into action, clearing the table for her first and only client of the day. Hopefully, she would be lucky. She quickly placed a few of her newer works on the door end of the butcher block expansion in the hopes of securing a sale.

Chapter V

Every Thelma needs a Louise

Samantha Cadwell, a well-traveled, 42-year-old, interior designer who never failed to amuse or enthuse, breezed through the unlocked screen door laden with bags of fabrics. Cara noticed she was also carrying a familiar striped, ribbon adorned box from Nero's Erotic Bakery. Sam's Gucci sunglasses, perched on top of her golden, shoulder length locks, slid down, and rested on her freckled, up-turned nose as she dumped her bags on the table. She slid them off and placed them in her Dior bag.

"Hey, there." Sam's bordeaux handbag spewed random design papers that cascaded to the floor. Cara helped her unload and organize. Her friend looked like a poster girl for Ralph Lauren leisure wear. Sam's style changed with her mood and Cara marveled how she threw seamless outfits together with what looked like haphazard ease, but Cara knew better. Sam plotted every golden detail.

"Nice outfit, Sam! Did you just literally call me from a parking spot around the corner?"

"Yes! And so glad you're here. Besides, I know your yoga schedule."

Cara rolled her eyes and smiled. "Summer still doesn't."

"Well, you know. Kids!" Sam smirked.

Cara glossed over her outfit. She was wearing tight black jeans with a mustard paisley patterned shirt. Her outerwear was a cleverly designed multi-colored tweed jacket, gathered at the waist, sloping to a rounded, longer bustle in the back. She took off her stylish jacket and threw it over one of the chairs. Sam's dark cherry suede boots completed her fall outfit and added that special 'umph' that other women admired. Cara paled in comparison in her black yoga stretchies and loose, cien cashmere sweater.

"Nice suede boots!"

"Thanks. *Weitzman* sale. I brought prize winning *beignets* for breakfast. I just went to Nero's and these beauties are hot out of the oven. In five minutes, you'll be thanking me."

"I thought I recognized that box. The scent wafting out of there is devilishly good. Are the pastries penis shaped like the last ones you tempted me with?" Cara smiled, eyebrows rising.

Samantha laughed as she unpacked her bag. "No, honey. I need you to concentrate today. While I was at the bakery, examining baked body parts, Nero hired me to remodel his kitchen in his new country cottage in Southampton. I'll need lots of tiles and pottery. Work for both of us. Yay!"

"Oh, yeah!" Cara smiled. "I so need a new project. The holidays are coming, and I want my children home this Christmas."

"Ditto, so could I, and this job is a big one. I brought some pottery pictures from my last European trip. I would like to replicate some of the colors and designs I saw in Spain and Portugal. Nero is leaning toward a Greek erotica theme, no surprise there, but I was thinking we could do a Mediterranean mix. He wants me to wow him with my ideas and I need your help."

"Greek erotica? I'm wowed. At least someone is thinking sex." Cara giggled.

"Sex and sugar is all those two have on their brains. Their baked goods are your first clue."

"So true. Let's see what you have."

As Sam lined up her colorful fabric options, Cara glanced at the black and white striped box with the lemon-yellow ribbon. It was beautifully wrapped. A designer's dream presentation that totally resonated with her.

"That Neo-Classical bakery has been a great addition to our community. I can't imagine living without Nero and Jonny's naughty pastries. Decaf?"

"Sure, honey. Serve it up."

Samantha pulled out colorful pictures of Spanish Roman-Celtic pottery and Castilian Renaissance tiles. She unwrapped richly patterned Portuguese ceramics as well as a few erotic Greek mosaic tiles. Cara scrutinized the careful arrangement on the table as she filled the coffee maker with water.

"Nero found these at a flea market abroad and would like me to accent his kitchen with similar designs and colors. Can you figure out a marriage of all these styles? What do you think?"

"Sure can. It may be more a marriage of color than style though." Cara winked enthusiastically. "A kitchen of Greek erotica, how inspiring! That will keep me motivated for days." Cara laughed. "Boy, am I in need of romance!"

"I can just imagine what happens on Nero and Jonny's kitchen table when they aren't baking." Sam laughed.

"We won't go there." Pointing to the other samples Cara observed, "Research should be a blast. I can't wait to start. These are hand painted designs. I have a few similar ones. I bought them in Spain and Portugal years ago, when I still had the luxury of travel."

"Ok then…. let's see what you have. Nero and Jonny are pretty intent on the erotic touch. It better be authentic and sexy."

"I don't have Greek erotica, but I do have Mediterranean pottery with those same colors. Don't know about sexy, however the colors work. Let's start with that. Coffee is ready."

Cara watched as Sam unwrapped the beignets and lined up two napkins featuring Neo Classical male nude sculptures, an eye-catching prop from the bakery.

"Oh! How distracting!" Cara winked, holding up one of the napkins.

"Focus baby, focus."

Cara watched Sam's eyes gravitate toward her new work.

"Are these your new pieces? They're fabulous!"

"Thanks … …fresh out of the kiln with no client in sight."

"I'll have to work on that."

Cara filled their muddled, aqua glazed mugs and walked into her adjoining shelved, storage room. She reappeared with a small selection of different sized bowls, decorated in stylized floral patterns in various shades of blues, greens, yellows, pinks and peach. She could see Samantha's eyes light up as she plopped them down with a measured thud.

"Wow, look how these match." Sam held up a fabric sample and placed it strategically next to one of the bowls. "The colors work surprisingly well. You're a color whiz. I always knew that. I'll need a few big show pieces and a lot of decorative tiles. I plan to incorporate the tiles randomly into a neutral ecru backsplash. They don't all have to be the same. I'd like to mix subjects but keep the overall color scheme the same. Can I take a few of these with me to show Nero?" Samantha asked, sipping her coffee.

"Absolutely," Cara chimed, reaching for her sketchpad. "I'll start some sketches and assemble a few tile color samples. Once we have the colors locked, I can work on design. I'll have them ready in a few days, ok? In the meantime, figure out the numbers and quantities needed."

"Got it. I'll be driving out to Southampton to take some measurements."

Business concluded, the two women sat back and relaxed, enjoying their decadent morning treat.

"Did I tell you about the time I was lost in a grotto in southern Portugal?" Sam asked.

Cara shook her head, "No, pray, tell."

"A handsome, dark-eyed native came to my rescue. He gifted me this bowl, after a fun day frolicking together. I will leave the rest up to your imagination." Samantha pointed and winked.

"Oh, come on."

"Or about the time I was in Mexico for Spring break? I visited a ceramics factory and ended up going out to dinner with one of the owners. Got some great pottery, too."

"Where in Mexico? You have to be so careful where you visit these days."

"You have to be mindful everywhere. All countries have their not so safe areas."

"I suppose, but parts of Mexico sound particularly frightening. Let me share what I read this morning." Cara pulled up the article about the man being found speared with a fire-iron.

"Yikes. Tampico is obviously not one of the safer areas. It's a port city, so I imagine drugs circulate through there."

"I've read about a few of these types of scenarios. It fascinates and scares me at the same time. Let's get back to your conquests. You were saying…"

Cara felt like a perpetual wallflower listening to her friend's encounters.

"Listen, Sam, I wanted to show you a website I discovered this morning. There's a gallery in Paris that currently is showing an interesting ceramic collage show. I've never seen anything like it. Check this out." She opened the website.

"Wow, that looks pretty cool. Who is the artist? Wait, is this the artist or owner? He looks interesting too."

"Yes, my sentiments exactly. What do you think about the art though?"

"Cool, but not for Nero. He's more traditional in his likes."

"By the way, Sam, we really should check out all the upcoming auctions for ceramics. They're generally a good source of inspiration and sometimes you get lucky with a piece or two."

"You mean someone else might have a penchant for Greek nudes?"

"Exactly."

"Sounds good. Let me know when you want to go."

"I'll check the preview schedule. We can also study the Greek pottery section in the Met one day."

"Good idea!"

Cara studied her animated friend as she chatted away. After Samantha's husband died at the hands of a drunk driver, she started her own business, despite not needing the money. Her husband's death left Samantha with a broken heart, but a flush bank account, unlike Cara. Sam rebounded by immersing herself in completing her unfinished interior design degree and starting her own business. This venture put her in contact with a cross section of interesting people and she quickly blossomed into a well-respected professional with a steady flow of assignments. Her captivating, humorous impressions and caring disposition were her unmistakable assets. She also had a wicked sense of style. Cara was thankful for her business and treasured Sam's friendship.

Cara was aware that her keen sense of color and Samantha's acute style were a marriage made in design heaven. They began working together on a few lucrative projects and became close friends in the process. Sam's *joie de vivre* was infinitely catching and often lifted Cara up when work was slow or tedious. She also proved to be a big boost in Cara's stuttering business.

When Samantha left, Cara sat down at the kitchen table with the remaining Portuguese pieces and pulled out her sketch pad. *A new job! Thank God!* The Christmas reunion was beginning to look more promising. Maybe they could all get away for a few days after all.

"Just what I needed." she mumbled out loud. *Thank-you, God for sending Samantha my way.* Inspired, Cara worked through lunch and most of the afternoon. For once the phone didn't ring. She looked at the upcoming auction schedules online and wrote down a few dates in her studio calendar. Reminded by her post-it-note, she managed to get the email regarding the holidays out to her children.

Chapter VI

The Heat is On

JFK airport moaned with its usual chaos. The arrival screen showed the Aero Mexico plane from Mexico City landing slightly behind schedule. Standing next to an associate dressed in a t-shirt emblazoned with the Metropolitan Museum of Art logo, Carlos waited anxiously near the baggage claim area for Fernando Flores to appear. The associate was yet another nephew from Fernando's expansive family. Fortunately, one of the more delightful ones.

Craning, Carlos spotted his boss's trademark black fedora. Behind him, a big head with long, shiny black hair advanced expeditiously. Carlos grimaced. Jose!

"I see them, Angel. You ready?"

"I was born ready, but never ready enough for Fernando."

Carlos chuckled. He knew exactly what Angel meant.

Fernando and Jose approached the baggage claim area with purpose. Their last visit to New York had been in a warmer season and Fernando did not look happy, but Carlos knew, business always took precedence, regardless of the season. Slowly, he approached his boss, but his eyes gravitated toward Jose. Despite the frigid weather, Jose still wore his thin, white, muscle revealing, t-shirt, a blank backdrop for his beloved silver and turquoise cross. Carlos wondered if he slept with it on. His outer wear consisted of a light-weight black leather jacket and a pair of tattered jeans. Fernando needed to buy his cousin a wool sweater, scarf and hat Carlos decided. New York was freezing and they had no time to be sick.

Business was good and expansion was necessary for survival these days. Carlos wasn't confident Fernando's business plan would work, but it wasn't his call to make. He followed orders and managed books.

He hoped to save more money if things worked out. He wasn't even close to his personal goal despite not having a huge overhead. He sent his sister Hermosa, a moderate monthly check to help with her rent in Mexico City and put whatever was left in his savings. Room, board, and wheels were covered by Fernando when they traveled. In Tampico, he rented a small studio apartment. He had few expenses, and his worldly possessions were scant. In fact, they could fit in one suitcase. His parent's home and boat had been sold to pay for Hermosa's and his education. His jeep was owned and covered by Fernando's company. Since Fernando covered expenses, Carlos was happy to work from anywhere. If it weren't for Fernando, Carlos would never have left Mexico. The clock was ticking, but timing was everything. Carlos was a patient man while his bank account inched upward from triple digits.

Fernando's nephew worked in the shipping department of the Metropolitan Museum of Art, hence the logo on his t-shirt. Fernando had taught Angel everything he knew; how to produce quality pottery, how to sell it, how to pack breakables properly and now he would teach him how to market. Fernando had congratulated himself when he heard his nephew landed a plum job in the shipping department at the prestigious museum. What a feat! Now it was pay back time for Angel. Carlos had not yet shared Fernando's more devious plans, despite being in New York a few days prior to his boss's arrival. Making all the accommodation arrangements had taken up his time. He would let Fernando share the news himself.

Fernando walked around the conveyor belt, scouting his luggage. As Carlos and Angel approached, they heard Fernando's assertive voice.

"Look, our bags are here. Grab them, Jose." Fernando's laser sharp emerald eyes scanned the anticipating crowd until he found his mark.

"Angel, Carlos, *Amigos. Hola.*"

Carlos noticed the order the names were uttered. Fernando didn't miss a beat. The waiting party advanced. Carlos smiled tentatively letting Angel step forward and hug his uncle. Fernando tipped his forefinger to the edge of his fedora at Carlos.

"*Hola! Que tal?*" he asked.

"Good, Fernando. Welcome to New York. Good flight?"

"Ok. Jose kept me entertained. Cold here." He raised his shoulders and swept his hands up and down his opposite arms. "Angel, how's the job?"

"Fine, Fernando. Thanks to your training, I'm doing well. I'm helping out in the ceramics reproduction department too. I feel a raise coming soon."

Carlos chuckled.

Fernando laughed. "That's what I like to hear. Carlos, I trust our apartment is ready?"

"Yes. Ready and stocked." White smiles mitigated the unmistakable tension.

Only Jose could stand to spend hours upon hours with Fernando and vice versa. They had a close, but dysfunctional relationship that Carlos didn't envy one bit. After shaking hands, Angel scurried in grasshopper fashion to secure the luggage and place it on a waiting cart, his nerves, showing. When Fernando called, everyone jumped to attention. Jose's unexpected presence was disconcerting and added another level of stress, but Carlos would deal with it, as always. Fernando's evil right-hand man was not to be trusted and required extra vigilance. The four men exited the airport to a waiting black SUV and within nanoseconds disappeared into the noisy, merging traffic.

Chapter VII

Double Trouble

Around five o'clock Cara's phone rang. She looked at the caller ID. It was Samson, Summer's twin.

"Hey, Samson. What's new in Paris?"

"Nothing crazy, Mom. Just wanted to say hi."

Unlike Jasper, Samson called frequently. Hearing his voice always made Cara realize how much she missed her children. If she had her choice, she would elect to have them all nearby. Sadly, she no longer had a choice. All three were adults.

"Any breaking news at the Associated Press I should know about?" she asked.

"No breaking news that you haven't already perused this morning, as I know you."

Cara liked being the nucleus of her family; everyone deferred to her for family updates, which pleased her immensely. Small pleasures.

"What are you up to?" Samson asked.

"The usual," Cara replied as she continued sketching in her pad. "Designing erotica for a client." She waited for Samson's response. It took a few seconds. She counted, three, two one.…

"What? Erotica? Did I hear you correctly? Or is this a bad connection?"

Cara laughed. "Sam and I are doing a special project for Nero. A new classic Greek tile kitchen for the sweet men, who love to bake. What? You didn't think I would be hip enough for erotica?"

"Not exactly, Mom. Erotica in the kitchen? Is that a thing?"

"It is now. Sensuality while baking is a plus, don't you think? Besides, how else would they come up with their novel pastry ideas? Greek and Roman erotica has been around since the sixth century B.C."

"If you say so."

"So how does Paris compare to Hong Kong, Samson?" Cara asked curiously.

"Paris is great! I love this city. I've been doing a lot of walking. So much to see everywhere."

Samson always worked on interesting stories that required travel. He'd started his career in Hong Kong as a foreign correspondent's assistant and then moved to Paris after a brief interim stay in New York. Cara missed him. "I still regret not visiting you in Hong Kong, but I plan to make it to Paris," Cara replied, wistfully. She traveled vicariously through her children these days, but she vowed to change that if her business picked up. It was difficult having children who chose to live so far from home, but she consoled herself with the fact that Summer was close.

"I just got an assignment to cover the *Berlinale* in February. I'll be covering the international film circuit in Berlin, the *Golden Bear Awards*. So excited."

Cara's eyebrows jumped. "Holy cow! Aren't you the lucky one! Have you told Summer yet?" she inquired sitting back and eyeing her sketch.

"Not yet, you're the first to know."

"Thanks, can I tell her? By the way, did you get my email about the holidays? I want everyone to congregate here this year."

"Yes, you can. Sounds good, Mom. Can't give you the affirmative yet as it depends on work, but count me in anyway."

"Please try. Jasper already agreed. Between you and me, I think he's a little homesick."

"Jasper? Really?"

They chatted for a few minutes until Samson yawned.

"I'll let you go back to your anatomy lesson. Night, Mom. Love you."

The six-hour time difference was catching up to him. Cara was excited for Samson and imagined herself in Berlin at the film festival, but only for a second. Who was she kidding? Only a winning lottery ticket would get her there.

She surveyed her drawings with a critical eye and decided to call it a day. Locking the outside door, she turned off all the lights and set the alarm and headed to the warmth of her cozy kitchen. Once there, Cara stretched as if doing a salutation, then bent into an airplane posture to see what her dinner possibilities were in the fridge. What could she make that was simple and quick? An omelet? A frittata? She settled on the latter and got to work cutting up onions and little, red potatoes. She called Summer to see how the script changes were progressing. At least now she had some exciting news to share. Summer didn't answer. Her voice mailbox was perpetually full. Disappointed, Cara hung up and concentrated on chopping a zucchini. A few minutes later, her phone rang. It was Summer.

"Hi, Mom, are you ready to hear more script changes? I've been working all day."

"Sure thing. You have my full attention. I'm making frittatas and that takes time."

"Yum."

Cara sautéed the vegetables and added the egg mixture. She listened intently, adding her opinions when asked. Finally, she blurted out Samson's news.

"Wow, that is so awesome. He has the best job ever! I would kill to be his assistant on that trip."

"Get in line, honey. I haven't been anywhere since your Aunt Betsy's funeral two years ago."

They chatted a while longer. Together, they concluded they needed to get out of New York. Maybe after the holidays? New Years?

"Wouldn't it be fun to go to the Berlinale?"

"Yes. It would, Summer." It was agreed that once again the boys had all the fun and the girls just treaded water. A change was imminent.

Cara thought about Summer's graduation from NYU in film and television. "I think the last time we were all in one place was your graduation and that's what, a year and a half ago?"

"Yeah, I guess so."

"How is Harley's film project going?"

"Still working on it for miniscule pay."

The experience was priceless, but starvation was not a long-term option, Cara kept trying to impress upon her. Since work was so sporadic, Summer had time to dally on her own projects and apply for grant opportunities whenever applicable. Summer was temporarily content with this arrangement. Cara was merely appeased that one of her three children was close to home and occasionally free for dinner. She worried about Summer's future though.

"Well, one step at a time. How about dinner next week?"

"Ok. I'll call you on Sunday when I know my schedule. Bye, Mom."

As Cara flipped her frittata onto an eye-popping dinner plate adorned with generous fuchsia roses, the phone rang again. It was Summer with one more script change. Thank God Summer lived in the same time zone.

"You know, Mom. Maybe we should try to go to Paris after the holidays. We could stay with Samson and then go to the *Berlinale* while he's there. Jasper could join us. That would be so fun."

"You know, I thought that as well. It certainly would. Now there's a goal worth working hard for. Save your pennies. Oh, that's right. You don't have spare pennies."

"Mom!"

Chapter VIII

Lights! Camera! Action!

Cara sat at her computer Friday morning sipping Rooibos tea. She was scanning world news. Her eye roamed over an article about a man in jail in South America for maliciously killing two women. The most disturbing aspect of the story was that he was permitted to marry and procreate while incarcerated. *Should those genes really be passed on?* Next a ferry captain was sentenced to 36 years in prison for abandoning ship, leaving 300 school children to die. Cara shuddered at the thought of those poor children following directions only to drown with their life vests on. Finally, she read about the impending snowstorm anticipated in the northern states. She looked up and peered out of her window. The morning sun was hidden in folds of dark, metallic waves. There wasn't a single animal in sight. Even the plump woodchuck dubbed Harry, who lunched regularly on her vegetation, was nowhere in sight. Was he in hibernation now? To end her morning news on a positive note, she pulled up Fereaux Galleries and studied their new art show and the owner's picture. She wondered if her more creative work would be of interest to him. Should she send him an email? She decided to think about it. That would require updating her website first and maybe photographing some of her newer pieces professionally. Presentation was everything. All her ducks needed to be in a row before she could attempt reaching out. She studied his face again and wondered if he would like her artist portrait as much as she liked his.

Cara savored the last sip of tea and shuffled off to the shower. Her cell phone notified her of an incoming text. She peeked at the screen and decided to shower first. It was Summer with an urgent message to call her back. Summer's calls were never quick, and she needed to begin her day. While drying her long, hazelnut, sun-streaked hair, Cara noticed another urgent text. Summer was relentless when she wanted Cara's attention. *What could be so pressing?*

Cara lined her bright blue eyes with a smoldering ember charcoal pencil, added some coal mascara, softly tinted moisturizer, and her favorite soft cherry lip gloss. Done. She threw on her favorite, faded size eight jeans, a white, flower embroidered, Italian cotton shirt, and a cozy, magenta cashmere sweater. One brief look in the mirror convinced her that at 47 she still looked good, save a wrinkle here and there. Who was counting anyway?

The house felt chilly and empty. She slipped into her electric blue uggs, minus socks and settled into the warmth of her studio, rearranging erotica sketches on the table. She called Summer back as she brewed Columbian decaf. Sam was coming to view her ideas. Summer picked up on the first ring.

"Mom, are you ready for this? Remember the film proposal I drafted and submitted?"

"The one you keep changing?"

"Yes, that one! I got the Independent Filmmakers Grant. Yahoo!!!" Summer's voice went up a few octaves.

"OMG, does that mean you have enough funds to shoot your film?"

"Yes!"

"In Paris?"

"Yes!"

Cara whistled incredulously as she stopped arranging her drawings. Stunning developments.

"Wahoo, I'm going to Paris, Mom! And you are too. Are you still there?"

"Yes, I'm processing." Cara could hear the joy in Summer's voice.

"I just discovered the email. I was too excited to read the details. I'll forward it to you. Tell me what fine print I missed. Later."

"Ok then. Oh, and Summer, congrats," Cara mumbled through her descending brain fog. She sat quietly for a moment staring into space. Now all three children would be abroad. Exciting, but terrifying. Suddenly she felt abandoned and very alone. Cara, who preferred her family close, was losing the last one in the nest, even though Summer wasn't technically in the nest anymore. As she waited for her coffee to finish brewing, she thought about her love of travel. Here was a window of opportunity, so why wasn't she thrilled? Her mind wandered to the Fereaux gallery, and she perked up. A visit there could possibly be an adventure in itself.

Cara poured coffee into her favorite pink and lilac peony mug, sat down on one of the eight barstools surrounding her studio table and searched her email. Sure enough, Summer's grant was approved. Sighing, she reread the email, clutching her feel good mug tightly with both hands. The world around her was forever changing and yet she stood still.

Footsteps shifted her attention to the studio door as Samantha waltzed in, peach umbrella wedged under her arm. Cara smiled as Sam dumped the contents of her embrace, from under her minty rain cape, on the expansive oak table.

"Hello. Surprise. The drawings are done. What have you got there?"

Cara needed time to process and fully digest Summer's life changing news. She stayed mum about Summer's phone call. Samantha's timing was perfect and a good diversion. Her attention shifted to Sam and away from her imploding holiday plans.

"Ideas, fabrics and architectural plans. We have work to do."

"Ok then. Coffee? I have some auction dates for us to consider."

Chapter IX

Christmas Where?

The following few days Cara was busy with getting orders out. She worked on the first few designs Samantha approved and spent a lot of time listening to Summer's jubilant elation and subsequent panic. Summer was carefully planning her trip abroad and trying to assemble a small team. Easier said than done since most of her esteemed colleagues already had jobs, time constraints or projects of their own. Cara listened to how the joy turned to frustration.

"I can't find the right people, Mom."

Cara could hear the exasperation in her daughter's voice.

"Kelly can't take time off from a new job, David is in LA on a freelance project and Mica just accepted work that will keep her busy through Easter. I'm running out of good people to ask." Summer's frustration was real.

Cara heard from Samson too. Samson liked to share his life and loves. He was currently enamored with a Parisian girl named

Natalie Saint Claire. Natalie worked in the media department of a major auction house, *Beaussant Lefevre*. Samson explained, with gusto, how he and Natalie met at an art media event at the *Pompidou Centre*. He sounded light-hearted and drunk with love. Samson was elated to hear that Summer would be joining him in Paris. Cara could hear the bubbling glee in his voice. Samson and Summer had always been close.

"We'll have so much fun. When is she coming?"

"After the holidays, I hope. You know, Summer will be busy working, Samson." Cara reminded him.

"I know, Mom! Me too. There are weekends and evenings, Ms. Killjoy."

"Right." *Not in movie making land.* Cara refrained from voicing this revelation out loud. She could visualize her son leaning back in his desk chair, pleased. She thought about all the times she saw Summer filming and editing for hours, regardless of the day or time. She knew what being on location meant. Very long days. Pure exhaustion. Hours of scheduling and rescheduling. Dealing with peoples' constantly changing needs. Editing wasn't any better except now you were locked in a closet with a computer and oblivious to the outside world. Samson would figure it out soon enough.

The following few weeks were work as usual for Cara, but chaotic for Summer. Cara kept getting frustrated reports that Summer's team wasn't coming together as she envisioned. She listened patiently and finally suggested hiring abroad. This idea was first met with vehement resistance, then a few days later reluctantly revisited and finally, a week later, decided upon.

"I mean… I guess I could hire people in Paris, but that will take extra time." Summer lamented. "How will I find them?"

"The same way you find them here. It may even work out better in the end. These would be professionals that can help with local bureaucracy too. That could be a big plus abroad." Cara argued.

"I suppose," Summer replied half-heartedly.

It meant leaving a little earlier than expected. Instead of leaving for Paris in January, Summer would have to leave before the holidays. Cara was crushed. Her much-anticipated holiday reunion, with all her children at home, had just officially imploded.

Summer quickly remedied the family's disappointment by announcing her intention of inviting everyone to Paris for the holidays. She argued, since two out of three family members were already there and a third was close, in Barcelona, it made perfect sense. Why shouldn't they all celebrate the holidays abroad?

"Come on, Mom. Christmas in Paris! How fun is that?"

"Christmas is my busiest time," Cara complained. "I can't just leave that time of year."

"Then come the day before and stay through New Years. Get all your orders out early."

Cara looked at the sliced strawberries floating in her water. Lunch was liquid and brief these days, shakes, soups, flavored water. She sighed and reluctantly agreed.

"Ok, I suppose I could try. I can't afford a hotel though."

"No worries. You'll stay with me, and Jasper can stay with Samson. We already discussed it."

"Really? You don't even have a place to stay yet."

"I'll make sure I get one with a sleeper, I promise."

"Ok then. Let's talk when you do."

The thought of spending Christmas alone was depressing beyond words. She would have to manage somehow. No expensive dinners out or extra non-vital expenditures. Samson readily agreed with Summer since now he wasn't keen on leaving Natalie. Jasper, as always, was flexible despite his steady workload. Within a few days, and a flood of emails and phone calls back and forth, the decision was final. The holidays would be spent in Paris one way or another. The Crenston family started booking their flights. Cara felt a tinge of excitement in her belly.

Chapter X

A Sense of the Familiar

The Mexican restaurant, *Casa Carlitos*, near Union Square was quiet between lunch and dinner. Carlos, Angel, Jose and Fernando were huddled at a back table, away from the bar, discussing business over a leisurely, late lunch. Whenever the waiter ventured over, Fernando smiled and exchanged a few pleasantries, his demeanor demanding privacy. Carlos looked down at his plate, his baseball cap shielding his face from view. Once the waiter left, the intense discussions resumed. Humming, hushed voices zipped back and forth over the colorful tile table. A blaring radio afforded them the privacy they needed.

Fernando, his black fedora sloping downward, rested his snake eyes on his cousin's face. "This plan must be well executed. We can't afford any mistakes. This is not Mexico. I cannot fix things my usual way." His eyes rotated from Carlos to Angel.

Hearing that, Carlos felt a wave of relief.

"Are you sure about the dates of the shipment?"

"Yes, Boss. This is the schedule. Of course, schedules can always change and sometimes we don't know until the last minute, but I'll be in touch if that happens. Don't worry. You'll know as soon as I know."

Fernando studied his nephew's face for a sign of uncertainty. Carlos shifted back and forth between the two but saw no one waver. It seemed Fernando had taught Angel confidence too. Eyes still lingering on the youthful, eager face, Fernando broke into a blinding smile. "Of course, Angel."

Carlos nodded silently still gaging the interaction. He trusted Angel more than Fernando, but he knew Fernando ruled by instilling fear. No one dared to or wanted to make mistakes around Fernando; sloppy work had consequences. If they did, there was no guarantee that blame would not be passed on unfairly just to cover tracks. Some events were just out of anyone's control though and that mere thought made Carlos uneasy. Not so much for himself, because Carlos had learned how to handle Fernando. He knew to keep calm, keep his head down and stay silent until the storm was weathered. Carlos had earned Fernando's trust over the years. He was reliable and made few mistakes. His specialty was catching other people's mistakes, especially the financial kind. However, any new blood that had yet to learn the ropes, he was fearful for. He remembered being in that unenviable position all to well.

After lunch, coffee was ordered. The conversation became less charged as the boss inquired about personal matters.

"How is your girlfriend these days? Still the same one?" Fernando asked.

"Yes. For now. She's sweet as sugar and doesn't ask questions. Works for me." Carlos replied. Changing the subject before Fernando talked about meeting her, he deflected, "You should see Angel's girl. What a knockout."

Fernando immediately looked interested. "Really? Tell me about her, Angel. Do you have a picture?"

As Angel chatted about his girlfriend, Carlos caught the waiter eyeing their table with renewed interest. Glancing at his phone, he realized they had been there for over two hours. He motioned for the check. It appeared the boss had dropped business discussions, satisfied that everything was in order. Carlos hoped things would run smoothly or there would be hell to pay for Angel. He also desperately wanted a financial bonus, which he was assured if things rolled as they should. Fernando did spread his wealth when the sun shone, one of his few nice attributes. Carlos reminded himself of the Mexican saying, *Money is a good servant, but an evil master.*

Chapter XI

Up, Up, and Away

November passed in a flash. Cara and Summer spent Thanksgiving in a Little Italy restaurant. Cooking for two was out of the question as both were extremely busy. Jasper and Samson worked through it since Thanksgiving was not a holiday Europeans celebrated. Samantha visited relatives. Cara kept up the pace and worked diligently to finish her orders. Her motivation was singular. Cara knew Summer was working around the clock to finalize her script, yet again, and assemble a skeleton crew, which in the end consisted of two people, Ted Braxton, a competent producer and all-around assistant, and Hope Hoshino, a trusted cinematographer from Los Angeles, with solid referrals. Both Ted and Hope were free lancers, so they were able to travel. Most of the equipment, the actors and the props would be rented, hired, and assembled abroad. Cara was pleased that Summer gave herself time to do that. She was confident that her daughter had reached the best possible decision under the circumstances.

Ted established a home base over the internet through Airbnb. He used his impeccable organization skills to find a lovely, spacious apartment in the Marais district. An older couple, who spent Christmas through Spring in Nice, was thrilled to rent their penthouse apartment during the cold months. They could leave December 1st. Their children would join them for the holidays in Southern France this year.

On December 1st Summer and her skeleton crew left for Paris. That morning Cara was close to tears as she sipped her tea in front of her laptop. Reading the world news didn't help. Numerous Indian women, who had undergone a government sponsored sterilization procedure for a mere ten dollars, had died. Countless others were fighting for their lives.

"Good Lord." Cara quipped. *How is this still possible?*

She said a quick prayer for the families and breathed a sigh of relief that she lived in a safer place, medically speaking. Her thoughts were interrupted when Summer called from JFK airport, mid-morning, to say good-bye. Summer was at her gate, waiting to board Air France.

"Bye, Mom. In 24 days we'll all be together. I can't wait! It'll be so much fun. I'll keep you posted on our progress. Keep checking your email."

"Of course!" Cara promised. "Send pictures and text when you arrive. Safe travels and call whenever you can. I'm curious if the apartment is as good as it looks on the internet."

She tried hard to sound cheerful, but her heart felt like a lead balloon. When she hung up the phone, the balloon ruptured, and the floodgate of tears breached her paisley flannel shirt. After she calmed down, she left for a calming yoga class. On her way home, she stopped at the Apple store and treated herself to a tangerine tablet. The bright tangerine color lifted her spirits in a Zen-like way. She was certain the devise would be useful for her business and her impending trip. When she got home, she tested the picture quality on some of her new, more sculptural work to finally update her website. She wanted her site to sparkle and reflect her talent before she peddled her work at Fereaux Galleries. Cara decided she also needed a new artist picture for her Bio. She texted Samantha.

Chapter XII

The Fedora Takes Manhattan

The weather in New York was frigid, especially by Mexican standards. Carlos walked to the nearest Starbucks from the AirBnb rental. Pulling down his charcoal wool hat and pushing up his matching scarf, shoulders hunched, he half ran the last block to the coffee haven. He was glad the scheduled meeting was at the apartment as he was in no mood to travel around the city in sub-freezing temps. How could people live here? He wasn't cut out for this weather and couldn't wait to leave. Paris was cold, but New York was definitely colder. *Soon.*

He entered Starbucks and ordered a variety of complicated coffee drinks. For himself, he kept it simple. "Add one medium *café latte* to that order, please."

Waiting for his little tray of coffees, he thought about his upcoming meeting. Fernando exhaled pressure these days. When he smelled opportunity, he was relentless. He had the sensitivity of a pit bull and the drive of a racehorse, pushing himself and his people to their melting point. Carlos had been quick to volunteer for the coffee run despite the frigid temps just to escape the tension his boss radiated in the apartment.

Back inside, coffee distributed, Carlos studied the auction catalogues with Fernando hovering over his shoulder. Thankfully, the warm brew loaded with sugar, sweetened Fernando's mood a tad. Carlos watched as Fernando wrote little notations in red marker next to pottery images in his catalogue. Clearly, he admired the lines and colors of numerous pieces depicted. He had a definite appreciation for quality work. The vessels were exquisite, even to Carlos's untrained eye. Carlos's expertise was numbers, not fine art or ceramics, but he was learning a lot about this medium from his boss.

Seconds later, Jose walked in with a Mexican food order. The fitted wool sock hat Fernando bought for him looked absurd on his watermelon head, but Jose had picked it out and insisted it was what he needed. Carlos studied the high, turquoise and black horizontally-striped knit framing Jose's wide face and smiled. *The Cat in the Hat* had nothing on Fernando's cousin, he decided with an internal grin.

The meeting started when Angel arrived. He opened his laptop and pulled up floor plans of the Met's secure areas. Everyone gathered around Angel to listen. Angel's computer skills were unsurpassed in the Flores organization. Carlos wasn't far behind him. He paid attention and was a quick understudy.

The men sat around the table eating tacos and scouring the printed catalogues, marking them up according to Fernando's specifications. He insisted they all be on the same page. After a couple of hours of scheming, Fernando leaned back in his chair, satisfied. His plan was in place. Angel would be immensely useful.

"Jose, get the tequila. Let's do a round of shots."

As Jose poured the shot glasses, Carlos crunched the numbers on his calculator, dreaming of what he could do with that kind of money. When the men weren't looking, he poured his tequila into the nearest plant.

Chapter XIII

Auction Fiasco

Cara scanned her emails daily for news from everyone, the proverbial dangling carrot. She was delighted to hear even the smallest peep from her children. Any news, however dull, was better than no news.

These days, Cara reversed her routine and read her personal emails first. She woke up and immediately reached for her smart phone. She needed that immediate lift that only her family could provide. Samson and Summer did not disappoint. Jasper surprised her occasionally. There was hope for him yet.

Scrolling through local and world news, she noticed a brief article mentioning the de-accessioning of some noteworthy pottery at the Metropolitan Museum of Art. It was to be sold at one of the upcoming auctions she already had marked in her calendar. Cara decided to go to the viewing. She also made a mental note to text Samantha. It appeared there were some Spanish and Greek pieces represented in the lots. The previous auctions she had checked had proven fruitless, but this one looked rather promising with its Mediterranean representation.

Later that week, Cara traveled to Sotheby's for the pre-auction viewing. She took her new tangerine tablet with her and tested the picture quality on the pieces she knew Samantha would be interested in. The detail images were astoundingly clear. She marveled at the camera quality of her new Apple device and felt like the cat who stole the cream. She could certainly deduct the tablet as a business expense. Examining her pictures, she decided the auction was worth returning to. She texted Samantha to make a date.

The following Monday, they arrived at Sotheby's a little early, so Cara could show Samantha the relevant lots for sale. She brought her tablet to add sales information to her files.

"Check these out, Sam. The colors would work great in Nero's new kitchen, don't you think?"

"Yes, I so agree. Do you think we have a chance?"

"Don't know. Depends on who shows up for the auction, internet and phone bids included. If many dealers come, then no. If they don't, we have a fighting chance."

Twenty minutes later, Samantha handed the auctioneer's staff a few written bids, just in case some pieces "bought in" or didn't sell. Sometimes deals could be struck if the seller was willing to negotiate. There was always that possibility. They seated themselves four seats in, in the back row, so they could escape unnoticed after the pieces they had their eyes on were auctioned.

Just after the first lot sold, three men sat down in the same row, taking the last three seats by the aisle. Cara's gaze traveled across the empty seat between them, to a pair of strikingly rough hands with dirty fingernails. She watched the rough-skinned, suntanned hands scribbling quick notes in a printed-out catalogue and showing them to the associate seated beside him. *An artist?*

Her eyes traveled upward and she observed the associate studying the notes with piercing green eyes. He had jet black hair and wore a black fedora that cast a shadow over his chiseled features. She noticed that his hands, in comparison were smooth and finely manicured. He also seemed to favor distinctive gold jewelry. A huge gold Rolex and a substantial lion's head ring with ruby eyes caught Cara's immediate attention. *Wow.*

Cara glanced back at the man with the dirty fingernails with renewed interest. He wore a black baseball cap with golden letters stitched on it over his long, loose hair fashioned in a mullet hairstyle. She curiously leaned in to discreetly read the word "champagne" embroidered in elegant gold cursive on the front of his cap. The man with the champagne taste, oblivious to her stares, removed his black leather jacket revealing bulging muscles covered with an array of *chicanno* tattoos on his arms and shoulders underneath a thin, white cotton t-shirt. Around his thick neck was a large silver cross with beautiful, *sleeping beauty* turquoise stones. His eyes were ebony coals and the corner creases of his eyes and mouth were shifted downward as if in a funeral march. She studied the tattoos for a moment; a skull with a red rose covered his upper right arm and a multicolored, patterned griffin the left. Stylized sun symbols and various totem-type symbols ran down his inside forearms. The man gave Cara the chills.

The younger, third man, in the aisle seat, looked more approachable. His casual dress made his black, pointed lizard-skin cowboy boots pop. While the man with the fedora bid on an upcoming lot, the younger man carefully folded his black and cobalt blue tweed wool jacket, ocean-blue sweater, charcoal beanie and scarf and neatly placed them on the floor beside his aisle chair. His shiny, onyx hair was combed into a tidy ponytail, revealing a singular, thick 22kt gold hoop earring. The deep, golden color was a dead giveaway. Through his white shirt, she spotted a single tattoo; it was the same skull tattoo with a red rose. His facial features were distinct; a broken nose, a small but visible scar through his eyebrow, pronounced cheek bones, all topping the most sensuous lips. He also had the longest, dark lashes she had ever seen on a man. He had a 'bad boy' appeal.

Her eyes moved back to the man with the black fedora. Sitting in the middle, he appeared to be in charge, the boss perhaps. The other two kept leaning in seeking his approval as they scanned the auction catalogues and exchanged quickly jotted notes and muffled retorts. She wondered if he also had a similar tattoo.

Periodically, the men surveyed the room and spoke quietly in Spanish. They continued to capture Cara's attention because they stood out from the 'known' clientele. Over the years, Cara recognized many of the usual suspects, the artists, the dealers, the designers and the various collectors, even if she did not know them all personally. While artists and collectors sometimes came in unlikely packaging, these three men looked like they belonged in a different world entirely. Cara was intrigued.

"Hey, Sam. Check out the three guys in our row." She sat back and watched Sam lean slightly forward to get a good look.

"Whoa...it looks like a scene from *The Godfather,* Spanish style. Hope they don't bid against us. That's all I care about."

Cara giggled quietly. "Doesn't seem likely, but you never can tell." Her eyes kept gravitating back to her neighbors with unexplainable fascination. Samantha, oblivious to the men, focused on the auction. Their first lot of interest was coming up momentarily.

When the auctioneer pointed to the Greek vase the women had earmarked in their catalogue, Samantha raised her hand to bid. Beside them, the man with the golden hoop earring raised his hand too. Further in the front, a third hand shot up. Then a fourth.

"Lot number 33 is one of the finest examples of Greek pottery we have in today's auction. Do I hear a bid for 1575?"

Samantha's hand shot up again, but so did their neighbor's. The prices increased steadily in measured increments until the vase was finally sold for way more than Samantha could justify to her client.

"Can you believe that vase sold for $15,500? Let's try again for Lot 38. That might be more affordable."

"These guys next to us are bidding on the same pieces we are. They must have deep pockets."

"Yes, but they didn't get the vase either. They just drove the price up."

"Right, Lot 38 is coming up. How high should we go?"

"I'll signal you when to stop. If it goes past 2000, let it go."

Much later, Samantha nudged Cara as their final lot came and went. The Mediterranean ceramics they were interested in had been lost to various bidders, including one to the men next to them. "Surprise, surprise," she thought. She shifted her attention to the auctioneer.

Samantha groaned. "No luck today. Shall we go?"

"Yeah. I doubt we can outbid these people. Let's try one more time. Lot 65 looks good. Then we can leave."

After losing out to another higher bid, the two ladies scrambled in their seats and gathered their belongings. The consolation was that they were now in possession of exceptional pictures of the ceramics they admired. It helped to have a visual source when sketching designs.

"No worries, Sam, I got fabulous pictures to work from. I can recreate some of the designs and capture the essence of the pieces. All for a more reasonable price, if that makes you feel better."

"Damn though," Samantha muttered. "I really would have liked one or two originals."

"It's hit or miss with these auctions. Sometimes I get lucky, and sometimes I don't even get close. Guess today was one of those days. This sale was written up because of the museum pieces," Cara offered her client, consolingly. "It attracted a bigger crowd with some new faces. Some of those ceramics were magnificent".

"Yes," sighed Sam as she pulled on her cherry beret. "Back to the drawing board. It was worth the trip. I got an education, and you were inspired. I suppose that's the best we can hope for today."

"Appears so," Cara agreed, putting down her tablet to button her coat. Grabbing her handbag from the floor, she stuffed her auction papers inside. She cast a downward glance at the three men as she passed their seats and studied their heads huddled together. As she and Sam tip-toed to the door, she felt a tap on her shoulder. She jumped. The man with the golden hoop earring briefly surveyed her surprised face. Looking into his warm, milk-chocolate eyes, she decided they were kind, but too quick to shift away from her own. His face was expressionless, statue-like and belied the warmth in his eyes.

"I think you forgot this." He held out the tablet she had left on her chair.

"Oh yes, thank you so much! You just averted a potential disaster."

He nodded, showing no reaction. Cara again, admired his beautiful long eye lashes, the kind most women would pay big money for. Before she could utter another syllable, he returned to his seat. Cara couldn't help but wonder what his business was and why he was here. Was he a dealer or a collector? Or was he here representing someone else? She guessed he was only a little older than her children, in his early to mid-thirties perhaps?

Two days later, Cara was reading the morning news and noticed a small paragraph with the caption, "Art Theft at Sotheby's." Horrified, she discovered that some of the pottery from the Metropolitan Museum was stolen from the decorative arts department or loading docks at Sotheby's. As anticipated, these items were some of the higher priced pieces they had examined, the ones that exceeded Sam's budget. Cara quickly checked her tablet. She was certain that she was in possession of several of the stolen items' images. She remembered them clearly. Checking her notes and notated picture sheets, she verified her suspicions. Reaching for her phone, she called Samantha.

"Sam, you're not going to believe this. I'm so glad I took all those detailed pictures at Sotheby's. There was a robbery after we left and a few pieces we liked were among those stolen."

"Oh, my! You'll have to show me which ones. Send me the article. I sure am glad we didn't bid on them with Nero's money. That could have been a disastrous mess."

"Yeah. Who could have stolen those ceramics? They have good security there. I'll have them on my radar now. I'm familiar with how they look."

"Honestly, what are the chances of them popping up? They'll probably be sold on the black market, don't you think?"

"Maybe, but you never know."

Chapter XIV

La Vie Parisienne

When the Air France plane landed in Paris at Charles de Gaulle Airport, Summer and her two friends gathered their luggage, hailed a taxi and headed to the apartment on Rue Malher. "Wow, I can't believe we made it," Summer remarked, dropping her suitcases in the foyer, and flopping down on the nearest chair. The days leading up to their departure had been hectic. Ted rolled the girls' suitcases into the living room and walked into the kitchen to investigate. Hope followed him.

"Nice kitchen. We'll definitely hang in here."

"What are we doing for food tonight? Dinner out after we nap?"

"Yes."

The past weeks' pressures and the seven-hour flight had exhausted everyone's reserves. It was an ungodly early morning hour on a Sunday, so no one felt compelled to do anything but hop into bed. They arrived at the apartment, briefly marveling at the location and size, then melted onto the nearest, appealing mattress.

"I choose the yellow room. It has an extra bed for when my mother comes. Ted, go ahead and take the master." Summer offered. "Does that sound ok, Hope?"

"Sure, Summer. As long as my room has a soft bed, I don't care which room is mine. We can share the other bathroom."

"The blue room works for me. I appreciate not sharing a bathroom with you girls. No offense."

"None taken. We might just feel the same way about you." Summer chuckled. "See you in a few hours, guys."

The next morning, Summer faintly heard Ted showering and puttering around the apartment. She listened to him tiptoeing past her door, then the front door closed softly. She secretly hoped he was looking for the nearest bakery. Her tummy was rumbling. In Paris, bakeries dotted the cityscape.

When Ted returned, she could smell a fragrant French roast brewing and hear dishes clanging. Ted was making just the right amount of noise to get her attention. She lay listening to the unfamiliar apartment and street sounds, unable to move despite the compelling scents.

"That smells incredible," Summer heard Hope say a short while later. She could visualize Hope's small nose wrinkling with enthusiasm. She heard Ted pour coffee and she listened to their conversation, still unable to rise and shine.

"Sleep ok?"

"Yes, thanks. You?"

"Yeah. It appears Summer is still out. Shall we clang a few pots?" Laughter.

Earlier, when the front door clicked, Summer woke up, feeling slightly disoriented. She glanced at the unfamiliar surroundings and the realization that she was in Paris sunk in. She stretched and rolled over. When she heard Ted return, her eyelids fluttered. Had she been in New York, she would have snoozed longer. She took in the sunny room, with its fine nuances. The walls were painted a soft lemon yellow, and the furniture was in a French empire style. There was a large dresser, a desk and chair with shelves over it and a lovely impressionist style painting. By the tall window stood a comfortable, straight backed Louis XV armchair with a white tray table next to it. The view faced the Seine. Summer pulled out Samson's number from the side pocket of her handbag and looked across the river from her comfortable bed. She was excited to see her brother, but it was too early to call. She stayed in bed listening to the sounds of her new temporary home, familiarizing herself.

Eventually, hopping out of bed, she pulled back the sheer, ivory curtains. They would stay in the open position for the next six months. She slipped on her grey sweatpants under the spacious white t-shirt she slept in and followed the fragrant coffee scent.

Her bedroom was the closest of four to the living room. It was also smaller than Hope's and Ted's, but it had a door to the wrap around terrace that enticed her. The flat was a horizontal, railroad apartment. On one end, were the four bedrooms and on the other end were the kitchen and entry way. Summer tumbled out of her sunny room in her trademark cushioned, plush boy sweat socks, a reminder of her two brothers. She walked through a series of French doors bridging the living and dining room to the kitchen. The apartment boasted a long wrap around terrace that faced southwest. It ran from the kitchen and living room, past Summer's room to the master bedroom, occupied by Ted.

Hope's bedroom, opposite Ted's, and the spare bedroom, opposite Summer's, faced the courtyard side of the building and had no terrace. Hope's bedroom was a floral vision in lilac with Louis XVI furniture. Discovering the details of this gorgeous, but pleasantly weathered, apartment, proved to be fascinating. She walked through the Louis XIV living room into the dining room and continued, following the tantalizing scent to the adjoining kitchen.

After her short discovery walk, Summer entered the kitchen and viewed the French doors that lead out to the penthouse terrace. The kitchen had a servant's entrance where the service elevators stopped, just a few feet from the elaborate and more formal, bird cage elevator at the main entrance. Outside the kitchen terrace doors, a table with chairs, bordered by large planters along a shoulder-high wall, divided their terrace from the neighbors. Summer shifted her focus to her friends seated around an old, weathered pine table. She joined the conversation.

"Morning. How did you all sleep?" Summer inquired as she picked a cushioned wooden chair. She glanced around at the beautifully detailed, white-washed, pine cabinets, taking in rows of radiant pottery. *Mom would approve.* This was clearly a French country kitchen with expressive pottery, copper pots trimmed with blue and white enamel handles and old-fashioned jam jars lining the weathered cupboard shelves. The floors were a rustic, white, wide-plank pine and showed their advancing age. Many interesting stories must have unfurled here. If only those boards could talk. Summer stood by the pine table as Ted poured her a cup of coffee that smelled heavenly. Starbucks be damned.

"Great. Like Louis XVI himself. Milk? Sugar?"

"Just milk."

She took a big sip and stared at the rich brown liquid swirling in her cup. The scent alone was starting to revive her tired bones.

"Those pastries smell divine, Ted. Where did you get them so early?"

"There's a yummy bakery right on the corner of this block. We're in luck. There's also a nice café nearby."

Hope pointed to the chair next to her. She picked up her own coffee mug and marveled at the stylized bird design.

"Morning, Summer. It was the smell of good French roast that got me out of bed. I'm a 'good coffee' addict, especially in the AM. Try one of these pastries. I could easily give up avocado toast for a few months. Sit."

Summer squinted at Hope's sleek, shiny, jet-black hair cascading down her white, quilted bathrobe. Underneath it she detected a slinky, silk fuchsia nightgown. Hope's delicate, embroidered, dark red silk slippers were strewn under the table and her bare feet resting up top another chair, revealed a dark red polish. She noticed Ted eyeing Hope's attire too. Hope looked like a delicate China doll. Summer knew she couldn't be underestimated though. By no means a doll or delicate, Hope exuded energy once you spent time with her. She was one fearless, tough cookie in a small package.

"What about you, Hope? How was your first night?"

"I slept like a corpse."

Summer glanced over at her. She was chewing on an almond croissant with gusto.

"Did you see the living room? It looks like a Catherine Deneuve movie set."

"I know. We'll have to explore after breakfast. First things, first."

"What's the plan for today, girls?"

"This smells and tastes so awesome. Thanks, Ted. I was thinking we could just bum around our neighborhood for the first day." Summer reached for a croissant and broke off the tip. "You know, jet lag and all."

Ted nodded.

His resourcefulness was impressive. Summer perused the breakfast delights: flavored croissants, *pain au chocolat,* a freshly baked French bread with country butter and an array of awesome looking jams and cheeses.

"Anything for my ladies. Dig in." Ted swept his hand over the length of the table."How does everyone like their rooms? We can still switch if anyone wants to."

"I'm good." Hope smiled.

"Summer?"

"I'm good, too."

"I'm happy in the blue room. Feeling a Picasso vibe in there." The blue master bedroom had a comfortable, tufted double bed flanked by two small mirrored nightstands. On the opposite wall were large twin dressers with a distressed full-length mirror between them. There was a Picasso reproduction on the wall. The room had a decent walk-in closet that must have been part of a renovation at some point. The de Fontenay's belongings were piled high in there, boxes towering to the ceiling. They only spared a few dresser drawers and a small corner of the closet for hanging clothes.

"They didn't leave me a lot of closet space, but I'm fine with that." Ted answered.

Hope and Summer's eyes met and they winked in unison. Ted liked clothes. For the next half-hour they sat around the worn kitchen table, relishing the setting and leisurely enjoying their first French breakfast together. To Summer the kitchen was reminiscent of her mom's studio, replete with pottery and weathered wood. The stylistic differences were minimal. The kitchen looked and felt like home. This would be her favorite room, especially with that incredible terrace, a valuable extension come nice weather. They drank café au lait, ate pain au chocolat, and ignored the unpacked bags still lingering in the living room.

"This kitchen reminds me of our kitchen at home. My mom will love this. She's coming for Christmas, by the way. I should give her a call. She was seriously bummed when I left."

"Send her some pictures," Hope suggested.

"Good idea. She's such a visual person. She'll love that."

"Nothing like caffeine and chocolate to rev your engines girls. I think we should scout possible locations today instead of just bumming. Never too early to start. What do you say?"

Summer nodded silently; her mouth stuffed. Crumbs airborne, she murmured an emphatic "yes". Hope agreed. They briefly planned their day in the neighborhood, and their work week, dividing up the tasks to be accomplished.

"Ted, tomorrow can you start checking into hiring crew and equipment? I'm so nervous about that."

"Yeah. Don't worry. I'll be on it."

"Hope, you and I will spread our wings and scope out locations and research permits for them. How about we walk around the Marais and visit the Centre Pompidou in the Beaubourg area this afternoon? It's close and we might get some ideas."

"I remember that from my last visit; the area has a crazy, artsy vibe." Ted pulled out the map he found in the kitchen drawer and they huddled around it.

"I think we truly lucked out with this apartment and location. Ted, you rock."

"I know."

Chapter XV

Joy and Life Along the Costa Brava

Jasper looked around his little, windowless office. Life in the international division of Rothschild Espana, a private bank, was good. It was a conservative outfit that suited Jasper perfectly, although his Spanish language classes in high school and college had not helped much in Catalonia. They barely prepared him for the different dialect or for working in Barcelona, but somehow, he thrived. He was a quick learner. An internship at the bank following his junior year abroad cemented his job offer. His old boss, Adriano Aldana, welcomed him back with open arms.

Jasper enjoyed living in Barcelona. He loved the city architecture, the climate, the proximity to beautiful beaches and the fact that it was one of Europe's principal seaports. Barcelona, a gateway to a plethora of Mediterranean islands as well as to all of southern Europe, was an incredibly beautiful part of the world. He was awed by the unusual architecture designed by *Antoni Gaudi*; the *Sagrada Familia*, the *Casa Mila* and *Park Guell*. Despite not being artistically inclined, he recognized that Gaudi's vision was unique, certainly different from what he was used to in New York.

Jasper easily navigated Barcelona's thriving business district and knew all the best local restaurants within his first month there. He enjoyed Sangria and tappas after work and he seamlessly immersed himself in Spanish culture, adapting to the slower pace. Jasper found company with his colleagues and business associates from other institutions. Enrique Banderas was his new best friend and sports soul mate. They bonded over soccer.

He reflected on the small close circle of friends he'd built through networking. On week ends, he enjoyed soccer games with Enrique, the beach, wine bars and all the trendy, new hot spots. Jasper's morning commute to the office was all of fifteen to twenty-five minutes depending on whether he drove or took the bus and his workday ended punctually, so his free time was substantial.

Today he took the bus to work. On his way out, he chatted with Clemente, his ever-present superintendent. "Morning, Clemente. Nice day today."

"*Buenos dias*, Jasper. How was your weekend? Clemente winked. "Off to work?"

"*Si*, it was sweet and too short."

"Isn't that always the case?"

"Yes. Have a good day." Jasper continued walking. He knew Clemente would chit-chat about nothing for an hour if he permitted him. Clemente loved to pry. When sober, he lived vicariously through his renters. During the day, he appeared sober but at night and on weekends, he enjoyed his Spanish red wine and the local pub, his alternate home.

Jasper worked hard but was content to spend weekends relaxing. This upcoming weekend he had plans with friends on

Friday night and a date on Saturday night. Nothing serious. At 27, Jasper knew he still had plenty of time to meet the right girl.

Jasper was headed to his weekly morning conference with his boss to discuss the status of their accounts and projects. "Maria, are we meeting in the conference room or Adriano's office?

"Adriano's office," Maria instructed him over the intercom. Jasper chuckled. Whenever he encouraged Maria to use the intercom, she jumped at the opportunity to hear her voice broadcasting. Jasper loved to egg her on and she in turn basked in his attention. He grabbed his materials and sauntered down the hall to Adriano's comfortable corner office, a spacious room with a window, but no view. When the last coffee was poured, the meeting began.

"Did everyone have a good weekend?" Adriano asked looking around the group. The replies were largely affirmative.

"Ok then, lets see where things stand with current accounts. Jasper, can you start?"

"Sure, Adriano."

Jasper, always organized and ready, summarized the status of his work from the past week. He loved his job and he considered himself lucky to have Adriano Aldana as his boss.

Chapter XVI

The Secret to Life? Butter!

Samson looked out over the uneven Parisian roof tops, circling down to the *bateaux mouches,* or tourist boats on the swiftly moving Seine River. His office was tiny, but the spectacular view more than compensated for the sparse furniture and miniscule room size. He worked on the left bank, in the Saint Germain district, on the *Quai de la Tournelle.* He was directly across the river from Summer, and he couldn't wait to see his twin sister. In fact, he couldn't stop his mind from wandering this morning.

Samson and Summer had always been tight, and he missed her tremendously. Not only did they look alike, slim, with blond, generous waves and infectious smiles; they also shared a kindred artistic sensibility and a keen sense of adventure. Both were passionate about their chosen fields and had no problem working through holidays and days off to accomplish their goals.

Samson thought about Jasper. Jasper worked hard, but he also liked to play hard. Jasper was the dark horse in the family, physically and mentally. His dark hair and eyes let him blend in easily with his adopted culture. He was conservative, but easy going, social, but private and Jasper was fiercely independent.

Jasper was like Grandpa Joseph, according to his mom, the grandfather that died before Samson and Summer were born. Samson was looking forward to seeing his sister, Jasper and his mom; it had been a while and he missed his family.

Lost in a daydream, the phone jolted him back to reality. He let it go to voicemail. Soon enough he would begin his workday, but for the moment, he was content to enjoy his breakfast--*café au lait,* a *croissant,* and a banana. His mind wandered to his dinner plans with Summer and Natalie. He wondered what Summer would think of his girlfriend and vice versa. He hoped they'd connect. It mattered a great deal to him. He picked up the phone and called Summer, knowing she would be up early. Jet lag worked that way. Summer's melodic voice chimed in his ear over the Paris traffic. The French sure liked their car horns, never missing an opportunity to blast them.

"Bonjour, Samson," Summer sang into his ear with her best 'faux' French accent.

"Hey, girl…. are you fully awake?"

"Barely. What do you think?" Summer chuckled.

Samson smiled as he looked out over the river. "Some things never change. So glad you're here. Natalie picked a great restaurant for your welcome dinner tonight. I imagine you'll still be functioning later? May I suggest a powernap for this afternoon? What's your game plan for the week?"

"Sleep, French food and scouting and no, I don't have time for naps." Summer replied. "Can't wait to meet Natalie. What's she like?"

"She's fun, pretty, sexy. I really like her. Hope you will too, because you'll be seeing a lot of her. Real French food is fabulous, by the way. I'm enjoying an almond croissant right now."

"Trust me. I know. Ted already spoiled us this morning. He discovered a great bakery on our block. As for Natalie, I'll give her the once over and let you know if I approve," Summer teased. "Ted and Hope will join us. I think you'll like them. Text me the address of the restaurant, ok? Later, Dude!"

Samson grinned. It was good to have his twin sister close. She never failed to put a smile on his face.

Dinner was scheduled for eight on the *Ile Saint Louis*. Natalie chose a traditional French restaurant and everyone happily obliged. They were all in the mood for an authentic French meal. Samson and Natalie got there first and organized a long table with a *banquette*. They ordered a bottle of red and white wine. A few minutes later, Summer, Hope and Ted sauntered in. Summer hugged her brother who couldn't stop smiling. The warmth in the two sets of blue eyes radiated around the table and set the mood for the evening. Introductions, followed by small talk, quickly transitioned to laughter and uninhibited chatter. Was it the wine or the heated Parisian bread and butter? French food worked like magic. Either way, good karma boomeranged around the dinner table from every perspective, including the neighboring table.

Soon the subject turned to Summer's movie. What was she doing? Did she have actors? Where did she plan to shoot? Everyone had ideas and they got bounced around the table like a beach ball. Then the conversation shifted to Natalie's work and Samson's travels. It was a heart- warming night among new and old friends. A couple wine bottles later, Natalie promised to help Summer with resources and valuable contacts. Samson offered to help with media coverage and Ted made friends with the two men at the neighboring table, Pierre and Claude, who first eavesdropped, then ended up staying and lingering over dessert to ingratiate themselves with valuable resource suggestions. They left with the American group's phone numbers and promised to help with the film.

"I look forward to hearing from you, Pierre. Thanks again for all your suggestions."

"*De rien, mon ami,* it's nothing, Ted. We're happy to help. Nice meeting you all."

The welcome dinner could not have gone better and everyone left on a high note for their own reasons. Paris was clearly an inspiring city.

Chapter XVII

Cause You Gotta Have Friends

Summer quickly realized that Ted Baxter was having the time of his life in Paris. Living in a penthouse apartment in the city of lights, working on a movie with friends, and meeting two delightful men he could relate to, was only the tip of the iceberg for his adventurous soul. It turned out that Pierre worked for a technical design firm and Claude worked in advertising. Both men, like Ted, adored theater and all three enjoyed the visual arts. The Frenchmen knew every worthwhile gallery and every upcoming attraction. They also knew all the best gay bars. Ted had struck gold on his first night out. Summer secretly hoped he wouldn't get too distracted.

In a few days, Summer realized that Pierre really did have friends in theater. Friends of friends proved to be helpful in a variety of ways. Ted was not only having fun with his new *amis,* but his work life was made so much easier by association. Summer happily reaped the benefits. Pierre's friends introduced Ted to contacts, who all pointed him in the direction of a small theater in Montmartre.

Summer was pleased when Ted secured the theater for auditions during the day. They started to set up casting calls.

Mimi, the theater manager, and a close friend of Pierre's from their university days, was pleased to help. Ted also, courtesy of Pierre, Claude, and Mimi, found places to rent the needed equipment for Summer and Hope to assess. The theater office had a comprehensive list of recommendations and resources he, Hope and Summer could weed through. They were in business.

"Wow, Ted. We hit a goldmine with Pierre and Mimi."

"I know. She's super connected, as is Pierre. I think it may be nice to take her to dinner one night. She really has shared tons of valuable info."

"Definitely. Let's do it. Can you set it up?"

"Yeah."

One dinner later, Summer was privy to a plethora of resources that promised to propel the movie set forward in a big way. Ted's tall, lean, blondish Ken doll appearance didn't hurt in getting results either. Pierre and Claude were bedazzled by the handsome American and were thrilled to assist on the movie project for only a credit mention. Ted inspired them.

Summer had hired Ted for his impeccable organizational skills and his sunny disposition. She had thoroughly enjoyed working with him on previous projects and was impressed with his networking skills. She also suspected Ted would respect her creative vision. Thankfully, she had kept his number on speed dial. It was paying off big time when she needed it most.

At dinner in the apartment one night, Summer told him how she felt.

"Ted, you're doing an awesome job. The theater was a real find, and I can't wait to start auditions. I'm beyond thrilled. We're right on schedule, maybe even ahead, although you can never be ahead enough in this business. Thanks for your quick work."

"Thanks, Summer."

"I really like living and working with you," she said with a dazzling smile.

"I appreciate that. Pierre has been extremely helpful and he's just fun to hang with. I already consider him a good friend. Stumbling onto him was pure luck."

"For sure. But it's your knack for putting things together that has made this a smooth start so keep up the great work."

"Thanks. It's nice when things come together."

Ted was exceptionally personable and could melt the most hardened obstacles when needed, but resources did not grow on trees. Summer knew he worked hard at it. Summer was well-aware of his valuable people skills when she selected him. Basically, Ted was everything Summer was not. Ted made friends and lasting contacts in nanoseconds, while Summer generally bonded over common interests over time. Her overwhelming shyness and her serious stubborn streak could drive mankind to extinction. Summer was well-aware of her attributes and shortcomings.

She enjoyed teaming up with Hope. Hope and Summer brought out the best in each other. Together, they weeded through the theater resource list and dissected equipment for rental. Hope totally knew what she was doing when it came to equipment. Once that was accomplished, they scouted shooting locations, applied for permits, and interviewed possible camera and lighting crew. Ted, in the meantime, prearranged the first round of auditions. He worked at a furious pace thanks to Mimi. Summer had met her match in terms of work ethic. Her team was awesome, and she knew it.

The first day of auditions Summer discovered only maybes. "What do you think of these three actors?" she asked as she placed head shots on the dinner table for consideration.

Hope grimaced. "I think these two don't look fantastic on camera and the third one didn't memorize his lines. Never a good sign."

"I agree with Hope. That could slow us down substantially," Ted voiced.

"I think we need to keep looking, Summer."

The first round of auditions came and went with no stand outs. Summer realized the audition process would take more time. It always did.

A few days later Summer tried again. "Let's go over more pictures and footage tomorrow night. I liked one or two people."

Again Hope voted her down. "The camera doesn't lie, honey. We need to keep looking."

After yet another day of auditions, Hope and Summer argued the pros and cons of all their prospects. Ted, busy with dinner prep, listened, occasionally siding with one or the other. The days were too hectic for positive affirmations, so most evenings were spent looking at audition footage. Seeing audition tapes the second time round was key. Often it revealed nuances that were missed earlier. Sometimes Samson and Natalie came to join them and one weekend Pierre, Claude and Mimi added their opinions, although Summer wasn't about to let anyone, but Hope change her mind. She trusted Hope and valued her insight and camera expertise.

"Hope, I totally trust your judgment, but we have to make some progress soon. If you think this batch won't work on camera, let's start from scratch. I don't like our last options after reviewing them again."

"Good. People change in front of the camera lens. If we have doubts now, I know we'll have regrets later."

After more long and unsuccessful audition days, Summer was excited to come home to an invitation from Pierre and Claude. She needed a break. The events they were invited to around Paris were fun and led to more contacts and friends, many of whom proved to be useful in pre-production. While some leads materialized, others were quickly discarded. There were crew additions, location possibilities, and clothing endorsements to be assembled. Everything needed careful scrutiny. Time just whizzed by as they weeded things out.

Summer realized there weren't enough nights in the week for all the invitations received. Many had to be skipped in the interest of viewing audition tapes. In general, the events were great networking opportunities, but they also swallowed valuable time. Most of the group's social activities centered around dinner since everyone was busy during the day. Unfortunately, dinners in

Paris were never quick. French people socialized and grazed over dinner. Many nights Ted went out alone with Pierre and Claude to meet crew prospects, while the girls were busy fighting over audition tapes. Ted was happy to escape.

Cara could hear the frustration in Summer's voice when she called.

"Mom, I haven't done as much sight seeing as I would like because our days are long and I come home wiped. We've gone to some great restaurants and seen some cool art, but in small increments. Right now we're swamped with auditions and not finding anyone. They totally consume me and will continue to until I find my two leads."

"Gee, I hope you'll have some time for fun when I come."

"Not if I don't finalize my actors, Mom. Pray."

"My fingers and toes are crossed."

Weekends were a 30/70 balance of fun and organizing the following work week. Every Sunday, time was set aside to discuss the following weeks' goals. Either brunch or dinner or both were used to discuss the upcoming schedule. Once the prep work for the film was established, Summer knew they would have even less time to socialize. Continued planning, filming and finally, rough editing would be even more time-consuming, exhausting work.

They would have to preview footage to know if any reshoots were needed.

And yet somehow, despite the arduous schedule, Hope managed to find an attentive French lover. Summer regarded Kais, who was originally from Tunisia, but currently living in Paris, with suspicion. She needed Hope's full attention and Kais was trouble right from the start. Hope met Kais while she and Summer auditioned for crew. They didn't hire him as he was too inexperienced, but Kais asked Hope out to dinner and worked on her relentlessly, hoping she would change her mind. Luckily the fascination fizzled due to his demanding nature. The relationship was doomed to end with a bang. Kais was peeved he wouldn't be hired, and Hope felt exasperated and used. Summer sighed with relief. When all was said and done, Hope didn't like complications no matter how attractive they were.

"He's way too controlling. I can't stand a man who tries to manipulate me. Too bad because we did have fun."

"When you weren't fighting."

"Yeah, I guess so."

"It's better you realize that early on. He would be hell on set."

Summer expected her team's full commitment and dedication to her film as time and budget were limited. In essence Ted and Hope did not disappoint, but some of the Paris hires were proving to be more difficult. Some lacked time or serious commitment and others were not up front from the start. It took a while to separate the white diamonds from the black industrial duds. Once those obstacles were overcome, pre-production moved smoothly. Summer held her breath, waiting for the inevitable hiccup that every film prep encounters.

The group's other new friendship finds were colorful characters that also contributed in some way: there was Alma, who had a vintage clothing store at the *Porte de Cligancourt* Flea Market, (*Les Puces*), Bette, a designer who worked with Claude in advertising, and Mimi's posse of course. Occasionally, Natalie and Samson brought friends too. Bette, together with Claude, were on board to help with designing the title sequencing. Summer was thankful for all the enthusiasm and helping hands. She could utilize all of them. Delegating was her strength.

Dinner conversations with friends, rarely revolved around the premise of the movie. The focus was on logistics and technicalities. Summer guarded her script. Although it was written, Summer was still working out many of the set details which meant that the script would have to be tweaked accordingly. Much would have to be decided as they went along, depending on what permits they could secure and which locations presented themselves. Summer was starting to feel overwhelmed, despite all the well-intentioned help.

When not lamenting over film problems, conversation centered around life in Paris compared to New York: the food, the restaurants, the current health issues and always, current events.

"Chinese food in the US tastes way different than in Paris" Hope remarked one night.

Summer had to agree. "They must use French ingredients or different spices."

One meal they giggled over a recent article about a Chinese hospital having a machine that simulated childbirth. The machine was designed to give men the birthing experience by inducing electric shocks. The goal of this experience was to elicit more empathy for women. They laughed about another article that featured a study Mc Gill University did. The study researched why some people are bad dancers. The article concluded that "beat-deafness" is a biological syndrome. This concept had Claude in hysterics since Pierre was not a good dancer and it was a point of contention. Claude loved to dance.

"Pierre, I think they had you in mind when they started this study."

"Let me remind you, *cher* Claude, I have many other hidden talents."

"True. Some are still in hiding, I think."

"Aren't you funny tonight!"

They also focused on the grave news from Africa, regarding a newly discovered bacterial disease. World news was at their fingertips and much more relevant than in New York. The proximity of European countries made world news so much more real.

Life in Paris was never boring and neither were their conversations. The days seemed to fly by and Summer was beginning to worry they wouldn't get it all done in time to shoot in January. She worried about not finding actors to do her script justice and most of all, she worried that she would not have time to spend with her mom and Jasper when they came to visit. They still hadn't cast a single role!

Chapter XVIII

Travel Jitters

For Cara, December did not fly by. In fact Cara was counting down the days till she left for Europe. She longed for Summer and the boys and although she was super busy, she missed talking to her daughter on a daily basis. One day in mid-December, she pulled out her suitcase and started throwing her favorite clothes inside. The half-packed suitcase in her bedroom was a welcome reminder of her upcoming travel plans. It radiated a warm vibe with its mere presence on her bedroom floor.

Her departure date was still more than a week away and work was going well. Samantha was pleased with the final Greek erotica sketches. Nero had approved them and a second batch of sample tiles were in the works. Things were moving in the right direction and she was making money. She planned to continue sketching in Paris and resume fabrication upon her return. Her project was firmly under control. Talking to Samantha one evening, after receiving a hefty deposit, she finalized their schedule.

"Thanks, for the payment. I'll finish all the samples before I leave so you and Nero can take your time deciding over the holidays. It's always best to look at tiles on location and at

"

different times of day and night. Once you decide, I can amend or duplicate them rather quickly when I return."

"Great, Cara. I think that will work well. We'll need to start the minute you get back though. The kitchen demolition is done and the new floor is in. I hope to have some appliances and cabinetry installed soon. How long does it take to make the tiles in large numbers?"

"Not that long once the design is set. Two or three weeks of intense work should do it." Cara assured her. "By the way, did you check out my updated website? I added a lot of new work. I also added the new bio picture you took of me. Let me know what you think."

"Will do. Instagram too?"

"Yes."

In mid-December, Cara hosted a BYOB ceramic class as a final financial boost before her travels. She invited her clients and friends to come to the studio and pick out a clay vessel. She taught them how to glaze it with colors of their choosing. These gatherings were always successful and a good source for personalized holiday gifts. Everyone enjoyed creating a "masterpiece" while sipping wine. It brought out the holiday spirit and often generated additional sales. Cara's holiday tradition was in its 5th year and running strong.

Talking to Summer the next day, she listened to the progress report. "I'm glad to hear you're collecting contacts. Ted seems to be very competent."

"Oh yeah! He really kicks ass. Hope and I can concentrate on auditions, locations and permits, which is totally helpful. We already reserved all our equipment and hired a skeleton crew."

"Great. That's a big step forward then. I know petty organization isn't your forte'."

"Understatement of the year, Mom."

"And how are auditions going?"

"Eh…. that is our soft spot. No standouts yet."

"Well, good luck with that. The right leads will show up… eventually."

"Eventually, is what worries me. We're on a tight schedule."

Cara could feel her daughter's pain. Nonetheless she was confident Summer knew how to direct a winning film once the leading actors were found. At least everything else was progressing expeditiously, despite no solid leads on the horizon. Summer's persistence would pay off. She never waivered from her vision and she never gave up until she had what she wanted. She also rarely compromised on the big issues. What worried Cara most was that Summer would have no time for her family over the holiday. She had envisioned their joint reunion and sight-seeing, like old times, a family affair.

Chapter XIX

Strange Bedfellows

Jasper was sipping his coffee and preparing for his Monday morning meeting with Adriano. After a whirlwind weekend, he found the task particularly cumbersome today. These days, weekends seemed to fly by while Mondays dragged indefinitely. It wasn't that he didn't like what he did because he still enjoyed working at the bank, but lately Mondays felt like recovery days. By Tuesday morning, things looked up and they continued upward until Friday. Sunday night is when the cycle began all over again. His phone rang.

"Jasper, can you come to my office? I want to see you before the meeting."

"Sure, Adriano, be right there." Jasper grabbed his notes and sprinted down the hall. When he entered, Adriano was in deep conversation with a tall, muscular man whose face was partially shadowed by a black fedora, which he made no effort to remove. Jasper was intrigued.

Adriano motioned him closer. "Jasper, this is Mr. Fernando Flores. He's a new client with the bank."

"Hello, Mr. Flores. Pleased to meet you." Jasper shook Fernando's hand. An unexpected chill crept up his spine when

Fernando's piercing jade eyes raked over him. Something about Fernando Flores's aura reeked of dangerous unpredictability. His smile revealed immaculately capped, snow-white teeth, but while the corners of Fernando's mouth curved upward, his eyes slanted downward in a dangerous glare. They appeared calculating and cold, evaluating Jasper, a cobra ready to strike.

"Mr. Flores has opened several accounts with us for his import/export company and new restaurant. He does large volume business, and we'll service him with his investments and transactions as needed."

Jasper listened attentively and nodded, but Adriano offered nothing more. "Great. Welcome, Mr. Flores. I look forward to assisting you with whatever I can."

Adriano smiled. "Mr. Flores, Jasper is my trusted assistant and will be available any time I am not, should you need quick action. You can cc him on transaction emails."

"Got it." Fernando Flores smiled woodenly and nodded once. He stood up and shook Adriano's hand. "Thank you. My accountant will be in touch."

"You have our information and direct lines. Please don't hesitate to reach out with questions."

"I will, don't worry. My accountant, Carlos Ortiz handles most of our transactions. I trust him."

"I look forward to hearing from Mr. Ortiz then."

When Flores left, Adriano dismissed Jasper with a wave.

"Ok. I need a few minutes. Tell everyone we'll meet in the conference room in ten. You and I will continue to discuss this account in private, after the meeting, ok?"

Jasper nodded silently. That was not Adriano's usual modus operandi. In Jasper's quick summation, Adriano was patting himself on the back over his new plum client. He wasn't sharing any new developments just yet. Jasper suspected that Adriano had worked hard to score Fernando Flores and perhaps he was nervous the higher brass would intervene. Either way, something about Flores made Jasper uneasy. He couldn't quite put his finger on it.

After the general meeting, Adriano motioned Jasper back to his office.

"Mr. Flores is a coup for us. His deposits amount to huge money. Look at these opening figures!" Adriano moved his laptop to face Jasper. "You and I will lock in his investments. We're never out of the office at the same time and we're always in contact, so this should work perfectly."

Jasper whistled and nodded. "Congratulations, Adriano. I hope this translates into a raise for you. You deserve it."

"Thank you, Jasper, I hope so too, but for now, I would prefer to keep things on the down low," Adriano admitted, "I don't know much about Fernando as he's from Mexico, however, the bankers in South America vouched for him. They offered little else though and Google provided few clues but the company is legit. No strikes against it as far as I can see. I'm excited about this prospect. We have his business accounts in Europe. His personal savings accounts are elsewhere. Mexico and Paris, maybe?"

"Hmm. What's his business?"

"Mr. Flores owns a ceramics import/export business. They manufacture in Mexico and ship all over the world. It appears to be extremely lucrative. Not too long ago, he purchased a restaurant in Barcelona, *El Toro*. He already runs one in Paris. The one here is located near a large luxury hotel, Majestic Hotel and Spa. It's a great location in the Gothic quarter."

"I see."

Jasper felt Adriano's eyes on him, but he couldn't quite muster the required enthusiasm. Something about this account made him uneasy, despite the encouraging numbers. He knew Adriano would rely on his discretion, so he would do his best to keep this account under his hat. All negative vibes would be kept to himself. After all, he had nothing concrete to object to and he certainly didn't want to throw shade on Adriano's success. He was certain Adriano would do his due diligence.

Adriano summoned Jasper into his office. "Listen, Jasper. Fernando Flores invited us to dine at *El Toro* on Friday night. Are you free?"

"Of course. Thanks, Adriano. What time?" Prepping for his first business dinner would be exciting. Adriano generally met his clients alone while Jasper assisted with all transactions at the bank. He was pleased to be included. "Tell me a little more about the restaurant. And… are we going directly from work?"

"No. We'll meet there at 9pm. You can dress casually, but nice. Here's the address." Adriano slid a business card across his desk.

Jasper nodded and copied the address into his cell phone calendar. Looking up, he waited to see if Adriano would reveal more, but Adriano was already reaching for his phone. Jasper knew he was dismissed and quietly exited the office, closing the door behind him. Adriano was not a fan of the firm's open-door policy.

Chapter XX

Search for the Perfect Frenchman

Summer and Hope were walking from the metro stop to the theater in Montmartre. As they progressed up the winding cobblestone streets, a breathtaking, luminescent linen white *Sacre Coeur Basilica* loomed majestically at the top of the hill. The Roman Catholic church, dedicated to the Sacred Heart of Jesus and built by Paul Abadie from 1875 to 1914, rested on Paris's highest point. One of the city's most prized treasures, Summer was in awe. She couldn't think of a more inspiring neighborhood to work in. Actors, artists, dancers, and tourists, all assembled under the *Sacre Coeur's* protective eye, enjoying the spectacular view over Paris cabarets, rooftops and architectural masterpieces.

The *funicular,* tirelessly shuttled the tourist population that did not want to climb the grand staircase to see the nineteen-ton bell, the largest heart-shaped mosaic and the statues of national saints. The cultural monument, a truly spectacular sight, was one Summer never got tired of admiring on her daily pilgrimage to the theater.

At the theater, Ted was diligently organizing auditions and call backs. Summer desperately needed two main characters for her film and a handful of supporting roles. They were coming up empty. Her story involved a love triangle with a comical multicultural twist. She was on the hunt for very specific requirements. Today, she hoped to find a male lead. The clock was ticking.

Summer watched Hope's head swivel back and forth in the narrow streets as she peered into open doorways. "The neighborhood really comes alive after dark. I'm going to have to check this out one of these nights after work."

"Yeah, we always say that and then we can't wait to get home."

"True," Hope sighed. "Do you think we'll find our leading man today?"

"Who knows? When we do, I hope he speaks English with a killer French accent," Summer gushed. "I love the way that sounds."

"I hope the camera loves him," Hope countered. "So far, I haven't been blown away. I'm thinking we may have to settle, for time reasons. Maybe we should reconsider some of the discards."

"No way. I'm not giving up."

They were walking through *Pigalle* known for its transgender and topless nightclubs. The two girls navigated the narrow sidewalks while curiously examining each cubbyhole. Manicured fingers seductively beckoned them inside, but the girls had their own agenda and waved as they passed. Montmartre boasted a colorful cast of characters, unique to that section of Paris. Finally, they turned onto a cobblestone street and headed up the hill, closer to the looming Sacre Coeur Basilica.

When they arrived, the girls identified themselves to the person in the box office and walked in, their eyes adjusted to the changing light. Ted was talking to a group of men seated in the first few rows. When he saw the girls, he pointed to the camera and lighting person. Hope took her spot and immediately started making some basic adjustments. Someone in the shadows was manning the lights. Hope went to chat with him.

After some introductions, Summer took charge, telling people where to stand, what to read and what lighting she wanted. Hope adjusted her equipment accordingly. Her trusty helpers had already set things up to her liking. After numerous days of auditions everyone knew the drill.

Ted, always early, had instructed and prepared the theater for their arrival. Since the girls reviewed audition tapes late into the night, he did the morning prep by himself and let them saunter in at a more reasonable hour. Sometimes Mimi helped him. He was the ultimate, reliable professional and he knew exactly what the girls required. He handled the actors' arrival, gathering their headshots and personal information and ordered lunch for all crew members. His active social life never interfered with his daily chores. Ted managed all with efficiency and grace.

Summer looked around the theater. "Ok, Ted. Put number one on stage. Hope, you ready?"

"Yup."

They filmed another round of auditions, cutting the obvious NOs short and extending those that mattered. By the time they left the theater they had four hours of film for seven plus hours of work. Out of 50 or so prospects, three actors were up for serious consideration, worthy of a call back. The rest were excused on the spot. A handful were signed up as possible extras and asked to return. There was no time for emails.

This was week two of auditions. The following short week before Christmas, they would have to repeat the same drill with the ladies. Picking the right actors was paramount for success and Summer was determined to get it done before the holidays, but they were now running behind schedule as the male lead took more time than anticipated.

The process was nerve-wracking for Summer. She tried to assess people's approach to the scene, their delivery, their general disposition, and their appeal in person and on camera. Hope took a very clinical approach, while Ted offered his insights occasionally, but in the end, Summer knew he trusted her and Hope to work it out. He had a different expertise and he preferred to stick to that. The girls gave him free reign and he gladly did the same for them. Summer appreciated that. She had decided early on that she didn't want an Assistant Director.

Summer had a clear vision, but Hope knew what and who would work on camera. Their ideas didn't always match up. Things took time to work out. In the end though, Summer trusted that Hope knew how to capture her vision effectively. She "got" Summer. They worked in sync, but agreement didn't always come easy. Summer was often fueled by emotion, and it was Hope's job to cut the fat and get to the hard camera facts. They had their share of heated arguments, but in the end, Summer always listened to what Hope had to say. Hope was a good cinematographer and Summer relied heavily on her input. By the end of the week, they agreed on the male lead.

Over the week-end Summer spoke to her mother.

"How's everything going in Paris? Have you picked your leading roles yet?"

"We have the main man and the male supporting roles filled, but not the leading lady," Summer lamented. "We'll start auditions for women on Monday. We're a week behind schedule, but I suppose it could be worse. We took longer than anticipated with the guys."

"Isn't that our universal problem?" Cara countered.

"Funny, Mom. We're also looking for an affordable long-term sound technician. Our current one got another job. We need to get those contracts signed asap before anyone else bails. I hope to have our leading lady before you come."

"Good. Keep at it. You'll find what you need. I'm sure of it. Good Luck."

Summer heard her mother lock the studio door. She was on speaker. "What does the leading man look like and what's his name? "

"His name is Alain Besson. He's a little short, but he's gorgeous with chestnut hair and hazel eyes that change color in different lighting, according to Hope. He's also built like a rock. Hope and Ted are fighting over him as we speak," Summer joked as she eyed Alain's picture on the dining room table. "However, Ted is two heads taller and gay which Alain is not, so I think Hope will win."

Cara laughed. "Seriously?"

"No. No one gets to mess with my leads until the film is shot."

They chatted for a few more minutes and then signed off.

"Miss you, Summer. I'll see you end of next week. Email me if you want me to bring anything from New York."

"I miss Nero's cinnamon penises."

"With all those amazing French pastries around? Really?" Cara laughed.

"Yes. They're singular." Summer yawned.

"They are damn good, especially the chocolate tipped ones. I'll bring a box."

"Ok, Mom. Can't wait to see you. Your room will be ready," Summer promised. She hung up and walked into the empty bedroom to make sure things were still ok. Right now, it was filled with equipment, but that would soon be moved to a corner in the living room, the room least used in the apartment. Life on Rue Malher revolved around the kitchen table.

Chapter XXI

It Takes a Thief

Cara hung up her phone and sashayed to the bedroom feeling happy. Her children had that effect. Inspired, she threw another freshly washed sweater into her open suitcase. It was almost full, and she still had six days to go. Would she need another bag? No. She decided she would just have to weed out a few garments at the end. Difficult choices!

The following morning, Cara turned on her laptop and surveyed the morning news. Her eyes zeroed in on the caption, "Priceless pottery stolen from the Metropolitan Museum of Art." The article covered the theft of a pottery crate earmarked for auction at Sotheby's. It had been in storage at the museum and pulled out of the deep freeze for re-evaluation. Periodically, the museum's curators decided to de accession art to have funds to buy new art.

They had undertaken this two-step venture after a little house cleaning and inventory analysis. Big donors were scarce these days so inventory had to be updated as such. A sign of the times. Somewhere in transit, the shipment had disappeared. It left the Met loading dock according to paperwork, but what arrived at Sotheby's was an empty weighted box. The shipment had mysteriously been switched and oddly, the security cameras experienced a brief lapse in footage, a tidbit the press was not briefed on.

Cara read the article carefully and shook her head in disbelief. She looked at the picture of one of the stolen items and noted how similar it looked to the Sotheby's pottery that was already missing. *Terrible. Where were the security cameras?* Her mind involuntarily drifted to the three men from the last auction. She was curious if they attended this auction as well. If they did, they would have been disappointed. Their bidding centered heavily on the Met's pieces last time.

Two robberies in one month. Was this starting to be a pattern? Or just a total lapse of security? *Could this be an inside job? It has to be.* Was it the same thieves with a specific request for Mediterranean ceramics from the Met? Where were they selling the stolen goods? In the USA? The police offered little insight or else they weren't sharing with the press. Cara carefully studied the pottery patterns and made a quick sketch. She took a picture of the article and her sketch for future reference and added it to her Mediterranean Pottery file. As an afterthought, she copied it to a new file marked "Stolen Ceramics."

Finally, she flipped through the Fereaux gallery site to see their new mounted exhibit. It was a group show that centered around the theme of 'Architectural Art in the Age of Technology'. The drawings were fascinating and very minimalist. Cara decided not to miss visiting the gallery. Maybe she could even meet the intriguing owner! *Now there's a thought worth entertaining!*

Chapter XXII

Into the Lion's Den

Jasper arrived at *El Toro* ten minutes early. Adriano was already planted at the bar. *"Hola,* Adriano. Nice place. Good crowd."

The inside and outside bar were packed. It was Friday night and people were drinking and devouring sumptuous looking finger foods wrapped in phylo dough or bathed in premium Spanish olive oil.

"Yes. I got here a little early. It's been filling up quickly."

The clientele was an upscale one and they were clearly enjoying the fact that it was the end of the work week. There was no sense of urgency to dine. Spanish custom was a late dinner around ten. As a result, there were more people at the two bars than in the dining area, save a few tourists.

"I bet he'll do well here. I was just going to order a carafe of *sangria.* You interested?"

"Yes, thank you."

A band was setting up in the dining area while an energetic DJ hyped the crowd with current pop hits. *Enrique Iglesias's* sexy voice filtered through the speakers. The mood was relaxed, and the music captured and inspired the Friday night crowd. The first alcohol-fueled dancers hit the small dance floor.

Seconds after Adriano ordered a half pitcher of sangria for them, Fernando appeared, flashing his immaculate smile. Jasper studied his appearance as he greeted Adriano. He was dressed in black jeans and a custom tailored, white, textured shirt. Gold sparkled everywhere, in his ear, around his neck, around his wrist, on his belt buckle and on his ring finger. Jasper noticed the striking gold lion's head ring with an insignia carved in the surrounding shank. He made a mental note to examine the ring closer. The lion had ruby eyes and he was roaring. Discretion and mindful of etiquette, prevented Jasper from asking Fernando outright about this unusual piece of jewelry. Upon a closer look, Jasper also discovered a tattoo shine through the sheer white shirt sleeve; it was a skull with ruby red roses.

"Welcome, Gentlemen." Jasper's eyes followed the generous sweep of Fernando's bejeweled hand. "So glad you could make it. You're my guests tonight."

Fernando gestured to the bartender not to charge Adriano for the sangria, then turned back to face them. "We have a great band starting at 10:30pm. You'll join me at my table over there. In the meantime, make yourselves comfortable. Relax. I'll be back shortly. I have one more thing to take care of."

His smile sparkled, but his eyes were murky pools of hunter green. Fernando turned and walked to his office, leaving his exotic bloom scent behind to waft up Jasper's nose. Jasper sneezed.

When Fernando reappeared, he was flanked by two sexy blondes. He motioned for Jasper and Adriano to come sit at a sheltered, elevated, round table half-way between the indoor and outdoor bars. The space heater was strategically placed to keep them toasty for when the night cooled down. The table was far enough from the band to have an intimate conversation, but still enjoy the music. Once the drinks were ordered, food began to arrive on eye popping platters. Jasper was starving. As he reached for an appetizer he remarked on the beautiful pottery the food was served on. It had a distinct Mediterranean style, with added flair.

"Your dishes are beautiful, Mr. Flores."

"Fernando. Thank you. We fabricate the dishes in Mexico, in my factory. These designs are exclusive to our restaurant."

Fernando appeared pleased that Jasper noticed the dishes and proudly talked about their unique pattern. "My family has been making pottery for four generations," he informed Jasper, bursting with pride. We make many patterns, not just Mexican.

"They really are spectacular," Jasper remarked. "I love the vibrant colors. Those must be special glazes."

"Yes, they are! Family secret."

"Do you have a restaurant in Mexico too?"

"No, in Paris."

Jasper thought about it and decided not to mention his mother's business. When Fernando wasn't looking, he flipped the bread plate to see the trademark insignia. It was a lion's head with ruby eyes. There was no name.

Fernando's assistant and general manager joined the group for dinner. Jasper eyed the large silver cross with turquoise stones around the man's neck. It popped on his stark white t- shirt. The cross did not have the refined appearance of Spanish jewelry, Jasper was accustomed to seeing in downtown Barcelona, but the turquoise stones were the color of Caribbean waters. The piece was reminiscent of rustic Mexican silver, with a textured design. Jasper recognized the style from past family trips, south of the border. *These guys sure love their jewelry.*

Jasper's eyes traveled to Jose's crooked teeth, a stark comparison to Fernando's perfect movie star smile. He wondered if Fernando offered his employees a dental plan. This employee would certainly benefit from the option. He observed the man's dirty fingernails which he found surprising for a restaurant manager. He hoped he wasn't involved in food preparation. *What does this man really do for Flores?* When Jose took his leather jacket off, Jasper experienced a sensory overload of frightening tattoos.

"Let me introduce Jose, my cousin and general operations manager. He'll be joining us for dinner. The ladies are Ana and Sofia. Ladies, Adriano Aldana and his assistant, Jasper."

"Hello," Jasper smiled. He turned to Ana, who was seated next to him and started polite conversation.

Despite his initial reservations, Jasper predicted a memorable night. The sweet *sangria* was starting to dull his senses. *One more sip and I might like the host.* Fernando's generosity and welcoming demeanor were compelling. The sweetness of the night and the drink were erasing his uneasy feeling. Jasper started to relax. Adriano's guard was definitely down, while Jasper was fighting a losing battle to keep his intact. He felt a little guilty about not staying 'on his toes,' but he vowed he would stop drinking after his third glass. Maybe food would help. Was Ana giving him the eye or was it his imagination?

Chapter XXIII

The Chance of a Lifetime

At the theater in Montmartre, Summer, Hope and Ted picked their leading lady, a Polish transplant to Paris, named Helena Majewski. It took the full week and countless auditions, but Helena Majewski was worth the search. After call backs and intense negotiations, Summer and Hope finally agreed. They offered Helena the part on Thursday evening and her ecstatic reaction was priceless.

"Thank you so much! I'm incredibly excited," she gushed, smiling from ear to ear. She did a little skip and squeezed Summer's arm affectionately. Not terribly professional, but heart-warming.

Helena would look good on camera. Her resume was spotty, a point of contention, but Summer was confident. Helena started as an au pair in Paris, before she was 'discovered' at the department store, *Au Printemps*, while shopping with a friend. According to Helena, she finished her one-year au pair contract and switched to modeling. Modeling paid the bills, she'd told Summer, but secretly she was hoping to break into acting. For the past year, she was immersed in acting and dance lessons and it appeared they were paying off. Summer liked her. She had style and seemed very genuine, which came across on camera. She also memorized her lines well.

Summer could sense that Helena was delighted to be part of an American film. She knew she was taking a risk giving Helena her first leading role, but Summer had a good feeling.

"Summer, thank you for the opportunity. Since the pay is not so good, I'll still have to model when I get an assignment, but I can make both work. I promise."

Summer sensed that Helena was pleased with herself for landing the lead role. It would keep her motivated. She suspected that Helena had visions of Hollywood circling her brain. Summer was ready to deliver the goods and make her dreams come true.

Helena was a striking presence. Her skillfully high-lighted, walnut brown hair framed an expressive round face, graced with cobalt blue eyes, a pleasing straight nose and generous lips. Her long-lashed eyes were accented by high cheek bones and a contagious smile flanked by one dimple. In heels, Helena towered over Alain, but Summer didn't seem to mind so Helena didn't either. Helena was used to being taller than most French men, including her Latin lover, she told Summer. Only Ted could look Helena straight in the eye and that he did with suspicion. Summer noticed a strange vibe.

"Why don't you like Helena?"

"I don't trust her. She strikes me as an opportunist that doesn't quite have the goods."

"Well, you're probably right. She's a total novice, but I think she's hungry enough to give me what I want. I would like to give her a chance. She seems genuinely committed and eager to learn. Hope says she looks spectacular on camera. Besides, the price is right."

"That is true. Just know, I'll be on her ass if she slips up."

"Hope? What do you think?"

"I say we give her a chance. Like you said, she looks amazing on camera." Hope gave them both a thumbs up.

"Put her on probation so we have the option to part ways if we need to. Nicola could be our back up." Ted, being his ever-efficient self, always had a contingency plan.

"My sentiments exactly. I think she'll work out though." Hope nodded confidently.

Summer realized Helena sensed Ted's apprehension, but she also believed Helena was determined not to mess up this golden opportunity. Helena had never been to the United States and she was dying to see New York and Los Angeles. She made no secret of that.

"Perhaps this film will be Helena's ticket to New York and my ticket to the Cannes Film Festival." Summer told her mom that night. "Here's to hoping."

When addressing the height issue with Alain and Helena during rehearsals, Summer assured them both. "Don't worry. We'll make it work. Height is a non-issue. The camera has many angles. Hope can do magic with that lens."

Alain seemed unperturbed. His confidence was annoyingly rock solid. Helena relaxed after hearing Summer's assurances. Perhaps she had already come to terms with being taller than many men.

Summer was confident Hope could make her shots and they both felt the height difference added a comedic element that could be exploited. Hope knew how to calculate camera angles and Summer was already thinking about how she would add comedy. Together, they'd turn this little discrepancy into an unexpected advantage.

Summer urged Helena and Alain to study the first few scenes of the script while she and Hope finalized the shooting permits for all their locations. Shooting would begin immediately after the holidays, in January. The actors needed to know their lines by then.

Bureaucracy worked slower in France and during the holidays it didn't work at all. Nonetheless, the Malher group was moving forward with actors and crew in place. Hopefully, the paperwork wouldn't slow them down too much.

"This is the best holiday gift ever. Knowing I have my cast and crew set. I hope nothing changes over the holidays and I hope no one gets a new job they can't refuse." Summer sighed with guarded relief. "Ted, are all the contracts signed? We need to have them locked and sent to New York."

"Working on it."

Chapter XXIV

The Best Laid Plans

The day before her departure, Cara had her suitcase packed and next to the door. Into her hand luggage, she had squeezed her in flight reading, Nero's baked penises and her favorite electronics. She packed her phone, numerous chargers, adapters, and her new tangerine tablet. She intended to take killer pictures in Paris and edit them for her blog. She'd also be checking her email regularly and preferred the larger screen for both. Cara loaded her tangerine tablet with tons of pictures from her ceramics studio to share with her children.

Her conversations with Summer, in the days before she left, were encouraging. With her actors and crew in place, Summer would be able to spend a little unscheduled time with family and friends. Cara knew that would be just what she needed before delving into the long hours of filming on location. She was sure filming in a busy city like Paris would bring its own added challenges. A good rest beforehand constituted the calm before the storm.

Her last day in the studio, Samantha stopped by to drop off a Christmas gift.

"Nero sends his love. The tiles are already in his possession and being argued over with Jonny. I'm staying away until after the holidays and their decision is made. Merry Christmas, Cara. I wanted to give you a little something for your trip."

"Thanks, Sam. What a sweet looking box. My gift for you will be bought in Paris, so you'll have to wait until after the holidays, I'm afraid."

"It sounds like it'll be well worth the wait. Go on. Open it."

Cara tugged at the sparkly red ribbon and tore off the royal blue paper to reveal a small silver box. When she opened it, she smiled."

"A *fleur-de-lis* pendant! How appropriate. I love it, Sam." She hugged her friend and motioned for her to add the delicate two-tone pendant to the gold link chain around her neck. "This was the emblem of the French monarchy, wasn't it?"

"Yes, but I'm giving it to you as a flower symbol of protection for you and your family. It's an 18kt stylized iris with three tiny diamonds, one in each leaf for each of your children. I know you will have a fabulous time with them. Shit, I wish I could spend the holidays in Paris with you all."

"How thoughtful, Sam. I absolutely love the idea behind it. Maybe you'll come next trip?"

"I'd love that. Wait … there'll be another trip?"

"Summer will be there for six plus months. I sure hope so."

"Ok. I'm in."

When the car service arrived the night before Christmas Eve to take her to the airport, every detail of Cara's business had been handled. The holiday orders were shipped and Samantha had a portfolio of sketches accompanied by a batch of tile samples for Nero. Cara had even sent out her holiday newsletter warning everyone of her absence. As soon as she set the alarm and locked the front door, Cara left her current life behind without a second thought. She was ready for adventure. For the next few weeks, she was making a clean break. Sam had the spare keys and promised to check on things while she was away. Cara left unencumbered and ready for action or so she thought.

Chapter XXV

Paths Crossing and Converging

Jasper arrived in Paris the day before his mother's arrival. The plan was to stay with Samson, so they could catch up. He would sleep on Samson's fold out couch.

"You know I like my privacy, Mom. Plus, I don't know Ted and Hope so it might be a little awkward if we both descend on them."

"That's fine, Jasper. I kind of like the idea of my own bedroom anyway," Cara teased.

It was also collectively decided they would spend Christmas in the apartment on Rue Malher as Samson's apartment was tiny. Since Ted and Hope were not going home for the holidays, they would all spend Christmas together. Ted's parents were deceased, and Hope's were in LA. She opted not to take the long flight home during the holiday rush. Cara was fine with everything. She was excited to have all her children in one place, friends happily included.

After checking in at the Air France counter, Cara waited in the winding security check line, surveying the masses. Generally, she disliked traveling this time of year but today, for obvious reasons, she took it in stride. Her excitement outweighed her apprehension.

Her eyes drifted aimlessly around the S shaped line of interesting characters. She stopped dead at the sight of two familiar faces. She zeroed in on a black baseball cap with the word *Champagne* embroidered on it in delicate cursive gold letters. Squinting, she was reasonably certain this was the man from the Sotheby's auction. She looked for the silver and turquoise cross around his neck and found it.

When his companion looked up, she noticed his bright gold hoop earring and sleek ponytail. She also recognized the black and cobalt blue tweed jacket from the day of the auction. *These guys sure don't change their clothes much… or their jewelry!*

Cara couldn't help but stare when the two men were motioned aside by security and escorted into a private room. She advanced to the conveyor belt and got preoccupied with her own security check, losing sight of them. Once through security, she browsed the magazine racks, picked up a yogurt and headed to the gate. As she stood in line to board the aircraft, she noticed the men arriving at her gate. *They're on my flight!* What were the chances? Her interest renewed, she inconspicuously took a few pictures and texted the best one to Sam with the caption,

Remember these characters from the Sotheby's auction? They're on my flight! Small world. LOL.

Sam texted back a smiley face with rolling eyes.

Find out if they bought the pottery I wanted. Maybe they'll sell.

You have a one-track mind, Sam. I'm wondering if they have the stolen pottery. Should I check their hand luggage? Ha ha."

I dare you. Nero is standing next to me, sending you air kisses. He loves all the tiles and still can't decide. Good thing he has a healthy supply of eggnog plus two weeks to make his decision. Have a safe trip.

Thanks! I'm sure Jonny will help if Nero lets him.

No chance.

Cara chuckled. When she boarded the plane, the men were already seated in first class. She made sure to walk down their aisle in the wide body plane. The man with the turquoise cross was looking out the window at the luggage being stowed in the underbelly of the plane while the man with the pirate earring was listening to music and looking at his laptop. Both seemed preoccupied and didn't notice her file by. As she wheeled her hand luggage past them, she pretended to get one wheel stuck. She turned around to look at the computer screen and spotted pictures of Mediterranean pottery. *Damn! Wish I could sit here.* Her seat was in coach at least ten rows and one curtain away. She concentrated on finding her aisle seat and settled in.

Jasper and Samson were picking Cara up from the airport. The thought of seeing her boys warmed her heart. She texted them that she was leaving on time, her heart fluttering at the mere thought.

"Yes!!! I'm going to Paris," she muttered doing a mental fist pump.

She pulled out her tangerine tablet and studied her ceramic pictures. The tablet would be very useful if she could only hold on to it. For some inexplicable reason it had a knack for disappearing on her. It was too big for her handbag and too small for her laptop case, thus it never found a reliable home. Maybe she could find a stylish bag in Paris that could house both her handbag items and her new electronics. She had bought a neoprene sleeve for the tablet, but she still didn't have the right shoulder bag to throw it in.

After dinner, a movie, and a cat nap, the plane started its descent. Cara could barely contain her excitement. She hadn't slept despite being exhausted. Every time she closed her eyes, her thoughts raced. Resting her weary bones was proving to be harder than an ice bucket challenge. At the baggage claim, the belt creaked into action. She turned her attention to the luggage chute. Waiting for her suitcase, she scanned the area for the Latin men. They hadn't yet arrived despite exiting the plane first. She spotted her boys through the arrivals window and waved emphatically from afar. Moments later, her bag shot out of the chute and she left the restricted area, butterflies dancing samba in her stomach.

"Hey, guys! I'm so happy to see you! How is everyone?"

"Great, Mom. Welcome to Paris! How was your flight?"

"As good as can be expected when you're sitting in a straight jacket for six plus hours. I worked on organizing my picture files. I have a lot to show you. I even updated my website recently."

"Can't wait." Samson replied.

"If it's pottery, I can."

"Funny, Jasper." Cara smirked.

Samson cringed. "Ouch."

Cara hugged her boys and they all started chatting simultaneously. She let them take her bags while she fired tons of questions their way.

"Jasper, how was your first night in Paris? Did you meet Natalie?" Cara asked curiously.

"Last night was catch up night. Samson and I had dinner near his apartment…alone. Summer had to work. She found her female lead, I'm supposed to tell you. Natalie will join us tomorrow night."

"I know! That means she can relax a little. Tonight is Christmas Eve. French families celebrate Christmas Eve together and go to church if I remember correctly. I look forward to meeting Natalie, Samson." Cara winked. She looked around for the men. They had arrived and were arranging their mega luggage on a cart.

"Mom, Samson, see those two Mexican men? The one with the baseball cap looks exactly like my client's CEO. His name is Jose Flores."

"They're Mexican?"

"Yes, my client, Fernando Flores, is Mexican and lives in Barcelona. He owns a restaurant by the harbor. I'm pretty sure that's his cousin. I had dinner with him. If it is, he sure gets around. If it isn't, he could easily be a double."

"I keep running into those guys. They were at the Sotheby's auction I went to with Sam and now they were on my flight to Paris. What do you know about them?"

"Like I said, they have a couple of restaurants. They also have a ceramics factory in Mexico.

They export their wares around the world."

"Interesting. I'll have to check them out. By the way, there was another robbery of antique ceramics from the Met. I told you about the first robbery. Sam and I were joking it was them."

Cara watched Jasper nod thoughtfully.

"I was kidding, Jasper."

"Hmmm."

They walked to Natalie's car and piled the bags into the back. After squeezing themselves into the small *Renault Captur*, Cara and Jasper peered out of the passenger windows at the two Mexicans exiting the airport. A dark SUV was waiting. This must be a business trip Cara surmised. How sad to be traveling for business during the holidays. She decided to check out ceramic auctions while in Paris. Maybe she would run into them again. She wanted to know who these Mexicans into ceramics were and what their story was. *What does their factory produce? Is it quality pottery?* Perhaps she would quiz Jasper some more.

Chapter XXVI

Away from the Evil Eye, Life in Paris Improves

Carlos and Jose got into the black van and greeted the driver, a fellow Mexican. Fernando used his own people whenever he could. He trusted no one. His trip to Paris was no exception. The driver informed them that Fernando was waiting at the restaurant. He also informed Carlos his renovated office was ready.

"Great. *Muchas gracias*," Carlos replied. "It'll be nice to not work out of the apartment. How does it look?"

"Like an office. Did you have a good rest on the plane? Fernando has a day of work planned."

"A little movie watching, a little sleep. We'll manage."

Jose stayed silent. He wasn't a talker unless he was acting as Fernando's informant. Supreme caution was exercised around Jose at F&S Enterprises. For the rest of the ride Carlos put in his earbuds and listened to *Enrique Iglesias, Pitbull and Daddy Yankee*. He didn't enjoy Jose's company and he wasn't in the mood to pretend otherwise. He was also particularly glad to be out of a confined space with Fernando Flores's number one mole.

Jose, annoyingly, spent a good portion of the plane ride trying to look over at his emails, so Carlos turned his screen and kept his correspondence hidden. He also pretended to nap.

Carlos was looking forward to a new beginning, removed from the Barcelona flagship. His base of operations would be the new Paris office and restaurant and he was thankful for the opportunity to disengage himself from the Flores family's roving eye. Not having to see Fernando and Jose on a daily basis and not having to constantly commute between Barcelona and Paris was refreshing and a relief. Happy to flee the pressure cooker surrounding Fernando and gaining some autonomy was a dream in the making. Living in Paris as opposed to traveling to Paris to check on operations would be a vast improvement in his lifestyle too. He planned to spend more time with his new girlfriend, the only ray of sunshine in his life. He had met her the first few months he was setting up the restaurant and he counted his blessings to have found such a sparkling gem.

Carlos turned up the music and watched the world go by, happy to be back in Paris. Now he just had to get through lunch with Fernando and go over their finances. After that, he was free for a while. Well, as free as he could possibly be under Fernando's umbrella. It was a step in the right direction.

Chapter XXVII

Paris is Always a Good Idea

Cara was thrilled to be in Paris. The first couple of hours were peaceful and filled with joy at seeing her children. She settled into her small bedroom, while Summer caught her up on the new movie developments.

"So, we have our two lead characters now. Hope and I are thrilled."

"Wonderful news. Does that mean you'll have some playtime over the holidays?" Cara asked cautiously as she surveyed her room, deciding where to put her belongings.

"Well, some of the pressure is off, but there are still logistics and paperwork to reconcile. It never ends, Mom." Summer fidgeted with her hair, wrapping a blonde lock around her slender finger.

"I thought the French take their holidays seriously?" Cara replied.

"Yes and no. The film world is the same everywhere. We work by our own schedule and standards. However, we are subject to their bureaucracy and right now all official offices are closed and on vacation, so nothing happens until January 2nd."

Cara looked around her room. It had a dirty white ironwork double bed, framed by two white-washed oak night tables with matching carved wood angel lamps. The doorway and bed faced a wall of windows underneath which there was a day bed with an ornate off-white scrolled metal frame. Summer helped Cara lift her suitcase onto it and then plopped herself beside it.

"Shall I open your suitcase?"

"Yes, please. I have some goodies for you. Oh and here are Nero's treats. They should probably go to the kitchen."

"Gee thanks, Mom. I was dreaming of these. I'll taste-test one now." She opened the box and fished one out. "Mmmm."

"Look at my new tangerine tablet. Don't you love the color? I took lots of pictures to show you."

"Cool, Mom. Let's see the pictures."

"Later. Too tired now."

"Nice *fleur-de-lis* necklace. Is it new?"

"Yes. Sam gave it to me for Christmas. It has a little diamond in each leaf for each of you. It's a symbol of protection for all of us, she said. I absolutely love it."

"Didn't know we needed protection."

"You never know what turns life may take." Cara tapped her pendant and yawned.

Perpendicular to the couch was a tall, narrow bookshelf. Cara spotted no English reading material. She was relieved she brought her own. There was no dresser, but the small walk-in closet had shelving. Her room had antique white walls with soft mint accents that portrayed a garden appeal. An exquisite painting depicting lilac trees, reminiscent of the *Cote d'Azur* hung over the bed. Summer, sprawled comfortably on the daybed, talked incessantly as Cara took in her new surroundings and unpacked a few more items, but her strength was waning. She lay down, trying to listen to Summer, but she could feel her eyes shutting and her consciousness slipping. "Summer, honey, I'm losing concentration. So tired now. Can we talk in a few hours?"

"Sure, Mom."

"Wake me before dinner," Cara murmured as she waved Summer out of the room, eyelids half closed. She was drifting off to dreamland at a record pace. She felt a soft kiss on her cheek as she closed her eyes.

The first night, Cara dined with Summer, Samson, Jasper, Ted and Hope and went to bed early, despite her mid-day nap. Madame Balon, the housekeeper that came with the ABNB, had left a deathly good welcome meal in the refrigerator, *Coq au Vin* with red potatoes and green beans. For dessert they had chocolate *éclairs* from the corner bakery and tangerines from Morocco. Christmas Day, Jasper and Samson came over for brunch and everyone slouched around the apartment enjoying each others company. Gifts were exchanged. In the afternoon they took a walk around the neighborhood just to get some brisk air.

The night after Christmas, a Saturday, the 'extended' family met them for dinner at a local restaurant: the group included Natalie, Pierre, Claude, and Mimi. Alma and Bette joined them later that night for wine, cheese, and fruits. Natalie brought a box of rainbow meringues. Cara decided she liked Natalie. She appeared to make Samson happy, and he literally glowed around her.

What a nice circle of friends, Cara thought as she drifted off to sleep that night in her minty cocoon. *Paris is always a good idea. Didn't Audrey Hepburn say that? Or was it Sam? How right they were.*

Chapter XXVIII

The Values of Good Help and a Small World

Cara soon realized that part of the reason pre-production had run smoothly was due to Madame Balon's dedicated help. Twice a week Madame came to the rue Malher apartment to clean and cook. Tuesday to do the heavy cleaning and prepare a simple meal and Friday to do light housework and prepare a gourmet meal for the weekend. Friday nights Summer and her crew were spent. Madame Balon made the most wonderful French dishes and placed them in the refrigerator for Summer's team to discover when they returned home after a long, tiring day and week. The de Fontenays had left her number in case Summer needed a housekeeper and Ted wasted no time making the arrangements. Having her come an extra day was golden. Twice a week they enjoyed a French culinary surprise.

"Madame Balon is worth her weight in gold. Everything she cooks is so delicious!" Cara remarked one morning. "Do you think she would share recipes?"

"I don't know, Mom. You have to ask her," Summer replied. "Actually, on second thought, a bribe might be more effective."

Ted raised an eyebrow, "Good luck with that, Cara. I asked her for a recipe recently and she pretended not to understand. I suggest a trade, pottery for *coq au vin* ingredients."

"You know, I think I saw her pull out her own baggie of premixed spices. Talk about French national secrets," Cara laughed.

"Sounds about right." Ted rolled his eyes. "She's as sweet as *mousse au chocolat,* but it will take more than a few *Kirs* to pry any recipes out of that woman's mental vault.

During one of their late-night chats, Summer informed Cara how happy she was with her crew from New York. "Ted has excelled at organizing our lives at home and on set. His natural ability to network has set us up with the theater for auditions and an entire crew from the theaters resource list. Hope has worked tirelessly by my side through the entire audition process, equipment rental, location scouting and securing of permits. We've only had minor hiccups so far."

"That's fantastic. Count your blessings. What do you still have pending?"

"Costume planning, hiring additional crew, scheduling. Ted is taking care of the crew, Hope and I will do everything else."

"It sounds manageable. Maybe we can work on wardrobe while I'm here. I can help with that too. Do you have a list?"

"Only a partial one. Yes, maybe you can help with that. We need to visit the flea markets for accent props. *Cliagnecourt* is the biggest."

"Sounds like a plan. I can also scout for pottery there, right?"
"Maybe. Not sure."

Besides Madame Balon's contributions, Ted's delicious decorations, which he picked up at *Les Halles*, made their apartment a home. Fresh flowers, wreaths with painted nuts and ribbons, festive candles which he lit all around the kitchen at dinner; all these touches contributed to a wonderful, cozy atmosphere. Their grand old rental was a warm, festive home filled with content faces. Ted took pictures of the holiday decorations and forwarded them to Monsieur and Madame de Fontenay in Nice. Their apartment never looked better and the de Fontenays concurred when they replied. They were pleased with their thoughtful tenants, *"les Americaines"*. Of course they didn't see the havoc in Summer's room. Lightning struck daily there.

"We can only hope that Madame Balon does not send them those pictures," Cara said one day. "They would freak."

"I don't think she knows how to use that feature on her phone. She barely texts," Summer remarked. "Ted tries."

The following day, after making everyone's beds on Madame B's day off, Cara decided to visit some pottery studios while Summer, Hope and Ted worked on set. Jasper was planning to visit Samson's office and have lunch with him. Cara chose not to join them. She liked the idea of giving the boys some time alone. She also had her own agenda. Dinner plans were made, and everyone went their separate ways. Before leaving, Cara searched for her tablet to take pictures. It was not in its usual spot on her night table. After turning her room upside down, she headed to the kitchen, trying not to panic. Passing through the living room, she spotted it on the dining room table. She sighed with relief. Madame Balon must have moved it there when she cleaned and forgotten to put it back. Next time, Cara would have to put it in her bag to avoid another panic attack. The search had cost her 25 valuable minutes of her morning, not to mention lightyears of stress. Her pictures were priceless, and they weren't on the cloud.

Once out of the house, she walked around Paris, taking more pictures. She stopped for a late lunch in a charming bistro and walked home, arriving completely ragged. When she took off her shoes she discovered a huge hole in her sock. Plopping her tired bones on top of her neatly made bed, she fell into a satisfying slumber. Paris was exhausting.

Cara carefully gathered information regarding pottery auctions from Natalie and the internet and sent them to Samantha. "Should I check these out while I'm here?" Sam's reply was swift.

"YES! Please do. Send pictures too. We can always use a few more accents."

Cara loved her Instagram account and shared poignant pictures daily. She kept her picture files organized in separate folders and accessed them as needed.

The first auction she attended was at Brissonneau. She stopped to marvel at the decorative antiques and modern furniture. As her picture collection grew, so did her inspiration. At Brissonneau she looked at everything, but she bought nothing. Sam agreed.

The second auction Cara planned to attend was at Natalie's workplace, Beaussant Lefevre.

"Jasper, do you want to join me today at Natalie's auction house? They're having a viewing before the ceramics auction. Natalie said she would give us a tour behind the scenes."

"Sure, sounds good."

They met around ten and walked around the viewing room, admiring the eclectic pieces. Cara explained the process of a few items to Jasper. Natalie came to greet them and give them an inside tour. When she left, Cara examined a colorful grouping of bowls, similar to the stolen pottery in New York. *They look remarkably similar!* She took pictures and sent them to Sam. She also made a mental note to check the pictures from New York on her tablet. She needed the larger screen to see the details. On a whim, she left a written bid. When they were seated at lunch, a couple hours later, Cara inquired about Jasper's Mexican client.

"So, tell me about your new clients. What's their story?"

"Well…they own a ceramics factory in Tampico, Mexico. They've had it for four generations and Fernando Flores is immensely proud of it. The pottery is nice. I saw it close up."

"What's the name of their business?"

"F & S Enterprises."

"Are the men we saw all related?"

"Jose, the man with the turquoise cross is Fernando's cousin. He doesn't talk much. I never met the other man we saw. I don't know a whole lot more."

They spent the remainder of the day at the *Gare d'Orsay*, a museum housed in a former train station.

The next day, Cara and Jasper went to the morning auction. Cara didn't bid on anything. Mid-auction they left for lunch to a nearby bistro. After lunch, they parted ways. Jasper went to Samson's apartment and Cara returned to Beaussant Lefevre for part two of the auction. She seated herself in the last row and perused the catalogue. Most of the people appeared to be dealers. Many knew each other, similar to New York. When the auction began, Cara noticed the two Mexican men from the airport, Jose, and the younger man. They were seated across the room, toward the back. With them was a third man, one Cara had never seen before. They were watching the auction proceedings, but only their French companion was bidding. Nothing was acquired. He was being outbid every time he raised his hand. She wondered if the man who returned her tablet in New York would remember her, but he showed no sign of recognition. She left her seat and went to the lady's room.

When she returned, she inconspicuously raised her tablet as if reading and snapped a picture, catching a side view of the three men. Stopping behind them, she listened. They were speaking in Spanish. Cara overheard one of the Mexicans address the third man as Alphonse, but her language skills only covered basic French, not Spanish, so she gave up. Perhaps Natalie could shed some light once she described them and showed her the picture. She was determined to find out who they were. Not wanting to wait for the lot she bid on since it was one of the last, she took one last look at the men and left. Their continuous resurgence captivated her.

That night, dinner was a home affair. The Malher residents sat in the warmth of their festive kitchen and discussed the days' events.

"What's for dinner, Ted? Any luck with Madame Balon and recipes?" Cara asked.

"No, honey…. that woman does not believe in sharing. Tonight, we'll have to contend with my limited chef skills."

"Bet they're better than mine," Cara mused. She grabbed a lettuce head and started washing it. Samson and Jasper arrived with more wine and Natalie added another box of meringues. This time they were chocolate. Cara started to wonder if they had a sale on meringues somewhere.

Over dinner, Summer and Hope caught everyone up on film proceedings and Cara described her auction experiences. She briefly mentioned how small the art world was and told the group about seeing the same men in New York at a Sotheby's auction. She pulled up her airport and auction pictures on the tablet and showed them to Natalie. Natalie didn't recognize the two

Mexicans, but she did know Alphonse. Jasper did a double take at the auction picture and interrupted before Natalie could elaborate.

"Holy crap, Mom! That is definitely Jose Flores," he interrupted. "I thought that was him at the airport! I can't believe he came to the auction after I left."

Cara's eyes widened, "The art world is smaller than you think. You sure there's nothing else you can tell me about them?"

"I'm sure. They have tons of money, and they own restaurants. That's all I know."

"What was their restaurant in Barcelona like?"

"It's pretty successful. It's in a nice area, near a popular hotel."

"Natalie, what do you know about Alphonse?"

"Alphonse Cretin is a shady arts dealer from Southern France. He's built a reputation on dealing with questionable provenances and he has an impressive arsenal of clients he buys and sells for. I don't know who most of his clients are though. I'm not sure anyone does. He's very discreet about sharing. I wouldn't trust Cretin as far as I could spit."

"Hmmm, interesting. Would he deal in stolen merchandise?"

"Very possible."

Cara pulled out her tablet and googled F&S Enterprises. The two restaurants popped up. The pottery business didn't. Next, she googled Fernando Flores. Nothing. Jose Flores. Nothing. She wrote down the name and address of the restaurant in Paris, *Au Coeur de Lion*. The translation was "Lion's Heart." Fernando's striking ruby ring came to mind.

"Does the ceramics business have a different name?"

"Not that I know of."

"How do you say 'Lion' in Spanish?

"*Leon.*"

"I wonder if the name of the factory has that in its name?"

"Interesting thought. His ceramics have a lion's head mark when you flip them over. Try *Corazon de Leon* or *Cabeza de Leon.*

"Bingo!"

"Which is it?"

"*Corazon de Leon.*" Cara scrolled around the website. "Wow, their stuff is good. I'm impressed."

The next day, Cara was notified by the auction house that the written bid she left for the bowls was accepted. The bowls did not sell at auction and the seller was willing to accept her lower bid. She was happy for her success. She eagerly emailed Samantha, attaching pictures. "Success. I got two beautiful bowls! I also saw the Mexicans from NY at the Paris auction."

"So glad they didn't outbid us this time."

"The ceramics world is shrinking. Those guys have a substantial ceramics factory in Mexico and export to Europe," she wrote. "They keep resurfacing wherever I go. Check out their website." She attached the link.

"The plot thickens," Sam replied. "Were there any thefts at this auction? Lol"

Chapter XXIX

Paying the Price

Carlos stepped out of the shower and grabbed a towel. He was going to a business dinner with Fernando, Jose, and Alphonse Cretin to discuss past and future ventures. Fernando put Cretin up at the Vendome Hotel which Carlos knew was costing his boss a pretty penny. The auction, the day before, had been successful and the ceramics Alphonse consigned on their behalf had all sold. He even managed to drive the prices up a little with discreet counter bidding. A few pieces sold lower than anticipated, but nonetheless, everything sold. The original works Alphonse successfully sold in Monaco for substantial sums. His rich Russian contacts were thrilled. Business was good, which put Fernando and therefore Carlos, in a great mood.

Carlos reached for his beloved Swiss Army watch, the one he had bought for his father's fiftieth birthday with his first big paycheck and grabbed his wallet. The hoop earring from his mother, never left his ear. It was all he had to remember them by, besides fond memories and a few pictures. He left the apartment slightly anxious knowing that Fernando was planning to propose a different kind of business deal to Alphonse. Carlos had his doubts about the direction this discussion would take. Alphonse was useful in selling their hot ceramic wares, but beyond that Carlos didn't think Alphonse would come through. The man lacked balls and gumption. Furthermore, the Frenchman was very high strung, a trait that did not mix well with F&S's profile.

Carlos pictured Alphonse getting ready for dinner in the plush hotel. He could envision Alphonse mooning over his reflection and spritzing his cologne in questionable places. The man smelled like a whore house on Sunday and just the memory of his sensory assaults made Carlos frown.

Meeting at the restaurant a half hour early, Fernando, Jose and Carlos discussed business over a drink. At eight on the dot, a cologne cloud floated through the dining room announcing Alphonse's arrival. Carlos detected Alphonse's guarded demeanor. Fernando's deceptively generous gestures put him somewhat at ease, however a nervous eye twitch and the repetitive stroking of his mustache were a dead giveaway. Carlos could relate to how Alphonse felt, only he had learned to mask his anxiousness over the years. Acquiring a poker face took years of practice. Fernando had a way of keeping you on your toes, so adopting a poker demeanor secured his survival when things got tense, which happened frequently.

Wine flowed freely and a three-course meal appeared in a well-timed sequence. The food was superb and the pleasantries crossing the table could have made a glacier melt. Over coffee Fernando assumed a more serious air and the mood shifted. He revealed his new business proposal. As Alphonse listened, he increasingly fidgeted in his seat, becoming visibly agitated as if he had a wedgie that needed arranging. He asked few questions, averted his eyes continuously and said nothing until all of Fernando's cards were on the table. Then he shook his head no. Carlos cringed inside, but his face was impassive.

With carefully chosen words, to not offend his host, Alphonse explained why he had to turn down Fernando's offer. Carlos studied the veins in his hands. It was exactly what he expected. Alphonse's rejection would not bode well with Fernando.

"Fernando, I can't accept this proposal because as a rule, I don't work with illegal goods. I also prefer to stay within my area of expertise."

"Are you sure? It could be very lucrative for you."

All at the table understood the implications except for poor Alphonse.

"Here's the thing, Fernando. I can sell items with provenance even if it is questionable and I can move certain high-quality goods without, but I don't know the business you are asking me about and I cannot be of assistance there. Impossible! I don't have that clientele. I only deal in art, nothing else. That is where my skill set lies. Furthermore, my clients are confidential by their choice, so I couldn't make an introduction even if I thought it was appropriate, which I don't."

Carlos looked at Alphonse's apologetic smile and guessed Alphonse had a reputation to consider, meager as it was. Carlos shifted in his seat and played with the water in his glass. He took a sip and looked around the restaurant, as he waited for Fernando's response. He sighed with relief when he realized no one was paying attention to them. He prayed Fernando would keep his temper in check. Fernando was livid. Carlos knew the signs.

"Well, then there isn't much more to discuss. Thank-you for your services." Fernando smiled through clenched teeth.

Carlos knew Fernando was seething inside. His ventilating nostrils were a sure sign to insiders as were his tapping fingers. It signaled the meeting was over. Jose cleared his throat but said nothing. Alphonse took a shallow breath.

Carlos had done some research and knew Alphonse was broke, living above his means. Nonetheless, he'd strongly advised against including the Frenchman in their internal operations. Alphonse was too skittish, and they were already experiencing enough force from local rivals who felt their turf was being invaded in France. Alphonse would never be able to stand up to that kind of pressure. Fernando thought otherwise. He felt a desperate man could always be bought. Bought maybe, but not pushed into something so risky and tough. Carlos knew Fernando was enraged that Alphonse turned down his generous offer and it worried him. He glanced at Fernando, who nodded at Jose, his eyes, a blazing dark green. In Carlos's estimation, it would only take seconds before Fernando blew a gasket.

Carlos shifted in his seat. "Gentlemen, should we ask for the bill?"

Fernando ignored him and held out a business check to Alphonse.

"Jose, please take Alphonse back to his hotel and see that he is taken care of." Fernando directed.

A chill ran through Carlos's body.

Alphonse pocketed his substantial check and assured them he did not need an escort, but Fernando insisted, his plastic smile frozen in place. Carlos stayed silent and studied his neatly trimmed fingernails.

"Jose will pay your hotel bill. Thank you for your service." Fernando smiled. Alphonse was sweating profusely. He thanked Fernando and Carlos, extending a clammy hand to all and left with Jose, taking his fading perfume cloud with him. Carlos excused himself to get the car. "I'll be waiting for you outside, Fernando."

At the hotel, Jose pulled his baseball cap down over his eyes and turned his collar up as he walked a few paces behind an increasingly nervous Alphonse. The lobby was empty and there was no one at the desk. They made no attempt at conversation or eye contact as Alphonse pushed the up button at the elevator with a faint smile. When the doors opened Alphonse extended his hand to say good night. Jose ignored it and ushered Alphonse into the elevator, quickly pressing the door close button. On Alphonse's landing, he held the elevator door open for Alphonse to exit first. Alphonse did so with noticeable hesitation. Jose knew he was scaring Alphonse, and he was enjoying every second of his domination over the diminutive Frenchman.

Jose walked down the long hallway to Alphonse's suite. He guessed correctly that Alphonse was staring at his insane arm and back muscles. His workouts were agonizing, and he was proud of his hard-earned rippled physique. It paid off at crucial times. At the door, Jose extended his rough-hewn hand for the key card. Reluctantly, Alphonse handed it to him. Jose smirked. Once in the room, Jose sat down and motioned for Alphonse to sit down on the couch next to him. Jose took a paper packet out of his pocket and carefully unfolded it, revealing a white powder. Alphonse shook his head no.

"*Non, merci.*"

Undeterred, Jose carefully crushed the powder and drew thin lines on a small hardcover book, delivered from the interior of his jacket. Inserting a thin metal tube into Alphonse's nose, he forcefully swatted Alphonse's head down to the table, ordering him to inhale.

"I think you should have an idea of what you're missing. You made a big mistake tonight, my friend."

Alphonse, slightly tipsy and too frightened to further object, did as he was told. Jose watched the squirming Frenchman inhale line after line. When Jose saw what looked like an overwhelming rush surge through Alphonse's body, he knew he had to act quickly. He tore off Alphonse's clothes and touched him firmly like Alphonse had never been touched before. Alphonse, totally defenseless, succumbed in a wordless scream. He was an easy mark for the sadistic Mexican.

Chapter XXX

Another Pink Slip

Carlos was listening to the Sunday morning news around 10am in his small, high-tech kitchen, sipping Mexican coffee. His angelic girlfriend was sleeping. He turned the radio up just a little louder. A few decibels more and he swore his French improved.

From what Carlos could decipher, housekeeping knocked on the door of Suite 113 early Sunday morning. When no one replied, they entered. The screams could be heard the length of the corridor and beyond. The man they found was gagged and sprawled awkwardly on the couch. His body was bruised, contorted, and spit naked. He was dead.

When the police arrived, they identified Alphonse Cretin, a decorative arts dealer with a slightly tainted reputation. He had once been accused of selling art copies as genuine and was cleared, but in the world of art you never live down a blemish to your reputation. The art world has an elephant's memory, akin to the internet. His small overnight case had been picked through and overturned. There was nothing major missing as far as the police could tell. Alphonse's wallet and personal ID's were accounted for, although his wallet was empty. Oddly, there was no cell phone. There were traces of drugs on the coffee table. At first look, his death appeared to be random, an unintended overdose in the throes of S&M passion. More news on the case would follow as details were uncovered, the newscaster promised before switching to the next breaking topic.

Carlos wondered how Fernando would handle these new developments if they spiraled out of control. So far, the police were looking for a sexual deviant, but that could change at any given moment once a possible motif was established. Ominous feelings were creeping into Carlos's gut. Damn Fernando and damn creepy Jose. Europe was not Mexico. Police could not be intimidated or paid off so easily. Under his breath, he cursed Fernando for letting his cousin loose on Alphonse. Jose should have stayed in Mexico. Carlos didn't trust those two hotheads not to mess things up. He didn't want to go back to Mexico. He liked his new life in Paris and more importantly, his autonomy away from the close scrutiny of the Flores family. He would have to seriously hasten his plan for the future, expedite his savings. This was a warning he knew not to ignore. Carlos picked up the phone and called Fernando.

"Just heard the news. You listening?"

"Yes. What a shame the man with the extensive art connections was so weak. A man with no balls. He could have made a lot of money with us. Dealing with that whining Frenchman was a big mistake. You were right."

"That admission doesn't make me feel any better, Fernando. I don't like the attention this may generate. We had dinner with him the night he died in a restaurant full of witnesses. I hope no hotel cameras captured Jose's portrait."

"Don't worry. Jose cleaned his tracks and took precautions. He said no one was at the desk when he arrived, and he left through the back. We're back in Barcelona with iron clad alibis. We flew home after dinner and there is no flight log that includes our names. The pilot knows what to say. Good thing the pottery sale was concluded before Alphonse could trip us up. From now on, Jose and I will handle the sales. We secured the man's list of contacts from his smartphone."

"Ok, Fernando. Just be careful. Please!" He couldn't believe he was saying this to Fernando. Only a year ago, he wouldn't have dared.

Carlos disconnected his phone not at all convinced Fernando and Jose were capable of being level-headed. Those two rabble-rousers could easily ruin everything they worked so hard to build in Europe. Carlos shook his head as he looked out the window. He heard someone stir in the next room and decided to go back to bed to let off some steam.

Chapter XXXI

Only the Art Dealers Die Young (The Meringues, Not So Much)

On Sunday, Cara and her clan decided to go to the flea market at *Porte de Cliagnecourt* to make a dent in the costume shopping list. They hopped on the metro after a lavish croissant and omelet breakfast and arrived around noon. Helena was waiting for them at the subway entrance when they arrived. It was a cool, sunny day and the market was hopping.

First stop was Alma's booth. Summer bought a few vintage items for Helena's character. Helena looked fabulous in everything, so the choices were easy. She and Hope found a few more vintage outfits and accessories for supporting characters as they forged on. Ted shopped for himself, finding a unique cashmere scarf and soft leather boots. Most of the clothing for the movie would be borrowed, but it was nice to start with a few stand out mood pieces. Once Helena's character was outfitted and accessorized, she departed for home.

"I'm going to leave if you're done shopping for me. My boyfriend is off today. He had a business dinner last night so I'm looking forward to some time with him. Love all the outfits, Summer. Thank you."

"Great, Helena. Thanks for meeting us. See you tomorrow."

Cara browsed through the furniture and decorative arts section and picked up a small floral milk jug. She contemplated buying sneakers to replace her trendy, choking new shoes. Her feet were gathering hurtful blisters with each step. Luckily everyone was ready to leave just when she fingered the tenth pair of ugly sneakers with disdain. She hobbled back to the *metro* and thankfully plopped down in an open seat for the long ride back home.

"I'm used to walking in New York. but not in these so called 'comfortable' shoes. What a joke! They're nothing I thought they would be. I'm going to need a couple of band aids Summer."

"No problem. I have band aids and worn sneakers for you. Want to trade shoes for the ride home? Will that help?"

"Yes, and yes. Gel band-aids, that is what I need. Here, slide over your shoes. Can you carry me home too?"

"Sorry, Mom. Trading shoes is the best I can offer."

"I'll take it. Remind me to wear my old boots for the rest of the vacation. I don't think my feet will recover any time soon. Ahhh your shoes feel better. Thanks."

"You're lucky we wear the same size."

"Today, truly."

Arriving at home, the group dropped their purchases in the living room and ventured into the kitchen. Summer opened the refrigerator while Cara wiggled her frozen toes and took off her socks to examine the damage.

"My hunger pangs are scary."

"My blisters are even scarier," Cara countered. "I need a footbath, aloe lotion, gel band aids and a pair of your triple ply sweat socks, Summer. If not, I'll be wheelchair bound."

Hope giggled. "Been there. My first week here I had a horrendous blister. Took a week to heal."

"Not the encouragement I need to hear, Hope."

Hope giggled some more. "This is why I stick to sneakers or uggs now."

Natalie's meringue box was still sitting on the counter. Ted made coffee and dumped the meringues on a plate. They dropped like lead. "It seems that meringues have a short shelf life. These have morphed into alien rocks." He picked one up and dropped it with a thunk. Ted emptied the plate into the adjoining guest toilet and flushed. "So much for these duds."

Summer pulled out a tin box of homemade chocolate covered butter cookies and refilled the plate. After carefully slicing and dicing, she added apples and cheese slivers. "Bless, Madame Balon. She always leaves us with something special."

Cara dapped a warm washcloth on her heals and rubbed lotion on her blisters moaning softly.

"Yay, my sweet tooth is content" said Summer as she chewed on her cookie and reached for an apple wedge with her other hand.

"When your hunger pangs are satisfied, can you concentrate on my blisters?"

"Sure thing, Mom. Give me a minute. First things first."

Cara glanced at the internet news on her tablet. It was rare for her to go a full day without checking world events.

"My news junkie adrenalin is pumping. I need a quick fix. New York City could have sunk under its weight, and I wouldn't know, being here."

Ted turned on the flat screen in the kitchen and Cara found herself face to face with Alphonse.

"Oh my God … is that Alphonse the art dealer? What are they saying?"

"It looks like he was murdered, Mom."

"Whaaat?" Cara's hand shot up to her *fleur de lis* pendant. She gave it a reassuring tug and googled Alphonse's name. A news flash popped up. His picture was featured with the caption, "Art Dealer Found Dead at the Vendome Hotel." Eyes widening, Cara put on her reading glasses. "Somebody translate, please," she asked, not fully trusting her French language skills. "I want to get this right. I sat near this man at auction yesterday. What happened to him?"

Summer pondered while eating a cheese slice. "Really? No kidding? What did you do to him, Mom? Slip some arsenic in his *café au lait*?"

Cara shot Summer a worried look. "No, seriously. He was at the Beaussant auction with the two Mexicans from my flight. The two who were at the Sotheby's auction in New York. I told you about them. Remember, I mentioned it the other night and showed you the pictures?"

"I wasn't really paying attention. Here let me see." Summer translated, "The article is pretty brief and doesn't really say what happened. Apparently traces of drugs were found in his room, so it appears to be an overdose. The police suspect a kinky sex act gone wrong as he was found nude and scuffed up, but that is all they're saying. Murder is suspected, but not confirmed. Reports from the medical examiner will shed more light. Creepy company you keep, Mom. Let me get you those band aids now."

A chill crept up Cara's spine. Summer got up to go to her bathroom and Cara went to the one off the kitchen. Upon her return, Cara announced, "I just exercised target practice on a cloud of floating meringues that refuse to be flushed. Anybody know anything about this?"

Ted belched a laugh. "I threw them out because they were hard-core missiles and completely inedible; I was sure they would dissolve. They're pure sugar." Hope and Summer dissolved into silly laughter.

"Natalie is trying to crack our perfect American teeth."

"French water pressure. It falters on the top floor."

"Forget the meringues, girls, dinner is almost ready" Ted announced. "Set the table. We're having lamb stew with vegetables. I prepared it early this morning while you all were getting your beauty sleep. Claude's recipe."

"It smells delicious."

"I hope Claude's recipe is safer than Natalie's dessert. We only have three toilets and now we're down to two for four people. Workable, but not an ideal ratio."

"Funny, Summer." That elicited another wave of giggles from Hope and Summer.

"Here, Cara, start passing the crudité. The girls are incapacitated. Can you also pop the cork on the second red wine and pour me another glass? The lamb got most of the first bottle."

"Not the way I cook," Jasper grinned as he and Samson walked in the door. "I would drink more than the lamb."

"Hey, Jasper, Samson. You're just in time for my virgin lamb stew experiment."

"Here, some reserves since the lamb was thirsty." Jasper and Samson each plopped two wine bottles on the table.

"That stew smells awesome. You cooked that?"

"Yes, at the crack of dawn."

"Wow, I don't think I've ever cooked anything remotely similar in my Barcelona kitchen. Maybe an omelet on a Sunday."

"Jasper, your idea of cooking is reheating tappas from the bar, the night before."

"True, I admit it." Jasper laughed as he poured red wine into two glasses, handing one to his brother and one to Cara. He looked at Summer. "Wine refills anyone? Or maybe I should skip you. It looks like you had a head start."

"No, I didn't! Hope and I are just tired and silly. Keep pouring." Summer laughed. "Ted, this really does smell amazing."

They gathered around the large rustic kitchen table for their hearty French *paysanne* meal. Ted lit some candles and opened another bottle of Merlot. Dinner on Rue Malher was a *gourmand* experience, especially when Ted was wearing the chef's apron. He unknowingly had that magic *cordon bleu* touch.

"Madame B watch out. Your American competition has arrived. This stew is good," Cara remarked.

Conversation around the dinner table soon centered around movie censorship, following a recent cyber bully story. The computer system of a major movie house in Hollywood had been hacked, creating havoc. Private emails between a director and an actor, of an upcoming film, were exposed. The controversial movie discussed was cancelled out of fear of reprisal, thereby setting a scary precedent. Whether the movie was worth the fight was irrelevant they all agreed. What happened to freedom of speech? Over dessert, the subject shifted to the Hotel Vendome death. Alphonse's demise was shocking to Natalie according to Samson; her world was tightly knit and Alphonse was a colorful, if not celebrated, fixture in it. Murder close to home was never a good feeling.

Jasper looked thoughtful. The Fernando Flores connection was real and becoming more suspicious by the day. Bad news seemed to follow that group around.

The next morning, Cara entered the kitchen early to empty the dishwasher and prepare breakfast. She started a load of laundry while brewing coffee and making toast. When she went to the bathroom a while later to throw the clothes into the dryer, the meringues were still bobbing in the toilet. *Dear Lord. They taste like sugared chalk and float like styrofoam. Some desserts should just be visual decoration.*

Chapter XXXII

The Meaning of Fete in Paris

Time was slipping by, and Cara was counting the days. New Year's Eve was around the corner and Jasper was returning to Barcelona on New Year's Day. Cara wondered how they should ring in the new year. Should she make a restaurant reservation? Should they have a small dinner party at home? Seven days had flown by in the blink of an eye. Considering the harmonious co-existence at Rue Malher, she wanted a memorable ending to her first vacation week. Cara also wanted Jasper to have a fabulous last night with his siblings. She didn't want him to leave, but Adriano needed him in the office in early January for important strategy meetings. The beginning of the year was when the bank reviewed all of their stats and set their new goals.

The ambiance in Paris had been effortless and relaxed. A good break for all from life's daily stresses. Maybe being in Paris was part of the miracle; the city of lights was a magical place. All had enjoyed their holidays and time off.

"Any thoughts on New Years Eve?" Cara asked Summer over breakfast one morning.

"I got nothing. You coming to rehearsals today?"

"Yes."

"Ok, see you later. Gotta run, Mom."

Later that day their dilemma was solved. Helena invited them to a New Years Eve celebration, Paris style. Cara was thrilled when she heard the exchange.

Helena arrived waving an invitation. "You must come to this party guys. It'll be incredible! Give me your head count and I'll make sure to get you tickets."

"My mom will still be here. Are there older people coming too?"

"Absolutely! She'll have a fabulous time. There will be a steep cover charge, but trust me, it'll be so worth it. Everything is included in that price. All my model friends, male and female, will be there."

"Can I bring two friends?"

"Yes, Ted. Summer, just give me the final head count tomorrow and I'll get the tickets."

"Ok, Helena. Thanks so much. It sounds like fun."

Ted and Hope were sold. Cara knew that Jasper, who had not yet met Helena, but who had carefully studied her pictures on Summer's laptop, would be thrilled. Jasper's fascination with Helena had become a running joke between Cara and Summer.

"You got Helena, a gorgeous model, for your movie, Summer? How did you manage that? She looks amazing." He asked his little sister incredulously.

"Ted found her in the first round of auditions. We all thought she was perfect for the part."

Summer and Cara chuckled at Jasper's predictable reaction.

"She certainly is," Jasper replied, winking. "I can't wait to meet her."

Summer rolled her eyes. "I bet."

Cara smiled at the memory. Meeting Helena would be a perfect ending to Jasper's Paris trip. That night Cara told Samson and Jasper about the invitation.

"It'll be fun, guys. I forecast a memorable night. Are you in?"

"Ok, Mom, we're on board. Sounds like a blast."

Chapter XXXIII

A Chance Encounter

Cara was dreaming about her next Paris adventure, a visit to *Fereaux Galleries*, when she heard an unfamiliar sound. She woke up to rain splashing against her windowpanes. It was grey out and Summer, Hope and Ted had already left. They were planning to interview additional crew at the theater and schedule another afternoon of punishing rehearsals. Helena was a pleasure and came prepared, but Alain needed help and slowed things down considerably. Summer would have to resort to scare tactics and hope he would come to the set more prepared when filming started.

Cara showered and pulled on black leggings, a long, pale blue shirt and an equally long, braided, charcoal colored cashmere sweater. For her trademark splash of color, she added a tangerine & cobalt blue paisley scarf. She grabbed her comfortable black boots and a black, hooded raincoat before heading out the door. After the flea market fiasco, she had given up on fancy footwear. Her feet thanked her by rejuvenating and healing her insufferable blisters.

There was no left-over coffee in the kitchen this morning and she didn't feel like making a new pot for one person, so she decided to have a leisure breakfast at the corner café. As an afterthought, she grabbed her tablet and threw it into a plastic shoulder bag. She wouldn't be taking scenic photos today, but she could read the newspaper and check her emails while having café au lait and a croissant. Thankfully, the cafe had Wi-Fi.

As she entered, she noticed a striking man sitting comfortably on the *banquette* having breakfast alone. He was reading the café's morning newspaper. Something about him felt familiar and inviting. She chose the table next to him, sharing the same *banquette*. When his phone rang, she overheard someone say, "Bonjour Francois."

The rest of the conversation was quick, and business related, but she couldn't help notice his deep, baritone voice. It glided over her like a *Barry White* song at sunset. She motioned to the waiter and ordered her usual while sneaking peeks at the man's profile as he chatted on his phone. Suddenly she experienced an epiphany. The man was the owner of *Fereaux Galleries*!

He had tiny laugh lines in the creases of his eyes and mouth and a narrow, straight nose. Cara felt her heart flutter. When he disconnected his cell and their eyes met, she was sure it was him. Caught, she smiled. Francois returned the smile, lingering for a moment longer than expected. As he studied her face a slight curve formed at the corner of his lips. Embarrassed, Cara looked away. If only she could find her words, but she was tongue-tied; she couldn't come up with a single clever thing to say in French.

While looking down she could feel Francois's eyes on her. Under her lashes, she saw him pull his jacket on and arrange his wool scarf in slow motion, his eyes never leaving her face as if willing her to look up. He glanced at the bill and placed money on the table. Next, he reached into the inside pocket of his coat and pulled out a folded, printed flyer which he placed on her table. It was an invitation to an art show opening on Friday night, right after New Years Eve.

"If you are interested in art and are free Friday evening, you might enjoy this exhibit and a glass of champagne on me," he said in flawless English. His rich voice and direct stare made her face heat up. Was she blushing? This was the man whose blog and site she followed religiously for the past few months. Where was her courage?

"Merci. How did you know I speak English?" Cara asked, one eyebrow disappearing under her bangs.

"I heard your accent when you ordered. I promise you'll enjoy yourself. You should come. The gallery is close to here," he smiled convincingly.

Cara studied the invitation and before she could look up and respond, he was gone. The gallery really wasn't far. How had she not noticed that before? She decided to walk past it on her way home in the evening and check it out. She had planned to go there all vacation, but somehow it got pushed off to the last few days. Now she had even more of an incentive to snoop. She spent the rest of her time at the café lamenting over her silence in his presence. Why hadn't she struck up a conversation? He was right next to her. What were the chances of such an amazing coincidence?

After Francois's departure, she scanned the daily paper regarding the murder, but there was nothing new reported that the previous evening news hadn't already covered. She emailed additional pictures of her auction purchase to Samantha and filled her in on her brief encounter at the café. "I was just invited to an art opening by the handsome Frenchman from the gallery site I showed you. Fereaux Galleries. He was having breakfast next to me in our corner café. Can you believe it? Should I go?"

The answer was immediate. "*Bien Sur.* If that isn't fate, what is? Go! Live a little dangerously for the two of us. I'm currently arguing with the tile guy putting down additional flooring in Nero's kitchen and let me tell you, he's really far removed from a handsome Frenchman. More like a short, overweight, bald Italian who is subjecting me to his drooping pants and lack of humor."

Cara replied with a laughing emoji. "Decision made."

When Cara finished her second *café au lait,* she slipped the tablet into its sleeve and paid her bill. She put on her coat and walked to the metro to get her ceramics at Beaussant Lefevre. As she walked past the café windows, the waiter came running after her.

"Madame, your tablet. You forgot it on the *banquette.*"

"*Merci! Merci beaucoup.*" Cara thanked him profusely. She sighed with relief. The impromptu invitation from Francois Fereaux had her head spinning. Luckily, leaving a good tip had its perks. This was a subtle reminder to back up her pictures when she got home. She couldn't bear to lose the memories on her tablet, nor her picture inventory.

Chapter XXXIV

Shop till You Drop, Parisian Style

The day before New Year's Eve was reserved for shopping. Nobody had anticipated or packed for a fancy New Years Eve party. Jasper could borrow clothes from Samson, but everyone else came up empty, so it was decided that a shopping day was in order. Ted let Pierre take him around Saint Germain. Summer and Hope wanted choices, so Cara suggested spending the day at Galeries Lafayette, a major department store so large you could easily spend days in it and still only see a fraction of its goods. When the doors opened at Galeries Lafayette, the three ladies were among the first to march in.

Cara found a dress first; a sleek, black crepe cocktail dress from an unknown French designer, with black lace accents in all the right places. The dress had a deep V neck with lace inlay, three quarter, lace sleeves and a five-inch lace hem that ended just above the knee.

"How do I look, girls?" Cara twirled around.

"How does it feel, Mom? It looks pretty hot."

"I feel hot." Cara joked. "Can you take a picture with my tablet?"

"Sure, Mom."

Cara studied the picture of herself. "This is as smoking as I'll ever be. The dress is a keeper."

"Wow, that was a quick choice."

"When you know, you know."

Hope decided on black, flowing silk pants and a cropped, cherry red tank trimmed in sequins.

"I must have these black silk pants. They are the bomb."

"The top matches the streak in your hair."

"Yeah, you look great, Hope. Especially with that itsy-bitsy fire tank," Summer teased.

Hope held up a sheer black glitter scarf to wear as a wrap.

"To quench the fire when it gets too hot. I wouldn't want to be too distracting with my itsy-bitsy fire tank." Hope laughed. Cara took a few more pictures.

"Too late. I already have this vision in my head. Men will be following you into the lady's room, tongues hanging out." Summer joked. "All Parisian restraint abandoned."

Summer was torn between a fitted sleeveless, midnight blue textured and asymmetrically- layered silk dress with a plunging scoop neck or a strapless black sequin number with a full skirt and fuchsia tulle layer peaking from beneath. Cara took a picture of both outfits and abstained from the vote. Hope and the saleslady voted for the navy dress. Summer acquiesced after studying Cara's pictures. As usual, she kept second guessing herself all the way to the shoe department. Once Summer discovered beautiful navy silk pumps with intermittent, scattered rhinestone stars, she happily bought the shoes and forgot about the black dress. Problem solved.

Secretly, Cara was glad Summer had skipped the tulle petticoat dress. What Cara loved in simplicity, Summer usually celebrated with sequins, tulle and pomp. Somehow Cara's understated elegance skipped a generation.

"I just love the silver stars; these are perfect. I think I have a rhinestone star hair pin that may top this look off." Summer exclaimed as she examined her twinkling shoes. Cara rolled her eyes and smiled at Hope.

"She always had a weakness for glitter. When she was seven she insisted on an aqua sequined mermaid dress for Halloween. I think we still have that tucked away somewhere."

"Yeah. You never know what you might need for a movie, so leave that dress right where it is."

Hope smirked. "In that case, I'll save my sequin top for you when I'm done with it."

"Now for shoes …. hope they have something comfortable to go with my sizzling dress," Cara muttered. "My feet have barely recovered from the blisters I sustained."

"Yeah. And we want to dance New Years Eve. Make sure you can, Cara."

"Yeah. Comfort over style. I got the message."

Hope opted for a sleek black silk platform, open toe, sling back shoe with dangerously high heels, Prada style. "Oh yes, now I don't have to shorten my silk pants. I just grew three inches."

After agonizing about comfort over the wow factor, Cara decided on simple black suede pumps with kitten heels.

"Suede should be soft enough for dancing in new shoes. And look at all these rhinestone clip-on buckles! I love them."

She added delicate, sparkly buttons in a lightning bolt design to her shoes and took a picture. "These will do. Ahh and they feel good too. Now I just need a dance partner."

"You're looking at her."

"Thanks, Hope. Good to know."

Satisfied, the women continued their quest in the coat department.

"Check out this black velvet cape coat. Wow, I love the red silk lining. I am so getting this. I can skip a few dinners out for this baby." Hope marveled.

"Mom, how does this look?"

Summer swirled in a midnight blue wool coat with a flare skirt and tailored top. It was adorned with small, violet velvet-covered buttons. The shawl collar and pocket flaps were trimmed in matching violet, crushed velvet.

"Nice. Take it. You'll wear that a lot, I bet."

Cara refrained from a coat purchase, since she came to Paris with a dressy black fur-lined raincoat. She did however pick a lengthy, violet velvet shawl with subtle glitter threads running through its lacy flip side.

"This is so beautiful I could faint! I can't resist this amethyst color. Sam will fight me to borrow this," she laughed. "Which reminds me, I need a gift for Sam. Something a little less extravagant though. She likes casual stuff she can wear every day."

"I suggest you wait till the January sales, Mom."

"Good idea. Another reason to come back. I like it here." Cara took a few pictures of possible gifts for Samantha, so she could check for them after the holidays.

Purchases in hand, the women headed to the makeup department.

"We need new faces for these kickass outfits, girls. Let's get a make-over." Cara sat down on the first make-up throne and pointed to the other two. Within minutes, she purchased a new foundation. Wanting to take a selfie to remember the eye make-up the sales lady had transformed her with, she realized her tablet was missing. She franticly checked all her bags. Gone.

"Oh my God! Summer, guard my treasures. I think I left my tablet on the accessory counter upstairs. I'm going to race back while you guys finish your makeovers."

"Oh no! Go."

When Cara got to the accessory counter, she didn't see her tablet. She circled around the entire counter, but the tablet was not there. Her heart was pounding. How could she have forgotten! She waited for the saleslady to reappear.

"Excuse me, did you see a tangerine-colored tablet anywhere on the counter? I left it here just a few minutes ago."

"No, I'm sorry. I saw nothing."

"Is the blonde saleslady still here?"

"Francesca? She just left for lunch. Run to the elevator. Perhaps you can catch her."

Cara sprinted in that direction, calling Francesca's name. The blonde woman turned just as the elevator door opened. Cara saw that she was holding a tangerine tablet.

"My tablet, I forgot it on the counter!"

"Oh yes! I was going to put it in the office while I went to lunch. I'm so glad you caught me."

"Me too. *Merci!*"

Cara clutched her tablet and scurried back to the escalator to rejoin the girls. They were still in the same spot she left them at. Arriving breathless, Cara held up her tablet.

"Good news. My, don't you two look transformed."

"Let's hope we can duplicate this when the time comes."

"My pictures should help."

Cara waited patiently, then documented their transformation. She carefully placed the tablet into the sleeve and into her shopping bag.

"You both look insane. Can I take you for a late lunch? We have to show off these faces somewhere," Cara laughed. "Besides, I'm starving. Shopping with you girls is strenuous work."

"Oh yeah. I could go for a late lunch."

"Good. Racing around for a rogue tablet made me ravenous."

"What is it with you and that thing? You're forever misplacing it. You should attach a tracking device."

"What a bright idea, Summer. I think Apple already thought of that." Cara rolled her eyes.

"Well, activate it and get cloud storage too, for heaven's sake."

"When I come back for January sales, I'll buy myself a stylish handbag that fits the tablet. That would help."

"Good idea, Mom. I would still consider activating that tracking App though."

"Yes, I will…when I have a moment.

Makeup purchases in hand the women made one last stop at the perfume counter on their way out. They experimented with Fleur Fatale, Chanel N 5, Thierry Mugler's Alien and Dior's Hypnotic Poison. Hope picked Allure.

"That's a classic, Hope. You'll love it."

"I already do!"

Summer decided on a light fruity scent from Biotherm. Cara took a bunch of samples. Around 3pm, before anyone fainted from hunger, they left Galeries Lafayette, and stopped for a *croque monsieur* and a *citron presse* at a nearby café.

"I declare today a whopping success. You girls will be the toast of the New Years Eve party."

"Mom, I seriously doubt that, considering that a whole modeling agency will be present."

"Details."

Chapter XXXV

Guys Just Want to Have Fun

Ted and Pierre browsed through the little boutiques in the side streets off Boulevard Saint Germain and stopped for a leisurely late lunch. Ted had found fine black wool pants and black patent leather loafers, so half of his outfit was in the bag. Pierre bought a sweater. After lunch, they decided to go to Galeries Lafayette for the final touches. There they found an unusually stitched, pale pink dress shirt for Ted and a black silk shirt for Pierre. They both bought silk bow ties on a whim, a dark fuchsia one for Ted and a striped one in varying shades of deep purple and magenta for Pierre.

"I haven't worn one of these since … … … ever. This calls for a jacket." Ted winked.

They looked through the men's department for dinner jackets and Ted found a daring, dark teal Mugler jacket with silk lapels and matching teal, silk buttons. It was a fortune, even on sale, but Ted could not leave without it.

"This is so mine," he exclaimed with conviction. "I'll skip champagne for a week or the next month if I have to, but I gotta have this jacket."

"What are you drinking New Year's Eve?"

"Water, but I'll look fabulous doing it."

Purchases completed, the men called Claude and arranged to meet in a nearby pub. On the way out, Ted topped off his purchase with a cologne by Gaultier. The cologne was neatly packaged in a simple silver can but the bottle inside was in the shape of a man's athletic chest.

"I love the packaging of this scent. So sensual!" Ted observed.

"So Gaultier." Pierre smiled. "And now we go for a double *Kir Royale*. My treat since you can't afford anything anymore."

Ted squelched a laugh.

Shopping mission accomplished, the men settled in a nearby pub and ordered drinks. Seated next to them was one of the Mexican men from Cara's photos. Ted was certain it was him. He was alone and on his phone speaking rapidly in Spanish. He sounded annoyed. From what Ted could glean, he was turning down a New Years Eve invitation. *Who turns down a New Year's Eve party in Paris?*

"How do the girls do this?" Pierre asked sipping his drink. "I'm wiped, totally *creve'*."

"Me too."

Tired from the shopping agenda, everyone lounged around the kitchen, waiting for Madame Balon's prepared meal.

"Madame Balon made us grilled chicken and potato gratin. I'm heating it now."

"Oh good. That looks delicious; I'm salivating just looking at it." Cara reached for vegetables in the refrigerator.

"Summer and Hope, can you make a salad? I pre-washed the ingredients this morning. I'll grill a few veggies," Cara said, cutting and sprinkling them with a lemon/fig/olive oil mixture. Ted opened a bottle of rose wine and heated a leftover *baguette*, after sprinkling it with water. Madame B had shared this simple trick to refresh day old bread and it worked like a charm.

"I do wish she would share a few recipes too."

"Don't push it. Cara, before I forget…I saw one of your Mexican art dealers this afternoon when I was having drinks with Pierre. We stopped at a pub near Galeries Lafayette."

"Really? Which one? Was he with anyone?"

"No, but he was conversing with someone on the phone in Spanish. It sounded like a disagreement about New Years Eve plans. He had a ponytail and a gold hoop earring. Don't remember the name of the pub."

"Ok. I know who. Hmmm."

An animated dinner discussion about shopping events followed and one by one they pulled out their purchases for collective examination. Cara had her tablet ready.

"Ok, here's the verdict. Ted's teal jacket is the closest to pure French couture. Bravo, Ted. Hope's fire tank is the sexiest piece so far and Summer's midnight blue dress the most sophisticated. My lightning shoe snaps are the most fantastical. Harry Potter would love them."

"Agreed. Let's hope the New Years Eve party is less strenuous and worth all this effort and expense," remarked Ted.

"I predict it will be so worth it." Cara assured everyone.

After draining a second glass of wine, everyone retired to their bedrooms, fully content, the anticipation of New Year's Eve festivities percolating in their brains.

Chapter XXXVI

The Calm Before the Storm

On December 31st the residents of the Rue Malher penthouse slept in. Only Ted was up early and did the honors by brewing coffee and doing the bakery run. Upon his return, Cara joined him in the kitchen and prepared a fruit platter with mango, tangerine, and pineapple slices. One by one the other two appeared for their *café au lait* and *croissants* with a side of fruit slices.

"I don't miss my American breakfast, Cara remarked. When in Paris… Hey guys, did you all see Helena's invitation? It's beautiful." Cara propped it prominently against a colorful jug planted with poinsettias. The oversized card donned two large champagne flutes outlined with multicolored glitter on black textured paper. Gold script inside the glasses gave the pertinent details. Cocktail Hour would begin at 8:30pm, dinner at 9:30pm and dancing would continue until dot dot dot.

"Yes, this invitation is pretty classy." Hope fingered the raised gold letters. "It's gonna be an awesome night, knowing Helena. We'll see Paris's beautiful people. Will this get all of us in?"

"Yes, I gave her all our names with the payment. They'll have a list by the door."

"The cream of the Paris modeling world will attend. Those male models might just float my boat."

"I bet, Ted."

"So what is everyone up to today?"

"Hope and I have hair appointments at 11:30am." Summer ran her fingers through her messy mop.

"Oh, good. You need a transformation. That hair has been in a messy bun every day I've been here."

"Yeah …. it's time for change."

"I'm going to work on my tablet and organize picture folders. Then a nap and some primping. It takes time to look this beautiful."

"Funny, Mom. You sure you don't want to come with us? Maybe they could squeeze you in?"

"I'm absolutely sure."

When everyone was out, Cara settled at the kitchen table with another cup of coffee to research F&S Enterprises in peace. There was nothing new on F&S, but on the ceramic's website, she discovered a new section featuring 'Mediterranean Pottery'. Looking through it, she recognized a few patterns. Her heartbeat faster. She compared the patterns to her photo file on stolen pottery. They were strikingly similar. She sat back and exhaled through her teeth.

While the apartment was quiet, she retired for a power nap. It was going to be a long night. When she awoke, there was excitement in the air. The kids were back. She made more coffee, put out some snacks and gave herself a manicure. Propping the art exhibit invitation next to the New Years Eve one, she wondered who might be interested. The gallery walk-by had captured her attention and she definitely planned on making an appearance. She hoped to engage Francois in a conversation this time.

Chapter XXXVII

Bad Moon Rising

Fernando Flores, wearing nothing but his towel, looked down at the nude, platinum blonde occupying his bed. She was out cold. He had out-partied her by a long shot. No surprise there. *No stamina, this girl.*

New Years Eve was under control. The restaurant was sold out. His staff was working diligently under Jose's close direction to prepare for a kick-ass party. He was a little ticked off that Carlos wasn't coming to Barcelona for the celebration, especially since the Paris restaurant was closed, but he didn't want to push the issue any more than he already had. Carlos had resisted pretty vehemently. He was doing a damn good job with business, so that boat didn't need to be rocked. Besides, the guy was not a party animal. Never was. Unlike Jose, Carlos liked his space and quiet time. He took work super seriously and seemed to thrive on privacy. Fernando knew that and let him be since he produced brilliantly, but he found it difficult to understand. He considered Carlos an odd ball.

Turning back to face his silky sheets, Fernando decided to let his date sleep off the drugs. She would only be in the way this morning and he had business to take care of. She served her purpose. The phone rang. It was Carlos on video chat.

"Carlos, did you change your mind? He asked hopefully. "I'm planning a spectacular party. I could easily have a few ladies here for you to choose from. What do you say?"

"I can imagine. I know how amazing your parties are. Thanks, Fernando, but I think I will stay in Paris and take it easy. I'm tired and have a cold. Good time to rest and catch up on things. Have a blast."

Fernando eyed Carlos fidgeting in his office chair. He frowned. "Ok then. Suit yourself."

"Thanks. I just called to wish you a Happy New Year, Fernando. We did good this year. May the next year be just as sweet and prosperous."

"Yes, thanks, *compadre*. Have a good one. *Feliz Ano Nuevo*."

"*Feliz Ano Nuevo*. Happy New Year."

Chapter XXXVIII

Dancing the Night Away

Cara and her extended family entered the beautifully decorated night club fashionably late. She looked around in awe. There were metallic colored streamers and colorful ornaments filling every crevice. The tables were a vision of metallic perfection with sparkling centerpieces in metallic shades of copper, gold, \and silver. White flowers with sparkling black ornaments offset by yellow ribbons added another color explosion. The tablecloths were stark white with festive, colored metallic threads running through at random intervals. Each table had a bottle of red and white wine on it. She regretted not bringing her tablet, but her cell phone camera was more practical considering her tiny handbag.

"This place is amazing. The decorations are exquisite," she exclaimed. "I've never seen anything like it and I've been to a party or two."

"Wow," said Hope, swiveling on her platforms as she took in a sweeping view.

"Cool," Summer exclaimed. "Wish I could film here."

Cara nudged Ted and pointed to Pierre and Claude at the bar. They waved. Pierre was talking to a tall, handsome man who immediately caught Cara's eye, despite the distance. Her distance eyesight was still remarkably good, especially when it included handsome men. Close up was trickier.

"*Bonsoir*, everyone." Cara could see Ted studying the man's profile with interest. She decided instantaneously they were an excellent match. "This place is incredible. So festive."

Pierre introduced the Greek God. "*Salut*, Ted. This is Jean-Michel. I told him all about you and your project. He's dying to meet you."

Cara greeted the men and turned to order a drink a few feet away. She knew when to give someone space.

Cara and Summer looked around at all the incredibly stylish people but didn't spot Helena. Observing the spectacular venue around her, Cara was thankful for the shopping day and outfit splurge. She would have felt completely inadequate with anything in her suitcase.

"I'm so glad we went shopping," she whispered to Summer. "You look stunning, honey."

"Thanks, Mom."

"Jasper, let's go see where our table is."

Without difficulty, they spotted 'Table 20' next to the second bar.

"Good spot," Jasper observed. "We won't miss a thing from here." The table was away from the stage and speakers, where the DJ was working his magic, but only one table away from the dance floor.

A handsome Frenchman approached Hope and pointed to the dance floor.

"There goes my dance partner." Cara laughed.

Hope nodded to the guy and winked at Cara. "Later… …rest your feet."

Cara smiled. This would be a magical night. She sensed fairy dust in the air.

While Cara and Jasper planted themselves at the table, Summer and Samson followed Natalie from room to room, eyeing the generous lay out and stopping to meet and greet. "*Salut, Tout le monde.* These are my American friends. Let me introduce you.

Moving on, they converged at the bar with drinks in hand. Pierre introduced his friend Jean-Michel to those not present earlier.

"Nice to meet you, Jean-Michel. Do you work in the arts too? Your outfit is spectacular."

"*Merci, Madame.* I'm a stylist by profession." Cara could see that Ted was completely smitten. Ted was not easily swayed, but Jean-Michel was worth the swoon.

"Well that certainly makes sense. You probably dressed half the beautiful people here," she said surveying the room with a hand gesture.

"I did help a few. I work with Helena's agency a lot." Cara could see how proud he was of his accomplishments. She promised to check out his work.

Close to dinner time, Helena arrived looking absolutely divine. She sported expertly mussed up, sparkly beach hair, long, diamond pendant earrings and flawless makeup. Her silver sequined mini dress and black silk Leboutin heels accentuated her killer curves and shapely legs. A long black feather boa was slung casually around her toned shoulders. Helena knew how to command attention. Her smoldering red lips and startling silver eye shadow served to enhance her fine facial features. Cara looked over to Jasper. He was still surveying the crowd and hadn't spotted Helena yet.

Helena easily worked the room, approaching groups of people with confidence. Cara watched her skillfully inch her way over to the bar. Helena had come with a date. He looked rather inconspicuous trailing behind her in his navy wool trousers and a simple but expensive-looking navy silk shirt. His long, shiny hair was combed back, revealing gold in his ear. He was handsome in a rogue kind of way. Not at all what Cara pictured Helena liking. He also looked vaguely familiar.

When Helena spotted Summer, she waved, and approached as if on a catwalk. Cara watched Jasper's face as he studied Helena's approach with fascination. His eyes alternated between Helena's face and hips. She stopped next to Summer and greeted everyone, positioning herself next to Jasper. Cara chuckled. *Perfect.*

"*Bonsoir*, Good Evening, everyone. Doesn't this place look incredible?" She gracefully swept one arm behind her. "This is my boyfriend, Carlos." Helena stepped aside and Carlos appeared from behind her glamourous shadow.

"*Bonsoir*, Carlos," Summer smiled shyly. "Nice to finally meet you. Helena, you look beautiful tonight. Thank you so much for inviting us. This place is amazing. Let me introduce you to the rest of my family."

Cara blinked in rapid succession and swallowed an imagined hairball. A shocking thunderbolt or perhaps it was a strobe light, struck her inept. She took a step back as her eyes traveled over Carlos. Waiting in Helena's shadow until everyone greeted him, Cara took the opportunity to study Carlos up close while letting her heart palpitations subside. Tonight, he had his shining, black hair loose, no slicked back ponytail. Cara admired his thick, textured gold hoop earring. The deep, golden color looked striking against his bronze skin. He looked like a glamorous version from *Dead Men Tell No Tales*. Thankfully, the man did not seem to recognize Cara. His dark, unsmiling eyes scanned the crowd as he nodded quick hellos to everyone with what looked like a slight upturn of his full lips. Cara recaptured her composure and glanced at Jasper. Jasper looked mesmerized, but not by Carlos. His eyes were velcroed to Helena. He didn't seem to recognize Carlos. Cara smiled. Smitten men were so transparent.

Regaining her speech, Cara turned to Carlos, "Hi. Nice to meet you. Do you work at the agency too?" She admired his long, shifting lashes, remembering how they had impressed her at their first encounter in New York when he handed her the forgotten tangerine tablet.

"No. We met at a party," Carlos answered, looking into the distance.

"How nice. What do you do in Paris?" Cara asked.

"I manage a restaurant and help run an import/export business," he answered curtly.

"I assume your restaurant is closed tonight?"

"Yes," Carlos mumbled.

"From where do you import? And what is your product?" Cara persisted.

"Ceramics from Mexico. Our company has a factory there. We ship worldwide." Carlos clipped, looking bored. He shuffled from foot to foot. "Excuse me."

Before Cara could fire off another question, he walked away. Clearly he was not interested in chitchat and he certainly wasn't in a festive mood. On the contrary, Carlos had a brooding expression.

Helena seemed unperturbed. As if sensing his discomfort by osmosis, she signaled him. "Go check where our table is, *Cheri.*"

Cara turned her attention to Jasper and Helena, who were chatting. Jasper's face was lit up like a Christmas tree with extra fluorescent lights. She decided not to interrupt and turned to Samson, Natalie and Summer who were talking to another handsome Frenchman. *Damn, these people are stylish.* Natalie introduced him as a close family friend.

"This is Pascal. We grew up together. Our parents are close friends," she explained, linking her arm through his. "He's like my brother."

Cara liked Pascal's looks. His blue grey eyes twinkled fondly at Natalie. She studied his straight blond hair and genuine smile, accentuated by dimples and decided he was extremely likeable.

"Nice to meet you, Madame. Are you enjoying Paris?" Pascal asked.

Before Cara could answer, Summer jumped in.

"Oh yes, we're having a wonderful time. I don't think I'll be ready to leave in a few months. We love it here."

Pascal laughed. "A few months? An extended vacation? What have you done so far?" he asked enunciating with his hands. Summer ran down her short list of activities, embellishing her favorites.

"Not as much as one would think. I covered the main attractions only. I'm busy making a movie," Summer explained. "Helena is one of my leads." Summer half turned and pointed in Helena's direction.

Pascal smiled, eyebrows disappearing under falling hair. "You must tell me about your movie. I love films."

"Sure. Any time."

"Have you been to the new restaurant in the *Gare Saint Lazare* yet?"

"No," answered Summer, her eyes fluttering. "What have I missed?"

"I'll have to show you in exchange for movie details," Pascal winked.

Summer laughed. "Is that a bribe?"

"The best kind."

Cara listened and winked at Natalie. Natalie smiled and interjected, "Pascal, we're seated at table 20. Come visit." Natalie took Cara by one arm and Samson by the other and ushered them toward the table.

"Let's go get the best seats, so we don't miss anything. This will be a busy night. I think our circle is multiplying."

Once seated, Cara looked around the club taking inventory. Hope was on the dance floor with a different man, her red streak flying. Helena and Jasper were dancing next to her. Carlos was nowhere in sight, but Helena's boa was slung over a chair directly across the dance floor. Cara realized that Helena and Carlos were seated at one of the tables bought by the modeling agency. Cara looked over to the bar where Ted and his new friend, Jean-Michel, were deep in conversation. Ted had that blissful look people have when they find a long-lost treasure. Cara turned back to Natalie and Samson. "I'm so glad we decided to come. Everyone is having a great time. I love this place."

Natalie smiled. "Me too."

The first course was oysters. One by one everyone returned to table 20. Music and chatter filled the air, fueled by a continuous stream of liquor. Well-timed, subsequent food courses arrived, one more delicious than the next. The portions were small and simply garnished, but totally satisfying. Fine dining was interspersed by dancing and a constant flurry of visitors. Jean-Michel came to dance with Ted and Pascal brought his desert to 'catch up' with Natalie and finalize his dinner plans with Summer. He had come with a date, but according to Natalie, it was nothing serious.

"She's a friend; I know her," Natalie assured her.

Summer smiled at that revelation. "Oh good. I like him."

"Come on, Cara. Let's dance." Natalie grabbed Cara by the hand.

Helena spent much of her time on the dance floor with Jasper, alternating between him and another young man from her agency, while Jasper recuperated between song sets.

"I haven't danced this much in the last five years combined," Jasper confided to Cara.

"Believe me, honey, I know. Helena is a knockout and an awesome dancer. I wouldn't turn her down either. She's worth a few blisters."

"Yeah, did you get some pictures, Mom? No one in Barcelona will believe this. I need proof."

"No worries, I have you covered. I have everyone covered. Can you take a picture of me? I want to show Sam."

Across the dance floor, Cara observed Carlos sitting silently at his table, occasionally chatting with Helena's associates as they approached him. *What an odd man. Handsome when he doesn't frown. A quiet bad boy. What an oxymoron.*

Carlos was holding court, barely moving from his chair. When he did disappear periodically, he reappeared without warning from who knows where. The man moved like a jaguar. He seemed completely disinterested in everyone, but his dark, alert eyes kept a close watch on Helena. Helena didn't seem the least bit bothered that Carlos didn't dance and occasionally went over and chatted with him between songs, gently planting sensuous kisses on his lips while sitting on his lap and pulling him close with her boa. Only then did Cara see him smile. It was a beautiful smile that lit up his clouded features, ever so briefly. He, in turn, did not seem bothered by the fact that Helena danced with other men. He appeared secure in the knowledge that

Helena was his and his alone. Cara could tell that Carlos was proud and in control.

At midnight, table 20 was the place to be. Champagne flowed, hugs and kisses were dispersed freely, and new friendships were sealed as the family welcomed all who cared to stop by. Samson kissed Natalie. Pascal kissed Summer. Ted kissed Jean-Michel, Hope kissed her current dancing partner and Cara hugged and kissed Jasper. HAPPY NEW YEAR, *Bonne Annee, Bonne Santé* they chimed around the table. The good vibes were flowing. Across the dance floor, Carlos kissed Helena with intense passion, sparks igniting.

At midnight in Barcelona, Fernando toasted champagne glasses with Adriano, Adriano's date, Jose, Jose's date and his own date, the platinum blonde who currently shared his bed. The party was in full swing and he was in his element. The band he hired was worth every penny. Business boomed. Champagne flowed. People were happy. The New Year was off to a promising start. When Carlos texted him after midnight, Fernanado glanced at his lucky lion ring with the flashing ruby eyes and smiled. *Life is good.*

You're missing a sick party, Compadre. Happy New Year! He texted a group picture of his table mates and himself, fedora in place.

Carlos looked at the picture and grimaced. Then he deleted it, in shock that Fernando was now referring to him as his *compadre*. This was a new elevated status that he had yet to absorb. Regardless, he was relieved to be spending the night away from the Flores brood. Celebrating with Helena was a gift from God. He nuzzled Helena's neck when she came to sit on his lap between dances and counted his blessings. Her scent was intoxicating and her skin as smooth as silk. A wave of passion overcame him and after toasting at midnight he kissed her so passionately he momentarily forgot about the dangers surrounding him.

Well past midnight, after dancing up a storm, an exhausted Cara was alerted that her car service was waiting. Forever the observant gentleman, Ted knew Cara was toast; he had arranged for car service. Cara was grateful. It had been enough of a good time and a memorable start into the new year. She was happy to scoot. Everyone else continued the celebration. New Year's Eve could not have been more fun. Helena had been absolutely right.

Cara leaned back in the car and closed her eyes. Her head was spinning, and her ears ringing, but she was pleasantly tipsy and utterly content. Her only regret was that she didn't have a chance to talk to Carlos. He never left his table, not even when Helena came over to toast the new year. Carlos was an enigma.

Chapter XXXIX

The Morning After and
A New Beginning for All

Carlos woke up with Helena in his arms. As he watched her sleep, he reflected on New Years Eve. It was the most beautiful, sophisticated event he ever attended, and he had soaked up the atmosphere with every piece of his fiber. He particularly enjoyed sipping champagne with his gorgeous girlfriend perched on his knees. He was proud of how beautiful she had looked and how loving she had been all night. He liked to watch her dance and felt relieved she didn't force him to oblige. Dancing made him feel out of control and vulnerable- exposed, with no one to mind his back.

Carlos considered himself lucky to have escaped the Flores festivities and to have spent New Years Eve with someone he loved. He leaned over and kissed Helena gently on the head, then disengaged his arm. As he swung his legs over the side of the bed, she reached for him and pulled him back into her embrace. Carlos felt a heated surge. He lay back and let her hands travel over his body. Her touch was magnetic and elicited an immediate reaction. She kissed him passionately, letting her tongue tease his lips and search the inside of his mouth. He took a deep, ragged breath as he looked up at her straddling his hardness, a slow rhythm beginning. New Year's morning could not have started better.

A few minutes later they collapsed into the plush pillows, arms interlocked. The day ahead would be a lazy, relaxing one in their cozy apartment. The restaurant was open, but Carlos wasn't going in. He was happy to spend the day with Helena. Fernando not pushing him to appear in Barcelona had been a gift and he was extremely grateful. He would tell Fernando, he had a quiet New Year's Eve.

Fernando Flores woke up New Year's Day feeling hung over and horny. He glanced at the smooth back of the blonde nude sleeping next to him, maliciously eyeing her luscious curves. He wanted sex. After going to the bathroom to relieve himself and to get a glass of water for his parched mouth, he plopped back onto his bed and ran his hand between the blonde's legs, starting at the knees. Slowly he worked his way up her inner thighs, massaging in circular motions. She didn't move. The drugs in her system were dulling her senses. Fernando, now fully aroused, flipped her over and circled her nipples with his tongue. Still nothing more than a groan and dismissive hand flip swatting him away. Getting frustrated he spread her legs and thrust himself inside her... pushing. Her lack of participation and her failed response angered him, forcing him to thrust harder.

"No, Fernando, stop. I said no." Fernando ignored the protests and wildly satisfied himself before rolling over onto his back, spent. *Time to replace her.*

New Year's Day, Cara was the first person awake. She opened her eyes and reflected on the previous night. Her eyes traveled to her glamourous outfit flung over the chaise. The only thing missing New Year's Eve was a date. Her mind wandered to Francois and the gallery invitation on the kitchen table. She wished she could have invited him for the New Year's Eve celebration. No … surely, he had plans with his wife, or a gorgeous girlfriend. Men like Francois were rarely unattached. She felt a pang of jealousy or was it remorse? She wasn't sure.

All things considered, Cara knew she had experienced a wonderful night with her children, and she was thankful for that. She slowly swung her tired legs out of bed and tip toed to the closest bathroom. Having to share it with Hope and Summer, she was glad to, for once, be first. She showered and threw on her soft cotton leggings and a comfy oversized sweater. She was thankful for the Advil she had taken the night before. All the dancing made her bones creak, like a well-worn, wood staircase. The apartment was deathly quiet. Miraculously, even Ted slept in.

Cara brewed coffee; decaf for herself, regular for everyone else. She chopped vegetables for omelets and set the table. Next, she arranged a basket with an array of baked goods and preheated the oven. A short while later, Hope came out of her room looking rumpled and seeking French coffee.

"Mmm coffee … … just what my head and body crave."

"Morning. You were quite the dazzling dancer last night. That red streak just kept flying past our table."

Hope laughed, "Yup, always love a night of dancing. So cathartic. You didn't do too bad yourself. I guess the new shoes worked out?"

"Yes, but I'm still paying a price today. My bones were begging for a hot shower this morning. It was all worth it though." Cara laughed.

Hope was soon followed by Ted and Jean-Michel, who looked quite smitten.

Ahh, to be young. No wonder Ted slept in! Cara smiled and started taking *omelette* orders. "Ok, everyone. Tell me what you want in your *omelette*. Here are your choices." She pointed to the little bowls on the counter filled with cut up veggies, ham and cheese.

By noon, everyone in the apartment was accounted for and fed. New Year's Day brunch was casually served in shifts as people arrived and placed their orders. The brunch included Jasper, Samson, Natalie, Pierre and Claude. Pictures were viewed, dissected, exchanged and posted. They all reminisced about their most glam night ever and everyone had a story or two of their own to share. Laughter looped around the table and voices escalated.

Around four o'clock Samson and Natalie nudged Jasper. They were taking him to the airport before meeting her parents for an early dinner. Cara's heart hurt as she said goodbye to her oldest son. She missed him tremendously. Time well-spent made her realize how much. It was surprising how everyday life took over, and people went through their routines mechanically, not realizing how wonderful and necessary vacations were for good mental health. Once again she wished her family lived nearby.

"I plan on coming back in a few months. I'll let you know when," Cara urged. "Springtime in Paris is the best! Make plans to return too."

"'ll try, Mom, but I can't promise anything. It all depends on work," Jasper replied with a sad shrug. "I'm lucky I got the holidays. I don't have a lot of seniority, you know. I got lucky because Adriano didn't go away this year."

"I know, I know, but you do get six weeks of vacation a year. Use it." Cara whispered. blinking back tears. "I'll email you my itinerary as soon as I figure it out. Safe travels. Text me when you land and Jasper, keep me posted on your Mexican client," Cara added. "I'm sure there'll be more to share about those guys."

"You may be right there."

She hugged her son and sighed, a few tears escaping as she turned away. It was tough letting your children go.

Chapter XL

Art Appreciation or Lust?

Cara was still thinking about Francois Fereaux the next morning while lounging in bed. She wondered what party he had graced New Year's Eve. She had googled him and found out he was indeed the sole owner of the gallery he invited her to.

Alone in the apartment after everyone returned to work, she showered and searched the kitchen for coffee. Thankfully, Ted had brewed both regular and decaf. She poured herself a generous cup of decaf. In exchange for his thoughtfulness, she cleaned the breakfast dishes left in the sink. It was one of the small contributions she gladly made for a room in this wonderful apartment. She was thrilled everyone started the new year with fond memories of a glorious *fete,* and with budding friendships to explore. Her thoughts turned to Sam. She needed a gift. *Friends are so important in the garden of life.*

Cara prepared and ate her breakfast, checked her emails and took off on a leisurely stroll to the Louvre. In the afternoon, she returned to Galeries Lafayette and picked up a spectacular multi-colored woven cashmere scarf with a matching slouchy hat and gloves for Samantha. The predominantly rich shades of blues and greens with silver threads woven through were delicious. Sam would love it.

For herself, she scored a soft, caramel leather handbag with scalloped tangerine trim and a long shoulder strap. She almost left her tablet on the counter again after trying it unsuccessfully in the side pockets of various options. Luckily her tablet was where she left it this time. *Geez, I need to be more careful.* Hopefully the new bag would remedy the problem. The caramel bag appeared to be perfect. Her tablet, with sleeve, fit securely in an inside pocket.

Lingering over a *café au lait*, outside the department store, Cara mentally organized her last few days. There were two items left on her Paris to-do-list. She wanted to attend the party at Francois's gallery Friday night, and she was itching to check out Carlos's restaurant on Saturday. Curious to observe both men in their habitats, she imagined herself talking to Francois. She wondered if she would like him once she faced him in a 'real' conversation. No one had captured her interest like him in a very long while but looks could be deceiving. The fact that their meeting was so completely random made it even more exciting. She wasn't sure what she would glean from a visit to Carlos's restaurant, but she was hoping for a chat about ceramics. What was his company producing?

Who could she enlist to go with her to the gallery? The invitation was perched on the kitchen table but hadn't generated much interest. That evening, Cara asked around.

"Sorry, Cara, I have plans with Jean-Michel tomorrow night. He invited me to dinner."

"I have a friend visiting from the US. We're going to a show at Montmartre," said Hope.

Cara called Samson. "Let me check with Natalie. I think she made dinner plans for us with another couple. Sorry, Mom. I'll see you Saturday night for sure."

"I'm kind of tired, Mom. I might want a night in. Let me see how I feel tomorrow," said Summer. "Can I decide last minute?"

"Oh, come on. I'm leaving in two days. It's in walking distance and I promise to take you for a nice dinner after. We'll sit and relax."

"Oh, all right. Maybe I'll go…." Summer replied. Summer could generally be persuaded with good food and the promise of a relaxing ambiance.

Cara smiled. She was looking forward to seeing Francois. She hoped she wouldn't be disappointed. Carlos's place she would check out on her own. Summer would shut her down if she knew about those plans.

Chapter XLI

Blue Hair, Strawberry Prosecco and Art Sparks

Cara and Summer walked to *Fereaux Gallerie;* Cara dressed to slay, and Summer wore torn jeans and a stretched out black sweater. Her stylish black suede boots and colorful bangles saved the outfit.

The new exhibit featured a local Parisian painter and showcased large acrylic canvases with entwined, body parts seen through a microscopic lens. A 'through-the-looking-glass' and sometimes naughty keyhole perspective captured the viewers' attention. They were greeted at the entrance by a heavily tattooed girl with blue hair and a roving eye. After a quick check in, she handed them each a glass of sparkling wine with a luscious floating strawberry. Sipping their *Prosecco,* Summer and Cara moved with the flow around the gallery, studying the artwork. A young man started chatting with Summer.

Cara looked around for Francois. She spotted him across the gallery busy with the artist and a couple considering one of the paintings. She would have to patiently wait for an opportunity to say hello, as she certainly understood the importance of business.

She wondered if he would even acknowledge her, given how involved he was.

She drained her sparkling wine, nibbled on the strawberry, and walked to the bar for a refill. She needed liquid courage. Generally, she wasn't at a loss for words, but something about Francois left her tongue-tied. Glancing around the room, she examined the crowd. People-watching in Paris was infinitely more exciting than in New York. Parisians were so stylish. In New York the art crowd was just different, going for shock value. She settled her gaze on a middle-aged woman with the body of a 30-year-old. She was dressed in black right down to her long fake lashes and she moved with a dancer's grace. *French portion sizes probably made that figure possible,* The woman was there with a much younger man who was clearly her lover. Their intimacy was blatant. As Cara stared, mesmerized, she felt someone approach from behind and touch her arm.

"*Bonsoir*, I'm happy to see you made it. Do you like the show?"

Cara turned to face Francois. She would have recognized that rich baritone without turning. It traveled the length of her spine like a warm stream of water. "The show is really cool. Thanks for inviting me."

"Let me introduce myself. I'm Francois Fereaux and I'm really pleased you took a leap of faith and came." He extended his large, warm hand.

Cara instantly liked Francois. "Cara Crenston, visiting artist from NY."

"So you are an artist? I had a feeling."

Cara waited for him to continue, but he just studied her face. "What feeling? Could you elaborate? I'm naturally curious, you know." She paused and watched him search for words.

Francois took a moment before he answered. "When I look at you, I see alert, inquisitive eyes. I feel an openness to the environment and… I see a warm, caring smile. It's how you look at the world that's telling. It enhances your creative spirit. I also like the tasteful way in which you put yourself together. An all-around captivating package." His eyes took in her crimson suede pumps, black velvet leggings and floral silk shirt underneath a tailored faux Chanel blazer.

"Really? You noticed all that while paying your café bill?"

"That and more, but I don't want to scare you away now that I have you here. Are you familiar with the artist I'm showing tonight?" Francois's cool eyes searched her face intently, tuning out the crowded gallery.

"No, tell me about him." Cara wanted to hear him talk. His voice reverberated through her body and triggered arousing signals to dormant body parts.

Francois described his first encounter with the artist and why he offered him a one-man show. Cara listened, deciding Francois had an alluring style that could easily reel her into his orbit. She wanted to hear more. He also made her heart pound faster with his proximity. They chit-chatted for a few more minutes about the artist, the gallery and Cara's reason for coming to Paris, until Francois was summoned by some collectors. He smiled apologetically and left her side. As he departed, he brushed her arm. "Don't leave. I would like to talk to you some more."

She felt a warm rush charge through her body. Was it the second Prosecco in her bloodstream or Francois? She felt dizzy. In just a few minutes, she was completely charmed by this man. *Damn, why does this never happen in New York.*

Francois was not wearing a wedding ring. She noticed because he talked expressively with his hands. She looked around the gallery and noticed Summer was still engaged, so she went back to the bar and requested another strawberry for her bubbly. It added a nice flavor.

From across the gallery, Summer motioned to Cara with a cut-throat sign that she was ready to leave. Cara looked over to Francois, but he was busy talking to a group of people, his back turned to her. She wanted to say goodbye or catch his eye, but he was completely immersed. *Oh well.* If she had time, she would stop by the gallery before she left for NewYork and thank Francois for his kind invitation. Maybe then she could have an uninterrupted conversation with him. She would love that. Something about him drew her into his web, wanting more.

Cara and Summer slipped out of the gallery, but not before asking Miss Blue Hair for a restaurant recommendation. She had none as she didn't live in the area and usually left by metro after work. Mother and daughter strolled around looking for an appealing option. It didn't take long for them to find what they were looking for. They settled in a small, cozy restaurant for a leisurely family dinner over a glass of excellent red wine. Summer talked about her movie, but Cara's thoughts kept wandering back to Francois Fereaux and his sexy, velvet voice.

Chapter XLII

Tying Up Loose Ends

Cara was scheduled to leave Paris on Monday morning, so the good times were ending with a bang. Lamenting over breakfast Saturday morning she complained "Fun vacations pass way too quickly. I don't want to go home yet. Where did the time go?"

"It flies. Hope and I are working today. You're on your own, Mom. Do something fun. See you tonight?"

"Sure."

Before leaving Paris, Cara was determined to visit the restaurant, *Au Coeur de Lion.* After doing some window shopping, she stopped in there for lunch. The restaurant was located off the beaten path, near the *Place de Republique.* It had a traditional shoebox lay-out with *banquettes* running the length of the side walls and café tables and chairs facing them. There was a generous center aisle that led to an elaborate bar with a neat row of ten bar stools. The restrooms and the kitchen were down a small hallway, past the bar to the left. There was also a private dining room/party room across from the kitchen, in the back. After walking down the restaurant's center aisle, Cara opted to sit near the bar. Both tables near the windows were occupied. She sat down and studied the black board listing the specials. A waiter approached with a menu.

"*Bonjour.*"

"*Bonjour.* How long has this restaurant been here? I never noticed it before."

"We recently reopened, *Madame.* Renovations. New owners."

"Parisians?" Cara inquired.

"No, Mexicans. What will you have today?"

"*Salade Nicoise* and one chicken taco."

"Interesting combination. Anything to drink?"

"Water and a decaf *café au lait* please."

"Everything together?"

"Yes. American style."

Cara saw the waiter grimace. She looked around the restaurant but didn't see any familiar faces. Before her food arrived, she walked to the restroom to wash her hands. She explored all the side rooms, peering into the kitchen, the private dining room, which was empty and stopping at the door at the end of the hallway, marked *PRIVE'. That must be the office.* The bathrooms were right next to the kitchen, facing the private dining room.

Back at the table, she picked at her salad and devoured her tasty taco, under the staff's watchful eyes, two Mexicans behind the bar and the French waiter with an attitude. When they chatted with each other, she took a few pictures of the restaurant. She sent the pictures to Jasper in a quick text. Just as she was flagging the waiter for the bill, Carlos walked out of the office. Their eyes briefly met, but if he recognized her, he didn't show it. His face registered nothing, and his eyes swept past her to the other customers. The man had an enviable plastic demeanor. She decided he looked unapproachable, like New Year's Eve.

When Cara left the restaurant, she took the subway to the gallery. She wanted to stop by one last time hoping to catch Francois and engage in another chat with him … uninterrupted. When she arrived, the girl with the blue hair greeted her with enthusiasm. "*Bonjour.*"

"*Bonjour,* is Francois here?" Cara asked, smiling.

"So sorry. You just missed him. He left for the day. Can I give him a message?"

"Yes, give him my kind regards and thanks." She handed Miss Blue Hair a business card and asked her how the show went.

"It was good. We sold a few pieces opening night. Are you interested in anything?"

"No, not right now, thank you. I'll be flying back to New York City at noon on Monday. My luggage is already overflowing."

"We ship, you know. Francois will be sorry he missed you," she said politely. "I'll make sure he gets your message."

"I'm sorry I missed him too. Good luck with the show."

"*Merci.* Have a good trip. Will you be back?"

"Yes, in a few months, I hope."

"Fantastic. Here's Francois's card."

Cara left disappointed, but also determined to see Francois in the Spring. He had left an imprint on her brain and the feel of his voice was difficult to forget. Maybe she would email him a link to her website.

Chapter XLIII

Curious and 'Curiouser'

Carlos sat in his office working. He looked up at the security monitors to rest his eyes from numerical spreadsheets and the glare of the computer screen. There were only five occupied tables. His eyes focused on the woman sitting alone, taking pictures. She looked familiar. When she got up and explored the banquet room, stopping in front of his office door, he inhaled deeply. Was she going to knock or worse, barge in? He inhaled, then exhaled when she turned. *Whew.*

Carlos remembered meeting her and her family New Years Eve, but he needed a close-up look to be sure. When she returned to her table, he stretched and exited the office. Stopping at the bar for a water bottle, he looked around the restaurant as he waited for a glass with a lime sliver. *It's her. What is the filmmaker's chatty mother doing here taking pictures? How annoying.* He was determined not to converse with her. What did she want? He doubted it was a coincidence given where Summer lived. He took his frosted glass and walked back to the office before she could possibly engage him in conversation. He remembered how she fired questions at him New Years Eve. Downright nosy. He wondered if Summer had sent her in to check him out. Or worse. He picked up the phone to call Helena. It went straight to voicemail. Carlos was sure Helena didn't invite her. She would have told him. Privacy was something both he and Helena valued greatly. He would have to investigate this imposition.

Chapter XLIV

Chance Encounter,
Not Entirely by Chance

Saturday night Cara had dinner with Natalie, Samson, and Summer. The ambiance was mellow compared to previous dinners. She was sad to be leaving. Sunday, her last day in Paris, Cara visited the Rodin Museum with Samson and browsed through the stores off Boulevard Saint Michel and Saint Germain. Sunday night she shared an intimate dinner at the corner café with Summer. Cara was in no mood to go home. Samantha was the only anticipated bright spot. Thinking of Sam, she reached up and touched the *fleur de lis* pendant around her neck and smiled. It had brought her luck, hadn't it? Her vacation was filled with wonderful memories, and she got to spend the holidays with her children. What more could she ask for?

Sitting at the airport late Monday morning, Cara scrolled through pictures on her tablet. She had transferred her electronics to the new handbag with the generous side pocket. The old bag was now in Summer's possession. She perused the pictures of her children, their friends, exceptional ceramics, Paris, New Years Eve and of the apartment on Rue Malher. Streaming through all her memories, she regretted not taking a picture of Francois. Oh well…she would have to continue to look at his portrait on the gallery website.

Having time to spare, she sent Summer a thank you text for having the bright idea to celebrate the holidays in Paris. She also thanked her for her hospitality and the delectable impressions she was returning home with. What a great idea it had been to spend the holidays in Europe! She would never forget their glamorous New Year's Eve celebration.

Once on the Air France plane, Cara settled into her aisle seat hoping that the seat next to her would remain empty, however that wish was not to be granted. Minutes later, she peripherally noticed a middle-aged man in a navy baseball cap and dark sunglasses approaching and gesturing to the window seat. *Damn.*

"Excuse me. I believe the window seat is mine," he announced firmly in a melodious baritone.

Cara flinched. That voice…she would recognize it anywhere, anytime. Her eyes traveled upward in disbelief. When the man took off his glasses, Cara looked into warm, hazel eyes. Wavy dark blond hair escaped from the baseball cap as he took off his navy wool jacket and sky-blue scarf and folded them into the overhead compartment. He revealed a fit, toned body and was dressed comfortably in soft, worn jeans and a mossy green cashmere sweater.

When he sat down next to Cara he simply said, *"Bonjour a nouveau!* It looks like we are destined to meet again, and I must say, I'm quite glad about that. I missed the chance to say goodbye the other night. You didn't even leave a clue, like a Cinderella shoe or a DNA sample. How fortunate to have a second chance."

Cara laughed at the analogy. Heart fluttering, eyebrows twitching, she couldn't find the right words. When she found her voice she countered, "I did better than a glass slipper. I left a business card on Saturday. Did your assistant give it to you?"

"Yes, she did. Thank you. So you're not really Cinderella? You just look like her?"

"Well, thank you… I think. I never expected you to track me down so quickly. What takes you to New York if you don't mind my asking."

"I'm scouting for new talent. I have meetings with artists in New York and LA in the next few weeks. Very exciting." His gaze dropped to her enticing smile and dark red lips. Cara could feel heat rising into her neck and face. She was glad she had bothered to put on make-up for the flight home.

For the next six hours, Cara and Francois talked, teased, and connected. She learned he would be staying at the Bowery Hotel, which Cara knew well. That neighborhood was Samson and

Summer's old stomping ground. She was surprised to hear that he had stayed home New Years Eve preparing for the trip. Chances were, he didn't have a girlfriend then, but she didn't want to ask. She saw no wedding band.

Cara told him about her vacation and about her plans to return to Paris. She showed him a few pictures of her work on the tablet, and he kindly appeared impressed. He assured her that if he had time, he would stop by her studio. Before Cara left the plane, Francois Fereaux gave Cara his business card and urged her to visit his gallery on her next visit to Paris. She handed him her card and promised she would. She didn't tell him she had that planned days ago. Finally, he insisted on a selfie with both and asked her to send it to his phone.

The good vibes from the Paris trip never seem to end. As silly as it seemed, considering the distance, she was happy at the thought of seeing Francois again. Exiting the plane first, she smiled and mentally planned her return as she walked toward the baggage claim. Lost in thought while searching for her luggage, she patrolled the conveyor belt's rotation. When someone tapped her on the shoulder from behind and pointed, she jumped. Francois was running toward her waving. In his hand was her tablet.

"You forgot this in the seat pocket, Cara", he exclaimed. "I was hoping passport control would hurry so I could catch you here."

"Oh my God, thank you, Francois. I would have lost all my pictures," Cara exclaimed. "I haven't backed them up yet." She shuddered at the thought. "I'm seriously in your debt now. If time permits, let me take you for a drink in NYC one night. You have my number." She shocked herself with her new-found boldness.

"Good," said Francois. "I'll start thinking of all the ways you can repay me. A drink is a good start. I'll call you when I know my schedule." Their eyes lingered and she could feel her face flush.

"Until next time, Cara. *A bien tot,*" and with a quick hug and wave, he grabbed his bag off the conveyor belt and disappeared into the New York airport crowd. The man had a knack for quick exits, but boy did he leave lasting impressions.

Chapter XLV

Getting Her New York Groove Back

Once home and unpacked, Cara remembered to check the bowls she bought against the ones she saw at the Paris auction, the bowls on Flores's website and the bowls stolen in New York. She had been too busy in Paris, but this task had stayed on her mental checklist. In the comfort of her office niche, laptop, and tablet side by side, Cara carefully studied all the pictures. The similarities were overwhelming. The bowls all shared the same patterns, but they were not exactly alike. There were nuances of differences. The ceramics Cara bought had a slightly crude finish. Cara didn't have pictures of all the stolen pottery, but she wondered if she should contact the Met or Sotheby's with the images. Viewing them side by side was an eye opener. She decided to email her decorative arts contact at Sotheby's, attaching a few examples.

Cara was happy to be back in the comfort of her studio. She pulled out her sketches for Nero's country kitchen and made a few adjustments. *Funny how your perspective can change in two weeks.* She placed the purchased ceramics in front of her and studied her work.

A short while later, she picked up the phone and tried Summer. No answer. Sam was next on her call list. "Hi, Sam. Happy New Year! How's the project coming along?"

"Welcome back. Pretty good. Nero picked his tiles and approved some more sketches. When can I stop by?"

"Come tomorrow morning. I have a few more ideas to run past you. I can start working on the tiles right away. Guess who was sitting next to me on the plane coming home."

"Brad Pitt?"

"In coach? Guess again."

"The Mexican guys?

"No, not this time. And they fly first class, like Brad Pitt."

"You got me. I have nothing."

"Francois Fereaux, the gallery owner who handed me the invitation to his opening. Remember I texted you?"

"You're kidding me. Of course, I remember. How did that happen? Start spilling."

Chapter XLVI

Meant to Be?

The next day, on the morning of January 7th, the unthinkable happened. A terrorist attack by Islamic extremists on the inner sanctum of a French Satirical Magazine was executed with maliciously, fatal intent. Writers, cartoonists, and innocent people died, just for expressing their humor and thoughts. The brutal attack divided Paris even more from its unintegrated, Muslim communities. The following days were somber, but the conviction and resilience of the French people was something for the world to behold. They came out into the streets in full force, fearless. Not only in the heart of Paris did people unite, but also in French cities around the country, Toulouse, Nice etc. They proudly echoed the sentiment of one of the murdered magazine's cartoonists, "I would rather die standing, then live on my knees." –paraphrased from Emiliano Zapata

Freedom of speech is a powerful tool that cannot be compromised in a democracy. Cara immediately conference called Summer and Samson with a heavy heart. Uncharacteristically, they both answered the phone on first ring. She was relieved to hear their voices and opinions. They all agreed.

The following morning, Cara sat in front of her laptop in awe. It took extra time for the enormity of what happened to her beloved, adopted city, to sink in. The overwhelming response of the French citizens was heart-warming, reducing her to tears as she sipped her morning tea. Her call to Summer and Samson the day after the attack was reassuring to a point, but she couldn't convince them to stay home. Both Samson and Summer were out, in solidarity with the French people. A few days of film work would be lost as they too, took to the streets, one to march, the other to document and report.

"I'm reorganizing our upcoming shoots to accommodate days lost. We can't shoot while protests are going on. Our crew is on the streets."

"That will set you back, what, at least a week now?"

"Yes, it is what it is, Mom. Some things are beyond our control. The film crew is passionate. If filming goes well, we can make it up on the back end."

"Just be careful out there," Cara warned. They were now planning to start filming in the third week of January.

A few days later, Cara got an email back from Sotheby's. The experts wanted to have a look at Cara's pottery and pictures. Someone from the Met was coming to meet them. Could she be there on Monday morning with her pieces? "Of course. I'll see you then," she replied.

Later that day, Cara met Samantha for dinner. It was a catch-up dinner, but this time Cara did most of the talking. Samantha sat back and let story after story roll over her. Truth be told, she was astonished at her friend's active fourteen-day Paris sojourn. Tables were turning. Samantha was along for the ride. "Bring it on, Cara. I'm all ears."

"It's surprising how two weeks can change your whole perspective on life, but it did. I'm back in travel mode and I can't wait to book my next trip," Cara gushed. "I really love it there and I remember how much I love adventure."

Both women were in shock over the events in Paris and a good portion of the evening was spent on the subject. It felt as if someone in the family had died. Hearts heavy, shoulders slumped, over a glass of French wine, they discussed the tragedy and its possible repercussions. "I hope it doesn't affect Summer's schedule more than a week. She really cannot afford that."

"Knowing Summer, she'll make it work. By the way, did you hear from Mr. Wonderful?"

Cara shook her head and frowned. "No, maybe he cut his trip short? Or else he's just too busy with appointments. Who knows."

"Why don't you call him?"

"I don't feel comfortable calling him. He explicitly told me; he would call me when he had his schedule worked out. He's here on business, you know. I almost forgot. I brought your holiday gift. Care to open it?"

"Yes, please. A gift from Paris has got to be good." Sam untied the bow and rifled through the tissue paper in the gift bag. "Oh my God! Cashmere! I love these colors, and this feels so soft! I'll plan my whole outfit around these accents tomorrow. Thanks, honey."

"Your *fleur-de-lis* pendant did its job for me. I had the most amazing time with my family."

"And then some." Sam winked.

On Saturday morning Francois called. Cara instantly perked up.

"Hello, Cara. How are you?" His voice smoothed over her like molten wax.

"Hi, Francois. I've been busy, catching up with work. It's nice to hear from you. How is your talent scouting going?"

"Good, so far. I'm sure you saw the news?"

"Yes, I have. It worries me. And it makes me very sad."

"Yes, me too. I called my son a few times already. Guess we must wait and see what happens. Very unsettling. I need a good diversion to keep my mind off disasters at home. Any ideas?"

"I don't know, Francois," Cara teased. "What do you consider a good diversion?"

"You. Are you free for dinner tonight? I know it's short notice, but my schedule is tight and I never know when I'll have time. What do you think?"

"Yes. I am. I was afraid you might have returned early."

"No. This trip has been planned for a long time. I wouldn't go back unless it was a family emergency."

"How are your meetings going?"

"I'll give you details over dinner. It's been an interesting few days. I have to run. I still have a few appointments today."

They made plans to meet downtown. Mission accomplished. Cara wished him luck and hung-up smiling. Secretly she had hoped Francois would call, but she hadn't counted on it. Dating was not her expertise these days. Also, considering the events in Paris, she had been distracted, thinking of her own family. All thoughts of Francois and his sexy persona were pushed to the back of her brain. He was on a business trip, and he lived in Paris for Gods sake! Now that he had called, she decided she would go and have a fun night, no expectations. Francois was delightful to talk to and she welcomed the charge between them. She couldn't remember feeling like that since, forever.

Cara joyously spent the rest of the day primping and deciding what to wear. It had been a long while since her last date. It was a shame that the world events weighed so heavily on everyone's minds, but nonetheless, she tried to concentrate on the task at hand. She picked black velvet leggings, a flowing, asymmetrical, long, fitted ivory shirt and a black Chanel-like, wool jacket with colorful pink and purple trimmings. She added a hot pink cashmere scarf for color and warmth and a knee length, black faux fur jacket. Since it was January, she decided to wear black suede boots. The final touch was jewelry; stunning pink tourmaline earrings that dangled provocatively off a short, string of tiny diamonds. The earrings were a remnant from a past relationship, actually the best part of it, she thought, as she fastened the posts. She finished her look with her favorite pink sapphire and amethyst ring. Eyeing herself in the mirror, Cara felt confident and ready for anything. A continuation of Paris karma perhaps?

Around eight that evening, Cara waited for Francois in the lobby of the Bowery Hotel. Charging butterflies took over her stomach. Nervously, she sat by the fireplace and watched the flurry of activity. Francois appeared, a vision in different shades of blue and green. He was sporting a compelling grin and looked so handsome to Cara she had trouble keeping her cool. His navy wool jacket and sky-blue scarf were slung over his arm, and he carried a small, shiny bag, which he presented to her.

"*Bonsoir, Cherie,* I'm glad you could meet me. You look beautiful as usual. Here's a little surprise for you." Francois smiled and sat down. "*Voisi,* unpack it."

Cara peeked into the small bag. "Good things come in small packages they say. *Merci,* Francois."

Inside the sparkling, white bag was a small silver colored box with a raspberry bow. Cara untied the bow and lifted the lid. Her eyes zeroed in on a delicate ceramic lady's shoe, exquisitely hand painted. It opened with a tiny hinge.

"It's beautiful, Francois. So delicate. Thank you, *Merci beaucoup!*" Cara beamed. She leaned over to hug him, planting a kiss on his smoothly shaven cheek.

"I bought it from one of the artists I visited yesterday. It reminded me of you, Cinderella." Francois said warmly.

Cara felt the butterflies kick it up a notch.

"I carry mainly painting and illustration in my gallery, but occasionally I have sculpture and I guess, now maybe ceramics too. This artist made a miniature shoe and handbag collection out of ceramics and glass and it's quite charming and humorous. I'll show you the pictures over dinner. The shoes span trends over several centuries and countries, many presented in a comedic style," explained Francois. "I fell in love with the collection. They make good gifts. Are you hungry? I made a reservation nearby."

"Famished," Cara replied truthfully. He put on his coat, and they left the hotel walking closely together. When they got to the restaurant, Francois opened the door with one hand and put his arm around her with the other to usher her into the warmth.

Over dinner they talked a little about the tragedy in Paris. Francois was saddened that he wasn't home, but also a little relieved he left before it happened. Over their cozy candle lit dinner in Little Italy, Cara realized that Francois and she had more in common than she imagined. Francois admired some of the same artists as she, they loved to travel and they both adored movies and the theater. Francois wholeheartedly agreed with her on freedom of press and conversation flowed from one topic to the next rather seamlessly. Cara felt like she knew Francois forever.

"Do you have any children, Francois?"

"Yes, two. My son, Luc, works for an entertainment company in Paris and my daughter, Amelie, lives in London with her British husband and two children. They own a framing business. I get to see them quite a bit as I collaborate with a gallery there. I have a partnership in London."

Cara listened attentively.

"Luc and I have dinner at least once a week and I see Amelie when I travel to London a few times a year. I enjoy seeing my grandchildren. My ex-wife Madeleine, a journalist, remarried and relocated to southern France with her new husband."

"Well, you know where my children are. My husband died eight years ago," Cara explained. "No girlfriends?"

"No one in particular. The gallery is keeping me too busy. You?"

"No. Same here. I work a lot and when I'm not working, I'm trying to find new clients."

Francois talked about the artists he visited in New York and what aspects of their work he liked. He knew a great deal about art and Cara enjoyed his perspective. After dinner they went back to the hotel and had a drink by the fireplace. Francois walked Cara to a taxi and gently kissed her on the lips. Pleasure darts shot through her insides.

"I hope to see you soon, Cara. I'm leaving for California tomorrow evening, but I'll pass through New York again on my way home. Can I call you then?"

"That would be nice, Francois. I enjoyed dinner and your company. Thank you."

Francois placed his hands on her shoulders and gazed into her eyes. Then he leaned down and kissed both her cheeks. "A bien tot. See you soon, ok?"

Disappointed he didn't kiss her on the lips again, Cara waved goodbye as she got into the taxi. She felt alive after spending the evening with Francois. They had managed to make each other feel good, relieving all stress for a few fun hours. Sometimes you have to embrace what life offers, however fleeting it may be. Either way, a warm human connection was made and enjoyed. Paris Karma.

Chapter XLVII

Day of Reflection

On Saturday, Summer, along with Ted and Hope joined their friends on the streets of Paris to support the French people and to stand united for freedom of speech. Samson and Natalie joined them. It was a day for unity against extremism and terrorism and for freedom of expression, artistic and otherwise. It was an emotional experience, leaving Summer drained, but the day also yielded comfort and resolve in an increasingly unsettling world. On Sunday, the long healing process, for countless broken hearts around the world, began.

Chapter XLVIII

Inspiration Can Come
from Anywhere

Sunday, Cara resumed her work. Her vacation in Paris and her countless new pictures on the tablet inspired her to sit down in the studio and draw. Dinner with Francois had fueled her motivation.

Over the years, Cara made two types of pottery. First and foremost, she made conventional, functional pottery in pretty colors and recognizable patterns for business purposes, but whenever she had free time, she experimented with sculptural pieces which incorporated other materials like natural stones, crushed glass, or metals. These pieces often had organic patterns and bold color combinations or metallic glazes. She considered the latter pieces her personal art. They were not suitable as eating or drinking vessels since they utilized glazes and materials that weren't safe for consumption, but they were beautiful art forms. She was proud of this work, but rarely had the opportunity to show it. She needed an agent.

Cara participated in gallery shows on occasion, but these days, the commercial jobs kept her too busy to pursue this passion seriously. The need to make a living prevailed. There would always be time later, Cara comforted herself. *When I retire.* However, after two weeks in Paris and an inspirational dinner with Francois, she felt the need to harness into this "other" creativity and produce something totally non-functional and beautiful, something as unique as the little ceramic shoe Francois had given her. She spent the entire Sunday working in her warm studio. It was 20 degrees outside and she had nowhere else to be.

On Tuesday, an email from Sotheby's caught her attention. It was revealed that the bowls she bought in Paris were indeed loose replicas of the real bowls that were stolen from the Met a few months ago. The curator was surprised at the quality of the copies and how close the designs and colors were to the stolen pieces. Naturally, he could tell from the material of the bowls that they were not old, but rather recent. A red flag email went out from Sotheby's to dealers who bought and sold this type of merchandise.

The Met had registered the stolen pieces on the international Art Loss Register, a comprehensive database for stolen art. Both institutions, the Met and Sotheby's issued a joint state-ment/email for Art Business.com to warn people of the copies/forgeries. They thanked Cara for her visit and astute ob-servations. They also told her they'd contacted the auction house where she'd bought them. Cara was pleased she'd acted. The men she kept running into immediately came to mind, but she didn't want to take the risk of accusing someone incorrectly, so she re-plied with a simple, "You're welcome." Nonetheless, her antennae were up.

Chapter XLIX

Suspicions Kill

Carlos, seated in his cramped office at the restaurant, concentrated on his computer screen. He was deleting junk emails when an email marked urgent, from Fernando, popped up; he immediately opened it and whistled. Fernando had forwarded a communication from Sotheby's alerting all dealers to the possible copies/forgeries on the market. A picture example was included, which Carlos immediately recognized. Seconds later, the phone rang and hesitating briefly, he picked it up. He knew who it would be without checking the screen. Fernando was spitting mad.

"Did you see the email from Sotheby's?"

"Yes, I was just reading it. What are you thinking?" Carlos could picture Fernando in his spacious office, swiveling in his luxurious chair, cursing.

"We need to contact the lawyer. Good thing Alphonse is no longer around, that squirming worm."

"That would probably be wise, Fernando."

Jasper and Adriano were working hard on the Flores transactions. The amount of money coming in and out of Fernando Flores's accounts was substantial. Jasper continued to have an uneasy feeling, but could not find anything amiss, try as he might. The investments he was managing for Adriano were solid and pretty much standard, the same as those he managed for other clients. His radar was on high alert though, since large amounts of money were also being transferred weekly to various accounts in Paris, Marseille, and Mexico. He kept his suspicions to himself, wondering if Adriano felt the same way. If he did, Adriano didn't question the golden goose or its steady egg drop. Jasper decided to just do his job and follow instructions; it was not his place to question or snoop into legitimate transactions. Adriano was a smart man; if anything was amiss, he would handle it. After all, Fernando Flores was his client.

Fernando rarely came into the bank; his transactions were all handled electronically, mostly by his associate in Paris. Jasper was not copied on all communications, he suspected, and he did not accompany Adriano on any outside meetings. Jasper assumed Adriano met Fernando at the restaurant occasionally as he was out of the office often these days. Jasper had no regrets he wasn't included. He preferred it that way. The pictures his mother sent him of Fernando's restaurant stayed on his phone. Nothing was shared with Adriano. He couldn't put his finger on why, but he just didn't feel like the timing was right. *Maybe I don't want to know more about this client officially.*

Those pictures are interesting, Mom. The restaurant in Barcelona is much more impressive," he told her when she called.

"I'll send some more pictures, should I ever go there again. In the meantime, you can look online."

"I already did."

Jasper called Samson more frequently since the Paris trip. He missed his little brother and was considering going to Berlin for the Berlinale, if work permitted. The Berlin International Film Festival was fast approaching in early February and Samson was still scheduled to cover the event.

"Dude, the office is paying for my luxury room, and I can easily request two queen sized beds. Please come!" Samson urged him. "The events will be fun, Jasper. When will you ever have this opportunity again?" Samson argued convincingly.

Jasper knew Samson was right. "Probably never! Alright then. Let me check with Adriano if I can tack on a day to my weekend and make it really worth it." Jasper wanted to go for his own reasons. He needed to talk to someone about his suspicions and Samson was the only person he trusted, besides his mom. He couldn't risk talking to anyone in his world in Barcelona. It was too small, and people talked.

Chapter L

Vive l'Amour and
Filmmaking in Paris

Summer began shooting her film in the third week of January. Between the recent terrorist attacks and a few mundane setbacks, two and a half weeks late wasn't terrible. So far, they had accomplished a tremendous amount in only six and a half weeks.

The weather in Paris was frigid. Given the freezer temperatures, filming outdoors was put on hold for another week. The schedule was shifted around, and they began shooting the indoor scenes first. These took longer than anticipated. Well-oiled plans and Ted's precise scheduling skills were already being put to the test and succumbing to rifts, minor ones, but nonetheless rifts. One particularly cold weekend, Summer and Hope made more schedule changes, leaving poor Ted to coordinate the cast and crew. As usual, he made it work, but not without undue pain. "No movie ever sticks to the schedule 100%," Ted assured the girls. "We'll manage and make it work. No worries. Besides, it's good to get the indoor scenes done while the weather stinks. Come Spring, we'll want to be outdoors."

His flexible attitude was appreciated.

"Yeah, the natural outdoor lighting will be better for filming in another month," Hope added. "These dark days are challenging. Right now, I'm craving Southern Cali weather in a big way."

"Agreed. Paris winter weather is depressing. Even New York gets more sunshine than this." Summer voiced in frustration.

The cast and crew were ready and eager to start. The apartment on Rue Malher and the Montmartre theater were used as a home base and a place to store equipment, costumes, and props. Ted had organized everything to a T but even the best laid plans have hiccups. Delays were nothing new in the movie industry. You had to roll with the punches. Sick days for crew, retakes of scenes, equipment malfunction, all those mishaps were considered par for the course.

Ted was still seeing Jean-Michel and seemed to be in a perpetually good mood. He was unflappable and took each hiccup in stride. He was the steady balance in the girls' lives, their reliable rock. Summer realized that she depended on him more and more. Ted kept her sane when the days were long, arduous, and filled with unexpected surprises, not necessarily of the good variety.

Prior to shooting, Summer also went on her first dinner date with Pascal. She thought it went well. He must have too as they went on an immediate subsequent date to see an art exhibit. She enjoyed his company and knack for interesting conversation. Given their schedules it wasn't often they had time to meet, but when they did, there was a definite spark. Summer had found herself a French part-time lover.

Summer often wondered about Hope's emotional well-being. Hope dated a string of men, one she danced with New

Years Eve and the others she picked up here and there. Her last fling was an extra in the film. Hope's vivacious personality and boundless energy attracted men like magnets, but none of them stuck around for long. Few could keep up with her.

It appeared Hope liked being unattached, Summer noticed. Hope didn't want the burden of a lengthy attachment. She liked being on the move. *Well, to each his own.* Summer knew she herself could barely handle a single part-time relationship. No one judged.

Chapter LI

Art is in the Eye of the Beholder

Francois emailed Cara almost daily from California. He began sharing artists' work, asking her opinion. She was flattered. He was coming back to New York at the end of January, and he wanted to visit her studio. Thrilled, she stepped up production. His announced visit inspired her to work on her personal pieces whenever she could. She aimed to impress him. Having Francois possibly represent her in Europe would give her more of a reason to stay in touch and she wanted very much to stay in touch with this man. She hoped she wasn't being presumptuous, but what did she have to lose?

"What do you think, Sam? Will he like this piece?" she asked one morning.

"How could he not? It's gorgeous, Cara."

"He might not have the right market for my work though."

"That will be his call to make, but if he doesn't yet have a market, he can create one. It never hurts to try new things, for him and for you."

"I suppose so."

January business was generally slow, so Cara found time to work on Nero's tiles during the day and tackle her own work, nights, and weekends. She started a new series with sleek, elongated black silhouettes against muddled yellow or blue and purple backgrounds. The elongated silhouettes were stylish women, and the background colors were bright with a softness in hue. The black silhouettes served as a fetching contrast. Some of the silhouettes were playing instruments, some were dancing, and some were just figures conversing or strutting. All were stylized, made from sketches Cara had rendered first. She managed to complete three pieces. One was a large, organically shaped vase and the other two were large frame-less wall tiles. This was a departure from her usual work, and she felt particularly good about it. The inspiration came from the erotic Greek tiles she had done for Nero and Jonny. She silhouetted the black, slinky figures, against the colorful backgrounds, a simple but effective, eye-catching concept. She wondered what Francois would think. She finished the final glaze on the two 24 x 34 tiles the day before his arrival. Samantha stopped by to look and give her seal of approval.

"Those are wild, Cara. He'll love them. Nero loved his and you know how picky he can be." Sam gushed, swinging a glass of red wine to and fro. They were sharing a bottle of red wine in Cara's studio.

"Thanks."

"I need a new client with good taste so I can sell these for you. The tiles would look great in a seductive wet bar," Samantha volunteered as she poured herself another glass. "I can just picture it." Samantha dramatically draped herself over the studio sink, the back of her hand swishing over her forehead.

Cara laughed and reached for her wine glass. "Should I put them on my website? I don't usually put the art pieces on there. I always wanted them on a separate, serious artist site."

"I think you should either start a separate site or just put them in a connecting blog, folder or link if you don't have time to do a whole new separate website," answered Samantha thoughtfully. They should be shown, or no one will ever know what other talents you have. Let's see what Francois says" Samantha teased. "He's your newest art consultant and clearly knows how to market. Now show me those stolen ceramic pictures. We have a mystery to solve."

Chapter LII

Second Date and Whirlwind Romance

The next day Cara got up early and tidied her studio. Francois was coming around six to see her work and have dinner with her. Cara planned her dinner menu on a little notepad that doubled as her shopping list and drove to the market. She treated herself to a much-needed manicure/pedicure and picked up some fresh flowers at the indoor flower stand. Once back home, she prepped her dinner, straightened her living quarters, and took a leisurely hot shower. She slid on her favorite faded jeans, a winter floral silk shirt and eggplant suede, ballet flats with furry insides. No socks needed. The house was heated. To add a little sparkle, she wore diamond hoop earrings and a few amethysts, blue topaz, and pink sapphire bangles. "It will be a casual dinner at home," she told Francois.

"What can I bring, *Cherie*?"

"Just yourself. I have everything covered. You can relax."

Francois arrived punctually with a bottle of French champagne. It was good to see him and Cara suddenly realized that she had missed him. Surprising even herself, she gave him a prolonged hug. She felt a tingling right down to her toes when she inhaled his scent and felt his warmth.

Francois, slightly tan from the southern California sun looked equally happy. He greeted her French style, planting kisses on both cheeks and embracing her. Then he stood back and searched her face. "You and the food smell delicious."

Cara laughed self-consciously and ushered him in. "In what order may I ask?"

"You first, of course."

"Right answer. Welcome to my home."

"I think I missed you." he said genuinely. "Is that possible?"

Cara laughed again. "Anything is possible. That should make for a good evening then. How was your trip? I enjoyed reading your emails. It made me feel like I traveled with you."

"I wish you had, *Cherie*. I love California."

"That makes two of us. So, give me some of the highlights," Cara replied as she lead him into the kitchen. "By the way, I'm baking a chicken dish, and I made a vegetable casserole. I hope you will like it. Very American dishes. Would you like a glass of American wine from Long Island to start?"

"Absolutely." Francois examined the bottle from the Lenz winery. "I've been curious about Long Island wines. Are they any good?"

"Yes. This rose' is a little fruity."

"Nice."

Cara put the champagne in the refrigerator. "For dessert."

Wine glasses in hand, they toasted their reunion.

"Let me take you on a tour of my studio."

Francois trailed after her into the open studio space and looked around at the many shelves lined with colorful samples of her pottery. Cara shyly pointed to her new work.

"I've been busy this month." She had set her newest pieces out on the large wood table. Francois studied her work. His expression was calm and interested. She wondered what he thought and nervously shifted from foot to foot.

"Wow, those are magnificent, Cara. Where did your inspiration come from?"

"An erotica project I was working on for a client. Here, look at the photos." She handed him her photo book and sketches for Samantha.

"Oh la la and where did these tiles go?" he laughed.

"They were made for a kitchen design project for a sexy Italian baker."

"Hmmm… now I'm worried, Cara. I won't ask what his bedroom looks like."

"I wouldn't know." Cara laughed and described Nero's unique bakery, promising to take Francois on his next visit.

Francois seemed to genuinely like what he saw in the studio. He bombarded her with questions about her process. Then he took photos with his cell phone and said he would test his market with a few pieces to see if he could sell her work in Europe. Cara was thrilled. "Oh good. Which pieces do you like best?"

"I don't know. One of the tiles maybe? Let me think about it over dinner."

"You can come back into the studio later and pick whatever you think makes sense."

"Good, I make better decisions on a full stomach."

In the kitchen, Cara shoved her dishes into the oven. She gave Francois another glass of wine, a tour of the house and then set up for dinner as Francois sat at the kitchen counter. Conversation flowed from work to his California trip and beyond. After a few glasses of wine and a leisure dinner, the conversation shifted to more personal topics. Francois helped Cara clean up and as she loaded the dishwasher, she felt him brush against her. His presence was magnetic. She wondered what his touch would feel like.

"Shall we have champagne and strawberries by the fireplace?"

"Why not?"

Bellies full and kitchen cleared, they took their champagne glasses and strawberry bowls to the couch, by the electric fireplace. Cara changed the music to a more bluesy mix and turned off the bright kitchen lights.

"Your home is lovely, Cara. Very cozy. I especially like the fireplace."

"No mess with these logs." Cara laughed. "I don't have time to clean or chop wood."

"I understand. Who does? Your home has an artistic woman's touch everywhere I look."

Francois placed their glasses on the coffee table and reached for her, enveloping her in his arms. The chemistry was undeniable. Kissing her, softly at first, then more passionately, he separated her lips with his warm, probing tongue. Cara could feel her body respond. She felt a fire in her belly that hadn't been there earlier.

His kisses trailed down her neck to her collar bone, edging the border of her buttoned shirt. She closed her eyes and tilted her head back. Within seconds, Francois's hands and mouth touched spots that made Cara groan with pleasure. She helped him unbutton her silk shirt and let his hands travel across her scented skin, exploring her softness. Climbing into his lap, straddling him, she pulled off his sweater and T-shirt exploring his neck with her tongue. She could feel his hardness. Francois pushed her down onto the couch and let his mouth explore the curves of her body. Arching her back, Cara totally succumbed. His hands smoothed over her shoulders and pushed her bra straps down as his tongue traveled downward. He was a sensuous, gentle, and all-around thoughtful lover, everything she had anticipated.

The next morning, they made love in the shower and cooked breakfast together. They read the newspaper cover to cover and had breakfast in bed. Cara made mimosas with the left-over champagne. The Sunday Times was Cara's only remaining paper pleasure. Seeing red carpet activity, large and in color, allowed her to clip her favorite gowns. Today Suzanna Svelte's cut-out, deep purple dress caught her attention. *I wonder if Samson is seeing this up close.*

"I can't remember the last time I had champagne in bed, especially in the morning," Cara giggled.

"Relieved to hear that."

Francois picked three ceramic pieces to try in his gallery in Paris. The two new tiles and an older piece. He assured her he would cover shipping as they discussed logistics. Around noon they decided to go into the city and browse through art galleries.

They spent a leisurely Sunday strolling through Soho, ending with an early fondue dinner on Broome Street. They made plans for the following week and then separated with great difficulty; lips locked.

Cara hopped into a taxi while Francois walked back to his hotel. He looked like he was floating on air when she glanced through the rearview window. He turned and caught her looking, so, embarrassed, she waved and blew him a kiss.

It was a wonderful weekend and Cara didn't want to think about Francois's impending trip home. She would enjoy the one week he was here and after that, who knows? One day at a time. Cara viewed Francois as an extension of her wonderful Paris visit and knew it would have to end soon, but she elected not to dwell on it. Life was too short to worry about the inevitable. She would enjoy the here and now and savor the moment.

On Monday morning Francois called to invite Cara to stay in the hotel with him for his remaining days. "Just pack a small suitcase and stay here with me," he urged. "The room is large enough and comfortable. We'll make it a mini vacation. Our first together."

Cara thought for a moment about her weeks' schedule and then agreed, "Ok, I can come tonight. I need to finish a few things here first."

"Great. Text me when you know what time works. Let's have dinner together."

Cara could feel the butterflies returning, wreaking havoc with her insides. She had already cleared most of the week in anticipation of Francois's return. There was nothing pressing on her calendar that she couldn't put off until the following week. The last batch of Nero's tiles was almost complete. She could finish them today and glaze them over the weekend. Sam could pick them up late Monday. She texted Samantha and pulled her most stylish travel bag out of the closet. Then she agonized over what to pack.

Chapter LIII

Fantastic Film World in Berlin

Samson was preparing for his business trip to Berlin. Natalie was joining him for the opening weekend and Jasper was confirmed for an extended second. Adriano had given Jasper the extra day off. Samson was thrilled. He also invited Summer to come during the week, but she declined due to filming deadlines. All things considered that was probably for the best. Samson wanted to have time to catch up with colleagues. He always enjoyed the social aspect of his job and looked forward to seeing the foreign press from other cities. Summer would have been an easy guest, but the pressure to produce was real, for both, respectively.

Summer's film was behind schedule and every day counted. Samson understood. There had been problems that caused added delays, but Summer was back on track and couldn't afford the break she explained. "I'm so sad and sorry I'm missing this incredible opportunity, Samson. I just can't get away. I think Hope and Ted would kill me."

"It's ok, Summer. I'll fill you in when I get back."

"Take lots of pictures."

"I will, I promise."

Samson knew when not to push. Summer was dedicated to a fault and could not be swayed when her mind was set. He promised to share pictures throughout his stay.

The festival looked promising. His hotel was located in the hub of activity, and he was getting industry invitations daily. Samson would be working around the clock, but he looked forward to it. He threw his favorite sneakers into the open suitcase in anticipation of doing a lot of walking.

Chapter LIV

Hooray for Hollywood...Briefly

Opening weekend at the Berlin Film Festival was a success. Samson and Natalie flitted from event to event. They had a wonderful time, despite Samson having to work a good portion of it. They visited screenings, enjoyed parties, and had dinner with some of Samson's colleagues. Celebrities walked in and out of their hotel and Natalie was tickled pink with their sightings. Pictures were shared with family and friends.

Meetings were taking place all over the hotel lobby, the adjoining banquet rooms, and the restaurant. The atmosphere was simultaneously eclectic and electric. Novelty was the order of the day. One of the celebrities occupying the top floor suites of their hotel was Suzanna Svelte, a beautiful A-list movie star. Her appearance on the red-carpet Saturday night left the audience breathless and insatiable. The press feverishly competed for photo ops and any utterings she chose to grace them with. A select few were lucky enough to interview her with her publicist hovering. Her star was shining brightly in the festival's crown. Suzanna's revealing, knock out, eggplant gown and impressive ruby drop earrings were featured on the internet and papers around the world on Sunday morning. Samson knew his mother would be following all.

Samson and Natalie were fortunate enough to see Suzanna up close. People were doing summersaults to breathe in Suzanna's exhales, whenever she left her room. Wherever Suzanna went, an entourage of crew, press and paparazzi followed. Natalie was thrilled with her glimpse into the film world for a brief interlude. Seeing Suzanna Svelte up close was the highlight of her stay. Sunday evening, she left Samson on a high note, wishing she could stay longer. However, there was work and bills had to be paid.

Less than 24 hours after Natalie's departure, there was a seismic shift in the hotel's landscape. The sparkling glamour of the previous week turned to ashen tragedy. All hell broke loose, early Monday morning.

Chapter LV

Dead Starlet and Live Thugs

Early Monday, after a night of shameless partying, Suzanna Svelte's lifeless body was discovered in her suite by her publicist. Overnight the atmosphere in the hotel lobby became frantic and oppressive. Ambulances, police, press, and paparazzi crossed paths, circling around each other like vultures. The hotel staff tried to maintain a certain decorum, but a stifling, hushed fog descended over the once vibrant lobby and restaurant. As the day unfolded, there was talk of drugs found in Suzanna's room. Hotel cameras mounted at strategic angles revealed the expected. The weekend parties had shown some shocking behavior in the crevices of the hotel.

Samson's schedule was unchanged, but he kept his ears, eyes and smartphone tuned to the drama. The next day, the papers revealed that drugs had most likely caused Suzanna's demise. An overdose was suspected, and the police were pouring over the hotel's camera footage to see who frequented the premises and who may have gained access to Suzanna's suite of rooms. Unfortunately, Suzanna had celebrated her success with a few hundred close friends in the adjoining suites so the people partying in her quarters were numerous. The security tapes went on for hours and showed plenty of illicit behavior. The source of the drugs was being investigated by a special narcotics squad. A powdered substance they discovered, seemed to be an unusually potent mixture, not the usual Berlin fare, but no details were disclosed publicly about this fact. Whoever supplied and killed the mega-star of the festival remained incognito. The pressure on law enforcement was intense.

"Oh my God, I cannot believe I was one of the last people to see her alive," Natalie exclaimed over the phone one night.

"You and a few hundred others. Shocking developments. Jasper will be seriously bummed. He was so excited to see her."

By mid-week, the police released a statement confirming that drugs had indeed killed the star. Suzanna had gone into cardiac arrest. Narcan had not worked or wasn't administered in a timely fashion. An investigation was launched into the drug mix and origin. Samson was getting tidbits of information when Jasper arrived in the lobby on Thursday evening. Jasper was gathering pertinent intelligence for a news update. The two brothers hugged warmly and Samson escorted Jasper to the elevator, handing over a spare key to their room, while filling him in on the newest inside knowledge.

"Go get settled. I'll come up soon. I'm trying to get some facts straight. Her publicist said he would issue a statement to the press."

"No problem," Jasper countered. "I was hoping to see her alive. Damn! Just my luck."

"Trust me. I know. She was pretty incredible up close. A true beauty."

"Double damn."

A few hours later, Samson and Jasper were seated in the hotel bar over a German draft beer, catching up on mutual news. They decided to have dinner at the far corner of the bar as they both were tired after a long day of work and travel. Samson briefed Jasper about his week, the events before and after Susanna's death and where the investigation currently stood. Jasper filled Samson in on his job, his boss and his activities in Barcelona. He also clued Jasper in regarding his biggest client, Fernando Flores. Jasper, for the first time, verbalized his suspicions out loud. It felt good to tell his brother because he didn't dare tell anyone in Barcelona. Most of his contacts were connected to the financial world and news traveled fast in the small financial community. Jasper was tight-lipped and this characteristic had always served him well in his line of work.

"In my opinion, if you have an uneasy gut, there must be something off about the guy and his business. Your instincts are usually pretty good, Bro." Samson chewed on a goat cheese stuffed Portobello mushroom. "Mmm, this is delicious. Have you done the obvious and googled him?"

"Yes, there was nothing unusual about his meager online profile." Jasper speared his fork into the shared appetizer.

"Here is my tablet. Take a look. In fact, there is very little that shows up at all. He imports and exports pottery. The ceramics business in Mexico is family-run and apparently extremely lucrative. All the pottery is manufactured there. He distributes the pottery around Europe from a warehouse in Barcelona. He also owns two restaurants, one in Barcelona and the other in Paris. Mom went to the one in Paris and I've been to the one in Barcelona with Adriano. Barcelona is a money maker. Always crowded. Not sure about Paris. It was empty when Mom visited. Can you check him out for me?"

"Looks and sounds like he is diversified. Restaurants are good for money laundering, of course. When I get back to Paris, I can try to rummage a little. I'm too swamped here." They speculated about Fernando Flores over one more drink and decided to call it a night. As Jasper walked away from the bar, Samson picked up his tablet.

"Hey, do you still want this?"

"Oh, damn. Yes! I keep misplacing this thing. You have no idea how many times I've forgotten it. It always finds its way back to me though."

"Until it doesn't. I know someone else who has the same issue. Her name starts with C."

"She's ten times worse."

"Hmmm. It only takes one mistake. We shall see who loses it first. Care to bet?"

"Sure, I say mom."

"What are the stakes?"

"A kick-ass dinner."

"Done."

They walked to the elevator and Samson pressed the up button. The doors opened and a man with a black baseball cap pulled low, exited. He had the word champagne stitched in gold letters across the front of the cap.

Samson and Jasper briefly caught a glimpse of a large silver cross with turquoise stones flashing beneath a black leather jacket. Instinctively two sets of eyes trailed the man. Jasper recognized Jose. Jose's eyes, two slits under the visor, were fixated on the revolving door. He didn't appear to notice Jasper. After he passed, Jasper nudged Samson.

"Check out that guy. That's Jose! Flores's cousin. Have you seen him here before?" As the elevator doors closed Jasper held the open button. Both men observed Jose exiting the hotel and stepping into a waiting car. Jasper let go of the open button and pressed their floor.

"Who? The one who likes champagne and big turquoise jewelry? No, don't think so."

"Yes! That was Fernando Flores's right-hand man, Jose. The one I just told you about. You saw him at the airport when mom arrived. Remember? What a strange coincidence."

"Vaguely. Are you sure it was the same guy?"

"Yes! I had dinner with him in Barcelona. I sat across from him. I'm positive! Besides, I would recognize that jewelry anywhere. He sure gets around. What do you suppose he was doing here?"

"I don't have a clue. People like celebrities and films and this is a popular festival."

"He doesn't strike me as the star struck kind, Samson. He showed no interests. He's all business. The man barely talks. When I had dinner with him and Fernando, he only responded to Fernando and he's a total yes man. There must be more to his being here. A business trip maybe? This is beyond odd."

"Special ceramics delivery?"

"Let's hope it's ceramics."

Chapter LVI

Let it Snow, Let it Snow

Cara's mini vacation at Francois's hotel was heavenly. It was hard to get out from under the fluffy covers every morning. Each day she accompanied him to various artist's studios, gathering inspiration along the way. At the end of the day, they shared intimate dinners in small out-of-the-way restaurants and three wonderful, passion fueled nights. One evening they splurged on theater tickets and another on a jazz bar. Their connection felt real. Time flew by and their liaison was cemented.

Together, they started planning Cara's trip to Paris. Francois seduced her with a list of places he would take her to, if only she would agree to come soon. Cara loosely planned the trip for late April which seemed a long way off. The day before Francois's planned departure, a snowstorm threatened the tri state area. Cara packed her overnight bag in the morning and left it with the concierge, before brunch. Thick, opaque flurries started to fall, and the sky looked ominously dark. The wind's teasing fingers breezed through her hair. She pulled out her black wool beanie and stuffed her locks inside.

"I'll leave after brunch. Trains may be delayed or suspended later, and I have work to finish for Monday. Excessive snow in

New York has its drawbacks and usually translates to delays." She needed to finish glazing Nero's tiles as Sam was coming to the studio on Monday to pick them up.

"I understand. Work is work. It was fantastic you could spend a few days with me. Thanks for that."

"It was fun. My treat today. I'm taking you to the Pain Quotidien for brunch. It's around the corner."

"It looks interesting," Francois observed.

She questioned him regarding its authenticity. "Does this prepare you for home? Is this authentic French?"

Francois's eyes traveled to the t-shirts the servers were wearing. The slogan *Don't Panic, we are Organic* made him laugh. "Maybe not completely authentic," he joked.

Le Pain Quotidien was one of Cara's favorite luncheon places in New York along with Sara Beth's Kitchen and The Smith. She had taken Francois to all of them. It turned out, Francois was partial to Sara Beth's.

They enjoyed a leisurely brunch while Francois told her more about his family. He couldn't wait to meet hers in April. He didn't remember seeing Summer at his gallery. After sharing a passionate, heart-felt hug and a coffee infused kiss, they parted. Cara walked to the subway and Francois trudged back to his hotel to pack, make phone calls and check the weather report.

That night his flight to Paris was cancelled. All three major airports around New York City closed due to the raging storm and hefty snow deposits. The conditions were white-out, over the top. Even the subways stopped running at 11pm.

Cara listened to the news. She checked her email while doing laundry, wondering if she would hear from Francois. When her phone rang, she dove for it.

"You're stuck with me *chere,* Cara." he said. My flight tonight is cancelled. Tomorrow's flights are cancelled until further notice and Monday's flights are fully booked. I'm waiting for a call back from the airline."

"I figured that. I heard the news. Why don't you come and stay with me until you can get a flight out, Francois? You'll leave whenever you can. Consider it our second mini vacation together except that I must work this time."

Francois laughed. "Me too. Are you sure that's ok? You're not sick of me yet?"

"Yes. Come. I won't see you for a few months after that, so if I do get sick of you, I have plenty of time to recover."

"That's a warm thought."

They agreed that Francois would come north the next day and stay until the airports reopened and flights were available. Cara closed her phone, secretly happy about the turn of events. She could not spend enough time with this man. He was so easy and fun to be with. She ate the slice of pizza she had picked up for dinner on the way home and got to work in her studio.

Late the next day, Cara picked Francois up from the train station. Her driveway and the streets were cleared by then. One month in the US had yielded a heavy load. They heaved his suitcase into her SUV and threw the hand luggage and painting roll on the back seat.

"Welcome back, *Cheri*. Long time," she joked.

Francois laughed, "Yes, for sure. Thanks for saving me from a boring day in the hotel. I promise not to disturb you too much while you work. It'll be hard though."

"Not just for you. Fortunately, I did a lot in the last 24 hours. I had a deadline that just got pushed to tomorrow because of the snow." Cara trailed a finger down his chest. He leaned in and kissed her.

Once in the car, she took him on a ten-minute tour of her immediate neighborhood, including Nero's bakery, where they stopped for rolls and pastries for the morning.

"In case we can't get out tomorrow. It's supposed to snow again tonight."

"I've never seen pastries like this before. Now I understand your racy tile connection."

They pulled into Cara's driveway and hauled Francois's suitcase into her bedroom. Cara headed into the kitchen to assemble something delicious for a late lunch. She heated a prepared corn chowder soup with turkey sausage and assembled a crudité plate. She also heated some apple cider with cinnamon sticks to sip by the fireplace. Francois was appreciative and ate everything with zest. The cider was an aromatic bonus.

The rest of the day was spent working on their respective computers in the studio. Cara also checked her kiln and unloaded and reloaded Nero's remaining glazed tiles. She felt comfortable working in silence, as if they had done so for years. When Francois finished his emails, he looked up and studied her face.

"Dinner? I just loaded the last batch. It's on a timer so we can leave. It's late, isn't it?"

Francois nodded and smiled, "Let me help you with dinner. Any mimosas left over? I think we deserve one."

"Yes, I don't have French Champagne, but I do have a nice Prosecco. No orange juice either, but I bought a tasty peach nectar. Or would you prefer your liquor without embellishments?"

"Even better."

As they closed the studio, Cara's phone signaled an incoming text. Sam was confirming that Cara was dropping the tiles at Nero's the next day. She could transfer them directly to his truck bound for Southampton.

In the kitchen, she gave Francois the Prosecco to open and pour. She also directed him to set the table. She started chopping vegetables. They sipped their drinks and chatted about artists as they prepared their meal. She baked potatoes, wrapped asparagus and goat cheese in thin chicken filets and popped everything into the oven. She liked an easy prep when she was working. She threw the remaining vegetables into a stock pot and added some vegetable stock and water simmering them until they were blanched. After transferring the vegetables to a casserole dish, she added an egg mixture and sprinkled panko and parmesan on top, popping it into the oven, next to the chicken.

"This will be lunch, tomorrow. I don't have time to prepare much during the day."

"Looks tasty."

"Dinner will be ready in twenty minutes. Would you like a cup of soup to start?"

"Yes, please." he replied, holding out two bowls. "Everything smells incredible. I can't believe how quickly you pulled a meal together."

Cara poured a ladle of her defrosted curried carrot-sweet potato soup into his bowl and waited for his reaction.

"Mmmm, *tres bon,*" Francois offered.

"It's a vegan recipe, I discovered recently. I make soup in advance and freeze a portion for busy days." Cara explained.

"Good strategy."

Cara handed him the bottle to refill their glasses. It was nice to have company. Outside the storm was picking up again, depositing another thick blanket of white. The wind chill factor lowered the temperature about ten degrees, but indoors it felt toasty. Romance added to the warmth. Cara's log-less fireplace, champagne, warm soup, and a hearty home cooked meal made for a magical mix. After dinner they snuggled on the couch under a fleece blanket as they watched the news and weather forecast. They didn't make it to the bedroom until much later.

The next day, Cara woke up early and prepared her rooibos tea. She made coffee for Francois, checked her email, the news, showered and checked the driveway. She was still snowed in. She texted Sam. When Francois sauntered in, they shared a late breakfast and parted. Cara retreated to the studio and Francois worked on his laptop at the kitchen counter. The time difference only allowed him to connect with his office in the morning. By late lunchtime his window to communicate and to receive immediate replies closed until the next day. Cara spent much of

Monday in and out of the studio, finishing the last of Nero's tiles. She was thankful for the extra snow day. Francois was patient and content to wait. When the tiles were ready she texted Sam. The snowplow had arrived in the nick of time.

Cara loaded the tiles into crates and placed them in her car. Francois helped. She left to drop them at Nero's bakery and pick up some sourdough rolls. When she returned, Francois greeted her at the door. It was something she could easily get used to.

"I was able to get a flight for Wednesday. The airline just confirmed me."

"Oh, good! I can't drive you to the airport though. I must make up for lost time from last week. I'll order you a car service. Is that ok?"

"Yes, of course. I understand. You're a working woman. Can I take you to dinner tonight, so you don't have to cook?"

"Yes! Thanks. That would be nice. Do you like Mexican food?"

"Sure."

That night in Cara's favorite Mexican restaurant, she filled Francois in regarding the pottery she bought in Paris and her meeting with Sotheby's. She told him about the art thefts and the men who kept popping up from New York to Paris. She showed him the stolen art files on her phone. Francois listened intently and promised to keep a watchful eye back in Paris. He appeared intrigued, but mostly he admired her tenacity. She couldn't tell if he believed there was a connection between the men and the stolen goods.

Once home, she made him hot tea and they settled in their favorite spot on the couch by the fireplace. Francois used the moment to confide a secret.

"Remember the day you stopped by my gallery and told my assistant you would be leaving the following day?"

Cara nodded. "Yes. I was disappointed I missed you."

"You shared your flight information. Do you remember that?" Francois took Cara's hand in his.

"Yes. I believe I might have." Cara replied, looking at him intently.

"I was so annoyed I missed you and I wanted to see you again so I changed my flight to yours. Luckily the seat next to you was free."

Cara looked at Francois dumbfounded. "Whaaaat? Really?"

"Yes, really. I was planning to come to New York anyway. I thought why not fly now with good company and have the opportunity to meet you." Francois kissed her hand.

"But you had all those appointments set up!" Cara exclaimed in disbelief.

"My assistant switched the appointments while we were on our flight. We were in contact with most of the artists for several months already. She just firmed up the new appointments. It all worked out."

"Miss Blue Hair? Well, I don't know what to say. I'm so glad you took the leap of faith."

Francois laughed. "Yes, Miss Blue Hair, also known as Annabelle."

He looked into her eyes and she could feel heat circulating. She leaned over and kissed his lips tenderly, sliding her fingers around his neck. She let the soft pillows of her fingertips glide underneath his sweater and t-shirt and slide up his back, gently along his spine. Circling back down around his waist she traveled the rim of his pants from back to front. She could hear his sharp intake of breath as she dipped her fingers into the front of his waistband stroking back and forth along his abs. He gasped and reached for her sweater, slipping it over her head. "Bedroom?" She whispered.

Cara was still digesting Francois's brazen confession when they cuddled in bed a while later. Who would have guessed that proactive romance was still alive in this century?

Chapter LVII

The Dark Side of Berlin

Friday night, Jasper and Samson were getting ready to go to a screening when Samson's phone rang. It was Summer.

"Hey. What the hell happened with Suzanna? Is there an inside scoop I should be privy to?" she teased.

"Hey. Nothing yet. We're in the dark too. Looks like too much partying did her in. It doesn't appear that she had a regular habit from what I'm gathering."

"Is Jasper having fun yet or is he still mourning the loss? I know he was dying to see her alive. Oh, and thanks for the pictures."

"You're welcome. He feels short-changed and sad. You wouldn't believe the week I've had. It's been crazy here. We're still getting updates daily. Suzanna had a big celebration that fateful night and it carried over into adjoining suites upstairs. Anyone could have supplied the drugs. There were tons of people in and out all night."

"Well, where are your investigative skills? They should be kicking in right about now."

"Funny, Summer. I'm here to do another job in case you've forgotten. The one I'm actually getting paid for. Besides, there's red and blue tape everywhere. By the way, remember the Mexican guys Mom kept obsessing about?"

"You mean the Flores brothers, Jasper's clients?"

"Cousins. Yes. One of them was here in the hotel. Jasper and I saw him in the lobby."

"Nooo! Which one? I would have followed him. If nothing else, you would have scored major brownie points with Mom."

"Hilarious, Summer. Just for that, I'll let you tell mom the news. That should tie you to the phone for a while. The cousin, the rough looking one with the turquoise cross."

"Turquoise cross? Oh…that will definitely be a long conversation. I don't have time for that these days. What do you think he was doing there?"

"Damned if I know. Jasper is seriously spooked though."

"Why?"

"Long story. Jasper can tell it better."

Samson filled Summer in on what little he knew about the movie star's death, his weekend with Natalie and the events he attended. He circumvented Summer's question and changed the subject not wanting to betray Jasper's confidence.

"How is the movie coming along?"

"Well, we're moving slowly, but we're moving," Summer replied. "There are always setbacks. One of our essential crew guys has the flu and one of the camera dollies is striking. A creaky wheel needs to be replaced, but for now we're troubleshooting to see if we can get it working with lots of lubricant. We'll resume shooting tomorrow," Summer explained. "It is what it is. How is Jasper enjoying the film festival? What is the best screening so far?"

"I'll send you my reviews."

"Oh, good. I'd like that."

"Here let me put Jasper on, so I can further investigate Suzanna's death for you. We're getting ready to go sleuthing soon," Samson teased.

"Right. Hopefully with some success this time. Talk to you Sunday night after Jasper leaves, ok? I'm sure you'll have this tiny mystery resolved by then. Keep sending those pictures, you tease. We love them. Bye."

Samson chuckled and handed his brother the phone.

Jasper, in his usually crisp manner, exchanged a few pleasantries with his sister.

"I think Samson pretty well covered it. Having fun so far, but I feel like I lost the lottery. I so wanted to see Suzanna up close and I didn't mean at the morgue."

"Well… …life sure threw you a curve ball, but look at the bright side. You're there. I'm not. Take lots of pictures and share, ok?"

"Yeah. See you soon."

"Yup. Mom said April."

"I'll try."

Jasper's phone calls were just as short as his emails, Samson noted. He communicated best in person, preferably over a meal and a drink or two. Besides… Summer could talk forever if you let her, like Cara, and Samson knew that Jasper was not inclined to give her that opportunity. He had places to go, stars to see, even if Suzanna was no longer an option.

The screening Jasper and Samson attended was fun, with plenty of celebrities to gawk at. It was held in one of the 20-plus participating Berlin theaters, not far from the hotel. The after-party took place in another hotel, nearby. Before going to the event, Samson had to upload his report to Paris. He briefly left Jasper in the lobby to nurse a Bellini and eavesdrop. He gave Jasper a newspaper featuring pictures from Suzanna's suite.

"Here, check for clues," he joked.

After Jasper departed for Barcelona, Samson's last days at the Berlinale were busy. He covered all the media events and the honorary *Golden Bear* awards. He wrote about how films were voted on, received, and judged. Time permitting, he also went to some of the special presentations. It was an exciting trip and a unique experience for him. When it came time to pack and go home, he was tired and ready. Samson exited the hotel and took a taxi to the airport. He collapsed on the plane and fell asleep until the plane touched down in Paris, but not before reading Jasper's email. Jasper had indeed found an incriminating clue. It appeared that some pottery in the newspaper pictures of the party suites was remarkably like F&S exports. Samson noticed that Jasper had copied Cara and Summer.

"Well, I'll be damned." Samson muttered to himself.

Chapter LVIII

The French Connection

Suzanna's untimely death was the buzz in the lobby and the talk of closing festival parties. Speculation was running rampant. Tributes to her had invaded the festival schedule and cast a shadow over events, but the film crowd was resilient, and life went on. Awards were received and thank-you speeches uttered.

The updates on Suzanna's death speculated that she had mixed cocaine with prescription drugs and a little too much alcohol. In short, she ingested conflicting substances, and the consequences were deadly. The origin of the drugs had yet to be determined, but the film world had already moved on to the next star. Only the police, press and her steadfast fans were still intent on solving what combination cocktail caused her death.

The drugs and the pottery found in Miss Svelte's suite were coincidentally similar to those found in the Hotel Vendome murder scene, but the police were not publicizing this fact. It was being investigated quietly to see if there indeed was a connection, which seemed likely to law enforcement. Narcotic investigators were exchanging information regarding the deadly drug mix. The homicide squad was studying the security tapes and interviewing hotel staff. Every agency had their eyes on the festival. As of now, the public was still in the dark about a lot of details and the police liked it that way. It gave them a head start in many respects. The press was parched, hanging around like buzzards in a desert.

Inspector Kralle was on the case in Berlin and he took a stingy approach, only releasing information as needed. The pressure was intense and the *Inspektor* immediately realized there were bigger, more important fish to fry with this high-profile demise. Big, high-profile cases were what he thrived on and he was dying to sink his teeth into some real evidence. The only problem was, with a large entourage like Suzanna's, there was little usable forensic evidence. Fingerprints were unhelpful because of sheer abundance and potential witnesses were disappearing to all parts of the world every day.

After examining Miss Svelte's room under a magnifying glass and receiving the initial coroner's results, Inspector Kralle called his counterpart in Paris, Inspector Arnaud. The drugs had to have come through Marseille; he determined. Inspector Arnaud filled him in on the Vendome Hotel investigation as well as a few other overdoses that revealed the same strain of powder. Arnaud believed the drugs were indeed coming to Paris from the south, most likely Marseille, he concurred. Inspector Kralle nodded thoughtfully at the phone. The French police, north and south, were already working together and Arnaud promised to keep Kralle up to date with any new developments. Timely communication was key. They had established a case connection and that was a promising start to trace the origin of this deadly strain of drugs.

Chapter LIX

The Plot Thickens

The rest of Jasper's weekend went smoothly. He was secretly pleased his brother had urged him to come to Berlin. His visit was well-documented with a slew of pictures on his tangerine tablet, the twin to his mom's. He happily shared the images with Cara and Summer, thoroughly enjoying their cheeky comments. Since his brother had little time to take pictures, the gesture was appreciated. No pressure on Samson.

Watching Samson work, Jasper realized Samson was quite the professional; he relished seeing his little brother in action. Pride swelled when he witnessed fellow colleagues bantering with Samson. Getting a first-hand glimpse into Samson's working world was an eye opener and it gave Jasper a better understanding of Samson's routine and workflow. It was very different from his own and it appeared much more glamorous than working at a bank, but Jasper knew that Samson made it look easy and fun because he had become a seasoned journalist, often writing under the intense pressure of tight deadlines.

Jasper was relieved that he had a chance to run his concerns regarding Fernando Flores past his brother. Samson's investigative training and open-minded approach offered valuable insights that Jasper sometimes overlooked. Or was it just in Samson's DNA to do that? Jasper wasn't sure. Samson had always been more observant, and he managed to see the humor in everything, but yet not miss a single detail.

Running into Jose still boggled Jasper's mind. It was on his brain Monday morning when he approached Adriano's office for the weekly briefing. Jasper said nothing to Adriano about his chance meeting, but it disturbed him that Jose was present in the hotel where Suzanna had died. Now he was eagerly waiting for a response from his mother and Samson regarding the pottery in Suzanna's suite. What in the world was Jose's reason for being there and more importantly, why did the sighting bother him? Was he blaming Jose for killing Suzanna before he had a chance to see her? That was a stretch or… maybe not?

Huge sums of money had been deposited into Fernando's accounts while Jasper was away. Apparently, Fernando was renting out the restaurant for events that paid well. A portion of the funds were being used to purchase a new apartment in Monaco, establishing another residency in Europe. The bank was writing a letter to indicate Fernando's good standing, one of the principality's top requirements. Jasper absorbed this information with interest. Fernando now owned homes in Tampico, Barcelona, Paris and Monaco. Monaco, a tax-free haven for the rich, was one of the richest countries in the world. *Is Fernando going to declare that his new home base?*

Jasper googled all of Fernando's real estate holdings based on their addresses. They were all listed under different corporate names some of which he was privy to. In Paris and Monaco his residences were modestly sized apartments overlooking the Seine and the Mediterranean Sea. In Barcelona, Fernando lived in the old town overlooking *Port Vell* Harbor. Tampico was also a major port, where Fernando enjoyed a water view. *Clearly… the man loves water.*

Fernando's import/export business was growing, and pottery was being shipped everywhere, according to Adriano. The pottery arrived in the Barcelona port from Mexico and was stored in the F&S warehouse near the harbor, as far as Jasper knew. The location served as F&S's distribution center in Europe. Jose oversaw the warehouse and shipping aspects in addition to assisting with the management of the restaurant. Carlos Ortiz ran the Paris office and restaurant. Carlos was F&S's general accountant. Jasper had to copy him and address him on all transactions for Flores. Apparently, Fernando trusted his two associates implicitly. Adriano confirmed that Fernando's twin brother and nephews ran the Mexican side of the business, but Jasper's bank had no interaction with them. Carlos handled all international transfers from Paris and now, Monaco.

From his visit to the restaurant, Jasper knew that many of Fernando's employees in Barcelona were Mexican, imported from home. Fernando surrounded himself with his own people. Jasper guessed that his Mexican workers understood the liabilities of crossing him. Europeans did not display that same kind of dedication. Jasper imagined that Fernando dealt with his people by inducing fear. He had that vibe. When Jasper visited the restaurant in Barcelona, the Mexican workers hopped for Fernando. Jasper bet that no one disobeyed or crossed Fernando Flores on either continent.

The more Jasper knew, the more he was curious about Fernando's business. Money was transferred from bank to bank, with no clear pattern. Jasper tried to follow the money trail via different corporations, and once was able to trace a wire to the Caribbean, but he couldn't be sure as the corporate names changed and were plentiful. He said nothing to Adriano and decided to distance himself from Fernando Flores wherever possible. He also made sure to always copy Adriano on every transaction. Jasper never accompanied Adriano outside the bank and followed instructions as needed, always confirming them by email. He never talked to Fernando directly. All client calls went to Adriano before the transactions trickled down to Jasper. Rarely did Jasper respond to messages from Carlos.

Even though he kept a professional distance, Jasper continued to feel uneasy. His gut told him Fernando Flores was dangerous and that a bomb would inevitably explode one day. Something about this business felt amiss, but Jasper could only guess. He knew nothing. He saw nothing. He had no evidence of anything. How could pottery generate so much money so fast? The restaurant business was known to generate unreported cash, but that wouldn't necessarily pass through the bank and in such large amounts. It was hard to fathom that pottery could accumulate that kind of cash. There had to be more to this money trail.

Jasper yearned to talk to his brother, but he didn't think he should discuss his mounting suspicions over the phone. He invited Samson to come down to Barcelona for a weekend and to his surprise, his brother accepted without hesitation. He was busy with Natalie for Valentine's Day, but he promised to come the weekend after.

"Natalie will never forgive me if I don't organize a 'special night' for her. She's an incurable romantic and she's been hinting for the past few weeks," he explained.

"No problem, Samson. I understand. I'm just glad you're coming. We'll have a blast. I promise."

"Sounds good, Bro."

Jasper was itching to share his recent findings with Samson. The banking world was too small to take a risk in Barcelona. He hesitated to share with his friend Enrique even though he would have liked to. Jasper longed to talk to his mother too, but he didn't want her to worry. He knew what she would say. Come home if you anticipate legal problems or safety issues.

For the first time since he'd arrived in Barcelona, Jasper felt alone and unsettled. He knew Fernando and Jose were not the upstanding people they purported to be at the bank. Did Adriano know this too?

Chapter LX

Beat the Press

Samson was meeting Summer, Hope, Ted and Natalie for dinner to tell them about his film festival trip. If the Malher group hadn't been so busy, they would have all enjoyed going to Berlin, but time was of the essence, and they had just ironed out numerous annoying problems. Over dinner, they listened to Samson's stories and tortured him with countless questions about Susanna Svelte's untimely demise. Neither Summer nor Samson mentioned Jasper's email regarding the Flores business. It was agreed they would discuss it in private.

Conversation shifted to world news. The group argued over a movie executive who announced a job change after her embarrassing emails were hacked and publicized. The legalities and moral issues were bounced around the table. Samson and Ted defended the press while Summer and Hope felt the press fanned the flames. Hacking into someone's email really was a privacy violation that should be punishable by law, they argued. No immediate conclusions were reached, and everyone left the table harboring their own convictions.

The following days, Samson was extremely busy catching up in the office and at home. By the end of the week, he was back on track. His thoughts shifted to Jasper and his impending trip to Barcelona. Sitting in front of his laptop, Samson decided to check out Fernando Flores. He didn't come up with anything unusual at first glance, however, when he searched Fernando's company, F&S Enterprises, a few articles, and affiliations popped up. One article in particular, captured Samson's attention. He remembered skimming the article recently, but it had slipped out of his mind until now. Was it mom who had pointed it out?

Deadly drugs were found at the scene in the Vendome murder, but no leads were cited by the police. The murdered man had some business dealings with F&S Enterprises, one of his many dubious clients. Samson attached the article to an email and sent it to Jasper. Then he booked his flight to Barcelona. It was time to listen to and possibly help his brother. He sensed Jasper's trepidation and suspected that Jasper needed his support. Jasper didn't share easily and Samson sensed this whole scene was eating at his brother's insides. He picked up his phone and left a voicemail.

"Jasper, my flight is booked. Free up the couch."

Chapter LXI

The Boys are Back in Town (Soon)

The next morning, Jasper arrived at his office early, coffee cup in one hand and his business briefcase in the other. The combination lock briefcase he had so disliked when Adriano gifted him, was now being used daily. Usually, he preferred a backpack, but these days he was thankful for the lock. Settling in at his desk he pulled out his personal laptop and looked at the news. First, like Cara, he perused international news while sipping his coffee. Next, he turned his attention to local updates. A short article caught his eye. The headlines read, "Police Search International Ships in Barcelona Harbor."

Under different circumstances, the article would not have captured Jasper's attention, but the name of one ship in the accompanying picture caught his eye. The *Corazon de Leones*. F&S Enterprises was one of the freight companies that used the ship. He printed the article and locked it into his briefcase. An incoming email confirmed Samson's flight information. Delighted that his little brother was coming to visit, Jasper thought about preparing for Samson's arrival.

That night, in the comfort of his home, he read his mom's email first. She confirmed the pottery in Suzanna's suite looked remarkably close to select stolen counterparts. She also verified that copies were being fabricated in Fernando's factory in Mexico. Next, he read the email from Samson and felt a chill creep up his spine. He deleted both emails after printing them and locked them into his briefcase. The dots were starting to connect, and it was scary to realize the pattern.

Tired, Jasper surveyed his small one-bedroom apartment. It had an L shaped configuration. A vision in ivory, there was a sleeper couch, a wall-mounted TV, and a modern, slanted bookshelf. The living room extended into a dining room which had a round, glass and tubular, chrome dinner table and four matching chairs. The small leg of the L was the alcove kitchen. He liked the layout because he could oversee everything with one clean sweep. Jasper opened the white wood kitchen cabinets to examine the contents. The shelves were mostly bare. He would need some supplies. Searching for his phone on the sandy, mottled granite counter to start a to-do list, he couldn't find it. *Where did I leave the damn thing?*

Opposite the front door, was Jasper's bedroom. He slept on a cream-colored Ludlow leather double bed placed in the center of the small square room. The bed was flanked by small square, metal, and glass bedside tables. On them were two matching chrome lamps. The apartment had ivory tile flooring throughout, with no carpets. He had all the essentials he needed to serve his minimalistic needs. When he studied his apartment from a critical perspective, he decided he could do with a few basics to make Samson comfortable. So far, Jasper had never entertained visitors from out of town. Discovering his phone on the nightstand, he started a shopping list. He needed sheets for the pull-out couch and another set of towels. Saturday would have to be a shopping day before Samson's arrival the following Thursday.

Impatient to remedy the apartment's shortcomings, Jasper drove to Barcelona's largest department store, *El Corte Ingles,* the next day. He bought a set of ivory cotton sheets, two sets of plush sky-blue towels and a set of textured white dishes for four. He decided to save his paper plate collection for future picnics. He also bought two pairs of fleece-lined house shoes on sale, for Samson and himself. On his way out, he picked up a nice shirt for work. Purchases in hand, he left the store and went to meet Enrique for a late dinner, stowing everything in the trunk of his leased car.

On Saturday, Jasper went back to the department store and bought a comfortable milk-chocolate brown leather recliner. He arranged for a Wednesday morning delivery, knowing his housekeeper would be there to receive it. He was immensely pleased with his luxurious purchase. Lastly, he made a copy of his keys for Samson.

The rest of the weekend, Jasper stocked his liquor cabinet and his refrigerator with snacks. He planned to invite Enrique and a few friends over for *tappas* and drinks to meet his brother, but mostly, he wanted to spend quality time with Samson to catch up on recent events. They had a lot to discuss.

Chapter LXII

Free Speech and Wicked Men

Cara sipped her morning tea in front of her laptop and shook her head at the screen. She was reading about the brutal attack on a Copenhagen Cafe that had hosted a free speech event. Under the heading, "Art, blasphemy, and the Freedom of Expression," it had been the target of an Islamic extremist. Disgusted, Cara closed the article and focused on her children's emails. Samson was on his way to visit Jasper in Barcelona and Summer was to resume shooting her film after a string of annoying setbacks. Film making was no picnic. So many stars had to align, literally and figuratively, for the process to be successful.

Francois sent her emails with updates on his gallery shows on a regular basis. He also sent her feedback generated from her three pieces now in his possession. There was interest, he promised. He sent her a separate, more personal email telling her what he would like to do to her. Cara blushed. She looked forward to hearing his thoughts on everything, especially the latter. She missed him. It seemed his New York artists' show was successful, and he hoped to sell most of the pieces. He ended with his usual "When are you coming?"

When Cara got to Samson and Jasper's replies regarding Suzanna Svelte and Alphonse, she paused. No doubt the pottery in the Berlin pictures looked like what she had seen at auction. Were her boys suggesting a connection to the Paris murder? Her skin crawled at the thought. She reached for her phone and called Jasper, then Samson. Both calls went to voicemail. Frustrated, she tried Summer.

Chapter LXIII

Trouble in Paradise

Carlos picked up the phone on first ring. Fernando's raspy voice attacked his ear without a greeting.

"Carlos, the boys at the dock alerted us about a police search this morning. Jose had everything under control. He sent the goods to you. We took them off the ship before the inspectors were due to arrive."

Carlos sat very still and listened, his mind racing. "On what premise did they do a search?"

"They said it was a random customs check to make sure all companies are reporting imports accurately."

"I'm not buying that. Who else got checked?"

"Our two warehouse neighbors and one other company in Warehouse 8."

"I don't like it, Fernando. Did our guy hear of any suspicions?"

"No, he just heard about the upcoming search the night before. Thank God Jose spent the night on the ship, moving goods."

"We got lucky this time. Give the guy a bonus."

"Trust me, I will."

"Fernando, I'm telling you, we better be extra careful. This stinks. I say we take a pause."

"I think you're a little too jumpy. We're fine. We came up smelling like a rose."

"If you say so. You're the boss. We may not be that lucky next time and trust me, there will be a next time. Keep me posted if anything, and I mean anything, unusual happens. It takes time to move funds from several accounts. And Fernando, don't keep any of the 'borrowed' goods. Send them home if you don't sell them to the Russians."

"Of course. Take it easy. It's all good."

Carlos, rolling his eyes, hung up and opened his laptop. He pulled up his financial spreadsheet and stared at it long and hard. He shifted a few funds around and studied it again. Once this next shipment arrived, he would squirrel some of the profits in case they needed to halt operations temporarily. He couldn't fathom why Fernando didn't feel worried. Paying people off was difficult business, especially here. In Mexico it was standard operating procedure. He would have to start making some contingency arrangements.

Chapter LXIV

Turning up like a bad Penny

On Tuesday morning Jasper was having breakfast and reading the daily news online at his desk. A short snippet about a second search on the *Corazon de Leones* caught his attention. After checking the international ship registry, *Maritime-Connector.com,* he confirmed the ship was indeed F&S property. It appeared that some of the stolen pottery from the Metropolitan Museum in New York had made an appearance in Barcelona via the ship. The pottery depicted looked eerily like some of the pieces he had seen on his mother's computer, but he wasn't sure. Jasper attached the article to an email and sent it to his mother with a brief translation. While his mom couldn't read Spanish, he knew she would be interested and resourceful enough to fill in the blanks. She would study the pottery in the picture and surely have an opinion.

Jasper was aware of her interaction with Sotheby's regarding the pottery she had seen in New York and Paris. Cara had a habit of copying all her children when she sent out contentious emails. Jasper was certain there was a connection here. How exactly the puzzle pieces all fit together still eluded him, but he could easily venture a guess or two and his thoughts weren't pretty.

Chapter LXV

Three Heads Are Better Than Two

Inspektor Kralle's phone rang. His spacious corner office was comfortable and impressive for his line of work, but given his workload, he rarely got to enjoy it. He spent most of his time in the field or in meetings elsewhere. Today, he was sipping coffee before a morning update in the conference room. "Kralle, here," he barked.

"*Bonjour*, Inspector Arnaud *ici*. How are you?"

"Swamped, as usual. Working on getting my blood pressure under control. My doctor has me drinking decaf and it's killing me in slow motion. I feel like either napping after lunch every day or killing my deputies, when what I really need is a lift. You?"

Arnaud laughed. *No pleasantries with this guy.* "That stinks. Sorry to hear it. I'm fine, thanks. I have some news regarding the Svelte case. We've had a couple more deaths from the same drug concoction. A model from a local Parisian agency and a young man, unrelated to the girl. Same stuff. We traced the goods, without a doubt, to Southern France. Marseille. No surprise there. We believe it was brought here on a ship that stops in Barcelona regularly. It comes from Mexico. I have reached out to

Inspector Abello in Barcelona. He confirmed the ship and recently searched it but found nothing. He did, however, find some antique stolen pottery, possibly from the Metropolitan Museum of Art in New York. I had my people check the stolen art register. I'll send you the pictures. I think there is a connection."

"What's the name of the ship?" Kralle asked.

"*Corazon de Leones*. It originates in Tampico, Mexico. They transport pottery made in Tampico, and a few other items, like fabrics. Sometimes they stop in New York along the way. The pottery company is affiliated with F&S Enterprises here in Barcelona. Their warehouse and European distribution center is at the harbor, but again, the warehouse is shared by three companies. Abello will keep us in the loop. He'll copy you."

"Very good. I'm beginning to see the big picture here. Thank you."

"Alphonse Cretin worked for them before he died, if you remember."

"Yes, I do."

"Also, a dock worker in Barcelona was caught handling a shipment of drugs, but he refused to talk. He swore he knew nothing about the shipment's contents; we couldn't link him to the cartel. Before Abello's people could interrogate him further, he was found dead. Bullet to the head in the dock's mens room. Shame."

"Front or side? Murder or suicide?"

"Murder. The perpetrator escaped through the bathroom window at dusk. Nothing on camera. Abello's men are checking out the pottery company because it's an unusually lucrative business as far as we can see. It's also linked to two restaurants, one in Barcelona and one in Paris. They must be laundering there. The other two companies are substantially smaller."

"Nice operation. I'm surprised they're sharing the port in Marseille without difficulty if you know what I mean. I'll look for your information. Thanks for the call."

Kralle hung up the phone and sat back contemplating the many connections. Clearly, there was a link here. The puzzle pieces were coming together at a snail's pace, but the important thing was that they were coming together at all.

Chapter LXVI

Reality Check, Please!

Samson arrived in Barcelona. He took a taxi to Jasper's apartment with instructions to pick up a set of keys left with Clemente, the superintendent of Jasper's apartment building. Jasper would be home around dinner time and treat him to a special welcome dinner, the text promised. Samson chatted briefly with Clemente, who was exceedingly curious, and let himself into Jasper's apartment. He immediately found his house shoes, towels, and a welcome note with an invitation to help himself to a beer. The fridge was well stocked, Samson noted. He looked around the light, clean, uncluttered apartment and chuckled to himself. Jasper had always been the most organized and uncomplicated member of the family. In fact, Jasper hated clutter with a passion. His bare, minimalistic apartment reflected his personality perfectly. Jasper liked things simple and streamlined. Samson took a quick shower, slipped into his new house shoes, clean boxers, a white t shirt and popped open a beer. He settled into the inviting recliner, his smart phone within reach, to wait for Jasper.

Jasper arrived home at 6pm, looking excited, but worn.

"Hey, Bro. Tough day?" Samson swung out of the recliner and gave his brother a bear hug.

"Not more than usual. There's weird stuff going on at the office. We'll talk over dinner. How are ya?"

"Good. Summer says hello. She wished she could have come too. Where are we going tonight?"

"I wanted to stay local. I figured you would be tired. There's a good place I hang out at a few streets away. Let me just shower and clean up, ok?"

"Sure. I'll get dressed. My rumbling stomach can wait a little longer."

"It'll be worth the wait, I promise."

A short while later, Jasper took Samson to his favorite local tavern for *paella* and *sangria*. They ordered a large pitcher from Juan Carlos, the restaurant owner and chatted with him about nothing in particular. Jasper asked Samson about the rest of his Berlin trip. After a few glasses of *sangria*, Jasper brought up F&S Enterprises. He pulled out his tablet.

"What do you think about the articles I sent?" he asked Samson.

"I think there is definitely something more going on here," Samson answered. "It appears that Flores is not only trading in Mexican ceramics and restaurant food. Has Adriano said anything to you regarding Flores?"

"No, not really," Jasper answered. "Adriano has been out of the office a lot lately. I haven't spoken to him directly. We've communicated by email. He even cancelled a few Monday meetings which is not the norm. What do you think Flores is trading in, stolen ceramics?"

"Worse. Sounds like it could be drugs, Bro. What else comes out of Mexico that generates big bucks? Machinery and drugs and we know it's not the first.

"Really? You think?"

"Yup, it sure looks that way. Certainly, wouldn't shock me. And the money is being laundered through the two restaurants and various corporations. The stolen ceramics are just the tip of the iceberg, I think."

"You should see how the Mexicans in his restaurant hop for him. They couldn't bend over fast or far enough. But … … drugs? Don't drug lords usually stay in Mexico?"

"Not any more it seems. This particular drug lord appears to have a legitimate business that lends itself to other locations. He must have a clever accountant."

"His accountant is Carlos Oritz. He runs the Paris office and restaurant. I copy him on all transactions."

"Carlos Ortiz? Are you sure? That's Helena's boyfriend's name. We met him New Year's Eve, remember?

"You're joking! The asocial guy? You think it's the same person? That is a common name." Jasper looked ghostly.

"Yes, I do. Mom has pictures of the Flores guys. We can double check with her."

"Holy Shit. It's a small world."

Jasper showed Samson the article about the *Corazon de Leones* raid he sent Cara and watched Samson digest this new information.

Samson sat back and contemplated. "I think the Spanish police is on to them. You better watch your back, Jasper. Don't do anything amiss," he advised his brother. "Remember, you're the outsider here, working on a guest visa in this country. I would hate to see you get blamed for something you didn't do. Has Adriano mentioned anything, anything at all?"

"Not a peep and I don't want to address my suspicions with him. He's not a stupid man. If anything is going on, he's choosing to ignore it. Maybe to keep Fernando's money flowing through our bank?"

"That or maybe he's protecting you."

Samson could see the wheels in Jasper's head turning. Jasper worked in a protected world at the bank; in fact, he lived in a safe bubble, until now. The fact that Jasper had a hard time grasping the signs of a drug cartel at work did not surprise Samson. They finished the pitcher of *sangria* and walked home in a happy, but guarded state, reminiscing about their Paris and Berlin experiences.

That night the restaurant called Jasper to tell him they found his tangerine tablet on the table.

"Thank you! I haven't even missed it yet. I'll come by in the morning to get it." That tablet sure was slippery. *Geez, I really need to be more careful. Especially now.*

Chapter LXVII

Risky Business

Carlos was facing Jose and Fernando over a cluttered desk in the Barcelona office for a session of troubleshooting. Fernando's face was serious.

"How did this happen? I thought we took care of everyone? Things were working so smoothly. Now we'll have to watch our backs every time we make a move. Put a hold on all distribution until the dust settles. You too Carlos, understand?"

"Si, Fernando", Carlos nodded. "We had our warning. We shouldn't be too surprised."

Fernando grimaced and ignored him. "Jose, do we have a rat? Or did our guy just not know about the second search?"

"He didn't know, Fernando. I had to take care of him anyway to make sure he stays in our pocket. Didn't want to chance it."

"Right. Find someone new quickly, regardless of the cost, but for heavens sake, make sure we can trust him. We need a customs inspector on our side, or we're cooked."

"I'll try to find someone." Jose replied gruffly. "It's not as easy as you may think. Not like Mexico."

Fernando gestured as if he knew the difficulty. Carlos decided to stay silent. There was no winning here.

"Now that that is settled, let's have something to eat. We'll talk finances later, Carlos."

They left the office and sat down for a late lunch in the restaurant.

Carlos knew how much Fernando hated mistakes. He had no qualms about erasing mistakes, swiftly, whatever it took. The man was ruthless and Jose was dangerously crazy. Carlos worried this lethal combination would be their undoing and ruin their international operations. Europe was not Mexico and the rules were different. Why hadn't Fernando listened to him the first time? Nothing got the police's attention more than unexplained murder coupled with drugs or theft. *How could they be so dense?*

Before returning to Paris, Carlos needed to get through dinner. He spent the afternoon going over the financial records. He had come to Barcelona prepared, but it never hurt to take a second look. Over dinner, Fernando, Jose, and he had their final meeting to discuss money. Fernando, a little uneasy, decided to disperse funds. "Some money needs to leave the country. Just in case. What do you suggest, Carlos?"

"That's fine, Fernando. I've been working on that already. We opened a resident account in Monaco. I also transferred funds to our corporation and of course the usual cash to Tampico," Carlos responded.

"We have a good amount of money here in Europe to keep things running smoothly. Investing in an income generating business and in real estate was a smart move. It gives us legitimate assets, but I want to keep the excess in Monaco for now. The restaurant is more than paying for itself. We don't need that much money here. The Paris restaurant is doing ok too, right?"

"Yes. We are ahead by an inch. Just give me a figure to transfer. What do you have in mind? I can do whatever you want."

"Oh, I don't know. Figure it out and tell me what numbers you think make sense. Make sure you have enough for operating costs in Paris and transfer the excess. I trust you."

"Ok, Fernando. I'll be on it and text you."

As Carlos sat listening to Fernando orate, his mind wandered to Helena. He was looking forward to getting back to Paris. Saturday nights were special to them; they always spent them together. They went to concerts, movies, special dinners and on a rare occasion, they met her friends. It surprised and worried him how much he loved spending his free time with her. He no longer liked being away for extended periods and he generally tried to schedule his trips during the week when they were both busy with work. Fernando didn't always make this easy. For some inexplicable reason he purposely scheduled meetings for Fridays so Carlos could spend the weekends in Barcelona. Carlos cringed at the thought.

"You don't want to stay till Sunday, Carlos? I have a few girls I can line up for tomorrow night."

"Tempting as it is, I have concert tickets for Saturday night and I usually spend Sunday mornings working on the books. I want to do all our transactions first thing Monday morning. That is crucial, especially given the turn of events. Thanks, Fernando, but if it is all the same to you, I am going to leave later tonight."

"Hmmm. I suppose. Suit yourself."

Carlos could tell Fernando wasn't pleased, but he couldn't care less. He did his job well and he knew he was indispensable now. Helena was the bright spot in his world and deserved his full attention. Luckily Fernando didn't push him again after dinner and drinks. Carlos had zero interest in spending another night in Fernando's and Jose's company. After the meeting, he grabbed his packed overnight bag and headed to the airport for a late flight out. A chartered private plane was waiting. So was Helena in a skimpy nightgown.

Chapter LXVIII

Curse of Clemente— Minding Everyone's Business

Friday morning, Samson heard Jasper shower and tip toe around the apartment before leaving for work. Samson was still so tired, he rolled over and fell back asleep as the door clicked shut. Around 10am he sprang into action after receiving a text from Jasper with directions to his office and an invitation to lunch. Samson was curious to meet his brother's coworkers and glimpse into Jasper's day to day world.

Showered and dressed, he grabbed a water bottle from the fridge. Studying the tourist city map Jasper left on the counter, he spied the street Jasper's office was on marked with a red X. Heading out the door, he rechecked his cell phone for Jasper's address. He decided to head to the general area first as he was early and do a little sight-seeing in the Barcelona financial district.

As Samson reached for the door handle to exit Jasper's apartment building, Clemente stuck his head out of the ground floor apartment and gave Samson a memorable, missing teeth smile. Samson thought of his many years of pumpkin carving as a child. Within seconds Clemente engaged Samson in conversation, offering helpful tips on what to see in Barcelona. Samson answered a few overly direct questions politely and edged his way to the door. Clemente, the human burr, walked him out, continuing his line of questioning in broken English.

"Clemente, which way is the bus stop. I don't want to be late."

Clemente pointed in the general direction, but not without checking what Samson's evening plans were. Samson shrugged and waved goodbye. "It will be Jasper's surprise. *Adios,* Clemente."

Clemente waved as he reached for a broom and began sweeping around the front door, swirling dust into every direction. Samson's Spanish was non-existent, and Clemente's English was rudimentary. This small fact aided Samson's timely escape. Jasper was never that lucky.

Maria, the receptionist in Jasper's office was also intrigued by Samson. Her beautiful dark eyes shifted from his longish blond hair down to his tight abs and back up again. It appeared she liked what she saw because her red lips curled up at the corners.

"YOU are Jasper's brother?" she asked somewhat incredulously, as she peered straight into Samson's blue eyes, barely blinking.

"*Si,*" Samson responded and winked, recognizing the suspicion registered on her face.

"How long are you staying?" Maria asked, before moving to pick up the intercom phone.

"Just for a long weekend." Samson answered dutifully.

"Too bad! Not enough time to really enjoy Barcelona." Maria countered, dark lashes fluttering around her delicious chocolate eyes. She dialed Jasper's extension in slow motion not moving her gaze off Samson.

Jasper came to fetch Samson in the reception area. "I see you've met Maria" he said with a slight smirk.

"Yes," Maria volunteered, smiling and still staring at Samson. "Why hasn't your brother ever visited before?"

Jasper shrugged. "Perhaps now he will, Maria,"

Samson knew his brother was playing with her. Samson followed Jasper into one of the hallways off the reception area. He snickered at Jasper's reaction to Maria feeling like he was back in high school. The ladies definitely responded to Samson, and it had always annoyed Jasper back then. "What do they see that I don't," Jasper used to tease him.

Jasper beamed at his brother, "You realize, Maria will give me the third degree when you leave. She'll not be able to resist questioning me from here to infinity."

"Deal with it. Spin tales…. Hey, maybe set her up with Clemente."

"Funny, Samson. I guess he caught you this morning then, did he? Uncanny, that guy. I try to dodge him every morning, unsuccessfully I might add. He's at the door, like clockwork. Here, let me introduce you to some of my co workers, but try not to dazzle them too much. We still have work to do."

"Funny. I see you haven't lost your sense of humor."

They briefly walked around a couple offices and said hello, exchanging small talk with the inhabitants. Everyone seemed to genuinely like Jasper, Samson noticed with affection. When they got to Adriano's office, Jasper knocked delicately and poked his head through the crack. Adriano was on the phone, but waved them in, eyeing Samson with interest. When he finished his call, he greeted Samson warmly.

"Welcome to Barcelona. I'm glad to finally meet someone from Jasper's family".

"Thank you," Samson responded, studying Adriano. "I've heard so many nice things about you. Please tell me you'll be joining us for lunch?"

"Thank you. So sorry, I can't today," Adriano replied shaking his head. "I need to leave the office for a lunch meeting shortly. Enjoy yourselves and don't rush back, Jasper." Adriano loosened his collar.

"Thanks, Adriano."

Adriano was dressed impeccably, and he was genuinely warm, Samson noted, but he perceived an underlying stress in Adriano's aura. As a working journalist, Samson was attuned to people's comfort levels, and he sensed that all was not well in Adriano's world. The men said their goodbyes and Jasper and Samson left. Over lunch, Samson revealed his opinion of Adriano.

"He seems very tense Jasper. Is he always like that?" he asked.

"No, not really. Only lately, I guess. He seemed particularly stressed these last few days. I've barely seen him. His office door is always closed which wasn't the case when I started working here. It was wide open back then."

"Hmm. Do you know who he's having lunch with?"

"No."

"Does Maria know his schedule?"

"No, usually I do, but he hasn't been keeping me in the loop lately."

"Hmmm. So what are our Friday night plans, pray tell. Clemente wanted to know, but I had to disappoint him."

Jasper laughed. "Typical. His nose is always in my business. I think he's waiting for an invitation that I assure you, will never be forthcoming. I thought we could have dinner at one of my favorite restaurants by the water tonight. My buddy, Enrique, will join us. We can hang out at the apartment after dinner, with a few more friends I invited in your honor."

"Sounds good. I'm flattered. But when do I meet your girlfriends?"

"Next trip, wise ass."

"Ok then. What should I do for the afternoon?" inquired Samson.

Jasper proceeded to rattle off the usual touristy venues for Samson, giving him a brief synopsis of each. Samson decided he had to see the Sagrada Familia Cathedral.

"Can we check out Fernando's restaurant tonight or is it out of the way?"

"I can drive you past it sometime this weekend, if you're curious. Not tonight though." Jasper answered.

"Ok. Text me if you want me to pick something up for later."

"Thanks, will do."

Samson arrived back at Jasper's apartment around 4:30pm. He managed to quietly slip into the building without arousing Clemente's ferocious appetite for small talk. Clemente's door was dangerously ajar, but he didn't appear. Samson skipped waiting for the elevator and lunged up the three flights, two steps at a time, congratulating himself on bypassing an encounter. Twice was enough. Three times would be overkill.

Key prepared, he quietly let himself into Jasper's apartment, closing the door in slow motion, barely clicking the lock. He took a water bottle from the fridge, gulped it down and then shed his clothes, as he headed for the shower. He turned on the radio and sang along at the top of his lungs. After his blitz shower, Samson discovered Jasper's incoming texts.

"If Adriano doesn't come back, I'm outta here at 4:45pm. Slow Friday."

"Great. I'm ready."

"As expected, Maria gave me the third degree after lunch."

"Hope you told her a good tall tale."

"Not tall enough. She wants a date." He added a laughing emoji.

Apparently, her inquisitive nature would not rest until she had all the facts about Samson. The final text read, *Get ready for a fun night, Bro.*

Chapter LXIX

Birthdays, Gypsies and
Sex Lives, Oh My!

Summer, Hope and Ted wrapped up their shoot at the Tuilleries Gardens. The crew was packing up and Summer and Hope were leaving for the apartment to look at the day's footage. They started shooting at 5:30am and were exhausted but pleased with the progress. Helena and Alain took direction well. Helena, especially, was very eager to please, which made filming so much easier. She came to the set with zest, always prepared, knowing her lines. When necessary, she redid her scenes with unequaled patience, never complaining. At 3:30pm they called it a day. Afternoon light changed the dynamic and cast and crew inevitably started to wilt.

It had been a productive week. Ted and the crew packed props to take back to the theater, where Ted stored it in a room with a secure lock. Basic equipment stayed on the truck. Summer and Hope arrived at the apartment and collapsed on the living room sofa.

"Good day, today. I'm toast though."

"Yeah, me too. Let's look at the footage later, ok?"

"Saturday morning?"

"Perfect."

"Mimi's birthday dinner tomorrow night should be fun. It'll be nice to see everyone and not have to think about work for an evening."

"Yeah. Did Ted get her a gift for us?"

"Yeah, I'm pretty sure he did. I think I'm going to take a power nap now. See you in a while." Hope dragged herself off the couch and ambled to her room. Summer's phone rang and she could barely move to look at the screen.

"Hi, honey, how was your day?"

"Good, but really tiring, Mom."

"Yeah, well it's the end of the week. That's to be expected. Do you have a minute to talk?"

"Sure, what's up?"

Her mother filled her in on the pottery developments and her thoughts on the articles Jasper sent her. Summer perked up. "How strange, Mom. Do you think it's the stolen pottery from the Met, you told me about?"

"Not sure, but it sure looks that way. I sent the articles and some of my pictures to my contact at Sotheby's. They agreed to investigate. We'll see where it leads. So, what are you doing this weekend?"

"You mean besides working? It's Mimi's birthday and we're taking her out for a special dinner tomorrow night. Tonight, Hope and I are going to catch up on sleep for at least ten hours. We'll go over the footage tomorrow morning."

"I understand. Say 'Hi' to everyone."

"Will do."

Saturday night everyone converged on a little restaurant on the Place de Tertre at Montmartre. The Malher group, including Jean Michel, Pascal, Pierre, Claude, and two of Mimi's closest friends, all arrived bearing gifts. Mimi, loved by all, was turning 28. Ted's innovative, collective gift was hiring a fortune teller to do an in depth reading to boost Mimi's romantic life. That promised to generate laughs and break the ice between new and old friends.

The lady arrived right after the first round of drinks was consumed. Dressed in a violet wrap dress and a scarlet, fringed wool scarf, she looked convincingly eccentric. To complete her statement outfit, she wore black lace stockings with black lace-up boots and a funky black wool visor cap pulled low over her charcoal-rimmed eyes and platinum blonde hair. The woman straddled a chair backwards, facing a shrinking birthday girl and balanced Mimi's arm on the ledge. Opening Mimi's palm, she started her magic. After a few intrusive questions, she went into a woven tale of love and deceit, possibly feeding on Mimi's reactions.

Her departure, after a half hour of pure adult, X-rated fun, started an ongoing and somewhat embarrassing debate about Mimi's sex life. A little more wine and a thorough review of the event left the table second guessing the validity of fortune telling. This spilled into a review of the occult in general and every thought was analyzed in detail, but not without plenty of laughter. It was a birthday dinner Mimi would not forget anytime soon.

After dinner, Helena and Carlos joined the group for dessert and drinks. Summer studied Helena's boyfriend with renewed interest. He had a somewhat fascinating tough, bad boy vibe and she wondered if it was real. He stayed unusually mum in the face of festivities and laughter, barely joining the conversation. Summer wondered why he felt so uncomfortable with them, yet so at ease with Helena. She did her best to include him, for Helena's sake. Did he indeed have something to hide? Her earlier conversation with her mom kept swirling through her head as she squinted at Carlos across the table. He wasn't uncomfortable; he just had no interest in making friends. *Why? What's his story?*

Chapter LXX

No News is Good News

Saturday morning Cara awoke from a terrifying dream. Mexican men were shadowing her family's dinner in a Paris restaurant, threatening them with bodily harm by sending cutthroat hand signals across the room. Terrified, Cara and her children left the table, single file, escaping through the restaurant kitchen. The dimly lit back-alley outside the restaurant proved to be a dead-end with a locked gate on one side and the Mexican men closing in on the other. She screamed and franticly rattled the gate as the twins argued and Jasper looked through the dumpster for a possible weapon. Just when he found a discarded broom handle, she woke up, sweating and gasping for air. It was the third cycle of this nightmare.

Momentarily disoriented, she reached for her smart phone to check her emails for any notes from her brood. She was restless and worried. Was this a sign? There were no messages from Samson or Summer, but there was a brief email from Jasper. Samson had arrived in Barcelona, and they were having a good time. Jasper just left lunch with Samson, and he was now bored in the office on a slow Friday afternoon. He sent her a selfie of Samson and himself at the restaurant.

Did she get his articles, he wondered and what were her thoughts? Also, could she send the pictures of the Flores men. Jasper and he were curious to see them. She took a deep breath and replied to his email, attaching her photos.

Happy you two are having fun. I've forwarded your articles with pottery pictures to Sotheby's. In my opinion the pottery looks like the pieces that were stolen, but you can never say for sure without examining the pieces close up. Reading between the lines, I would strongly urge you to watch your step with that client. .Do everything by the book and cover your butt by copying Adriano on every interaction. I'm sure you're already doing this as I know how meticulously you work. There could be more going on with that company than we think, if you know what I mean. Any particular reason you need the pictures?

The next email she opened was from Francois. It was brief, but it warmed her heart. He finished with, "When are you coming?" She sighed and closed her eyes. She longed to be in Europe near Francois and her children, but work was work and she couldn't afford to run off on a whim.

Determined to learn more about F&S Enterprises, she once again googled the company. Jasper was right. This sure was a fast-growing corporation. Adding a property and residence in Monaco was a smart move and a good place to park discretionary funds if you had them. Monaco residency required a healthy bank account and a list of conditions to be fulfilled, but the principality accepted anyone who could meet the criteria.

After making her tea, she looked at the equally grim world news. One of the New Delhi rapists unleashed his misplaced wisdom. He legitimately felt, if the victimized woman hadn't fought back and let herself be gang raped, she wouldn't have been killed. After all, why was a woman out at the movies at 9pm with a man she wasn't married to? She asked for it, was his explanation. Cara could feel her blood curdle. The men had raped the woman and then rammed a rod into her vagina, causing massive internal injuries, killing her. The thought process of some men in other parts of the world eluded her. Why were women always a target? Not a violent person by any means, Cara could visualize using the rod in a few choice places on the guy's body. She quickly erased that fleeting thought from her mind. You cannot fight violence with more violence; it only escalates. *Think Gandhi,* she half muttered to herself. Karma would hopefully come full circle.

In the meantime, she was temporarily appeased to know that her children were happy and safe… for now. However, the three Mexicans were on her radar, and she was determined not to drop her due diligence. She finished her tea and shuffled off to shower and start her day.

Chapter LXXI

Red Herring and Sangria do not Mix Well

Saturday morning Samson awoke to his phone's persistent ringtone. His sister was calling to see how his weekend was progressing. Summer filled him in on her film progress, then peppered him with questions.

"What have you done so far? What's Adriano like? And Enrique? How is Jasper's apartment? Any girls I should know about? What's going on with Jasper's client? Anything new we should be concerned about?

Samson answered all her questions patiently, except the last one, but Summer pressed on. She was wise to his tactics.

"Are you worried for Jasper? Mom seems to think that the Flores clan is smuggling stolen goods or worse."

"I think he's fine for now and, yes, mom may very well be right. I thought the same. Too much cash being made too quickly according to Jasper. His voice turned to a whisper. "Let's have dinner when I get back. I don't want to upset Jasper now. He may hear me."

Still feeling a little groggy from the *sangria* and the late night with the guys, Samson managed to satisfy Summer's curiosity on the more mundane questions. Years of practice.

"Alright then. I guess my timing may not be perfect. Call me when you can talk. I have a long day of reviewing film footage ahead. See you back in Paris. Dinner this week, ok?" she pushed.

"Absolutely," Samson replied. "When I'm fully sober and back in town, I'll call you. Have fun tonight."

Summer laughed as she hung up. "Bye, you lush."

Samson slowly swung his legs off the couch and sunk his feet into the wonderful fleece slippers. He wondered if Jasper had meant for him to take them home. They felt heavenly and he had no intention of leaving them behind.

Shuffling past Jasper's bed to the bathroom, he took a shower. Once refreshed and wrapped in a plush towel, Samson looked out the bathroom window. The sun felt warm on his face. The weather in Barcelona was definitely nicer than Paris. Today promised to be in the high 60's to low 70's according to the weather app. Warmer than usual. Samson was ready for action. He opened the bathroom door and saw Jasper stir.

"Jasper, you up?" he asked.

"I will be in a minute," said the muffled voice from inside the pillow. "Why did you let me have that last *sangria*?"

"I don't think that final one made the difference. You were already over the hill. Shall I get you a glass of ice water?"

"Yes, and a new head too."

"Tour of the city today?"

"Yeah, with a pair of really dark shades. I made dinner plans with some of my friends in *Placa de Sol*. You'll like that. We can check out some of the clubs at *Las Ramblas* too, but no drinks for me tonight. Only water." It was an ambitious plan considering the night before.

"Duly noted. Coffee and some food will change your mindset. Get moving."

On Sunday morning Samson awoke thankful he had one more day in Barcelona. He needed a day of party recovery. Samson had booked his return flight for Monday afternoon. His first-time visiting Jasper, he didn't want to rush in and out in two action-filled days. He was lucky to get the long weekend including Friday and Monday. This morning, he was particularly glad he'd made the decision to use two vacation days, despite Natalie's protests.

When Jasper woke up, they lounged in the apartment over coffee and shrimp, tomato and *chorizo* omelettes, using Jasper's snow-white dishes. After a quick clean-up, they headed out to the Picasso Museum. It was free on Sundays.

On their way to an early dinner, Jasper drove past Fernando's restaurant. He pulled up in front and urged Samson to pop his head inside. It was relatively quiet. Jasper didn't want to run into Fernando, so he waited in the car. The dinner crowd had not yet arrived, and the late lunch crowd had just left. Tables were being cleaned and set up. Samson walked through the restaurant out to the patio. When a pretty young woman spotted him and approached, he took a restaurant card and waved. Having seen enough, he sprinted for the door before she could reach him. Back in the car, he turned to Jasper.

"I really like the layout, with the inside/outside bars. It has a nice feel to it. Impressive venue. Is the food any good?"

"Yes, it is, but we're not eating here. Did you see anyone Mexican?"

"No. I only saw the hostess and I left before she got to me."

"Good."

They had an early dinner at Zinc Bar in Villa Emilia. A jazz band created a mellow atmosphere and provided a perfect ending for an action-packed weekend. To the waitress's surprise, they both drank bottled water with their meal.

"Thanks, for a great weekend, Bro. Life in Barcelona is pretty good. The only problem I see is your nefarious client."

"Yeah, unfortunately I'm stuck with him. Adriano is not letting this red herring go."

Chapter LXXII

The Sounds of Silence and the Perils of Spanish Coffee

Monday morning Jasper was up early for work and out the door before Samson could roll over and open an eye. His plan was to meet Samson at the office for lunch. From there, Samson would head to the airport. They had managed to dodge Clemente most of the weekend, but this morning Clemente was ready and waiting, broom in hand. When Jasper exited the elevator, Clemente stopped sweeping the lobby and leaned in on his broom, ready to chat. It appeared he had been waiting for Jasper. "Darn" Jasper whispered, through gritted teeth.

"Good party, Friday night. I heard your friends talking when they left at 3am." Clemente offered his irregular smile.

"Good morning, Clemente. Yes, I invited my friends over to meet my brother," Jasper answered edging toward the door. "We had *tappas* and a little too much *sangria*. You know how that goes. I hope we weren't too loud."

"No, no complaints from the neighbors. I met your brother. Handsome man. Same father? You don't look like brothers." Clemente smiled deviously, showing his collection of jagged teeth.

"Yes, Clemente. Same father, same mother. Samson and Summer look more like my mother. Me … like my father." Jasper put down his backpack and checked the mailbox. He slid the mail into his briefcase and closed it.

"How long is your brother staying?"

"Unfortunately, he's leaving today. Got to run. Work. Don't want to be late. Have a good day."

Before Clemente could answer, Jasper opened the door energetically and stepped out, letting the door swing shut with a vibrating bang. Rolling his eyes, he wondered if Samson could get by the Clemente fly trap unscathed today. He walked to the bus stop whistling. As he waited, he sent Samson a text wagering a bet on whether he could bypass Clemente without being caught. If Samson could, lunch was on him. An early morning dare, he knew his sibling would take seriously. He chuckled to himself as he pressed send.

It had been a really great weekend with his brother. He was still feeling the buzz. For the second time this year, Jasper realized that he missed having his family around. It had been particularly nice to have Samson to himself. When Summer was around, Jasper generally took the backseat. Samson and Summer were inseparable, two peas in a pod. He loved Summer too, but she changed the equation.

When Jasper arrived at his office's hallway, he noticed Adriano quietly closing his door. Jasper was fine with that as he was happy to read the morning news and sip his *café latte* in peace before the workday began. Nonetheless, he wondered what pressures Adriano was feeling and didn't share. This was not the Adriano Jasper knew and came to Barcelona for. Adriano normally would chit chat with Jasper before work, asking about his weekend and life in general. His peculiar silence made Jasper realize that Adriano was preoccupied with his own pressures and world.

At 9am Jasper called Samson and woke him up. Then he started work. He didn't move from his desk for the first two hours. A few friendly co-workers stopped in and asked about his weekend with Samson. Adriano's door remained shut all morning.

Precisely at 11am, Jasper heard hushed voices and sensed commotion in the hallway. Peeking outside, he saw an unknown battalion of dark suits enter Adriano's office. Moments later, Adriano left with two men while two others remained in his office. Curious, Jasper walked down the hall to Maria's reception desk. For once, Maria was speechless. She shook her head and shrugged her shoulders.

"What's going on?" Jasper asked.

"Investigators are in Adriano's office. I don't know why," she whispered, visibly frustrated. Jasper knew Maria took pride in knowing what happened on her turf. By now, a small group was assembling around Maria's desk. No one knew anything. Moments later, the elevator door opened, and the big brass arrived from higher floors. The group around Maria quickly dispersed. The executives walked to Adriano's office and firmly shut the door. Jasper found it hard to concentrate for the next hour until Samson's arrival at noon. The door to Adriano's office remained shut as Jasper strode to the elevator and down to the building lobby to meet Samson.

"Investigators are in Adriano's office searching for I don't know what and Adriano left with some guys I don't know," he greeted Samson. "Something big is going on. I wonder if the investigation has something to do with the Flores account." Jasper whispered looking over his shoulder. "Let's get out of here before I get called back."

They hurriedly walked down the street to a small, neighborhood restaurant and picked an isolated table in the back, away from the windows. Stashing Samson's bag under the *banquette,* they sat down to talk in low voices.

"Tell me what happened," Samson inquired, eyebrows raised. His investigative spirit was undoubtedly kicking in. Jasper relayed the few events of the morning. He was completely in the dark himself, probably a good thing, he concluded.

"It probably does have something to do with the Flores accounts," Samson speculated.

"Maybe they're investigating F&S. I always wondered about those huge sums of money coming in and out of their accounts. I know Mom doesn't make that much money with pottery. That's for damn sure."

They both laughed at the thought.

"By the way, Bro, I made it out of the apartment without Clemente seeing me. Maybe he was in the john reading the newspaper. That strong Spanish coffee will do it every time. Hate to tell you, lunch is on you."

"Damn. You have no idea how lucky you are. When I exited the elevator this morning, he was waiting with his mock broom. I was hoping he'd take off on it," Jasper laughed. "Lunch is definitely on me. You know what he asked me this morning? If we shared the same parents."

Samson laughed out loud. "Now that's just a tad too personal. He's a piece of work, that guy."

When they finished their lunch, Samson left for the airport and Jasper reluctantly returned to the office. Before leaving, Samson made Jasper promise to come back to Paris in April.

"Mom is coming and you really should come too. Coordinate with her."

Jasper promised. "I'll make it work somehow. I really want to come."

The rest of the workday passed without incident. The walls seemed to echo whispers, then reabsorb them again. People were speculating, but the men in Adriano's office remained a mystery. Jasper found it hard to concentrate given the tension. He hid behind his desk, his door only slightly ajar. All afternoon, he anticipated a knock, but it never came.

When Jasper arrived home that night, Clemente was waiting.

"*Hola*, Jasper, you forgot your backpack by the mailbox this morning. I hope you didn't need your tablet."

"Damn, thank you, Clemente! I didn't even notice it was missing. I was so busy all day. How did you know my tablet was in it?"

"I checked, of course. Nice color, tangerine. Did your brother leave? I didn't see him."

"Yes, we had lunch and he left from there. He has to work tomorrow."

"Sorry, I didn't have a chance to say goodbye. I was working here all morning. I don't know how I missed him."

"Maybe you took a coffee break?" Jasper chuckled as he pressed the elevator button.

Chapter LXXIII

Family Secrets and Beyond

Samson landed in Paris and took a car service to his apartment. He checked his email, called Natalie first, then Summer. Uncharacteristically, Summer picked up on the first ring.

"Hi, Summer. I'm back. Are you free for dinner tomorrow night? I have a lot of confidential things to discuss with you." Samson knew how to get his sister's immediate attention. Secrets were bait like no other.

"I can meet you after work for an early dinner if you come to my neighborhood. I'm so tired lately. We have such early mornings." Summer replied. "How was your trip?"

"Really fun, but also concerning. I'll fill you in when I see you."

"You're scaring me, Samson. Is Jasper ok?"

"For now, he is, but the future looks shaky. Something happened today before I left."

"Oh no! What?"

"Let me fill you in when I see you. I have to unpack and catch up on some work."

"Way to dangle a carrot."

"Good…my intention exactly. This way I know you won't cancel."

They agreed to meet at the corner brasserie, alone.

"Text when you leave work."

Samson placed his suitcase near the washer and pulled out his laptop. Once again, he searched Fernando Flores, his company, the individual restaurants and this time he added Carlos Ortiz to the search. There was no new information on Flores as far as he could see and there was absolutely nothing on Carlos Ortiz in conjunction with F&S Enterprises. It was as if the man didn't exist. However, the name Carlos Ortiz was as common as John Doe. Despite having viewed his mom's pictures of Carlos, he understood why Jasper felt like he was executing transactions for a phantom.

Chapter LXXIV

Paris Sleuthing Times Two

Cara was wrapped in her lavender bathrobe and planted in front of her laptop, searching for new dirt on F&S Enterprises. She checked almost daily now. Collaborating with Samson, they wholeheartedly believed that something illicit was going on with Jasper's client. Not wanting to alarm Jasper, they did their checking privately and exchanged their findings regularly, what little there was. The searches of the *Corazon de Leones* confirmed that the police thought the same. Cara was also in contact with her friend at Sotheby's regarding the stolen property. So far, there were no major new developments, but the proper channels had been set in motion. *Give them time and they'll hang themselves.*

She spent Saturday in the studio finishing various projects. Samantha stopped by and brought lunch from Nero's, mozzarella, and prosciutto sandwiches, garnished with sundried tomato and arugula on a brioche. "I figured you haven't eaten yet."

"You figured right. I'm starved. This looks yummy," Cara remarked, rubbing her tummy. "I hate stopping when I'm on a roll. Especially to do something as mundane as fixing food. Thanks so much."

You're welcome. So have you booked your next trip to Paris yet?" Samantha asked.

"Not yet, but I think I'll do it soon. Francois keeps asking me and I must confess, I would like to have something more concrete to look forward to. I miss the children and ....Francois too," Cara replied wistfully.

"Ahhh, springtime in Paris. Romance. It sounds perfect." Samantha sighed. "How long will you go for this time?"

"I'm not sure. I need to check my bank account. Summer says I should come for a month, but that sounds a bit excessive. I was thinking three weeks if no major projects come up and I can swing it financially," answered Cara.

"Well not having to pay for a hotel makes a huge difference already. What dates are you thinking?" Samantha asked tentatively.

"Why? Are you going to miss me?" Cara teased. She knew Sam didn't want to be without her for a month.

"Yeah, I hate to admit it."

"I might go end of April, beginning May maybe? I need to get my taxes in before I go. Also, the apartment rental is up end of May so there's that. Knowing Summer as I do, the last few weeks of filming will be hectic. I would rather miss that part." Cara laughed. "Why don't you come along for a week? You're almost done with Nero right?" Cara saw Samantha's eyes light up.

"Yes, I am. I thought you'd never ask. Maybe I will. I just might be able to swing a week, unless something urgent pops up. I don't have too much going on right now. Like Audrey Hepburn said, 'Paris is always a good idea'."

"Smart woman. Let me confirm it with Summer. Perhaps you can stay at the apartment too. There's another bed in the guest room if you don't mind bunking with me. Let's look at a calendar together."

"I can handle bunking for a week. If it's too much trouble for Summer, perhaps Francois can recommend a boutique hotel nearby?"

"Sure. I'll let you know."

They began to plan their trip over lunch. Then the topic slid back to ceramics and Cara filled Sam in on her stolen pottery theories. She left out Jasper's worries.

"That's wild, Cara. Are we going sleuthing in Paris? Inspector Clouseau-style?"

"We just might. We can start by checking out the auctions again."

"All right then. I'm in. I love a good mystery. Would that make me Cato?"

Chapter LXXV

Never Get Between
a Mother Hen and Her Chicks

Cara was sipping tea and perusing world news. A disturbing new story popped up on her feed. A 19-year-old Saudi Arabian woman, who was gang raped and spoke to the press about it, was severely punished for her disclosure.

"Good Grief," Cara voiced out loud. "Do women have any rights? Are these people insane?" *Sometimes seeing the severity of other peoples' problems puts our own in perspective.* Things could always be worse and in other parts of the world, they often were, in many respects. The phone interrupted her outrage. It was Summer.

"Hi, honey."

"Mom, you better plan your return trip to Europe soon. I think some weird shit is going on in Jasper's office," she whispered.

"What are you talking about?" Cara replied as she scanned her email with one eye. Nothing new from Jasper, she noted.

"Jasper's boss is being investigated and Samson thinks it has something to do with the Flores account. On Monday investigators stormed Adriano's office and walked him out. No handcuffs but he didn't say a word to Jasper."

"What? What did Jasper say?"

"I've only spoken to Samson, but he thinks Jasper's client is doing something illegal. Smuggling and dealing in stolen pottery or worse."

"But he's guessing, right?" Cara listened intently.

"Yes. No charges have been filed yet, but he's worried about Jasper. Jasper does all their transactions. What if Adriano implicates him?"

Summer's information confirmed what Cara was thinking and discussing with Samson, but she decided to not fan the flames.

"Thanks for filling me in, Summer. That does sound ominous, but why don't we wait and see what develops. Since Jasper only does transactions the bank executives instruct him to do, he should theoretically be fine, but I see why you and Samson are concerned. Keep me informed. I will try to touch base with Jasper. How's the film coming along?"

Summer lamented about her grueling schedule and all the mishaps that sparked small delays.

"Well, it sounds like you're on the right track. Some things are bound to go wrong. That's the nature of the beast, but all things considered, it sounds like you have things under control. Now let's see if Jasper does too. I'll send him my thoughts by email, and I promise I'll try to give him a call today."

Cara also promised to finalize her travel plans. "Sam will be coming along for one week. Is there room for her in the apartment? I thought she could sleep on the daybed in my room maybe?"

"Yeah, one week is probably ok, but let me run it past Ted and Hope. I just want to make sure they don't have guests coming at the same time. Send me the exact dates."

"Ok, honey. I'll email you when I decide. Let me know what they say."

"Yup. Gotta go. Talk soon."

If Jasper couldn't come to Paris, she could always shoot to Barcelona for a few days to see what was going on, Cara thought as she silenced her phone. Maybe she should stay in Paris for a month after all. She knew that Jasper would feel more comfortable talking face to face and frankly, she would too. Jasper's feathers were rarely ruffled, but it appeared they were now. Again, she wondered if the Mexicans were above board with their lucrative businesses, but she seriously doubted it.

She left her desk to prepare some coffee. She needed a strong cup, today. As the coffee brewed, she shot Jasper a carefully crafted email. She wanted to instruct him to be careful without scaring the daylights out of him. Surely, Samson and Summer already managed to do that.

Chapter LXXVI

Mother Knows Best
or So She Thinks

On Tuesday night Jasper checked his email before bed. His mom had written him a long letter to clam up and say nothing, should he be questioned by any officials. He needed to only discuss the apparent, his business transactions for F&S as instructed by Adriano.

"Do not try to protect Adriano; just be honest about your work," Cara had written. "If you feel uncomfortable, ask for council. 'I don't know,' is a safe answer. So is, 'I don't recall,' if you are in doubt about anything and want to check it first. You are not obligated to remember anything under pressure."

That would not be a problem since he knew nothing anyway. Normally, he didn't appreciate Summer's chattiness, but this time he was glad his sister had alerted mom. Her concern was comforting. Having his family rallying around him felt good right now.

The next day Jasper spotted a group email from Cara informing them of her anticipated Paris itinerary. She reminded them that she was only a phone call away and that flights can be changed if needed. Jasper smiled when he read that. He knew that was aimed at him. He would try his best to get to Paris. Besides, April was the rainy season in Barcelona. He loved the opportunity to escape that.

The week passed without incident and neither the investigators nor Adriano returned to the office. Adriano emailed Jasper with instructions for various accounts but offered no reason for his absence. He shared that he would temporarily be working from a place outside the office, but that he was available by email. The general office chatter was that one of the bank's clients was being audited. Suspicions abounded. Jasper was content with Adriano's arrangement. He appreciated the distance until this, whatever it was, blew over.

Lately, Adriano's silent presence had been unnerving. Jasper's calls to Adriano went unanswered, but he did receive and exchange emails with his boss. Jasper scanned the newspaper and internet daily for any new articles of interest that could possibly pertain to the investigation. The unofficial buzz around the office confirmed that the Flores account was the one that sparked the review of Adriano's work.

The following Monday, the investigators were back, holed up in Adriano's office. Working behind closed doors, they were parked there for most of the day. Lunch was delivered and no one surfaced except to go to the men's room. Jasper stayed in his office but left for lunch and extended bathroom breaks to escape the tension. The atmosphere outside his four walls simulated a brooding percolator on the verge of combustion. Heads were bowed, eyes averted, and the workforce's melodious tones were replaced by a cricket's steady machine-like hum. Everyone waited for the proverbial shoe to drop.

On Friday, management sent an email to all employees, requesting their presence at a bank meeting after closing. All departments were finally alerted that one of Adriano's accounts was being targeted for investigation, but that everything was fine at the bank. The bank was cooperating with the investigators and the bank's lawyers would be handling any inquiries. They were assured the bank did not misstep. Management was confident that the issue would soon be resolved. Everyone was advised to stay silent and do their work, as usual. They were instructed not to speak to any members of the press, if approached. The meeting was brief and unhelpful as far as Jasper was concerned. It offered a temporary band aid after a week of nail-biting silence.

Friday night Jasper met Enrique for happy hour. It was good to sit by the water and let the stress dissipate into the sea air. Clad in a t-shirt and jeans, sipping cool beers, Jasper was able to somewhat unwind. He didn't discuss work with Enrique or anyone else outside of the office. It wasn't that he didn't trust Enrique, but he just didn't want to call any unnecessary attention to his suspicions. He knew if he revealed one thing, Enrique would keep asking questions. Nothing was confirmed and Jasper didn't want to deal with intangibles. Besides, he was thankful for a subject change and some mindless bullshitting. Talking to Samson and communicating with the rest of his family filled his need to explore his fast-changing world. It was good to just let it go for a night.

In a few weeks, Jasper would be meeting his family in Paris. Hopefully, by then, the investigation would be resolved, although deep down he had his doubts. He wasn't sure why. Until then, Jasper intended to keep his nose clean. He was committed to staying uninvolved. Samson was right. It didn't escape him that he was a guest in a foreign country and needed to behave as such. He had never felt that way in Barcelona before. Until now, he always felt right at home. Mom had given him some sound advice and he had every intention of following it. His mother was a smart woman.

Chapter LXXVII

Paris Jitters

Cara and Samantha were having lunch in Cara's studio.

"I booked my Paris trip this morning. I'm arriving a week after you. I figure you need some quality time with Francois and your family first," Samantha said, winking.

"Perfect! I'll be ready for you when you come." Cara laughed. "I promise to scope out all of Francois's eligible friends and filter the winners in anticipation of your arrival."

"Oh, good! Nothing like pre-screened plums. Saves time and eliminates the prunes." Sam giggled.

"Definitely. Time is of the essence when you only have a week. Be ready for an active schedule. Living with Summer and her friends reverses the aging process by decades. They ooze action and they have no patience for stragglers," Cara warned.

"Duly noted," Samantha grinned. "I'm all action. Talking about screening the prunes, have you ever googled Francois's ex-wife?"

"No."

"Well, let's have a look. You know her name, right?"

"Yes. She goes by her maiden name. She's a journalist and works for *France Soir*. Let's check."

Sam leaned in.

"Scroll down to the picture"

Cara gasped. "She doesn't look anything like I imagined."

"She isn't exactly a knock-out, is she?" Sam waved her fork at the screen. "Why did they split?"

"He never told me and I didn't ask."

"I see that I will have more investigative work to do when I come to Paris. This is important information."

Cara laughed. They finished their lunch and began loading the last accent pieces of Sam's order into her SUV. She was delighted with the outcome. These works were the show pieces that promised to send the kitchen over the top. A house and garden magazine was already booked. Jonny and Nero loved the tiles and had baptized the kitchen with champagne and chocolate glazed *eclairs*, to rave reviews of their own.

"I will secure your final check from Nero, before the Paris trip," Sam promised. "They also promised to have us both over for dinner one night soon."

"Oh, good. I would love to see the final product in person, although your pictures are pretty awesome. They look good on my web portfolio. Thanks, Sam. Drive carefully."

The next morning, Cara sat in front of her laptop sipping tea, reading the Sunday news. Pope Francis, whom she respected immensely, had sent a long-needed message to all Armenians. He took a step toward closing the 100-year-old wound of the

Armenian people by labeling their slaughter in 1915 by the Ottomon Turks "the first genocide of the 20th century."

"I like this man," Cara thought out loud. *He truly is a pope who is unafraid to air his inner thoughts, despite the diplomatic consequences that may ensue. He's a pope who loves people.*

She scanned her emails hoping to see Jasper's flight information. She came up empty. Cara desperately wanted Jasper to come to Paris, so she could hear firsthand what was transpiring in his office. Jasper was reluctant to elaborate on the phone, which made Cara's mind wander to dark places and worry. Her older son was not a complainer. When Jasper talked, Cara listened.

To get her mind off her worries, she walked to the attic hatch and pulled out a suitcase. She would do laundry and start throwing a few things in. Sunday was a good day for ironing and packing. Now that her most pressing orders were done and delivered, her focus shifted. Perhaps Jasper would email her later. She'd keep checking.

Chapter LXXVIII

Brotherly Love

When Jasper's phone rang Sunday morning, he sprinted for it. Samson's voice calmed him immediately.

"Hey, Jasper. How are things at the office? Any new developments?"

"The same. We're still in the dark. There was an office meeting on Friday, but it yielded no telling insights. They just said they were investigating Adriano's clients, one in particular, but they still didn't confirm which one, officially. We all know it's Flores though. We were instructed not to speak to the press, so that means you.

"Ouch."

"I haven't seen Adriano in over a week," Jasper added, sounding somewhat irritated. "I tried calling him a couple times, but he doesn't pick up."

"Well, the press has a tidbit for you," Samson teased. "There was a blurb on the wire about stolen pottery being traced to Barcelona and Paris. It was confirmed that the pottery came from the Met in New York and was sold and bought illegally as we suspected. It also seems that convincing copies were made in

Mexico, prior to its arrival here. I will send you the article. It's very brief. Some Parisian art dealers are being questioned. Natalie heard about it at work and mom confirmed it with Sotheby's."

"Forgery, huh? Interesting. I bet they came here via the *Corazon de Leones*. Did they mention F&S?"

"No confirmation of the exact shipping route or the company name." answered Samson. "I'll keep you updated. In the meantime, did you book your trip?"

"Not yet. I need to clear it with Adriano and I can't track him down. I hope that won't be a problem."

"Email him. It's getting close." Samson replied. "Mom won't forgive you, if you don't come, and I won't either. I want to see you, Bro".

"Alright, alright," said Jasper. "I'm on it. I'll draft an email today. Trust me, I really want to come see you guys."

"Well, don't sit on your hands. Get to it, today!"

Chapter LXXIX

All Rats on Deck

Carlos was sitting in the sanctuary of Fernando's office in Barcelona. He disliked being summoned for unscheduled meetings, but operations were not running smoothly these days, and Fernando was appropriately agitated. Carlos knew Fernando would never admit that Carlos had been right when he preached extreme caution after the first raid, but he didn't need to. The strained silence in the air was telling enough. A strategy meeting was long overdue. The police were watching them now and the stolen pottery issue was focusing unnecessary attention on their other enterprise. They had more important things to worry about.

Fernando's inability to part with some of the stolen pieces in a timely manner had gotten them into a jam. Carlos was peeved. Fernando never seemed to grasp the severity of things, until trouble was at his doorstep. Then he dispatched Jose. That usually translated to disaster.

Without looking up, Carlos felt Fernando's eyes shift from him to Jose,

"The lawyers are handling the pottery problem and I have moved anything and everything incriminating out of the warehouse. However, I'm not happy we're on their radar. The Moroccans are breathing down my neck in Marseille and want us to stop shipping goods, until things have calmed down. One shipment is already on its way from Mexico, so I can't change that, but after it arrives, we'll take a break until things calm down. Understood?"

"Yes," said Jose, nodding obediently.

"Carlos, how are we on money? Even if we stop shipments temporarily, we're still in good shape, correct?"

"Yes, no problem. We are owed some money, and the restaurants are carrying themselves. The restaurant in Barcelona is making good money as you know, so we are more than flush. What concerns me most is what's going on at the warehouse. Are the guys at the harbor still on board, Jose?"

"Yes, for now. They're not Mexican, so things are dicey. They could turn if things get ugly."

"What about the banker, Fernando? Is he under control?"

"He's a liability now that he suspects something. I wasn't happy with the questions he asked me last meeting. I don't trust him and I can't bribe him. We should probably sweep his computer to check his emails. Maybe we need to send him a message too."

"I urge you to do that with great care, please. We're doing so well here in Europe. Now all eyes are on us. We don't need any more negative attention. Agreed, Fernando?" Carlos looked at his boss with pleading eyes.

"Yes, agreed." Fernando sounded aggrieved. "Don't worry."

"Do you think the banker's assistant has been alerted?

"I don't think so, but we can't be sure. I haven't seen Adriano's assistant, since I opened the accounts. I do believe he only follows instructions."

"Better to be sure."

"I know what to do."

In Tampico, Carlos never got involved with logistics. He strictly handled the books. He preferred that. Here in Europe, Fernando used his level head as a sounding board more than Carlos wanted. Fernando's brother was too far away to discuss every detail with. Unfortunately, Fernando only listened to Carlos half the time if at all.

While the freedom in Paris was intoxicating, the pressure was intense. Any day their house of cards could crumble and Carlos didn't thrive on gambling. Unlike the Flores men, Carlos preferred to play it safe, a true accountant by nature. Moving forward, he decided to be more proactive with their dummy corporations, so assets couldn't be easily seized if trouble continued. He wouldn't tell Fernando his strategy until he needed to, but he would make sure their money was protected.

Chapter LXXX

Burglars, Chatty Supers
and Bosses Flying

On Monday morning Jasper sent Adriano the email he drafted about his family reunion in Paris. Hoping for a quick reply, he checked his email continuously. None was forthcoming. Later that day, he got an email from his mom requesting his itinerary. He wrote her that he was working on it, but secretly, he was wondering if he would be permitted to leave this time. He didn't want to miss seeing his family, but he also doubted that his boss could allow his departure at this crucial time. Jasper longed for his family's support. He confided only in Samson, but he understood Summer and mom were being kept in the loop.

Late Monday, the bank's management approached him in his office.

"The investigators would like to ask you a few questions, but don't worry, our lawyers will be present."

"Of course," Jasper replied, feeling even more worried. He'd been wondering, waiting, and dreading this moment and frankly, he was surprised it had taken them this long. They invited him into Adriano's office and closed the door.

"We're looking at Adriano's accounts and we're investigating F&S Enterprises," the investigator introduced as Franco, began. "Has Adriano spoken to you about this account, and have you sat in on their meetings?"

"Yes, I have been working on the accounts with Adriano from the start. I was introduced to Fernando Flores when the account was first opened, but I have not seen him since the first week. I haven't been to any subsequent meetings here or out. Adriano goes alone. He emails me with transaction requests, and I take care of them. I copy him on all transactions made. I can show you."

"Yes, we saw. Thank you. Have you ever been asked to do any bank transfers for the client without Adriano's knowledge?"

"No, never."

"Who do you communicate with on their end?"

"No one really. Fernando Flores's associate in Paris takes care of most transfers for the company as far as I know. I see the funds go in and out, but I have nothing to do with that. I only handle their investment transactions as per Adriano. He double checks it and I send the confirmation to Carlos Ortiz, their accountant, but there is no dialogue."

Jasper sat quietly as they perused some records. Clearly, they were already completely familiar with his work. After a few more questions, Jasper was dismissed for the day. They would be needing his office. He would be notified when to come back to work.

"Please be available by phone if we have any questions. You can work from home. Take a company laptop with you. We'll keep you in the loop."

"Yes." Jasper grabbed his jacket and briefcase and left, his stomach in knots. Were they going to fire him if things with Adriano went south.

He headed straight home, calling Samson from the car. As usual, Samson's voice calmed him down.

"Chill, Jasper. You did nothing wrong, and your work is documented. They have nothing on you. Now Adriano, I'm not so sure about. Have you heard from him?"

"Only by email but only business related. You don't think Adriano planted anything in my computer, do you?" Jasper asked, suddenly panicked. "They asked me not to come into the office until further notice."

"I seriously doubt it, or they would have found it by now and besides, didn't you say he's been working from another location?"

"Yes, he hasn't been in the office for over a week."

"Really, Jasper. Stop worrying," Samson assured him. "Have a glass of *sangria* and put your feet up. Relax. Enjoy the day off."

"Easy for you to say."

Samson had succeeded in making him feel a touch less agitated, but Jasper was still unsettled when he arrived at his empty apartment. Now the quietness irked him, and his racing thoughts transferred him to dark places. He was glad he used his own laptop for all personal emails, even at work.

He changed into jeans and a t-shirt and went to the corner cafe with his laptop. It was a beautiful Spring Day and he needed to get out of the confines of his small apartment. The walls felt like they were closing in. He ordered an ice *cafe con leche* and checked round trip flights to Paris. He started drafting a vacation request, attaching his unanswered email to Adriano, to their mutual boss, copying human resources. He would wait to see what the next day would bring and send it. He sent mom a copy with the dates. Finally, he called his mother. He wanted to hear her voice. Her sound, well-intentioned advice was soothing to his ear.

That night Jasper checked his email and found that he had another day off. He would be reporting back to the office on Thursday, he was informed. He could take another day off.

The following morning, wondering what to do, Jasper went for a good Spanish breakfast. He brought his briefcase with the electronics and scanned the news. Nothing of interest caught his eye. Spontaneously, he decided to go gift shopping for his family. They were heavily on his mind and he needed to do something to occupy his time. He also needed some new shirts, since the dry cleaner conspired to kill his stash off one by one. Jasper paid the waiter and walked back to his apartment to drop off his briefcase with the small laptop and tablet inside. He saw Clemente in the lobby talking to a stranger, so he changed course for the garage. He was not in the mood for Clemente's grilling. Jasper dropped his bag in the car, covering it with his jacket and drove to *El Corte Ingles*. After an afternoon of shopping and an early dinner out, he headed back home, feeling rather pleased with his purchases.

When Jasper arrived home, he noticed his front door was unlocked. When he stepped inside, he gasped. The place had been torn apart. Cabinet doors were flung open, and the contents of drawers spilled onto the floor. His closet was ravaged with clothes strewn all around his bedroom. He immediately alerted Clemente who called the police. As Jasper looked around the apartment, he couldn't find anything missing. His flat screen TV was still screwed into the wall and his passport was still in the side pocket of his travel bag. The rest of his belongings, clothes, kitchen goods and furniture were all accounted for as far as he could see. He was thankful he had kept his electronics with him. Cash, he kept either in his wallet or in the bank. The ancient coin pendant, a graduation present from his mom, and his dad's steel and gold watch, he wore every day. He had nothing else of value.

Jasper was sure this search was related to Adriano and F&S Enterprises in some way, but he kept his suspicions to himself. Why were they searching his place? What did they hope to get? A report was filed and Jasper began to sort through the mess. Clemente, for once, had not seen or heard anything. His silence was completely uncharacteristic.

"How unusual," thought Jasper out loud. *The man who never shuts up and knows everyone's business has nothing to add. This is a first.*

Once alone, he pulled out two portable, external hard drives from his computer bag and plugged them into his computer and tablet. He hadn't backed anything up in a while and he didn't use the cloud other than for his travel pictures. After the back up was completed, Jasper hurried to the post office and mailed Samson the external hard drives in a padded express envelope. He gave Samson instructions to keep them safe. Jasper also included a quick note explaining his thoughts on the break in. He was nervous and felt violated. On his way home, he bought a new lock and a metal latch for his front door and more external hard drives.

Again, he backed up his computer and tablet overnight. It wouldn't hurt to have several copies. That night, he barely slept. The next morning, he instructed Clemente to install the extra latch on the inside of his door and to replace the damaged lock. He took all his electronics to work in his combination briefcase. Jasper got there early with his breakfast and studied the news as he ate.

The investigators had combed through his office, but as far as Jasper could see, nothing was amiss, not even the F&S files. His computer had been replaced with a new one, but all of his files were on it. He went to the lunchroom to get some coffee and passed by Maria's desk. Before he could speak, Maria volunteered, "They were holed up in your office for two days and they took your computer."

"I know, but they replaced it with a new one and all my files are on it," said Jasper. "Now tell me something I don't know. What do you hear from Adriano?" he asked.

"He's working from home, I think," she answered.

"He's not answering my emails."

"I know he's been here after hours to speak with management, but I don't know when he'll be back or if he'll be back for that matter. From what I hear, the police are conferring with him. Weird right?"

"Yes, this whole investigation is suspicious and unsettling."

"The investigators are done for now," she added. "They won't be back today. I'm not sure about tomorrow. I've heard rumors that the account they're investigating was making money from stolen goods. That's all I know."

"I guess we'll soon find out." Jasper nodded and walked to his office. The rest of the day was uneventful. He debated telling his superiors about his ransacked apartment but decided against it. The police could connect the dots themselves. Besides, there was no proven link and he didn't want the police to rummage through his belongings or worse, investigating him or his personal electronics.

Jasper pulled up his vacation request email and sent it to management. He wondered if he should bother to copy Adriano, but then he decided to keep Adriano in the loop. At this point he wasn't even sure if Adriano was still employed at the bank. He hoped so. Jasper longed to talk to Samson and his mom; he was itching to see his family to hear if they had a different take on his situation or just to discuss what he should do if anything. That night he went through his emails and deleted whatever he thought was questionable.

On Friday morning Jasper woke up happy the week was almost over. He was having trouble sleeping at night, because any sound in the apartment or stairwell left him breathing rapidly. He was exhausted. He dressed and headed out to the office early. Clemente was nowhere in sight. *What a relief or is it?* thought Jasper. *The one time I would have liked another body in the stairwell, he's in hiding. How very odd.* He wondered what Clemente might have seen or heard and not reported. Clemente could easily be bought, no doubt there. He could also be paid to look the other way. Loyalty was not his strong suit and the man loved to spend money on expensive booze.

Work was uneventful and slow. Jasper decided to have an early dinner on his way home, so he could get home before dark. Since the robbery, he was looking over his shoulder whenever he approached his building. His car did not leave the garage, because he didn't want to be caught underground alone. He took a crowded bus to his neighborhood and stopped at Juan Carlos's restaurant, a block away. After ordering a glass of *sangria* to calm his nerves, he pulled out his tablet. The evening news hit him like a ton of bricks, leaving him gasping for air. The headliner was "Executive from Rothschild Espana found dead in Hotel Miramar." He was staring at Adriano's pictured face in disbelief.

Chapter LXXXI

Paranoia is Legit If They Really Are Out to Get You

Jasper's heart did a somersault and nausea gripped his insides. He paid for his *sangria*, took his dinner to go and hurried home, hyperventilating every step. His knees buckling, he looked over his shoulder at least twenty times in the short walk from the restaurant to his building. Scrutinizing everyone on the sidewalk, he envisioned himself being grabbed from behind and forced into a waiting van with dark windows. He hated the thought of entering an empty lobby and stairwell, but he also didn't want to loiter outside until another resident came.

When he got to the building, Clemente was nowhere in sight. Clemente's apartment door off the lobby was firmly shut. Jasper felt light-headed as he pressed his ear to his apartment door before inserting the key. Prior to stepping over the threshold, he listened and took a sweeping view of the place. It looked the same. Once inside, he double bolted the door and turned on the TV, flipping back and forth between the local channels. He shrunk into his quilted, leather armchair, like a raisin in the sun. After he scanned all the channels, he popped back out of the chair to pace and pee. Restless, he ran the faucet and sat down on the closed toilet seat. A nervous wreck, he called Samson, praying his brother would pick up. *How is all this possible? What happened?*

"Samson, did you see the news? Adriano is dead. I think he was murdered."

"What?" Jasper heard Samson gasp.

"Yeah, he was found dead in a luxury hotel. They're calling it a drug overdose. Check the wire." His voice was shaky, and he was still hyperventilating. "I don't believe Adriano did drugs. I would have known or noticed. Listen, I also sent you a copy of my hard drives for safekeeping. You should get them any day. My apartment was broken into yesterday afternoon. They did a bang-up job and went through everything. I'm pretty sure they were after my electronics. Nothing was taken."

"WHAT? Holy Shit!"

Jasper could hear the surprise and mounting concern in his brother's voice. "Book your trip to Paris now. Jeez, you're just full of good news, aren't you? Nothing was missing from your apartment?"

"No, but I had all my electronics and valuables with me. I already reserved my trip. I just haven't paid yet because my boss hasn't responded to my vacation request. Call mom and tell her everything when she wakes up tomorrow. Tell Summer too, but don't tell her until later in the day. I don't want her to call me in the office tomorrow morning. You know how she is."

"Ok. Understood. Listen, lie low and stay in tonight. Let me see what I can find out. I'll call you tomorrow."

"Ok, but not at work."

"Right. I'll text there."

Jasper talked to Samson a little longer, letting Samson calm him down. When he disconnected his call, he turned off the water and resent the email asking for his vacation time. Then he took a long, hot shower. He warmed his dinner and nibbled at it. His stomach was in knots.

Again, Jasper could not catch a wink all night. He lay awake waiting for any unusual sounds. In the dark, he was convinced someone would be coming back for him or his electronics or both. Adriano's right-hand man who may know something he shouldn't, could be perceived as a liability. This thought made him quiver in bed. The next morning, after minimal rest, he woke up with a head cold.

The office was abuzz by the time the workday began. Mid-morning an email was sent out to all personnel citing Adriano Aldana's death at the Hotel Miramar. He was temporarily staying at the luxury hotel. His body was found by the police officer who was supposed to be guarding him. Surveillance cameras showed two, unknown police officers entering the room around 11pm and leaving about 15 minutes later. Their hats made it difficult to recognize them. They did not come or leave on the guest elevators, and no one seems to have noticed them in the stairwells. They were not recognized by the local police force, but their uniforms were legitimate. The hotel staff was still being interviewed. The police officer, legitimately shadowing Adriano, was tasered, locked in the men's room and sufficiently tied up, while his partner was ambushed in the hallway, knocked out cold from behind and stuffed into a broom closet in his underwear. The police guns were hidden in a maid's garbage cart. Adriano's death was a mystery; information was scant, although the investigation of one of his clients was mentioned. There were no suicide messages left. It appeared that Adriano died from a drug overdose. Interestingly, he was found nude on the couch of his suite. The police were investigating all leads. Inspector Abello was all over the case. Jasper remembered reading his name once before in connection to the raid on the *Corazon de Leones*.

Thoughts raced through his aching head. Adriano was not a party boy. Yes, he enjoyed a few drinks once in a while, but as far as Jasper knew and saw, he could swear that Adriano did not do drugs. He was as straight as an arrow. Jasper found it hard to believe that Adriano overdosed. Something about this scenario smelled fishy.

In the confines of his office, Jasper's knees folded, his hands trembled, and his body convulsed as he sunk into his swivel chair. He dry-heaved a few times and lunged for the garbage pail, no longer able to hold back. His insides were hurting. His head throbbed and he was scared. He rested his head between his knees.

He didn't feel safe in Barcelona anymore. He desperately wanted to leave. He thought about Paris and New York, places he thought he would feel safer, or would he? A possible drug cartel or smugglers ring had no borders; if they wanted to find him, they would. Jasper was confused and not sure of anything. He would not feel safe anywhere until he had some answers, or someone was caught for something. His world was crumbling fast and he didn't know where it left him. And the saddest part of the matter was that he knew nothing and had done nothing wrong.

Chapter LXXXII

Family Meddling Welcome

Samson sat at his desk in the office and stared out over the Seine. For the first time in his life, he was afraid for his older brother. He wanted Jasper out of Barcelona ASAP, at least until this nightmare was over. It was hard to concentrate on work. He got up and wandered into his boss's office to chat.

That night Samson called his mom. He held off on calling Summer, knowing she had a long day of shooting ahead; he wanted to respect Jasper's wishes. Summer's wake up time these days was 5am, so he refrained from worrying her, although it was excruciatingly difficult. Talking to his sister usually comforted him. They both liked to troubleshoot and arrive at conclusions together. Always had. As expected, his mother was alarmed.

"Oh my God, Samson. What the hell is going on there? Did you see anything on the wire? Should we call the Barcelona police directly? Or Jasper's bank manager? They're putting him in danger, I feel. This has all the markings of a cartel hit."

"I don't know, Mom. He can't really be in danger if he doesn't know anything, right? I mean, nothing was missing out of his apartment."

"Yeah, but he had his electronics with him you said. What if they come back for them? Or worse, hurt him for them. I mean what else would they be looking for in his apartment? He has nothing valuable really. It sounds to me like they're wondering what he knows."

"Well, the break in could be unrelated, Mom. A coincidence. Someone looking for cash perhaps."

"And nothing is taken? Unlikely. I mean think about it. A burglar would have taken something to made it worth his while. Were any other apartments broken into?"

"No."

"I rest my case. This is not random. Adriano's killers are looking for something and maybe they think Jasper has it. I feel sick to my stomach. "

Samson could hear the panic mounting in his mother's voice.

"We have to get him out of there. I'm going to email him right now. Who could blame him for leaving a job where people are turning up dead? Call me anytime if something is wrong or you hear anything new, ok? Day or night Samson. I mean it."

"Of course. I promise." He hung up, his mouth dry.

Chapter LXXXIII

Dirty Laundry

Jasper checked his email and discovered his mother's long message. She urged him to ask for police protection until the dust settled and answers were found. Then she called him for a long chat, despite the time difference. Jasper was wide awake, so he answered immediately.

"Jasper, fill me in. Samson just called, but I want to hear it in your own words. What the hell is happening?" He settled on the toilet seat and turned on the tap water as he filled her in.

"Promise me you'll talk to management about protection and coming to Paris."

"I promise, Mom, but it's not that simple."

"Yes, it is. Some circumstances simplify things. No one will fault you for wanting to leave right now. Do it. Say you have a family emergency if you have to."

The next morning the headline revealed a motive. Adriano was accused of money laundering for a "stolen art" business. Rare, stolen pottery that was traced to the Metropolitan Museum in New York, was being shipped to Mexico, copied, and then sold in Europe to a group of Russian collectors. The transactions appeared to take place in Monaco. The copies were distributed everywhere. The shipments came into Barcelona harbor first, then Marseille and finally Monaco. The Rothschild bank had branches in Barcelona and Paris and it was speculated that Adriano helped launder money for F&S Enterprises in both locations. One could only guess how much Adriano really knew and whether he had been threatened into participating.

The CEO of F&S Enterprises was currently being questioned regarding their pottery shipments on the *Corazon de Leones*. Fernando Flores was lawyered up and denying all knowledge of illegal art shipments. He acknowledged his pottery was carefully crafted after old motifs in Mexico and distributed in Europe. The antique pieces he copied were legitimately bought at auction he claimed through his lawyer. If the artwork sold was characterized incorrectly at resale, he was unaware. Since when is that a crime?

Chapter LXXXIV

Paris Idyll Interrupted

March in Paris was remarkably mild, unlike New York. April was beyond lovely with few showers. Summer, Hope and Ted were enjoying the late afternoon sun on their terrace. The frosted glass wind-shelter walls on their kitchen terrace, trapped Spring's first warm rays and kindly bounced them back onto their comfortable, cushioned armchairs. Together with Madame Balon, Ted, industrious as always, had uncovered and scrubbed the cedar table set and 3 armchairs. They found plush outdoor cushions tucked in the window benches on either side of the kitchen terrace door. Along the wind shelter, Ted planted purple, blue and yellow pansies in large, majestically carved pots thus adding a rainbow of color and a touch of nature to their private enclave. In the window boxes, he and Madame B started an herb garden including basil, dill, chives, and cilantro seeds. Green stubs were sprouting proudly, chives standing tall in the afternoon breeze.

The roof garden was a cozy sanctuary after a long, exhausting day of work. Sipping *cafe au lait* and munching on hazelnut biscotti, absinthe cake and multi-colored meringues, the trio sank into the cushioned reprieve. Sunshine, caffeine, and sugar were the only way to extract a lift this time of day. The five and 6am wake up calls were deathly and taking their expected toll. Summer's phone rang, disturbing the blissful moment. She barely could move out of her chair to reach the side table. Seconds after she answered, Summer's face clouded up.

Sitting up straight she listened, then answered in spurts, "Oh my God, when did this happen? And you're just telling me now? Really? Where's Jasper? Does mom know? Should we go get him? We can't just leave him there alone, Samson! Are the police keeping him there? Then why can't we get him? What CAN we do? Can I call him now? Alright. Keep me posted," Summer pleaded. She sank back into her cushioned chair looking whipped, beaten to the core. A few tears formed in her eyes.

Summer realized Ted and Hope were looking at each other in alarm, then at her, waiting patiently for Summer to speak only she didn't know if she could without bursting into tears. Summer's mind was racing, and her emotions were getting the better of her.

"Well?" Ted quizzed her after a few seconds.

Close to waterworks, Summer replied, "Jasper is in serious trouble...."

Chapter LXXXV

A Sigh of Relief

Jasper's head was spinning, and he had a splitting headache that not even Excedrin Plus could remedy. He checked his email repeatedly for a reply regarding his vacation time. The following Monday morning, after a harrowing weekend, in which he barely left his apartment, it came. He could leave for Paris, on Friday. Over the weekend, Enrique had left several messages, but Jasper couldn't move from his recliner to answer the phone. Nor would be leave his cocoon. He was scared stiff, his imagination in overdrive.

Management thought he could use a break, although this was not openly voiced. They granted him two of his six vacation weeks per calendar year. If they knew that his apartment had been broken into, they didn't address it and neither did Jasper. In the email, they assured him he had nothing to worry about as everyone knew he followed banking protocol meticulously. His transaction records spoke for themselves. Jasper made few mistakes. They asked that he be available by email and phone while away and they wished him a good trip. He readily agreed to be available and thanked them for the time, given the late notice. Jasper's heart took a small leap of joy.

For the first time since his arrival in Barcelona, Jasper felt that his work was being noticed and appreciated by the top brass. However, the circumstances didn't appease him. In fact, right now he could have cared less. Jasper knew he always had Adriano's appreciation, but this was different. Appreciation no longer mattered when his personal wellbeing was being threatened.

The email asked Jasper to meet with management one more time prior to leaving. Tomorrow at ten in the office conference room. A separate email, regarding Adriano's funeral Friday morning, circulated to all in the firm.

Back at the bank, Jasper's floor was still in shock, the office cog wheels moving in slow motion, as if stuck in a time loop. With Adriano's office door permanently closed one could easily imagine that he was still in there, working. Adriano had always been well liked despite everything that had transpired in recent weeks. His untimely death cast a wide shadow over the bank's third floor. Even Maria barely talked these days.

Jasper rushed to pay for his Friday flight reservation and sent the extended itinerary to his family. Now he just had to make it through the rest of the week. When Jasper's email was opened on both sides of the Atlantic, the Crenston family sighed in collective relief.

Chapter LXXXVI

On the Crest of the Wave

"Thank God," Cara uttered as she read Jasper's flight confirmation. She checked her suitcase, which was completely packed and by the door. "Just a few more days and I'm out of here," she mumbled to herself. Jasper's situation had put her on high alert. She was ready to jump on a plane at a moment's notice, if needed. After the frightening news about Adriano, Cara found it hard to concentrate on her final tasks, yet she knew she needed to leave her home and workshop in order. Her Spring/Summer orders were almost done, and she was in the process of packing and shipping them out. She had alerted her clients to save their new orders and re-orders for June. The phone rang, forcing Cara to stray from her mental 'to do' list.

"Hi, Cara, any new developments? How's Jasper?"

"Thankfully, no. I think I've reached my limit for surprises. The good news is he's confirmed to meet us in Paris; we're all so relieved. My suitcase has been ready and by the door for days, just in case. I'm so ready to go, Sam."

"What are you up to later? Free for a late lunch?"

"I can't. I must get these last few orders packed and shipped before I leave. Our next drink or lunch will have to be in Paris."

"Anything special I should bring for the trip? What can I bring for Summer?"

"Nero's pastries always work. Don't go crazy. Summer is well equipped in her apartment. Thanks!"

"Ok then…. baked anatomy it is. I will take you guys out to dinner once I get there. Listen, Cara, if there's anything I can do to help before you leave, let me know. Seriously."

"Thanks, Sam. I just might get back to you on that."

When she hung up, Cara resumed preparing her boxes for delivery and shipment. After loading the SUV, she sat down to finish her email blast to all her clients. She promised to come back with new pottery ideas. She coined her trip as a business trip and convinced her clients that inspiration is best gathered through world exposure, not in the confines of a studio 24/7.

"Artists need to spread their wings, the further their reach, the more interesting the results," she wrote in her blog.

She googled F&S and Adriano Aldana, looking for updates. The information on Adriano's death was the same. The descriptions of the Cretin case and the Aldana case appeared similar and both men had dealings with the Flores organizations, this much she knew for sure. Surely, the police did too. Was Flores making money with stolen ceramic goods and laundering in Jasper's bank? Or were drugs the real issue? From what she knew, drug money didn't go through banks. She would have to continue her research in Europe. Satisfied with her customer email blast, Cara pressed send. She quickly composed an email to Francois, confirming her new flight info and signed off with a written hug. She headed out the door to her loaded SUV to begin making local deliveries. The remaining batch of boxes would be packed later and shipped in the morning. After that, she was free.

Chapter LXXXVII

The Great Escape

At 10am Jasper took the elevator to the building's top floor and entered the conference room. A small group of the bank's most important executives were gathered around the intimidating ten-foot table and listened intently as Jasper spoke. He tried to stay calm explaining the status of his files, pulling them up one by one, but his nerves were apparent, and the executives weren't interested. They already had that information.

Jasper's voice wavered with emotion he couldn't control. Inside, he felt sick. His stomach was in a state of upheaval and his legs felt like Jello. Luckily, he was seated, or his knees would have surely buckled. He tried to answer slowly to collect his scattered thoughts. It took every ounce of effort he could muster to focus on the task at hand. Normally Jasper was calm, cool, and collected. It was shocking how life could change in an instant. The repercussions of Adriano's death were affecting his psyche, and he was turning into a blubbering, incoherent mess. After the briefing, the executives thanked him.

"We would like to ask you a few more personal questions that may be helpful in solving this crisis. Did Adriano ever do drugs to your knowledge?"

"Not to my knowledge," Jasper answered honestly, shaking his head for emphasis. "Never."

"Did Adriano frequent Fernando Flores's restaurant? "

"We were invited there once by Mr. Flores when the accounts were first opened, the first week, I think. I never went back, and I don't know if Adriano did. If he did, he didn't tell me." He placed emphasis on the word didn't.

"Did Adriano ever go to Fernando Flores's warehouse office for meetings?"

"I don't know. Adriano was out of the office more than usual lately, but he never told me where he was going. However, having said that, I was always able to reach him by phone, text or email. He never failed to respond," Jasper assured them.

This wasn't entirely true, but Jasper felt it was true enough. Overall, Adriano had been accessible and a good, conscientious boss and employee of the bank as far as he was concerned. Jasper had no intention of tarnishing Adriano's name in any way. Whatever the police found, they would have to find on their own. He wasn't going to throw Adriano under the bus now that he was gone. As Jasper left the conference room, he was reminded to be available by phone, but he was cleared for travel and wished a good visit with his family. He sighed with relief as he hit the elevator button with force. His trembling forefinger crimped under the pressure, and he winced with pain.

Chapter LXXXVIII

Chasing his Tail

Inspector Abello's department was stumped. The *Corazon de Leones* had come up clean. Yes, antique stolen pottery was discovered in the warehouse, but it was hard to pin on Flores as the warehouse housed numerous companies. F&S was not the only company receiving merchandise via the ship. Besides, many people had access to the warehouse according to Flores's lawyers. The unmarked crate the antique pottery was discovered in, had no paper trail. It sat in a lone corner. Invoices Flores produced, showed that he had legitimately bought some antique pottery at auction and that he used these particular pieces as samples for similar production. Those items were in his possession and he could verify their trail. His legal team was able to produce some records.

"This guy is smooth," Abello voiced in a department meeting. "Magic books. Of course, it would help if all this damn pottery didn't look the same," Abello mumbled to his team in frustration.

The fact that he was color blind didn't help his case either. He had to rely on art experts. Abello and his team had a strong hunch that Flores was connected to the drug trade, but they couldn't find any drugs on the ship or in the F&S area of the warehouse. They had spot checked the ship and the warehouse more than once. Even the dogs came up empty. Abello was annoyed. In fact, he was in an extremely foul mood. His underlings kept their distance, knowing the signs.

Now, to add to the conundrum and therefore his workload, Abello had a high-profile drug overdose on his hands, that he suspected was a murder. Adriano Aldana did not overdose by himself. From the information he and his people were gathering from the coroner's office and work associates, the man did not indulge. It appeared someone must have helped him along. Certain injuries were consistent with this theory. For now, he kept this fact under his hat. He hated feeding the press. Those vultures never got things right.

There were many similarities with the Alphonse Cretin case. Adriano might have made some ethical mistakes, or perhaps been scared into them, but he was not a druggie or a drug distribution enabler. He must have gotten sucked in somehow. Blackmailed or threatened perhaps? Abello trusted his people's and Arnaud's findings. The common denominator had to be Fernando Flores and his crew. In both cases, Fernando or his posse were nearby. Their pottery was showing up everywhere trouble brewed, like a sloth scoping a bird's nest.

What surprised Abello and his Parisian counterpart was that Flores had come to an understanding with the existing drug trade from Morocco. They both distributed through Marseilles. The Moroccans ruled the hashish trade and in no way would they share that market with any newcomers. Perhaps they were offered a good incentive to distribute Flores's magic powder? Maybe that was the angle to pursue more rigorously? He scratched his head, lost in thought.

Chapter LXXXIX

Final Farewell

Every morning Jasper left his apartment in fear. Shockingly, he never once ran into Clemente all week. Ironically, this was the time Jasper might have been glad to see his nosy, ratty superintendent. Yet the lobby was consistently empty when Jasper left the building. Clemente's newly acquired behavior was suspicious, totally foreign, and out of character. The man was exercising unduly restraint. Was he sick or just covering his hide in a foxhole? The week crept by in slow motion.

Friday morning Jasper dressed appropriately for the funeral, in a black suit and dark tie. He grabbed his suitcase for Paris, his briefcase with his electronics and locked up the apartment, rechecking the locks twice. He knocked on Clemente's door and reminded him that he would be away for 14 days. He gave Clemente his cell phone number for emergencies even though he knew Clemente already had it. Clemente barely cracked the door and asked no questions. At 8am Jasper took a bus to the office, not looking back. He was exceedingly happy to leave.

Around 9:30am he got into one of the limousines provided by the firm to go to Adriano's funeral. Jasper dreaded going. His hands were sweating, and his stomach was churning. Regardless of what Adriano might have done or not done, he had been a good boss and friend. He always treated Jasper fairly and respectfully. Jasper couldn't believe he was dead. The office would never be the same and Jasper no longer enjoyed going to work. Maybe a couple of weeks off would change his perspective, but he had serious doubts. The mood in the limo was somber; Jasper peered out of the window, as his coworkers chatted quietly. The ride to the cemetery was crushing him inside. This was almost as bad as his father's funeral years ago. He felt like screaming as he pressed his face against the window, fogging it up.

Chapter XC

The Usual and Unusual Suspects

Inspector Abello's team was planted around the funeral home, scrutinizing each arrival. Dark suits and sunglasses in place, they blended right in. They watched as Jasper got out of the company limousine with his briefcase in hand. A few other bank employees stayed by his side. Abello squinted.

"Who brings a briefcase to a funeral? Obviously, the contents is something he doesn't dare leave behind, in the limo?" He adjusted his earpiece.

The last arrival was Fernando Flores, who was flanked by two men. Security guards that doubled as drivers; Abello knew that from previous surveillance. Flores looked unperturbed as he glanced around the cemetery hall and respectfully stood in the back, head bowed, hands folded over his crotch. Upon viewing the casket, he made a sign of the cross. Abello's team looked at each other from across the hall.

"He has balls to show up here," one of his team members whispered into his earpiece. Abello agreed and felt a rush of heat up his neck. He pulled out a vial and popped a blood pressure pill.

Eyeing Flores, he noticed him spot Jasper and choose a seat in the last row of Jasper's section. The kid looked visibly ill. His pallor was a pasty grey. When he spotted Flores behind him, he looked even sicker. One hand was on the briefcase parked between his legs and the other on his stomach, trying to keep its contents down. He sat between Maria and a male colleague. They all looked shaken and stirred.

"I bet Flores would just love to get his hands on that briefcase," Abello mumbled to his team. "Let's make sure he doesn't."

Abello's people had debated whether to permit Jasper to leave the country, but Jasper's superiors were adamant.

"The kid is ok. He's badly shaken. Let him go see his family. He knows nothing," they said.

In any case, Jasper had come up clean and Abello was in close contact with Inspector Arnaud. Jasper would be on their radar one way or another. They had nothing on the kid and he wasn't a suspect, but one could never underestimate what he might have been privy to. He wasn't a talker. Either way, they wanted to protect and tail him. To cover all their bases. On the surface, the kid appeared to be clueless and scared, but who knew what he might have overheard or suspected on his own. Also, nothing had been stolen from Jasper's apartment, which was odd. The only concern was that Flores might take the kid himself if he thought Jasper was holding out. Abello would make sure he and his briefcase got to the airport without incident. An unmarked car would escort Jasper until he was safely on his flight. Arnaud had the Paris end covered.

Happy Arrivals... Sort of

At Cara's request, Jasper 's flight was timed, so he would arrive the same day and close to the same time as her own. She had rebooked her flight to depart a week earlier once she knew of Jasper's situation. She planned to share a taxi with Jasper to the Rue Malher apartment. Francois asked to pick her up, but she declined his sweet offer in favor of time alone with her son. First things first. Jasper's one-year contract with the bank was complete and Cara knew he could leave Barcelona if he so chose. He was there on a month-to-month basis now that Adriano hadn't renewed the contract with him. Cara hoped to convince Jasper to come home to New York.

"You have to convince him to leave Barcelona, Mom," Samson urged her in their last phone call.

"Yes, I know, but I don't want to bombard him this minute. In the end, it's his decision, his life. Let's hear what he has to say first."

"I'm getting a bad feeling about this Flores guy. If he is a drug trafficker too, he'll be ruthless if he thinks Jasper knows something he shouldn't. You know, in Mexico, people disappear into thin air; one day here, the next day gone without a trace."

"Believe me, I know, and I agree, but let's give him a chance to come to that conclusion himself. He isn't stupid and he is already nervous enough. We will talk to him when he is sitting across from us."

"He could be dead before he has a chance to get here, Mom."

"Stop scaring me, Samson. I have a long flight ahead and you are making it impossible for me to sit through it. We'll deal with everything when I get there. Please."

The week before Cara's departure had been crazy busy at the shop. Moving her trip up a week added to her stress, but adrenalin and fear for Jasper, pushed Cara to get the urgent orders out. She worked tirelessly around the clock. Her deadlines kept her mind focused on work instead of worrying over something beyond her control. Luckily, Sam had come to help.

The news from Barcelona only added to her mounting stress level. Once on the plane, Cara paced the aisles. Samson had fed into her fears even though she tried to keep calm when speaking to him. She couldn't relax despite being utterly exhausted. A few hours into her flight, she sank deep into her seat with a loud sigh and momentarily closed her eyes. Nuzzled comfortably, with a drink, pretzels, and a good movie, she started to unwind and plan her strategy to bring Jasper home.

Cara's plane landed first. It was midday. By the time she retrieved her bags, the arrival screen showed that Jasper's plane had landed too. Cara waited anxiously in the arrival hall. Forty minutes later, Jasper appeared looking thinner, worn out, but relieved to see her. They hugged and Cara could feel the tension in Jasper's lithe body. His eyes were just as glassy as her own and his hands and voice were slightly unsteady. Cara could sense the dangerous, emotional crack in Jasper's usually impenetrable armor. In the taxi, conversation centered around the funeral. Jasper didn't want to talk about anything private with another set of ears listening. They agreed to stop at the corner cafe on Rue Malher to catch up. No one would be at the apartment until later and they were starving.

They settled outside at the last table, away from the cafe doors, so they could talk privately. After Cara ordered two *citron presses*, *croque monsieurs*, and decaf *cappuccinos*, Jasper let loose. All the events of the past couple of months came pouring out. Cara listened attentively, without interrupting. When Jasper finished speaking, he sank back into his chair, visibly spent. The afternoon sun had shifted, and Cara reached for her jacket, pulling it around her shoulders. She felt chilled.

"What are you thinking of doing, now that Adriano is gone?" she asked carefully.

"I'm not sure. Adriano would have normally handled the new contract, but he didn't. My year is up, so I could either ask for a new agreement or to be transferred or I could just come home, I guess. I wasn't planning on coming home yet. I wanted to stay another year," Jasper answered.

Cara decided to stay silent for now, just nodding. The seed was already planted in Jasper's mind. She would broach the subject another day. She could see that he was emotionally conflicted and mentally exhausted. She also saw no point in adding to his fear. He understood the danger. She felt scared for her son, and she definitely did not want him to go back to Barcelona under any circumstances, but Cara bit her tongue. She had two weeks to sway him. Her restraint was killing her.

Flores was lawyered up and was free to do harm if he chose to. Jasper clearly was aware of this and understood the downside. There was no doubt in his mind that Flores was behind Adriano's death and now Cara believed the same, after listening to her son. They changed the subject and talked about Summer's progress. They were chatting about what to see in Paris this time around, when Ted walked by laden with groceries.

"*Bonjour,* Ted" Cara called out waving. "We're back."

"Cara, Jasper, *Comment ca va*? So nice to have you back. Summer and Hope will be home in a bit. We left the keys with the concierge for you. Did you not get them?" Ted asked looking concerned.

"Not yet. We never made it that far. The sun was so lovely, we decided to detour here. We were hungry for our favorite *croques*." Cara beamed. "Want to join us for an early *Kir*? My treat."

"Let's have one in the apartment. It's been a long day and I have groceries that need to be put away. Besides, our terrace should still be sunny now. We face southwest, you know. Are these your bags?" Ted offered.

"Yes," Cara replied, tired from the long flight and the leaden news.

"Thanks, Ted. Nice to see you too!" said Jasper.

"Welcome back!" Ted grabbed the handle of Cara's rolling suitcase, put the grocery bag on top and started walking down

Rue Malher. "C'mon, lets go home. Wait till you see the place. Madame Balon and I have been busy."

At the apartment Ted brought the suitcases into Cara's room and prepared drinks. Cara and Jasper marveled at the beautiful terrace with all its pansy pots and budding herbs. Comfortably nestled into the plush outdoor chairs, they chatted for a short while over *Kirs*. Cara then headed to her room for a nap until Hope and Summer returned home. Jasper, exhausted from nights of poor sleep and an emotional funeral, crashed on Summer's bed while Ted tip-toed around the apartment and prepped dinner. They would have a full house. Samson was joining them. *Bouillabaisse* and French bread with homemade *rouille* were on the menu.

A few hours later, all were once again assembled around the kitchen table for one of Ted's exquisite meals. It was just like old times, but there was an unspoken strain in the air. No one addressed Jasper's problem. Everyone could see that he needed a distraction.

For dessert, the housekeeper had baked a traditional *clafoutis* with black cherries. Ted added fresh cream. It was heavenly and worth every calorie. The oohs and ahhhs of pure content circled the table, making everyone smile, even Jasper. Cara and Ted once again schemed how they could pry the recipe out of Madame Balon. Should they tie her up and beat it out of her or barter for it with an American apple crisp recipe?

After dinner the inevitable question loomed, "What would Jasper's next move be?" It was carefully addressed, but no solutions were reached as no one dared to upset Jasper. He looked so fragile. It appeared everyone needed to sleep on it, especially Jasper. Spontaneously, he decided to stay the night and move to Samson's the next day. He would sleep on the daybed in Cara's room.

"Are you sure about that, Bro? I have a good bottle of wine waiting."

"Yeah. I'm really beat. Save it for another night. I'll be there."

Cara was pleased to have him close. Reluctantly, she retired to her room after dinner, while everyone else sipped wine and continued chatting. She hated missing out, but she couldn't keep her eyes open. It was hard to shake jet lag. Before going to sleep, she called Francois. Hearing his voice calmed her. "Can't wait to see you, *Cherie*."

Chapter XCII

Paris, Everyone's Home Away from Home

The next morning, Cara was the first body stirring. She showered, made coffee, and executed the bakery run. Buying bread in the *Boulangerie* was an art she had perfected last trip. There were important choices to be made. *Baguettes* could be *bien cuite* (well-done) or *moulee* (brownish and crusty) or pas *trop cuite, farinee,* (soft and slightly under-baked). One could request a *baguette entiere* (full) or a *demi* (half) *baguette.* Chez Crenston favored the *baguette bien cuite entiere.*

She also bought *brioche* rolls, almond *croissants* and a *pain au levain* (sourdough bread). She scanned over the jam selection and decided on a *confiture cassis et violette* (black current & violet) and a *confiture fraise et rhubarbe* (strawberry rhubarb), *Bonne Maman* style. For an afternoon coffee treat, she bought a box of fruity *meringues.* She stopped at the market for fresh fruits, *kefir* yogurt and milk. On the way back, she called Francois. His velvet voice made her smile. She invited him to join them for dinner. By the time she returned, Ted was up, sipping her freshly made coffee.

"Wow, thanks Cara. I was so tired this morning. Couldn't shake a leg out of bed."

"My pleasure, Ted. I love looking around that bakery. I gain a few pounds just imagining the possibilities, but then we walk off all our calories here anyway, so who cares."

"So true."

It was Saturday and the girls slept in; Jasper was still out cold, making up for nights lost. Pure emotional lethargy, Cara guessed. After breakfast, Summer and Hope had work to do and Ted needed to run errands. Dinner reservations were made and shared with everyone. They would regroup then.

Cara and Jasper decided to explore the new exhibit at Beaubourg and have lunch in the vicinity. She intended to stop by François's gallery after they ate. Jasper would be the first family member to meet her new French boyfriend. Summer never met Francois at the exhibit opening last trip. Cara knew meeting Francois would take Jasper's mind off his own worries and she was curious about his opinion. He wasn't always as perceptive as Samson, but he was a good judge of character.

Francois's touching welcome pleased Cara and visibly surprised Jasper. Cara observed Jasper eyeing Francois in his quiet, cordial manner. When they left the gallery, Jasper interrogated her. It was so uncharacteristic of him that it made Cara smile. He usually left that job to Samson and Summer. Cara was just happy to distract him. She noticed that he often briefly stopped, looking over his shoulder; apparently a recently acquired habit. It broke her heart a little.

It was another beautiful sunny, Spring Day and the streets were bustling. Cara was joyful to be in Paris and she couldn't help but notice Jasper's tense frame slowly relax, as the day progressed. His rigid shoulders dropped a few inches, releasing weeks of tired tension. He actually managed to smile and it warmed Cara's heart. The fact that Jasper liked Francois, warmed her heart too.

"He's really nice, Mom. I like him."

"Yes, he truly is."

"How did you meet him?"

"I discovered his website and blog in New York, so when I came to Paris, I wanted to check out his gallery. Summer and I went to an art opening there after you left, last trip. He came to New York for business after that and called me and we have been in touch ever since."

"Hmmm. Interesting. Have Summer and Samson met him then?"

"No. You are the first. I really enjoy his company. We have a lot in common."

"But he lives here right?"

"Yes."

Jasper nodded and gave her his full attention, but she decided to leave him hanging. She didn't want to sell Francois to her children. She wanted them to discover his merits on their own.

That evening the Rue Malher group was joined by Samson, Natalie, Jean-Michel, Pascal and Francois for dinner. Francois's son Luc, planned on joining them for dessert. Ted picked a spacious restaurant off the Boulevard Saint Germain and requested a long table with a *banquette* in case more friends appeared. Lively conversations dominated the night and in the end, Luc, Pierre and Claude joined the original ten for dessert and aperitifs. Cara noticed Samson and Summer interacting with Francois and she wondered what their impressions were.

For Cara it was like a warm homecoming with the added bonus of Francois. She relished having all her children, and the man who snuck into her life, in one place, however brief it would be. Cara took pictures to remember this happy reunion. She would add them to her growing Paris portfolio. She would have liked to capture the charged energy of the evening in a bottle, but memories and pictures would have to suffice.

"Can you send me a couple of those shots, Cara? This is such a nice occasion."

"Sure, Francois. Here, let me take one of you and Luc too."

By the end of the night, Summer made plans to shoot a scene in Francois's gallery, Luc promised to take Hope to a dinner theater at Montmartre and Jasper decided to spend one more night on Cara's day bed, despite Samson's protests.

"Really, Jasper?"

"Yeah. I promise I'll come tomorrow night. Mom and I have plans in the morning, so it'll just be easier to crash there. Besides, that daybed was more comfortable than your couch."

Cara guessed that Jasper felt totally comfortable in the apartment on Rue Malher, which was testament to the potency of its positive inhabitants. The vibe was good and clearly, he preferred having people around these days, the more, the better. Once Samson left for work, Jasper would be alone and Jasper hated being alone since his apartment was robbed. He told her that in the café their first night in Paris. She could see the difference in her son and it pained her. Life in Paris was good, but beneath the surface trouble was brewing, threatening to combust any day.

Negotiating the Maze, Pardon my French...

Inspector Abello was studying the cast of characters on his notorious wall of pictures. The list was expanding, but the trails still had too many deviations and missing segments. Flores was slippery and surrounded himself with the best black suits criminal money could buy. His lawyers had built a legal wall around him much to Abello's chagrin.

Flores, with his blinding, annoying smile, seemed to be enjoying the fact that his sparring lawyers were protecting him, successfully. His smug smile pissed Abello off. He had reached a temporary impasse, but he wasn't giving up, of course. He could taste success.

"I can't believe this son of a bitch is jerking us around. His profoundly annoying grin is ruining my day."

"We're on him, Boss. Give it a little more time. We'll nail him."

"Argh."

Generally speaking, he was able to keep a professional distance between himself and all his cases, but this one was irritating the crap out of him. The self-assured Mexican was really pressing his buttons. He picked up the phone to call Inspector Arnaud. Two heads were better than one. It wasn't the first international case they'd collaborated on and it wouldn't be the last. He was determined to not let this slippery crook get the better of him. Not on his turf!

"*Salut*, Arnaud. Glad I caught you."

They exchanged a few pleasantries and got down to business. Time was short. "You cannot believe the legal representation surrounding Flores. He wasted no time covering his assets. I know he has plenty to hide, I just can't prove it yet."

"Come on, you can't possibly be surprised. Covering those legal expenses is peanuts to him. Give it time. We'll get a break. We usually do."

"You sound like my detectives. It can't be soon enough for me. I will dance the flamenco for you when we catch him."

"Now that picture is worth waiting for." Arnaud chuckled.

Chapter XCIV

Film Basics 101

On Sunday, Summer and Hope continued going through their footage as Cara looked over their shoulders. "Looking good girls. The camera really loves Helena."

"That is Hope's skill, Mom. She makes my character's shine."

"Good job, Hope."

"Thanks, but the girl is beautiful! Summer and I work well together. We truly have a good collaboration going. She knows what she wants, and it makes my job so much easier. I also have a top-notch lighting team, which saves us time on set, but Helena makes it all possible."

"I guess checking the footage as you go along helps as well."

"Yes, it does. When we have time and energy to do it. Like today. Usually, we just do it on weekends."

It was advantageous to check the footage regularly since they would be leaving the country in a month or two and would no longer be able to reshoot any scenes. Cara knew that Summer was meticulous in this respect.

"So far, we reshot one scene and it cost us a full day. It was an important one though, so we had to get it right," Summer explained. "At this point, everyday counts, and a day lost is costly. Also, we must reshoot quickly as the seasons change and scenes look different; the foliage, the signage, or the natural lighting: it all could be off."

"Yes, I realize."

"So far, so good. Although we're still a little behind schedule, there is nothing we can't catch up on."

"Good to hear."

As a precaution, Ted emailed the de Fontenays regarding a possible extension on the apartment in case it was needed. The de Fontenays had balked but agreed to work with them. They wouldn't agree to a full month, but perhaps a full month wasn't needed?

"Would a week or two do," they asked?

"That would help. Even an extra week eases my pressure," said Summer.

Cara understood the urgency. "Good thinking, Ted."

"Good. I will confirm it girls."

Over breakfast, Summer invited Jasper and Cara to the set.

"Helena will be there looking as sexy as ever. She's doing a fabulous job, so you should come watch her for a bit." She winked at Jasper.

"I would love to," Cara replied. She was pleased to see Jasper smile. Maybe it would distract him for a few hours. "Jasper?"

Jasper nodded and gave Summer a thumbs up.

After a leisure breakfast, the girls went back to work and Ted mapped out their schedule for the upcoming week. He was notifying the cast and crew of minor schedule changes. Cara used the time to call Francois in the privacy of her bedroom. Just hearing his voice made her feel warm inside.

Later, Cara and Jasper set up their electronics on the kitchen table and checked their emails. They laughed when they realized they both had bought the exact same tangerine-colored tablets.

"I guess we are more alike than we think," Cara noted winking.

"You inspired me."

Cara uploaded her pictures from dinner and saved everything on her new external hard drive. She wasn't taking any chances with these priceless family photos. Since her tablet had a knack for disappearing on her, she wanted to make sure these memories were locked. She had yet to sync her tablet with her laptop at home. Jasper did the same, but for different reasons. Jasper and Cara worked for a solid hour.

"Hey, do you want to go for a walk? Give the girls some space?"

"Sure, Mom. Let's go. Maybe we can grab lunch in the café later?

"Sounds good."

The girls were arguing over the footage. Opinions boomeranged and heated discussions followed, but in the end, they always came to some kind of understanding. Ted was smart enough to stay out of it. He didn't bother to look up from his laptop.

"We're out of here, girls. I removed all serrated and blunt objects near you," Cara joked.

"Just wait till we start editing. Sparks and nun chucks will fly,"

"Thanks for the heads up. All the more reason for us to leave."

"Kidding, of course. Hope won't be in New York for the editing. I'll have to make those tough decisions alone."

Cara and Jasper exchanged looks. He raised his eyebrows.

"Ted, should we pick up anything for dinner on the way back?" Cara asked.

"Good question and thanks for asking. I'll text you a small shopping list later if that's ok. Right now, my mind is elsewhere."

"Perfect. See you later."

Cara was happy to escape. She sensed that Jasper was too. Summer could be intense.

Chapter XCV

Trust No One, Least of all
Those Close to You

Carlos was sitting in the rear office of *El Toro* with Fernando and Jose discussing business. Actually, Carlos mainly listened and answered the occasional question directed at him. That was his tried and tested strategy when he had to deal with the two cousins at the same time.

Fernando stood up and motioned toward the door. "Let's go for a drive."

Once in the passenger seat of the car, Carlos instinctively turned the radio on. Fernando was stretched out in the back seat.

"Drive to the harbor and park, Jose."

"The warehouse?"

"No, the scenic parking lot."

Carlos looked out of the car window and thought of Mexico. "Working harbors have a similar look everywhere, don't they?"

That was the point. They offered comfort to those who travelled by boat and convenience for those who needed the break and opportunity to unload and replenish on land. They also were picturesque and loved by people hooked on coastal living. To Carlos, a harbor was a touch of home. The boats on the Seine did not have the same appeal.

Fernando got right down to business as soon as they were stationary. "So far, we have everything under control, but we need to be careful. We're being watched like hawks. Abello is just waiting for us to slip up and obviously his team cannot be bribed or intimidated. This is not Mexico, my friends."

Carlos rolled his eyes as he looked out of the side window, waiting....

"Make sure this next shipment goes directly to Marseilles and not to our warehouse here, understood? I want it distributed immediately and then send the pottery to Monaco to be delivered to the Russians. Quick and no mistakes. Change the ship's itinerary. Come to Barcelona after Marseille. You can fly to Marseille and meet the ship there, Jose."

Jose nodded, looking grim. "Si, Fernando."

"You don't think you're being watched in Marseille as well?" Carlos asked trying to make his point cautiously.

"The Moroccans have us covered there. My brother promised the wrapping is air-tight and secure," Fernando continued. "We'll be fine. I pay everyone well to do their job properly."

"Yes, you do."

"Make sure the Marseille guys are paid half in advance, so they continue to be motivated, Carlos. Anyone who changes their mind, under the pressure, will be permanently replaced. You understand me, Jose?" Fernando continued.

"Yes, Boss. Carlos and I got it handled." Jose replied, stroking his turquoise cross.

"Yes," Carlos nodded, but in reality, he felt a knot of apprehension twisting in his gut. He hated the words, "replaced permanently". That had only one meaning with Fernando.

They chatted about logistics for another half hour and circled the car back to the restaurant. Carlos looked around the street, deliberately exiting in slow motion. He took the time to adjust his sunglasses, as he swept the premises and followed a few paces behind the two men. As they re-entered the restaurant, he took one last look over his shoulder and closed the screen door. He didn't see anyone, but he knew they were being watched. He could feel it in his gut. Upon his arrival, he noticed the non-descript van in the hotel garage. It was still there hours later, in the same spot.

Carlos disliked coming to Barcelona for what his boss dubbed an 'important' meeting. Fernando was getting paranoid and no longer wanted to talk on the phone, even the secure ones made him nervous. This made Carlos anxious, because his boss rarely buckled under pressure. Usually, he was overly confident, relying heavily on Jose, his enforcer.

Or maybe it was an excuse to force Carlos to come to Barcelona? That wouldn't surprise him either. Jose echoed his cousin's concerns, but then, he always agreed with Fernando. Carlos wondered if he had a brain of his own or if he was just too lazy to use it.

They could not afford any slip ups. Carlos didn't want to spend the rest of his life in a Spanish jail cell. He couldn't wait to get on a plane and go back to Paris. He was at his happiest, when he was saying good-bye to Fernando and Jose and hello to Helena. She was his one joy, his sweet reprieve at the end of a taxing day. Helena and his growing savings account comforted Carlos during stressful times. One day, he would make his move.

The Artist's Heart

After lunch, Cara and Jasper decided to part ways. Jasper was going to Samson's house to drop off his suitcase and Cara wanted to walk back to Francois's gallery before grocery shopping. They planned to all meet up later for dinner at Rue Malher. Cara felt uneasy letting Jasper go.

"Shall I walk you back to the apartment?"

"No, Mom, I got it. I'm fine. Really! See you later."

"Ok then. If you're sure… See you tonight." She texted Francois that she was on her way.

When she got to the gallery, Francois was waiting. Decaf cappuccinos and artist portfolios were set up for her opinion.

"Hello, Cara, dear, I have some good news. I have a check for you. Two of your pieces sold."

"Really? That's fantastic, Francois. Thank you! More money for me to fuel the local economy."

She waved the check in the air, ecstatic that he was successful selling her work. "I will have to show you some of my newer pieces later. I have tons of pictures." Cara smiled.

"I wouldn't expect anything different. You're a demon with that tablet. As a matter of fact, I wanted to ask you if you had time to start some new work when you get back. I think I might have a market for your work. There was definitely interest."

"I was too busy getting orders out before I left, but I plan to make some new designs when I return, unless I get bombarded with new orders again. It's a vicious cycle."

"You know, Cara. Those two pieces sold relatively quickly. I was thinking we could generate more interest with a show of your own. Perhaps in a few months? We would need at least a dozen works of art. What do you think?"

"Oh my God, that would be beyond awesome, Francois! I'll need time to get the right pieces together of course, but a few months should be doable. Mmm, this coffee is sooo good. Just what I needed. Thanks."

"Take all the time you want. Let me know when you're ready and we'll write it in the calendar. I do need a few months' notice though. We schedule our artists well in advance."

"Yes, of course. I know you need time to advertise and assemble. Thanks so much. This is really exciting, Francois."

She could feel Francois's warm, hazel eyes resting on her face as she studied the portfolios. It felt wonderful to be cared for.

"When can I take you to dinner? *Toute seule*? Alone?" he asked.

"Tomorrow, Cheri" she answered. "Tonight, I have a family dinner."

Francois took her into his arms and Cara could feel his body heat. Her mind wandered. Jasper's situation had somewhat overshadowed her reunion with Francois, but they were on a good track and now she would be on Francois's radar even longer with the planning of a one-woman show. Cara counted her blessings. Francois made her heart soar. She couldn't remember the last time she felt like that. *My own show! In Paris, no less. Ohh la la.*

Chapter XCVII

Nightmare in Paris

Jasper's first night at Samson's started out nicely. After the family dinner at Rue Malher, he and Samson walked across the river to Samson's apartment and talked for hours over a nightcap. Talking to his mom and Samson helped ease his racing mind, but Jasper still couldn't shake the eerie feeling that he was being watched. He compulsively looked over his shoulder while walking around Paris and he still had trouble sleeping without checking and rechecking the windows and doors. He never discovered anyone or anything unusual, yet he could not rid himself of that creepy feeling. For fear of being labeled paranoid, he kept his sentiments to himself.

"Perhaps mom is right about seeing a therapist," he mumbled to himself when Samson was in the bathroom. *I'm perpetually on the verge of freaking out.*

When Samson yawned and got ready for bed, Jasper checked his computer for news from Barcelona. There was nothing new. Further checking revealed no added articles referring to F&S Enterprises. Satisfied, he got ready for bed. It was after 2am in the morning when he finally drifted off to sleep.

During the night, his dreams tripped into nightmares. He was invited to *El Toro* with Adriano, but the dinner transpired differently than the one he had attended months earlier. In his dream Fernando informed them with his green-eyed, fake smile, "I hope you enjoyed your supper, gentlemen. It will be your last."

Jasper could feel sweat beads forming in the nape of his neck.

"What do you mean?" Adriano asked, taking it as a joke. "Are you closing?"

Smoke enveloped their dinner table and the lighting dimmed. "No, but you are. We no longer need your services, and you know too much. You shouldn't have asked so many questions, Adriano. I warned you not to snoop into our private affairs."

"But I know nothing," Jasper shouted confused and scared out of his wits. No one seemed to care or listen. It appeared he was guilty by association. Through the haze Jasper saw a gun appear in Jose's hand. It was pointed at Adriano and when the first shot was fired, Jasper bolted from the table and zig zagged out of the restaurant. He heard multiple shots follow as he exited at full speed, ducking as he ran. He heard Fernando's firm command, "Go after him."

Running past the restaurant windows, he saw Adriano slumped over the dinner table. Sprinting for his life, Jasper forged into the dark, narrow alleys of the Barcelona harbor area. Looking over his shoulder, he could see Jose gaining on him. At each juncture he looked back, anticipating someone striking from the shadows. Echoing footsteps urged him on. The shadows never quite caught up to him, but he couldn't stop to rest. He was running out of breath fast and his energy was waning.

Then, in the distance, Jasper saw his mother waving and beckoning him through the fog, backlit by a bright moon, but he couldn't get to her. She didn't seem to grasp his obstacles. He awoke panting in a cold sweat and shivered. He pulled the covers over his head. It was still dark out and he couldn't rid himself of this reoccurring nightmare for the remainder of the night. Every time he closed his eyes, it continued… relentlessly. Sleep, eluding him for hours, he woke up around 8 am feeling spent. Jasper resolved not to say anything to Samson.

"Everything ok?" Samson walked into the living room. "I heard you scream."

"No hiding anything from you! I've been having nightmares since the break-in."

"Understandable. They will pass in time."

"Thanks, Freud. I sure hope so. I wake up feeling so tired."

"Maybe you should talk to a professional?"

"Now you sound like mom."

"Just saying… Think about it." Samson nodded with a caring and encouraging look on his face, but he said nothing else.

Jasper was thankful for that. He knew his brother was thinking about telling him to leave Barcelona. He was getting that same look from Cara. He wondered if his nightmares were yet another sign to make a change. He was still floundering with the decision regarding his future. By day he wanted to sign for another year and by night he wanted to escape to the comforts of his home in New York. He wondered if the nightmares would cease if he decided to leave Barcelona.

Chapter XCVIII

It Takes a Thief

The next day, Summer, Hope and Ted were already gone when Cara woke up at 7am. After showering, she called Jasper to invite him for breakfast. She was busy brewing her *rooibus* tea when he picked up.

"How are you today? Didn't expect you to answer this early. I was going to leave you a voicemail."

"I didn't sleep well. In fact, I keep having reoccurring nightmares about Adriano."

"Geez, so sorry, Jasper. What can I do to help?"

"Not sure, Mom."

"Do you want to come back here to sleep? Will that help?"

"No, I'll be fine. This can't last forever. What are we doing today?"

"Shall we start with breakfast at the café? My treat."

"Perfect. See you in a half hour?"

"Ok."

Cara finished her tea and packed her bag with the tangerine tablet. She put on a little make-up and fussed with her hair. Without her usual equipment it was a hopeless cause. Exasperated, she pulled it back into a ponytail and added her rose gold hoop earrings, hoping they would distract from a bad hair day.

Arriving at the cafe first, she settled in a window spot and searched the sidewalks for Jasper. The day was a dismal grey and rain threatened. Fog surrounded the gorgeous architectural rooftops, creating an ominous vibe in the neighborhood's narrow streets. A few minutes later, she spotted him. He looked tired as he approached, blending in with the fog. She couldn't help but feel sorry for him. They placed their order and Cara decided to broach the subject of Jasper's future.

"First, tell me about this dream."

Jasper explained it in detail. The fact that the weather was foggy and similar to his dream was not lost on anyone.

Wanting to change the subject, Cara asked, "What were Samson's thoughts about Barcelona?"

"He thinks I should pack up and leave… …. ASAP," Jasper answered. "Honestly, without Adriano, it won't be the same for me. The general office climate is not great either, but that may subside over time."

"Yes, but it may take longer than you think. Murder has a lingering stigma."

"Yes, I'm afraid of that. I'm also worried about who I will be assigned to. No one currently there can replace Adriano. He was singular."

"Yes, I gathered that. After this morning's conversation, I was thinking, if you continue to have sleeping problems, maybe you should see a therapist to help you through the trauma. Adriano's death was traumatic for you, even if you don't perceive it that way."

"Yeah, maybe. I knew you were going to say that. Let's see how the next few days go."

"Ok but keep me informed. I'm here to help, Jasper."

"Thanks, Mom."

Jasper had calmed down somewhat, but the thought of going back to Barcelona made his hands twitch and his smile disappear instantly.

"So do you have any idea who will take over for Adriano?" Cara asked.

"No. Maybe management will have decided by the time I get back, but I kind of doubt it. Things don't happen quickly in Spain or in the company."

"I could start asking around about jobs for you, once I get back to New York. I would love it if you came home, Jasper," Cara volunteered.

"Thanks, Mom, but I think I need to handle this myself. Let's see what happens when I get back to Barcelona," Jasper countered, "I was happy there until this happened. There is a good chance I may leave, but I don't want to decide this moment. This thing with Adriano really shook me up. I started not to feel safe. I don't want to continue with Fernando's accounts either, but I think that's already handled. I just don't know what to do yet."

"Well, give it time. You'll figure it out. I would think that if the police find that he has dealt in stolen goods, they'll freeze your client's accounts anyway," Cara responded, pulling out her orange tablet.

"Yeah. Probably."

"Just promise you'll think about coming home, ok?" Cara half pleaded.

"I promise, Mom. Under the circumstances, I wouldn't feel terrible leaving. I love living in Barcelona but … … Right now, I'm still confused and undecided. I think you're right. Things will become clearer when I get back and see what's what."

"Let me show you the pictures from the other night." Cara changed the subject. She could see Jasper tensing up and she wanted him to relax. "Do you think Samson and Summer liked Francois?"

"Yes, I think so. He's very likeable, Mom."

They chatted and laughed over some of the pictures, while the tables near them began filling up with morning customers. Cara and Jasper decided to spend the day in Samson's neighborhood. When Cara got up to go to the lady's room, she saw Jasper motion for the check. "Here's some cash. Go ahead and pay. I'll be right back."

Jasper placed Cara's tangerine tablet on the banquette next to him and wrestled his own tablet into a neoprene cover, briefly placing it on the table. He turned to reach for his jacket on the back of his chair and slid his arms into the sleeves as he looked out the window. It was still raining. He motioned to the waiter to come get the cash just as Cara reappeared. Cara reached for her raincoat and the tablet on the table. Both tablets had black covers.

"Wait, that one is mine," said Jasper. He turned to the banquette to hand Cara her tablet, but it was no longer there.

"Where is mine?"

"Not sure. I thought I put it on the banquette." He looked around helplessly.

Cara looked at all the surrounding chairs, then, under the chairs and table. Her tablet was gone. She gasped in disbelief. She was gone for less than five minutes, and Jasper had stayed at the table!

The café was crowded, and no one paid any attention to them as they searched the vicinity. The waiter was sympathetic, but he saw nothing. He was busy. Cara was in a panic. She looked around frantically, asking the people around her. Who could have possibly swiped the tablet so quickly without Jasper noticing. Thank God, she had backed up all her pictures! This was not a good start to the day.

"I'm sorry, Mom. I didn't see anyone take it."

"It's not your fault, Jasper. Obviously, this was a professional who targeted us. We're lucky both didn't disappear."

Deep down Cara worried that Jasper was the intended target, but it could have been a common petty thief too. Just her luck. She decided to keep her thoughts to herself. Jasper did not need the extra stress; he was nervous and felt bad enough already without her adding to his misery. If Jasper thought the same, he didn't voice it, but he looked as if he had seen a ghost. Cara decided to downplay the loss despite feeling crestfallen.

"It looks like we've fallen victim to a Paris thief. How unfortunate."

Chapter XCIX

Follow the Money....
Or the Pottery......Or the Drugs?

Inspector Abello scanned the expert's report on the stolen pottery and smiled. Finally, he was getting somewhere. The ceramics found, could definitively be traced back to the Metropolitan Museum of Art in New York. Furthermore, the receipts Fernando Flores produced from the New York auction to account for the antique pottery in his possession, only accounted for a couple of items, not all. Several pieces found did not match the bills and they were from the crate nabbed from Sotheby's. Where were the rest of the stolen artworks?

The items in the Paris auction were imitations of more antique stolen goods from the Met, but the whereabouts of the originals were still a mystery. The auction house did not have a record of all the originals for sale. Similar items, yes. So, where and how did Fernando Flores get the crates from the Met and how did he dispose of them in Europe? He didn't have all the correct transaction records after all. Abello smiled to himself. "Caught ya."

To Abello, all the pottery looked the same, but apparently age and color accounted for substantial differences in price. Thank God for experts who could tell the difference. Arnaud had proven to be very helpful and committed in the quest for the museum goods, but there still were many loose ends. They knew Fernando Flores was involved in stealing from the Met and Sotheby's, but they were fuzzy on how it went down. New York police was working on that, but also not quite nailing it. Whatever art they found from the Met would go back there and the sold ceramics stolen from Sotheby's would be shipped back too. However, where did the remaining missing merchandise go? Frustrated, he picked up the phone to call his counterpart in Paris.

"Arnaud, do you have a minute?"

"Hello, Inspector Abello. I was wondering when I'd hear from you. How's it going?"

"Good, good. I would be even better if I knew what Flores did with all the missing pottery from the Met. I saw your report on the copies sold at auction in Paris. Tell me, did Fernando buy his own copies in order to fake records for the purchase of the originals?"

"Good question. I know that Alphonse consigned the pieces that Fernando had and now he is dead. Tracing Alphonse's consignments and Flores's purchases was no problem, but following the trail after that was where we had problems. Apparently, Alphonse had private clients that wanted to remain private. They paid him in untraceable ways. That is where the antique originals most likely went if they aren't still with Flores. We could not find any records in his office and Alphonse's cell phone was missing. What have you uncovered? What do Flores's lawyers say?"

"His lawyers argue that he never worked with Alphonse. Yes, they went to one auction together, but they did not do business. They merely discussed the possibility over dinner. It is their contention that the auction house misquoted the dates and had confused the ceramics, making simple, ignorant clerical or printing errors. Of course, you and I know that is bullshit. And then there is the problem of the copies. His lawyers are saying his copies were made from photos of the originals. They had pictures from the pre-auction viewings they went to in New York. There is no law against using antiques as inspiration. There are few copyright laws for antiquity, if any."

"But what about the copies that look like the pottery that hasn't resurfaced? What do the lawyers say about that?"

"Pictures served as a reference. What else can they say?"

"Pictures provide a very limited reference and are never as good as viewing an original, but we cannot prove otherwise. Our next step should be to go back to the Paris auction house and talk to the ceramics department. We need to go over their records one more time and investigate who did the appraisals and who wrote the descriptions for the catalogue. Maybe Flores got to them? I'm eager to see the buyers and seller's information and talk to the staff to get a feel for the department and its employees."

"Yes, agreed. I want to understand the whole process to see where and if an impropriety or switch could have happened in the chain. There couldn't have been that many opportunities to do that. Have your men talk to security and check them out. There is always the possibility of an inside job."

"Yes. I will do that and get back to you. Do you think the originals were consigned and then switched with the copies during public viewings?"

"I wonder. Anything is possible."

Abello did not want to reveal his hand publicly yet. Together, they decided to hold off on arresting Flores for the alleged pottery theft charges. It was doubtful the charges would stick. They would let Fernando believe the pottery mix up was indeed straightened out. There wasn't enough hard evidence, and the lawyers could keep them tied up in court for weeks or even years, Abello argued.

"Ok, I agree. Let's hold off until we have more concrete evidence. Let's focus on the drug trail." Arnaud coughed.

"This pottery stuff is confusing and tedious to follow, and it is only the tip of the iceberg. It's also somewhat harmless compared to the drug venture. Innocent people are dying from laced powder. I say we forfeit the tip of the iceberg for the whole glacier. Let's leave the pottery confusion for the insurance agents and art specialists to sort out. I don't know about you, but my manpower is limited."

"Yes, same. Good plan. Let's follow the drug trail."

"Good. I'm confident that we'll eventually nail Flores. Patience and diligence usually pay off. Besides, the drugs are killing people at an alarming rate. This stuff is deadly and potent, not to mention, highly addictive. Sooner or later, Flores will make a mistake and you and I will be right there, waiting."

Secretly, Abello was hoping Flores would piss off the Moroccans in Marseille. That would take care of him alright.

"Do you think you could rattle the cage a little with the Moroccans? If Flores crosses them, we might benefit."

"I can certainly try. That thought had crossed my mind too."

"Great minds think alike."

Inspector Abello smelled success. A big fish like Fernando Flores could deliver a huge feather in his international law enforcement cap. He could taste it. He was pleased that Arnaud understood his vibe and that he agreed to be patient and go along with the search for illegal drugs rather than just trying to make the art theft charges stick. Drug charges would land Flores in jail for a long time and that is exactly where Abello wanted him, behind bars, his very own Spanish curtain.

Chapter C

Art Confusion and Book Magic

Fernando and Jose were celebrating at *El Toro*. Carlos looked on, cautiously. He had been summoned by Fernando for yet another annoying meeting and was present when the call came in. Fernando's lawyer had called earlier to assure them that things were moving along without difficulty. The auction house records were inconsistent, and his purchase was legitimate. If the pottery's exact age was missing or incorrect in the auction house records, it was not Fernando's fault, nor could he be charged. Perhaps the originals had been switched while in the auction houses' care? There were no visible links between Alphonse and Fernando. No direct payment record had been uncovered.

"You will just return the few stolen pieces you have in your possession and be done with the 'misunderstanding', no harm done," Carlos heard the lawyer instruct Fernando over speaker phone. "The police can try to trace the timeline of those pieces, but that is no longer your problem."

"I'm happy to supply my sales records, Fernando chirped smugly.

It looked like the auction house would be on the hook for the mistake. Clearly the trail led elsewhere. Fernando was cleared. Carlos listened apprehensively. He wasn't convinced.

"Moving on, I have more good news," Carlos offered. My men located the American boy's tablet. They nabbed it at a café when he was having breakfast with his mother. No break in or injury required."

Carlos knew Fernando loved life when things moved smoothly; his mood could go from doom to exhilaration in seconds.

"Good work, Carlos. Let's see it."

"Sure." He got up to reach into his carry-on luggage. "I figure there is no reason to hurt the boy if he wasn't privy to Adriano's concerns."

"Right. Smart thinking. Abello has been up my ass enough. I don't think he would have let the kid leave the country if he knew anything, but it's always better to check things out myself. Champagne, boys?"

Jose poured a glass of chilled champagne for everyone. Carlos was not so sure their celebration was warranted, but he remained silent.

He let his mind wander while Fernando played with the electronics. He knew Fernando hated giving up the Metropolitan pieces because he loved them with a passion, but it was a small price to pay to get Abello off his back.

Fernando Flores's obsession with quality ceramics stemmed back to his roots in Mexico. His family had been in the ceramics business for four generations and Fernando admired, breathed, and dreamed about ceramics all day long. It was his passion in life, the fire in his belly more important than money or women.

However, in recent years, business had slowed, due to added competition. To stand out, they needed to expand their line and add more sophisticated designs. It was imperative to market in other parts of the world too or die a slow retail death in Mexico, which to Fernando would have been unthinkable. Tourism was not what it once was, and Mexicans could only afford so much. Drug distribution, combined with the export of his beloved ceramics, added the extra financial boost that helped the company flourish again.

Seeking out old European motifs had been Fernando's idea and it was a good one, but it was costly even though skilled labor in Mexico was cheap. They needed to get their hands on good models to make this strategy work. Fernando's nephew and connection at the Met made this possible. Once the copies were made, Fernando sold the originals on the black market through Alphonse, but some he just couldn't part with. His love for the craft, didn't allow him to let masterpieces slip through his sticky fingers. This worried Carlos. Evidence was something he wanted to get rid of, the sooner, the better.

Carlos didn't feel the same about the business. His father had started working for the *Corazon de Leon* factory when he was a child, long before the transition phase into drug distribution. Unfortunately, when his father voiced his concerns about the new addition, he was threatened. Both father and son got caught up, despite not wanting to and they were not permitted to leave. They knew too much about the company's inner workings. Carlos blamed Fernando and Jose for his family's downfall, but unlike his father, he had learned to keep his innermost thoughts buried deep inside. He accepted the accounting job in the ceramics factory to help his family, but it killed his family in slow succession. His time to strike back and break loose would come; he firmly believed that.

Select stolen pieces, Fernando stored with his family in Mexico, but a few chosen ones were shipped back to him and were in his possession in Barcelona. Fernando kept them in his hidden safe, only occasionally taking out one piece or another, to enjoy in his home or office. It was his inspiration, his obsession, his weakness. It was also Russian roulette in Carlos's humble opinion.

The only way to pay for the necessary expansion of the family business was through drug money. The drug money enabled them to hire the best crafts people, to travel for sales, to market to hotels and restaurants internationally and to establish and buy their own transportation method and hubs. Once he experienced success in Europe, Fernando Flores wanted to stay. He was more autonomous, away from his brother in Mexico, where the cartel kept them supplied and on a short, suffocating leash. They were under constant pressure to pay, ship and sell for the cartel. Like Carlos, they had no choice.

Carlos had jumped on board as an accountant in his early twenties when the European expansion was still a dream. A few years and trips later, Fernando fell in love with Barcelona and decided to expand his business there, far away from the cartel, who his brother Felipe was now fully enslaved to. Carlos was happy to step into the unknown. His life in Mexico had been bleak and oppressive with no chance of ever escaping. Here in Barcelona, Fernando was his own boss and in Paris, he let Carlos do his thing while maintaining the company's books and assets.

Carlos continued to handle all accounts pertaining to the various businesses. His occasional trips to Barcelona kept them all happy. As long as money was wired back to Mexico on a regular basis, they were free to realize their own dreams with the remaining profits, and those were substantial. Carlos made sure this set of books were known only to Fernando and himself. He wasn't even sure Jose knew the full extent of it. He guessed that Fernando only fed Jose what he wanted him to know.

With the ceramics business finally yielding a profit, and the lucrative restaurants in place, Fernando and Carlos hoped to create their own niche. Carlos's business and computer skills made him indispensable to Fernando. That would have never happened in Mexico. If the cartel realized their additional profits, they would have increased the pressure. Carlos was glad he had taken a chance and left his home. His skillset allowed for them to ship and sell just enough drugs to keep the cartel happy, without jeopardizing their own expanding business. Carlos made sure their payments to the cartel were exact and prompt.

Carlos knew if he stayed in Mexico, he would have been enslaved forever or worse, hunted, and jailed or killed by rivals, like the ruthless *Los Zetas Drug Cartel*. He would always live a life of looking over his shoulder, but at least here, he had a reprieve, a semblance of a 'normal life.'

It was as much freedom as they could ever hope to get. They paid to keep their families safe at home. That was the non-negotiable price they agreed to. However, Carlos sensed a change in the tide. They were now on the police's radar and that meant pressure of a different nature. Carlos longed for a simpler life with Helena, but he knew that was an insurmountable dream. His life would always be complicated if he was connected to the Flores dynasty and there was no getting out of this family business. He was into it as deep as the family members themselves and at this point, everyone counted on him to keep the magical books straight. Carlos was involved up to his eyeballs. He didn't even want to think about it because it scared him. For now, he lived day to day, for who knew what tomorrow would look like?

"Carlos, did you hear me?"

"No. What, Fernando?"

"I said, this tablet has an incredible picture library of ceramics. I've never seen anything like it. Tons of good work."

"Really? Who would have thought?"

Chapter CI

Love in the Afternoon

After searching the café to no avail and getting over the initial shock of being victimized, Cara and Jasper went to the Picasso Museum. They stopped for a light, late lunch, then parted ways. Jasper went to Samson's apartment and Cara headed to Francois's gallery.

Cara let Francois hug and appease her. "Don't be upset. We'll get you a new tablet and this violation will be ancient memory. I have a special afternoon planned for you, Cara."

"But it has to be tangerine-colored," Cara sniffled.

"Yes, I'm sure Apple still makes that color. Besides, you have everything on your external hard drive you said. What luck! *Pas de probleme*! No problem," Francois promised.

Cara nodded, but still felt defeated and victimized. However, if anyone could improve her mood, it was Francois. He had that magic power.

"Let me surprise you today."

Francois nudged her gently into a taxi and gave the driver directions. A few minutes later, they entered a store with rocks, the pretty gemological kind. Colorful examples of quartz, chalcedony, apatite, and tourmaline lined the shelves. Geodes with tantalizing crystals, small, exquisite stone carvings and ammonite fossils decorated the shelved perimeter of the small store. Cara felt her spirits lift. She focused on some rainbow hematite from Brazil. Its strong, metallic colors would look great combined with ceramics, she decided. Francois let Cara examine the room at her leisure and when she was ready with a tray full of favorites, he paid the bill.

"Thank you, Francois. These are beautiful. I'll use some in my ceramics."

"You're welcome. I'll be curious to see what you do."

"This one, I'll keep on my night table with the shoe you gave me. The colors are exquisite."

"I agree." He hugged her.

They walked around the neighborhood, browsing around the other galleries. The midday sun was delightful and helped lift her mood.

"Ready for a drink at my place?" Francois inquired. "I have a nice, sunny terrace, too."

"Ready. Can't wait to see it." Cara smiled. "And thanks again for the crystals. I'll be thinking of you when I incorporate them into my designs."

"In that case it was definitely my pleasure."

Francois lived on the top floor of an older building in walking distance of the gallery. While the building only was six stories tall,

the view was impressive from his penthouse terrace. Luckily, the surrounding buildings were lower. In the distance Cara could see the red tubes on the Pompidou Art Center. She liked Francois's home. It was centrally located and embedded in an artsy neighborhood. His walls also showcased some great art.

Looking around, Cara realized Francois had combined two apartments and renovated them, knocking down a wall or two for a more fluid floorplan. His kitchen opened to the dining area with a spacious bamboo counter on which there was a Japanese flower arrangement. The dining room opened to the living room with glass pocket doors. Exiting the living room, on the right, there was a short hallway with two bedrooms and two bathrooms. She liked the apartment's simple, straight, stream-lined furniture and its elaborate modern art display. The wall near the dining room had a large square painting in an abstract expressionist style, while the wall in the living room had a grouping of smaller, interestingly matched paintings by various artists. Both bedrooms showcased unique works of art.

"Your apartment is lovely Francois. It looks like an extension of your gallery. Very modern and high tech. How did you decide which art to hang?" Cara asked.

"It changes all the time, so you are absolutely right. It IS an extension of my gallery," Francois confirmed.

"There are only a few favorite pieces I keep, but the rest could be gone next time you come if I find something more pleasing. Would you like a glass of wine?"

Cara nodded. "Yes please."

He opened a bottle of red wine and poured two glasses, handing her one. They sipped their wine at the kitchen counter as the weather turned too nippy for the terrace, despite the late day sunshine. Francois lit a candle and settled into a barstool next to Cara.

"I'm taking you to a neighborhood restaurant tonight. It's small and simple, but the food is excellent, "he explained. "One of my favorite neighborhood spots."

"Perfect," Cara replied, planting a gentle kiss on his lips. Without another word, Francois pulled his chair closer and kissed her passionately. Cara melted under his touch. Francois's kisses traveled down the side of her neck and along her shoulder, as he unbuttoned her blouse. He continued blazing a trail to her cleavage with his soft warm fingertips and lips. Cara closed her eyes, rolled her head back and succumbed to the mood. The flutters in her stomach increased. Francois pulled her into his arms and led her toward his bedroom. Dinner could wait.

Chapter CII

The (Nearly) Invisible Man

The next day was another early one for the Rue Malher crew. Summer peeked in at her mother sleeping blissfully. Her date with Francois must have gone well as she was still smiling in her sleep. Summer chuckled to herself.

She gathered up her equipment and along with Hope and Ted tip-toed out the door. The filming was going really well, and Alain and Helena were completely in sync with Summer's vision. Summer explained her sets in detail, showing infinite patience. It paid off. Some days just flowed while others presented tricky problems, usually weather and equipment related. They didn't have too many actors to contend with, so that made a difference as well. In fact, there were generally more crew members than cast. For the past two weeks, they whizzed through their scenes, nailing the shots. They were in a productive groove and Summer hoped it would continue.

Street scenes were shot early in the morning. They saved the indoor scenes for bad weather days, whenever possible. Today was that kind of day. They were filming in a cafe near Montmartre. Around 3pm they stopped so the café could reopen for the after-work crowd. Alain left early as only Helena was needed for the final scene.

As they wrapped up, Summer noticed Carlos hanging around the crew. She remembered him from New Years Eve and Mimi's birthday dinner and was surprised to see that Helena still had this seemingly ill- tempered, unsmiling, guy in her life. *What could possibly be the appeal?* Try as she might, she could not see any redeeming qualities in Carlos. Helena was a beautiful, kind, and spunky woman; surely, she could have anyone she desired. *Why him? Mr. Grouch?* Summer was at a loss.

One of these days, she would broach the subject with Helena and find out what the deal was with Carlos. His connection to Jasper's client made him even more sinister to Summer. Was he part of an illegal business? Where did that leave Helena? Summer vowed to do some digging when she had the time, but right now she had zero extra time. Most days, she barely had time to pee.

Surprising Innermost Thoughts of a Felon

Carlos was mesmerized with Summer as she gently directed Helena. He observed Summer's collaboration and involvement with every aspect of filming; lighting, camera angles, shot set up, while simultaneously directing Helena's lines and moves. He had no doubt the American girl knew what she was doing. Perhaps his investment in Helena would pay off sooner than later, but even if it didn't, she was delightful in bed and worth every penny he spent. She gave him comfort and much-needed relaxation at the end of his aggravating days dealing with his business and its many problems. Just thinking about sex with Helena made his pants bulge.

With the constantly increasing stress Fernando and Jose were sending his way, Carlos needed a release. Drinking was not his pleasure. Neither were drugs. He had witnessed too many lives close to him destroyed by both. Sex was the only diversion he needed. In the past, a nice girlfriend here and there did the trick. Things always ended though because he didn't want to get married. He was careful not to get anyone pregnant. However,

Helena had rapidly become an addictive and compelling vice, so much more than just sex. Carlos could no longer imagine life without her.

Helena was beautiful and uncomplicated, a rare combination in his limited experience. She did not ask a lot of cumbersome questions and she was so grateful for everything he offered her. Carlos appreciated those simple facts and chose to reward them handsomely. Helena made his hot blood bubble like no other woman before. He no longer desired anyone else; Helena fulfilled his needs.

It irritated him now when Fernando tried to hook him up in Barcelona. Fernando just didn't get it, but that was fine. Carlos played along because he didn't want to show any weakness. If Fernando sensed softness, especially a softness toward Helena, he would become cruel. Carlos avoided talking about Helena at all costs and always changed the subject when asked about her. "She's an easy and skillful lay, so I keep her around," was his stock answer. It could not have been further from the truth. He kept her around because he loved her, and they were so good together. For that reason alone, he never brought her to Barcelona even though Fernando repeatedly invited her. Carlos would never tolerate putting Helena in danger.

"No, thanks, Fernando. I don't want her to get the wrong idea. I have her when I want her. That is enough. I don't want to rock the boat or pretend there is more to it."

Fernando ate up his answer and roared with laughter.

"You're cold, Carlos."

"I know. I've learned from the best."

This made Fernando laugh even harder after which Carlos could easily change the subject to Fernando's conquests. In truth,

Carlos and Helena were a perfect match. Carlos counted his lucky stars when he met her. What an incredible fluke that had been. It warmed his heart just thinking about that day.

As he watched Summer instruct Helena for the next scene, his mind wandered. He thought back to the night he first saw Helena. His guys had supplied drugs to the modeling agency party at his restaurant when he first spotted Helena on the security camera in his office. Her beauty captivated him, and he spied on her from the comfort of his reclining chair, never leaving the office. When the agency contacted him for yet another party a short while later, he gave them a good price to ensure their continued business. It was fun to have beautiful eye candy amongst his regular customers and staff, but secretly, he hoped Helena would come. He wanted to see her again.

He almost didn't go to the second party, but then he couldn't resist the urge to experience Helena up close. A modeling agency party, if nothing more, provided a night of entertainment for a lonely, horny guy, who still felt like an an outsider in Paris.

Carlos never intentionally started relationships as most women wanted too much and asked too many questions he couldn't afford to answer. He kept his life private, and his women trapped in a revolving door. The closer they tried to get, the quicker he shoved them out of his bed and life. Love never factored into the equation. Until Helena came along.

Carlos rarely drank, but nonetheless, he'd grabbed a glass of champagne and walked into the party. Helena immediately caught his eye. She was different from the other girls, more approachable, friendly, and less judgmental perhaps. What had impressed Carlos even more was that she had turned down free drugs the other party goers offered her; she preferred a glass or two of champagne. Seizing the moment, he offered her a glass of bubbly and watched her light up.

"Yes, thank you. Did you just get here?" She raised her glass and took a sip.

"No, this is my restaurant. I wanted to make sure everyone is happy and taken care of."

"Oh yes. We like this place. I'm Helena. What's your name?"

"Carlos. Can I get you a refill?"

"Not yet. I'm not a big drinker."

"I noticed."

Helena oozed sex appeal. Carlos could be charming and generous when he wanted to be and he wanted her badly. He didn't for a moment believe that his odds were good, but there was no harm in trying, he'd thought. That night he offered her all the free champagne she wanted which wasn't all that much and in return, she'd flirted with him quite shamelessly. To his surprise, she stayed until late and then agreed to leave the party with him, which morphed into an unforgettable night of passion for him. A night he would never forget. The angels were looking over him that fateful night; he was certain. Carlos knew after one night with Helena, he didn't want to let this girl go, ever. She drove him wild and soothed his soul at the same time. She was more than he could ever ask for in a woman and he knew going forward, he would do anything, anything at all to keep her in his orbit.

"Cut. It's a wrap for tonight. See you all tomorrow at 5am. Get some rest." Summer yanked Carlos out of his daydreams.

Chapter CIV

Standing by her Man

Helena glanced over and noticed Carlos had come early to pick her up. He often waited for her in his dark windowed van, but today he came in and observed her in action. She wondered if he liked what he saw. She smiled at him and blew him a kiss. He looked so good in his nicely fitted jeans and dark sunglasses.

Carlos's constant emotional and financial support had let her effloresce as an actress, a professional and a woman. Ever since Carlos plucked her from a modeling agency party and paid for her classes in acting, dancing as well as for her modeling photography portfolio, she was in demand. She absorbed everything like a sponge and with each lesson learned, she bloomed into a constantly morphing exotic flower. Carlos was generous in many ways. He paid for her Invisalign braces and her numerous dermatologist visits. He'd been a savior, putting her on an express path to success with all his resources. As far as Helena was concerned, he was her guardian angel.

Helena still couldn't wrap her pretty head around the kind of money Carlos made with marketing imported pottery and managing a small restaurant, but who was she to look a gift horse in the mouth. She appreciated that he was a hard-working man. Carlos had been nothing but loving and generous to her, so she chose not to question the details of his business. She respected his private nature and perhaps, the less she knew, the better.

When alone with Carlos, Helena truly enjoyed his sensual side. His kiss and smooth touch sent her heart racing and activated her libido without fail. She thrived on the power she exerted over him, when she decided to appeal to his manhood, but she did so carefully, never abusing her momentary dominance. Within seconds, she could change a bad mood to good, with just the hint of sex. Looking at Carlos in a certain way made him melt like putty in her fingers and she loved that fact, but she also knew not to push too far. He was so much stronger than her in every way. She wondered if he knew how much power he had over her.

When Carlos asked her to move in, after only two months of dating, she jumped at the opportunity to get out of her shared, sparse apartment. She didn't really enjoy living with two roommates much. It was a union of financial convenience. She never regretted the decision to share his spacious one-bedroom apartment. They lived in total harmony, and he meant the world to her. He was fun, kind and had a mysterious side that intrigued and excited her.

Few men satisfied Helena like Carlos could; he was loving, sexy and tantalizingly sensual. She was truly grateful for all he did for her, emotionally and physically. They had a mutual admiration and understanding of each others needs and weaknesses and they were both smart enough to not take advantage of either. Respecting unspoken boundaries worked in their favor. Since they both came from Catholic backgrounds, their cultural differences rarely came into play; on the contrary, they enhanced their relationship, and cemented their mutual fascination for each other. They were the "quintessential" couple, complete soul mates, a ying/yang combination if ever one existed.

When Summer called it a day, Helena grabbed her bag, her clothing and walked over to Carlos. "Bye, Summer. My set clothes need washing. I'll do that tonight and bring them back tomorrow morning."

"Ok, thanks. Please don't forget anything or our scenes won't match. Bye, Helena. Have a good night."

Chapter CV

Fernando's Sour Surprise

Carlos's phone rang as he waited for Helena. Fernando Flores filled him in on the information he gained from the tangerine tablet he had delivered.

"When I realized it was the mother's tablet instead of Adriano's assistant's, I was cursing like a sailor, but I think it shed some light on the fact that the boy knows nothing. He sent his family emails that tell me what I need to know. They are quite a nosy bunch."

"Good. Glad to hear that, Fernando. Sorry we got the wrong one. The mother and son have exactly the same tangerine-colored tablet. Wonder if they bought it in a clearance sale or something."

Fernando laughed. "Well, I'm not sorry. What really got my attention was her photo library. She makes and collects pottery herself. I'm telling you Carlos, this woman has an amazing collection and understanding of pottery. Apparently, she manufactures in New York. Google her. Cara Crenston. I have checked her out for the past 60 minutes and I still haven't seen everything."

"Really? Interesting. I'll do that. Please don't be inspired to contact her."

"No worries. I already copied the pictures in her library for future reference. Who would have guessed that the kid's mother would be so pottery prolific? What an unexpected surprise!"

Carlos could hear genuine admiration in Fernando's voice. Fernando reserved that kind of passion for pottery descriptions only, rarely for people.

"I'll check her out. Looks like they are a very creative family."

"What do you mean? Her son is a banker, and the other one is a journalist."

Carlos bit his tongue before he could mention Summer. Anything remotely close to Helena, he refused to discuss with Fernando or Jose or anyone for that matter. His employees didn't even know that Helena lived with him. She rarely came to the restaurant. Carlos took her out to dinner, all over Paris, the further away from the restaurant, the better.

"Journalism is creative too. So, what did the emails disclose?" Carlos desperately wanted to change the subject. He hoped Fernando would bite.

"I guess. I'll send you a few so you can see for yourself."

"Ok. Good."

When Carlos hung up he searched Cara Crenston's business on his phone. He saw that she was represented by a gallery in Paris and he decided to go check it out. Maybe he would buy a piece for Fernando's upcoming birthday. Pottery was the only thing that Fernando appreciated, the only thing that got him really excited. This thoughtful gesture might serve him well in the future. You couldn't score enough points to be on Fernando's good side, Carlos figured.

Chapter CVI

Mom Knows Best

The days with Francois and her family flew by for Cara and she enjoyed every minute. The second week was almost done, and Jasper was scheduled to return to Barcelona. Cara could not stomach the fact that Jasper had to return. Jasper didn't feel great about it either.

"I promise to call you, Mom. I'll keep you in the loop if anything happens."

"Yes, please. Call me if you need me to come. Barcelona is a short plane ride from Paris as you well know."

When Samson and Jasper left for the airport, Cara couldn't help but cry. She was worried sick. The stolen tablet had shaken her more than she admitted. Cara followed the news in Madrid daily and knew that Adriano's death remained unsolved.

Talking to Summer did not help matters.

"Really, Mom. He needs to quit and clear out of there. Can't you tell him to do that?"

"It's his decision, Summer. Let's hope he makes the right one. I gave him my opinion as did Samson. We hope he heard us."

"As did I, but will he listen?"

"Do you ever listen to others?"

"Really, Mom! This is a different situation."

There was no winning with Summer.

Jasper's flight left Sunday around noon and Samantha arrived at Rue Malher shortly after, the same day. Their paths must have crossed in the skies over Paris. Sam's presence distracted Cara in a good way. Sam reassured Cara that Jasper could handle himself, but deep down Cara was still worried. Sam didn't have all the facts. Cara made sure she touched base with Jasper daily. Hearing his voice gave her temporary peace of mind, but danger still lurked in the dark recesses of her brain.

Chapter CVII

Back in the Saddle

Jasper's first day back at the office was dull and sad. Maria's creviced frown echoed the sentiment. "Hello, there. I'm surprised to see you came back. We were placing bets."

"Really? So, who won?" Jasper asked with interest.

"Not me. How is your family? Your brother, Samson?"

"Everyone is fine. Thanks. Samson sends his warm regards. Anything new here?"

"Thank you. Absolutely nothing. No changes on our floor. We're holding our breath and keeping our heads down, noses close to the desk. It's a sad state of affairs here at the bank. "

"As I suspected," Jasper replied, pulling out his phone. "Let me show you a picture of my family in Paris." Maria leaned in captivated and curious as a cat. He knew she was interested. Jasper rarely shared his private world. Her own family life was an open book. Jasper had seen a picture of every niece, nephew and second cousin. Maria shared everything with those she liked. Those she didn't, got nothing.

"Everyone in your family is blond!" Maria remarked. "What happened to you?"

"I told you; I look like my dad."
"Hmmm, interesting. Was he Spanish?"
"No. American of German descent."

The office mood was unchanged. Adriano's office was still empty, the door closed. Adriano's clients had been temporarily redistributed to other employees and Jasper was asked to temporarily assist another associate, whom he didn't particularly connect with. The Flores accounts were already out of his hands and a legal team, together with management were overseeing them. They were not frozen.

Jasper was relieved he would not be dealing with Fernando in any capacity, but his uneasiness continued, especially when he left work and had to go home to his empty apartment. He missed his family tremendously. He would give his future in Barcelona some serious thought, but for the moment, he intended to sit tight and see what developed within the firm. They had yet to offer him a contract and a promotion.

Chapter CVIII

The Silica Hits the Fan

Inspector Abello's men were watching Flores, his restaurant, and his warehouse virtually around the clock. Shipments of pottery were coming in regularly and Abello made sure they were randomly checked in customs. Nothing irregular was ever discovered. This drove Abello nuts. He and Arnaud touched base weekly comparing drug deaths and drug leads, but neither one could find a substantial crack in Flores's operation, not in Barcelona and not in Marseilles. What were they missing? That guy was smoother than olive oil. His smile continued to irk Abello; it made him shudder and swear profusely.

He decided to randomly check in with customs one day when one of Flores's shipments was due to be checked. He rarely had time for a hands-on approach, but Flores inspired him. A crate was ripped open and the pottery carefully unwrapped and examined. Everything seemed to check out. As Abello peered into the half empty crate he noticed the thick protective crate lining. It was made of silica if he wasn't mistaken; not the usual styrofoam sheets or molded cardboard. It occurred to him that although silica offered good protection for a fragile shipment, it certainly was an expensive option. He questioned Flores's employees on why they used this lining as it was not particularly cost effective for so many crates. They shrugged explaining that the benefits were worth it as the items rarely broke, and the crates were reused. Abello ordered the silica to be cut open in one of the crates. He wanted to examine it himself.

He instructed his agent to utilize his Swiss army knife and slice into the depth of the silica. Embedded in the hefty silica slab was a three finger-thick layer of sky-blue paper. Abello asked for the paper to be removed. As the customs agent pulled the paper out and unfolded it, a narrow brick was exposed, and a white powdery substance spilled from around it. Abello fingered it, tasted it on the tip of his tongue and smiled. He had finally struck gold.

The dogs had not sniffed the drugs embedded in the silica or maybe they hadn't sniffed the right crates? Not every crate had drugs embedded in it. Either way, Flores had slipped by numerous random inspections. but now his ass was nailed to the warehouse wall. What a brilliant, but costly endeavor, the silica. Only drug money could offset the price of such expensive wrapping and crating Abello figured. He immediately ordered the shipment seized and the ship impounded. He had the brick sent to the lab and he made arrangements for Fernando Flores's and Jose's arrest pending lab confirmations. He wanted to question the brains of the operation himself. Small joys. At the end of the day, his men had discovered about 300 kilos of drugs in an unusually slender, elongated brick form. Each brick had a mark that led back to a Mexican cartel. Ironically, there was pride in the product.

As the silica was being sliced open, a customs agent texted Jose, who in turn alerted Fernando Flores. Within the hour, Flores boarded a private plane out of the country. His suitcases had been packed for weeks. They were loaded with cash and his favorite belongings. It paid off to be ready. Jose was instructed to follow, after retrieving some additional important documents, electronics, and valuables from the safe. On the way to Barcelona El Prat airport, Jose called Carlos and told him to disappear immediately.

Police stopped Jose at the security check before he could board the next flight to Mexico City and arrested him. He was traveling with a fake passport and if he hadn't been wearing his silver and turquoise cross, he would have made it out of the country without difficulty. The agent did not recognize him from the picture alert, but he did recognize the unique piece of jewelry around his thick neck. The suspect was wearing, a large silver cross set with strikingly beautiful turquoise stones, a one-of-a-kind piece and exquisite example of top-grade Mexican silver.

Chapter CIX

I Left My Heart...

Back in Paris, Carlos grabbed his half-packed suitcase and threw in a few more of his favorite possessions in record time. He secured a double bottomed bag loaded with cash from his safe, his few jewelry items, some documents, and his various IDs, one of which he slid into his always travel-ready multi pocketed tweed jacket and headed for Charles de Gaulle airport. He drove himself to the airport in a recently acquired rental car and abandoned the car in overnight parking. With a brown wavy-haired wig and baseball cap in place, he cleared the security check and waited to board the next plane to the Caribbean under the name of Julio Lopez. He paid for his one-way, first-class Air France ticket in cash.

While waiting to board, he transferred large amounts of money from European accounts in Barcelona and Paris, using numerous set up money grams and corporate names. He had closed his savings account in Mexico weeks earlier and transferred the funds to Hermosa and himself. He had also transferred the deed for the apartment in Monaco to a corporation owned by Felipe, Fernando's brother. Julio Lopez would be the designated pick-up person for the money grams, an expensive, well-executed ID ensured that. The money grams to various locations would not be traceable even if they required an ID for payment. Julio Lopez would cease to exist after the last pick up. When the flight took off, Carlos knew he had just narrowly escaped doomsday. For the past few months, Carlos had prepared for this day, mentally and physically. His internal radar was on high alert ever since the first customs check in Barcelona. Carlos knew his methodical preparation enabled him to orchestrate a speedy and uncomplicated departure. His affairs were in immaculate order just like the company books Fernando had entrusted him with.

From the Bahamas, Carlos intended to go somewhere in the world to start a new life. He had enough money stashed in various banks of the Caribbean to give him a fresh start. Lacing Fernando's drugs and skimming off the profit had been risky, but extremely lucrative. Carlos was patient, never getting too greedy. Little by little, he'd stashed more and more money into his offshore corporate accounts. If Fernando or Jose had ever found out, he would have been executed, sentenced to immediate death. He knew the risks, but his life was shit and he saw no other alternative to exit it unscathed.

Carlos's needs were simple. He wanted a business, a legitimate business of his own. He would make sure to never face Fernando Flores or Jose ever again. He hated them both with a vengeance. Being raised in a cartel environment had ruined his family and life and forced him into a line of work he absolutely despised. He was hereby cutting all ties with the Flores family, with his family, with Mexico and with his entire previous life. This was his self-designed witness protection program.

His dream had always been to start a new life with a new identity, free of the Flores clan. Finally, the time had come to reinvent himself. He was ready. He always thought he'd feel invigorated, but the one thing he hadn't counted on was falling in love with Helena. She was the wild card, the rose whose thorn was a pebble in his perfectly planned garden.

He wondered if the Spanish authorities would find Fernando Flores in Mexico and bring him to justice. Would Mexico dare extradite him? Probably not. Carlos knew that Fernando would never leave his family business. He would pay people off and continue his previous life with Jose enforcing his will in the shadows. They were both ruthless and strong, together. The cartel had their backs and Carlos knew they were not brave enough to start fresh, not brave enough to cut all ties with home or to meander off their twisted path. Fernando would never leave his factory and Jose would never leave Fernando.

Carlos's deepest, nagging regret was leaving Helena behind. It filled him with remorse and sadness. Helena was the unexpected in his otherwise flawless plan. Departing without saying goodbye to her was tremendously painful. She was the positive element in his miserable life, he never foresaw, the person he cherished most besides his sister, Hermosa, in Mexico City. Poor Hermosa, he hadn't seen her in a long while and phone calls from Europe had been difficult. It pained him unspeakably to let them both go. While on the plane, he studied Helena's Instagram picture on his new, clean tablet. A tear formed in the corner of his eye. Carlos never cried. The last time was when his mother died.

Helena was his unprotected underbelly, his soft spot, his true love, the only link besides Hermosa, that could possibly expose and hurt him. He knew Hermosa would rather die than unmask him. Helena, he guessed, was too loyal and savvy to reveal anything if she knew it, but Carlos never put her in that position. He made sure she knew nothing that could hurt her. He had protected her with his feigned indifference when around the restaurant employees.

Maybe one day, he would send for Helena and Hermosa, but not anytime soon. Too risky. Fernando and the police would be shadowing both women. Fernando would be watching Hermosa around the clock and the French police would be watching Helena. Carlos could conceivably never see the two women he loved most, ever again. The mere thought overwhelmed him. He chose hope and patience as an alternative because he couldn't bear to think of the first scenario.

Although madly in love with Helena, Carlos wasn't stupid. He knew what his survival required. Years of working for the cartel had taught him how to disappear, when to be silent and when and how to strike. Love was a sign of weakness that could and would be used against him, given the opportunity. Working for and watching Fernando Flores all these years had taught him well and made him strong. He counted his blessings that his exit from Paris was executed without a hitch. Had he been in the office, he may not have made it to the apartment and airport in time. Every second counted. His life was like surfing at Mavericks; one slip-up and it would be over in an instant. Lady Luck was on his side today and he was grateful for that.

Carlos sat back in his seat, eating peanuts and sipping water. He wondered if Fernando and Jose were equally fortunate with their escape plan. When would Fernando notice the money missing? The Flores family would wait for him to reappear with it. If he didn't show, they would start searching. He didn't have a lot of time to disappear. A week maybe? Two weeks? He sighed deeply and sank into his seat. As his racing mind slowed to a weary pace, Carlos began to mentally prepare for his new life. First and foremost, he needed to secure the transferred funds as Julio Lopez. Later, he could disburse them with his other new identity, Casimiro Santos. So far his plan was working smoother than Fernando's hair grease.

Chapter CX

Slip, Sliding Away

Abello contacted Arnaud within the hour to check Carlos's restaurant and apartment. French airports and train stations were placed on alert; picture bulletins sent out. However, Carlos could not be located; it appeared he had slipped out of the country unnoticed. None of his associates had seen him, not even for a promise of leniency when drugs were found in the restaurant office under loose floorboards. They had no clue about the drugs, they swore. They only worked in the restaurant for standard pay.

Carlos had vanished into thin air. Abello and Arnaud cursed in chorus when they realized both Carlos and Fernando were beyond their grasp. At least one of the three *banditos* was in custody. Hopefully, Jose Flores would shed some light on their mega-operation.

Chapter CXI

Good News Travels Fast

The next day at the office, Jasper heard the breaking news. The *Corazon de Leones* had been raided and drug shipments were found embedded in silica crate linings. Fernando Flores, the ship's owner, had vanished, pulled a Houdini, while his people were arrested. Jasper immediately called Samson.

"Samson, did you hear? Drugs were found on Fernando's ship and he skipped town, but Jose was arrested."

"Seriously? Spill. "

They talked as the news came in on the AP wire, tidbit after tidbit. Soon Samson was giving his brother the red-hot updates. Jasper was excited and relieved at the same time. He felt good that Fernando Flores's operation was rapidly becoming defunct. The thought that Fernando was still out there somewhere, made him uneasy. However, Jasper's educated guess was that Fernando hightailed it back to Mexico, as the cartels did not worry as much about being arrested or extradited there. Jasper thought he would be able to sleep a little better for the first time in months. When he finished talking to Samson, he called his mother.

"Mom, check your email. I forwarded some news. Flores's gang was busted for drugs, and he disappeared into thin air."

"Oh my God, are you serious? So, we were right all along to be suspicious! Tell me everything."

"It appears Fernando fled the country, but Jose and his restaurant crew are in custody."

"What about all his money at the bank?"

"Jose was caught on the way to the airport. The money is still here, I imagine. I don't have access to his account information anymore, so I really don't know."

"I'm happy for that. Honestly, who cares about the money anyway. I'm just glad he's gone."

"Well, I'm slightly curious."

They chatted for a few more minutes. "I already called Samson. You and he can fill Summer in. Do you think Carlos was affected too?"

"Good question. Summer will know from Helena, I suppose."

"Talk to you tomorrow?"

"Yes. Email me with any new developments. Love you. Bye"

Chapter CXII

News Junkies Unite

That night the Rue Malher apartment residents were glued to TV news. Samson came over to fill in the blanks. The news proved to be a major source of relief and cautious celebration. Cara and Samantha canceled dinner plans with Francois and his friend, but invited them over for a family dinner, American style, TV blaring. They politely declined and chose to reschedule their double date for another, more intimate night.

"Thank you for understanding, Francois."

"Of course, *Cherie*. I understand your excitement and relief."

"Thank you! I need to hear all the incoming news. I wouldn't be able to focus during a dinner out. Call you tomorrow?"

"Of course."

"This story is as exciting as a James Bond movie," Samantha opined. "Summer, you have an inside scoop for your next film. You all lived through parts of this horror. You can all contribute your angle to the story. This script could be a winner."

Samson agreed with Sam. "Summer, Sam has a point. You have a good story here. We can all help write it. Fill in the blanks from our perspectives."

"Don't think I haven't already thought about that Samson. Mom, your thoughts?"

"I can't think about that just yet. My knees are still shaking. I think we'll need a little distance first to digest it all, but it certainly sounds like a story with potential. You really would have to check with Jasper first though. He's been through a lot. Give him a little time, Summer."

Chapter CXIII

Jasper's Choice

The following day, Maria was holding court in the reception area, just like old times. Everyone was congregated around her desk discussing details of the drug sting. Speculation was running rampant, and opinions were offered on what would happen to Flores, if anything. Would Flores's legal team help Jose and the other Mexicans now in jail? Or would he abandon them as a lost cause? Would Flores be located? Extradited? Once again, bets were placed. This was more exciting than the office soccer pool.

And then there was the question of Flores's money. He had millions in his accounts. What would happen with that? More opinions were offered. If one or two employees were aware that the funds had already been transferred out, they didn't shed any informational light. After all, one dead body at the bank was sufficient.

The top question on everyone's mind was, where did Adriano stand in all of this? Did he know or suspect a drug trade? Was that his undoing? This issue was a big sore spot for Jasper. There were moments when he still could not believe that his mentor was gone. He walked past Adriano's office, expecting to see him beckon him in. It was a tough realization that Adriano was gone for good. Whatever Adriano did or didn't do, he did not deserve his untimely death. Adriano Aldana had been a good man. Jasper knew that the bank's third floor was forever stained with his innocent blood.

Extensive soul-searching aided Jasper with the decision to not renew his contract in Barcelona when it was finally offered. He decided to ask for a transfer. If that wasn't possible, he would resign. Maybe it was time for a change after all.

Later that day, he made an appointment with Adriano's boss for Wednesday morning, to discuss his future in the company. Without Adriano, Jasper had lost a major incentive to stay in Barcelona. Adriano was his ticket to promotion. He was also a joy to work for. Without him there, Jasper was floating between executives. His stellar working relationship with Adriano would be hard to duplicate with anyone else. Sometimes a fresh start in a new setting was better than trying to move forward from a bad experience in a stagnant one, Jasper reasoned. His family fully supported his decision. They hoped he would follow through and not be talked out of it in his Wednesday meeting.

Chapter CXIV

Three little words...

The following week, at Rue Malher, it was business as usual. Summer and Hope worked on the film, preparing for their weekly shoot and Ted continued to tirelessly organize everyone's lives. Cara and Sam relieved Ted in the kitchen on the nights Mme Balon did not cook. Ted was appreciative of the help. Sam and Cara continued their sight seeing and enjoyed a hilarious double date with Francois and his friend, who was delightful. Cara was pleased that Francois's friends were as nice as he, himself.

"Friends are a reflection of who you are and Francois is a gem," Sam offered one night. "His friend was really fun to hang with."

"Yes, I'm very fortunate to have met him," Cara reflected. 'I'm glad you're having a good time."

"Are you kidding? I'm having a fabulous time."

That night Jasper conference-called Cara and Samson to discuss his next move.

"Hi, guys. I made my decision. I'm going to ask for a transfer. If the bank can't find me a position in another branch, I'll resign. My meeting is tomorrow morning. I wanted to share my thoughts with you before I make this drastic move. Wish me luck."

"Of course. I think you're doing the right thing, Bro. Things have a way of working out the way they should. I believe that."

"Thanks. The office is just not the same without Adriano and I really hate coming home to my empty apartment. I'm ready for a change. My heart isn't into this anymore. I'll miss Barcelona and my friends, but not this job."

"Honey, you know you can always come home. We can figure things out and regroup in New York," Cara reminded him.

"Thanks, Mom."

Cara desperately wanted Jasper to come home, but she wanted him to arrive at that decision himself. She was pleased her exceedingly difficult, laid-back strategy had paid off.

"I can come to Barcelona next weekend and help you pack if you like."

"Yes. That would be great, Mom. Let me see what happens tomorrow. I'll let you know asap after the meeting."

"Sure, honey." Cara chuckled. Packing was not Jasper's forte.

"I think you made a good decision, Jasper. Maybe you can ask for a transfer to Paris?" Samson chimed in.

"Right. My French is rudimentary at best. Keep dreaming, Samson."

"Helena can teach you. You would speak French with a cute Polish accent."

"Hilarious, Samson. Does she still have a boyfriend?"

"Hmmm, not sure. We'll have to ask Summer. Carlos might have disappeared too."

When Jasper, Samson and Cara hung up, Cara picked up the phone to call Francois.

"I may be going to Barcelona this weekend to help Jasper pack. I think he decided to come back to NY with me. We'll know for sure on Wednesday."

"Oh, wonderful. You must be happy. When will you be back if you go? "

"Monday night."

"Can you come here Monday night? I don't like losing a whole weekend with you. I miss you."

"Yes. I'll miss you, too."

"I love you, Cara."

"And I love you. We still have time this week to see each other. I'm not leaving until Thursday evening or Friday morning, if I go."

"Good. What is your schedule tomorrow?"

When Cara disconnected her call, she was glowing. This long-distance relationship just might work out, she thought feeling her cheeks flushing. Once again, her calm and patient attitude was rewarding her with unexpected, sweet rewards. Today was just full of good news.

Chapter CXV

Heaven and Hell......
With No Goodbyes

Helena was in a panic. Carlos traveled frequently for business and didn't always share his whereabouts, but he always checked in. Now he was missing for a couple days without a word. He didn't answer her texts either which was very unusual. One night she noticed his suitcases were gone, along with some of his favorite clothes and belongings. When she heard his cell phones ring in the closet the next morning, she lost it. Carlos never forgot his cellphones.

While listening to the evening news that night, she was hit over the head with what felt like a ton of bricks. Her mind raced as she sunk into the nearest armchair, completely in shock. She totally did not see that coming.

When the police arrived with a warrant the following day, her situation became painfully clear. Carlos was gone for good. What kind of mess did he leave her in? Was she a suspect of some sort? Helena had never seen any drugs in their apartment, ever. She was questioned and allowed to stay, while the police searched the premises. She sat at the kitchen table, answering questions, waiting. When the search yielded nothing, she was told she could resume her life, but to not leave the country until further notice. As Helena looked around at the destruction in a daze, she knew her life would change forever. She realized that her 'guardian angel' had flown the coop, but in her heart, she also knew that one day she would hear from Carlos, when she least expected it. Carlos loved her. She was certain of that. And she still loved him, with all her heart. That night she cried herself to sleep.

What Helena regretted most was that Carlos never fully opened up to her. Had he been planning his exit for a while? She remembered no particular signs, no red flags, no secret phone calls. She wondered if she could have been more of a comfort to him. He must have been stressed.

She knew so little about his life prior to Paris. Helena had always respected his privacy, purposely not probing. She sensed a painful past. Should she have pushed? The only family Carlos spoke of was his sister in Mexico, but Helena had no contact information. She wondered if she could locate Hermosa Ortiz on social media. She would try.

Carlos did not leave her, Helena reasoned to herself. He fled the country or else he would have been arrested. Even though her heart was broken, Helena understood his silence; it was essential to his survival. Helena would have to be patient. In the meantime, she was forever thankful for the love and support she had received from this incredible man, however brief it was. Carlos had given her the tools to help launch herself and she would always be eternally grateful to him for this opportunity. Helena would never forget him. He stepped in when she needed it; no questions asked. Her heart ached for him, but her head understood what had happened and that it was inevitable. Despite this knowledge, she was in pain and in shock and in need of ice packs for her puffy eyes.

The police searched and searched but found nothing incriminating in their shared apartment. No drugs, no ID's, no business papers, nothing. They took Carlos's discarded electronics and left. Carlos must have kept whatever they were looking for in his locked office or taken it with him Helena surmised. Thank God, he didn't incriminate her, not that she thought he would. That was not Carlos's style. He had always been very careful and protective of her.

A few days later, the police dropped off some papers for Helena that Carlos had kept in the office safe. "These are yours," they told her. Helena took the envelope and threw it on the kitchen counter, not ready to tackle anything. When she finally looked at the papers a few days later, she saw that Carlos had transferred the deed for the apartment to her, weeks before his disappearance. He was preparing to leave and never said a thing to her! How worried he must have been these last few weeks or months? Helena noticed nothing unusual. It saddened her that he did not share his worries with her, but she was relieved that she still had a roof over her head. The apartment was paid in full.

Another night, while reminiscing and feeling exceptionally blue, she pulled out Carlos's favorite red dress, slipping it on to remember the good times. Feeling sad, she burrowed her fists deep inside the dress pockets, only to discover an envelope addressed to her with a large amount of cash. There was a heart drawn around her name, but no note. Helena burst into tears. A message from Carlos! She knew she could not share any of this with anyone. Helena would have to carry this burden and joy by herself.

Chapter CXVI

Jasper's Life Changing Decision, and Cara's Surprise of a Lifetime

That week, Jasper handed in his resignation. His boss could not locate a transfer position for him, but promised they would keep him in mind as opportunities would surely come up. The bank was sad to see him go, but they understood his reluctance to sign another contract in lieu of Adriano's demise. His change of heart, under the circumstances, was understandable. They would be delighted to write him a stellar recommendation.

On Friday morning, when Sam flew home to NY, Cara flew to Barcelona. She and Jasper spent the next two days packing to blasting *Enrique Iglesias* music and making shipping arrangements for Jasper's belongings. The beautiful leather recliner was picked up by Enrique, who almost wept at the gesture.

"Really? For me? I love it, Jasper." Enrique tapped his right fist on his heart.

"I'm going to miss you. We had some good times here."

"Well, you'll have to visit me in New York or wherever I end up eventually, Enrique."

"For sure, *Amigo*. I'll think of you every time I have a beer in this chair."

"Well, I guess you'll think of me a lot then." They exchanged meaningful looks and laughed.

"It's so nice to meet you, Enrique. I've heard so much about you. All good things, I might add."

"The pleasure is all mine, Mrs. Crenston."

It was clear to Cara why Jasper and Enrique were friends. She felt the close bond between them.

On Cara's last day in Barcelona, Jasper asked Cara to come to his office. He wanted to show her his hang out for the past year and take her to lunch. His apartment belongings were boxed and ready for shipping. Jasper would tie up the loose ends and come to Paris the following week, after which he and Cara would fly home together. His departure had come about rather quickly, but it only took a long weekend to pack up a year's worth of stuff.

When Cara arrived at the bank, Jasper met her in the lobby. They waited for the elevator together.

"I'm looking forward to visiting Summer on set and seeing Helena again. It was fun to watch them in action. I'm also thrilled to share Samson's apartment for another week. I hope he feels the same way."

"Of course he does. He told me it was great to have you around in Berlin and Paris. Those are memories you guys will share forever."

"I wanted to rehash these last couple of months over drinks with Samson. He fully understood my anxiety over the Flores debacle and offered the support I needed when I thought I was going to completely lose it. He kept me somewhat sane. I also wanted to talk to Summer about her next script. She mentioned something about wanting to write about the Flores family because she thought it would make a good story. I agree that it would, but I'm not sure I can relive that."

"We all understood your anxiety, Jasper. It was scary for us too. We just didn't want to tell you how scared we were so you wouldn't feel worse. It's crazy how your client popped up in all of our lives. Mind-blowing really. You can say no to Summer if you need more distance. Ultimately, it's your choice. However, I think it may prove to be cathartic. Obviously, it would have to be tackled as complete fiction."

"I'm thinking about it. I have mixed feelings. Maybe writing about this experience will help me come to terms with it. It could be freeing to some degree, I suppose. If nothing else, I may lose a few residual nightmares I still suffer from."

"Ok then. If you decide to go forward, I propose we all work together, pooling our 'Flores moments'. You know, Summer, and Ted will be in New York in just a few weeks after wrapping things up in Paris. We can all brainstorm over dinner."

"Maybe. For now, I just want to feel some space between myself and the whole incident, but I agree, anything is possible."

"Ok, moving on…. What is on your agenda for this last week?"

"Clemente found someone off his waiting list eager for my apartment. I'm going to see if they want to buy any of my furniture and kitchen supplies. I think he's trying to make amends.

"For what exactly?"

"I'm not sure, but I'll accept it for what its worth. I also need to wrap a few things up at the office and say goodbye to everyone."

"Makes sense."

"Are you ready for the full office tour? Here we are." They exited the elevator into the Spartan, ivory reception area.

"Yes, I'm curious to meet everyone. Is your office on this floor?"

"Yes, let me first introduce you to Maria, Mom. Maria, this is my mother, Cara Crenston."

"Pleased to meet you, Mrs. Crenston. Your son Samson looks just like you."

Cara laughed. "Yes, he and Summer look like me. Jasper looks more like his father. Nice to meet you, Maria."

"We're so sad that Jasper is leaving. Everyone will miss him."

"And he you, I'm sure."

"My office is down the hall, Mom." He started walking to cut Maria short.

Jasper showed her his tiny office and sadly pointed to Adriano's. Along the way, he introduced her to a few co workers. As Cara was saying goodbye to everyone, Adriano's boss appeared with a new face. In his hand, the man held a tangerine tablet. Jasper's boss introduced himself to Cara and then he introduced Inspector Abello.

"Inspector Abello has been overseeing the Fernando Flores case. He wanted to say hello to you both and thank you, Jasper, for your cooperation."

"Thank you. I don't feel that I was able to help all that much. Adriano shared very little, as you know. Nice to meet you, Inspector."

"You did fine Jasper and yes, I think you may be right about Adriano purposely not sharing his findings. I believe he was trying to protect you. From all the information I gathered, he was a good man who realized too late, the mess he got himself into. Nonetheless, if you think of anything at all regarding the Flores case, please contact me. Here is my card."

"I will gladly do that. I've read in the news that you have Jose Flores in custody. Is he shedding any light on the operation?"

"No. Only his lawyers are talking right now." Abello rolled his eyes.

"I don't know if this is helpful at all Inspector, but I briefly saw Jose in Berlin in the hotel where Suzanna Svelte died of an overdose. My brother, Samson, was covering the Berlin film festival and I visited him there for the weekend. Sadly, I arrived after Suzanna died."

Abello nodded; eyebrows raised. "What a shame. She was beautiful. Yes, that is exactly the kind of useful information I was talking about. Thank you. It helps us piece things together. Can you send me an email with the dates and anything else you may remember?"

"Certainly. I'm here for another week if you need to speak with me."

"Thank you. We may do that. To get a formal statement."

"Delighted to meet you, Inspector Abello. I'm very impressed with what I read about your investigative work on the case," Cara interrupted.

"Thank you kindly, Mrs. Crenston. You know, I'm happy to tell you we solved one more mystery that might be of interest to you."

"Really? To me? What would that be?"

"Yes, I was going to notify you and drop this off with your son, but since you're here, you can sign for it yourself. I believe this is your tangerine tablet?"

Jasper's jaw dropped as Cara's right hand flew up to cover her parting lips in disbelief.

"You're kidding! Wherever did you find it?" Cara was frozen in place as she processed the information.

"No, not kidding at all." He chuckled at Cara's shocked expression. Moments like this were priceless and he was clearly enjoying her astonishment.

"We found it in Fernando Flores's restaurant office. You may be interested to know that he greatly admired your ceramics. We saw that he exported many pictures of your work. I'm assuming he took that with him when he ran." Abello handed Cara her missing tablet, sporting a satisfying grin. He was enjoying her reaction.

"Be on the look-out for copies of your work from Mexico."

Jasper laughed nervously.

Cara belched an uncontrolled laugh. "Oh my goodness! My tablet! Thank you, Inspector. Well, I can certainly let you know if Flores becomes a client or worse, if he copies my designs," Cara replied, her hand moving from her mouth to her lucky *fleur-de-lis* necklace. She hugged the tablet to her chest. "I never thought I would see this device again. You have no idea how many times I lost it, but it always seems to find its way back to me. Nonetheless, I think I'll finally activate my tracking feature."

"Good idea, Mom."

"I was especially heartbroken about losing my pictures. By the way, I'll be having a show of my new work at a Paris gallery in a few months. Can I send you all an invitation?"

"Of course, but I'm afraid I'm not so knowledgeable about your craft, although I did learn a thing or two on this case."

"It's never too late to enjoy art, Inspector Abello. Thank you so much for retrieving my tablet. I will never, ever forget this visit to Barcelona. This story is film-worthy." She held up the tangerine tablet. "May I get a picture of everyone before my tablet disappears again?"

The End… ….for Now…..:)

**The Rogue Tangerine Tablet is Book 1
in the Crenston Family Suspense Series**

Good Karma is the Best Revenge, the sequel to **The Rogue Tangerine Tablet**, is about the power of love, and the ability to make lemonade by seizing the right moment to implement meaningful change. It's about hard work, fighting for what you believe in, persistence, and most of all, patiently building positive relationships predicated on the heart and soul.

The same cast of characters from **The Rogue Tangerine Tablet**, move forward to a new chapter in their respective lives. New alliances change their trajectory as is so often the case when time marches on and unpredictable situations explode. Unforeseen new developments promise to shake up the Crenston Family just when they thought they had their equilibrium balanced…. Cara's new romance is put to the test, Summer finds support for her next film venture but not without setbacks and Samson, her twin brother, suffers a broken heart. Her older brother, Jasper, changes his professional direction 180 degrees and Casi Santos (aka Carlos Ortiz) finally breaks free from the ruptured Flores cartel to follow his dream. However, the stakes for his escape are high. Will his daring departure end with a threat to his life? Will be ever see his cherished sister or Helena, the love of his life, again? Is his dream of having the freedom to build his own future worth walking away from all the people he loves?

Sequel Announcement

Island Allure and Black Magic is book three in the Crenston Family Suspense Series featuring the globe-trotting family and their extended inner circle. The Crenstons seem to have an uncanny propensity for encountering trouble, yet they always manage to bounce back with little more than minor scuffs and bruises. Their natural penchant for risk-taking has them escaping dangerous situations on more than one occasion, but in a pinch, the family always rallies and comes through as a team. Oblivious to their frequent walks on the fringes of disaster, they live life to the fullest, averting misfortune by a mere stroke of fortuity giving credence to the saying, "being in the right place at the right time." Will their good luck finally run out?

Then there are the Santos siblings, Casimir and Camila, formerly the Ortiz family from Tampico, Mexico. Hiding in plain sight, they recently found love on a Caribbean Island. Life should be smooth sailing ever since they broke away with millions, from the dangerous Flores cartel and their illicit smuggling operations, but their cartel past seems to lurk in the shadows, threatening to pop up like a geyser in Yellowstone Park.

Leaving their childhood home and mindfully cutting all mental and physical ties to their past, Casi and Camila are struggling to embrace a new life, however, the future, even a well-financed, rosy one, is never a straight path. When Casi gets a phone call from Maria Alfaro, his trusted Cuban private eye in Miami, the news surrounding his future brother-in-law shakes him to the core. To make matters worse, his loving, but vulnerable fiancée gets entangled with a dangerous psychic, thus inviting a new kind of danger into the fold. Good Karma doesn't last indefinitely.

Acknowledgement

I would like to thank:

George Varga, Louisa Cornell and Eilidh McKenzie for their helpful comments and edits. They were the first people to read the manuscript. Since they are all accomplished editors and writers, I value their input.

Donna McGullam and the Westhampton Writers Group for their useful insights and suggestions.

Lacegarden for digitally enhancing my naïve art book cover illustrations and making them shine.

Robert Sherman for his kind legal expertise.

About the Author

Bleue Rose was born in the land of incredible Alpine skiing, orgasmic chocolate and cheese riddled with air-holes. She continued to countries that favored sourdough, grilled sausage with spicy mustard and fermented apples expertly mulled into wine. Summers were idly passed in Europe's warmer countries where she acquired an undeniable taste for Mediterranean fare and their charming men. Her higher education years, enjoyed in the city of lights, placed priceless emphasis on an art education, modern dance experiences and sultry jazz clubs in the Latin Quarter. Engaging the five senses while surrounded by haute-couture and street grunge, her view of the creative world expanded exponentially. Home was a quaint walk-up in a street dotted with exceedingly social Greek restaurants and habit-forming French cafes. From there the big trek across the pond brought her to the big apple. This venture added an introduction to a new set of cultures and tastes. The world became familiar and smaller with quick Caribbean jaunts and explorations of the south and west. Of course, the internet added a whole new dimension of opportunities missed, so here we are now… …all incorporated into fabulous, far-away fiction.

www.ingramcontent.com/pod-product-compliance
Lightning Source LLC
Chambersburg PA
CBHW070929100726
47908CB00001B/153